Sabi Star

A Novel

by

Susan Hubert

SH
PUBLISHING

All characters in this publication are fictitious and any resemblance to real persons, living or dead, is purely coincidental

Published by Susan Hubert, 2013
Cover design © Duncan Watson

ISBN: 0797493905
ISBN-13: 978 0 7974 9390 2

The Author

Susan Hubert was born and lives in Zimbabwe. She read English and Psychology at the University of Natal, South Africa before teaching Mathematics to Advanced Level at high schools in Bulawayo, Zimbabwe. She stopped teaching in order to dedicate time to her son and support her husband in his efforts to retain their herd of cattle when the family farm was taken.

Dedication

To my friend Lenee Dahl Freemantle

and my son Jack Allard

Preface and Acknowledgements

This is a work of fiction – a novel dealing with issues that can be experienced and identified with anywhere in the world, but with a uniquely African flavour.

It is a pleasure to thank Robyn Foot, Frances Randell, Lisa Kaufman and Karen Vincent for checking the final proofs and for all their useful hints and suggestions, my parents, Chris and Moira Carver for their enthusiasm, my sister Nicola Lashbrook for her observations and Duncan Watson for his beautiful cover design. And massive thanks to my husband, Jeremy Hubert for his persistent motivational encouragement while producing this manuscript, without whom this project would not be complete.

1

Sabi

MY name is Sabi, but I think of myself as Sabi Star, in private of course, because if I started calling myself this in front of people I'm sure they would think I was really stupid. A sabi star is a pretty pink and white flower, small and star-shaped and they grow on the oddest looking plants that look a bit like baby baobab trees. These plants are very hardy, surviving the harshest of conditions in the low-lying, arid areas of my home country, Zimbabwe. This area is known as the Lowveld and it is here that I was born and it is here that a river once called the Sabi River runs. That is why my parents decided to give me this rather strange name.

The Sabi River is now known as the Save River so I

suppose I have to count myself lucky that I'm not called this. Sometimes, though I don't like being called 'Sabi', because it's different and I'm sure some people even snigger when I tell them my name but then, when I think of myself as Sabi Star, I realise it actually suits me because like the flower and the plant I'm also hardy and can survive the harshest of conditions.

I changed it in my mind to Sabi Star, umm, I guess when I was old enough to know what was happening and that was probably when I was about five or six. Up until then I just thought of myself as plain old 'Sabi', because that's what everyone called me; my gran, my dad, his friends, my friends, my teachers and everyone else I ever met. I haven't mentioned my mother in this list because she died just after my birth so I have no recollection of her calling me anything. This will always bring sadness even though I know nothing will change it.

When I was about six my gogo (that is the word the Africans use for grandmother) told me that my mother always called me Sabi Star when I was growing in her tummy. Once I heard this I retained it as my name. My gogo isn't really my grandmother, she being black, whereas I'm white. She is one of the maids in our house and when my mother died she was the one who brought me up. My dad was around too, but was never good at showing interest in me, so I have always spent most of my time when I'm at home with Gogo.

So when I got back from school for the Christmas holidays and went to say hello to my dad, I got the most terrible shock when he said, 'Dorca died last week, by the way,' as if he was telling me something irrelevant like we'd run out of my favourite cereal or something like that.

I looked at him in surprise, taking a while to register what I'd just heard; Dorca is my gogo, you see.

'Sorry?' I asked.

'You heard me. Dorca, she died last week, been sick for a while now. Most likely had AIDS.'

The significance of his words gradually dawned on me, and I could feel that funny feeling I always get creeping into my tummy when I get a shock.

'No Dad, surely not,' I managed to splutter, horrified.

'Fraid so. They've all got it you know, too bloody promiscuous they are, the lot of them.'

'No Dad, please, not my gogo, not my gogo dying.'

My throat started to contract as my eyes welled with tears.

'Dad no.' I cried.

'Oh for goodness sake,' my dad's current girlfriend, Sherry-Lee piped up from where she was standing behind me, 'she was just some stupid old Munt. Stop making such a fuss.'

I ignored her.

'But Dad, she wasn't even sick when I saw her last.'

I was desperately trying to find a reason for what he was saying to be untrue.

'Would have been. You just didn't notice.'

'But I know about AIDS, Dad, and I know Gogo, she wasn't like that,' I said with a slightly wobbly voice.

'Oh for God's sake, stop being such a drama queen, Sabi,' Sherry-Lee gave a deep sigh from behind me. 'You're unbelievable at times. Un-bloody-believable.'

I looked at my father, stunned, and then I ran from the room, pushing my way past Sherry-Lee, up the stairs, and along the passage to my bedroom. I slammed the door closed, locked it behind me and threw myself onto my bed, sobbing like I hadn't sobbed in a very long time.

Finally I calmed down a bit. I rolled onto my back and stared up at the ceiling while I tried to imagine how my life would be without Gogo around and I really struggled to do this. You see, whenever I think of home she is always very much a part of it. I felt the lump coming back into my throat as I thought about this and I had to swallow hard. Yes, it would have been easier to digest this terrible news if I'd known at least that she'd been sick, but I haven't been home once this last school term which means I was away for a whole three months. Dad's a miner and he was in Mozambique starting up a new venture there so I'd spent the three weekend breaks we had at my friend Sarah's house. If I'd come home for any of these weekends I would have seen just how sick poor Gogo was and then all of this wouldn't have been such a shock to me. I've seen other workers on my dad's mine dying of AIDS so I can recognise what the symptoms are, but I can't believe that Gogo would have got it by being promiscuous.

No, definitely not. I know all about promiscuity and Gogo just would not have behaved this way, with her thick glasses and the clean maid's uniform she always wore; no way. We've discussed promiscuity with Mrs Ngwenya, our Education for Living teacher at school, and sometimes I secretly worry that I might be, though. You see, often when I am alone in my room I get undressed and examine my breasts. They are small and quite shapely and Mr. Norris, the PE master at school has told me they are lovely. He tried to give me penny cools once if I showed them to him after swimming, but I knew he was joking so I just giggled and ran off. Mr. Norris is the coolest teacher at our school; all the girls really like him so I felt quite honoured that he joked with me about my breasts. Then another time he said that if I let him touch them he'd give me ten dollars for the tuck shop. His face went all funny when he said this which was strange but again I just giggled at his joke even though it was weird and for some reason it made me feel quite powerful, as if I had some hold over him. Different from when I am with boys my own age, not that I let them look at my breasts, either. However, I didn't know what to make of it when Mr. Norris implied on another occasion that if I took my swimming costume right off he would give me a lot more than ten dollars. Well, I could do with the money for the weekends we go to Harare for sports but I don't think it would really be worth it. He's definitely way too old, at least thirty, I'm sure, and his hands are rough so I certainly wouldn't want him to touch my fanny, let alone look at it.

However, some of the girls in my dorm touch themselves in funny places and maybe they think of Mr. Norris when they're doing it. I tried it once but it felt weird and I haven't done it again. My friend Tracey often wants me to do it after lights out but I'm always too scared we'll get caught by Miss Coburn, the hostel mistress. Tracey is taller than me and much bustier, but then she is over a year older. She says she's 'done it all the way' with my friend Mike but I don't believe her, or want to believe her because I actually think Mike likes me better. But Charity, who used to be in our class, has definitely 'done it all the way' with someone because she got pregnant last year and had to leave school. Gogo used to try and talk to me about these things but I'd pretend I knew everything and didn't need any more information. It was just too embarrassing for both of us, she talking about what she called 'the monthly waters' and why I must be careful with boys. Well at least she tried. My dad has simply ignored the fact that I'm growing up, except once when we were swimming at the Rawsons; he looked at me and said no, I couldn't swim and muttered something about needing a new swimming costume. I think that was the only time he's actually noticed that I am starting to look like a woman.

So yes, I really do know everything about being promiscuous and I really do know also that Gogo was not. On saying this, however, I have to accept that she must've done 'it' at least twice in her life because she has two children; Beauty, who also works in our house and Jabula who is a waiter or something like that at a wildlife conservancy near here. She had a husband called Enoch who used to work in our garden, but he died a few years ago. I had wanted to go with Gogo to his funeral but my dad wouldn't let me.

As I remembered this, I suddenly stopped dead in my thought tracks and turned quite cold as something occurred to me; has Gogo been buried yet? I needed to find out because I really have to go to her funeral if possible. There was no way I could ask my dad or Sherry-Lee about it after the way they'd behaved when they told me Gogo had died so I left my room and went instead to look for Beauty in the kitchen. I found Patience, our other maid in the scullery doing the ironing.

'Ah Sabi, sakubona,' she said when she saw me, a big smile spreading across her face.

I can speak Ndebele quite well, having grown up around Gogo who always spoke this language with her friends, but I feel very self-conscious when I use it so I just said hello back to Patience in English.

'I'm so sad about Gogo,' I continued.

Patience's face dropped in sympathy and she shook her head slowly from side to side. 'Ah, yes. Too bad, too terrible, too, too terrible, too.....'

'Where's Beauty?' I interrupted, as I know she has a tendency to repeat herself like this.

'She's taken time off since.'

'Oh yes, of course.' Stupid of me to think she'd be around when her mother had just died. 'Has Gogo been buried yet?' I asked.

'Ah no, tomorrow. Beauty wanted to wait for you to come back from school.'

This astonished me; that she should think of me like this. 'Do you know where she's going to be buried Patience?'

'In the compound, in the place where everyone is buried there.'

I have never spent much time in the compound, my dad usually not allowing me to go there, so have no idea where this place for burying is, but assumed there would be a crowd so I'd soon find it.

'Thank you Patience,' I said, 'I'll be there.'

I went back to my room then to decide on what to wear. I've never been to a funeral before, let alone a funeral for a black person, so have no idea how anyone dresses for them. I do see in the American movies I watch on television that most people wear black, but I don't have any black clothes. I opened my cupboard door and the first dress I saw was a dark blue, short sleeved dress Gogo made for me last year and I knew immediately that it would be ideal. To be honest, this is one thing I won't miss about Gogo, her dressmaking. She has made my clothes for me ever since I was a baby and although she was very good at sewing they just weren't ever very trendy and now that I've turned fifteen this is important, otherwise people will make fun of me. I hope that now she isn't around to make them any more Dad will be forced to give me some money to go and buy stuff that I actually want. This is something I'm going to have to talk to him about when Sherry-Lee leaves to go back to Bulawayo. Not that I don't have some fairly nice clothes. My gran sent me a really cool pair of jeans for Christmas last year and Sarah's mother has bought me some trendy shirts and shorts over the years. I think she may be aware of my predicament.

*

I got to the compound just as the truck carrying Gogo's coffin arrived from Gwanda, the small town which is closest to our mine. I hadn't thought before about where Gogo would've been since she'd died, but now I realised she must've been in the mortuary in Gwanda, because the truck had 'Hamba Kahele Burial Services-Gwanda' painted on the side of it. I was very relieved about this because it's too hot here at this time of the year for her to have not been in a mortuary. We do have a large cold room outside the kitchen, which might have done in the case of an emergency, I suppose, but thankfully this was obviously not needed.

I managed to get to the grave before the coffin had even been taken out of the truck but most of the people there knew me and immediately pushed me forward so that I was standing right next to the hole. I felt bad about this but Beauty was there, sobbing quietly and she grabbed my hand and held it very tightly in hers and wouldn't let it go. I looked at Beauty crying next to me and felt her wet hand in mine and I thought I should start crying too, but I couldn't. I was still having a hard time trying to get my head around what had happened.

There were lots of people standing about, some wearing black but some in quite bright clothes and there were some ladies in their church outfits, brown skirts and white shirts and little brown hats on their heads. These ladies were all singing their African church songs very loudly, songs that go on and on and are quite repetitive. I looked around and saw Jabula carrying the coffin from the truck with some other men. I turned back again and focused on the hole and waited while they brought the coffin to the graveside and I felt very uncomfortable when they put it on the opposite side of the grave to me. I stared at it and imagined poor Gogo lying in it and wished like crazy that I wasn't so close, but even though Beauty had let go of my hand by now I felt it would be rude to move off; I knew they were treating me like one of the family by having me stand at the graveside with them.

It didn't take very long for me to realise that Gogo must've been a Catholic because a Catholic priest materialised from somewhere and started waving his incense container around. Even though we were in the fresh air the smell of the incense was very strong and it made me feel a little sick, especially as I was starting to get very hot, standing in the sun as we were. The priest spoke in Ndebele and everyone prayed and although I could understand what the priest was saying I just pretended to join in with the prayers. The songs were in Ndebele too, but I really did not know the words so I just hummed along as best I could. I was greatly relieved when the priest put down his incense container and picked up a bowl of holy water and started flicking this at the coffin. I was feeling uncomfortably hot now and also a bit giddy, so it was almost a relief when a few drops of holy water landed on me. I wished the priest would flick the whole bowl my way.

And I'm afraid to say that that is all I remember about Gogo's funeral because as far as I knew, one minute I was thinking how nice it would be to have the whole bowl of holy water poured over my head and the next minute I was lying on a bed in a dark, stuffy room. When I discovered this I was very confused for a moment, but as soon as I moved my head on the pillow an old woman who I'd never seen before quickly came forward and stood next to the bed looking down at me. She was wearing the dark brown church outfit that I'd noticed quite a few of the ladies wearing at the funeral and she had thick glasses similar to the glasses Gogo used to wear. This made me wonder what was going to happen to those glasses.

Before I could think any more along these lines, however, she bent towards me and smiled as she said, 'Umntanami, you fell asleep.' This confused me further because I knew I could not have fallen asleep at the graveside, but then I realised that I must have fainted. I put my hand up to my forehead, which was still slightly sticky, and I could feel that the underarms of my blue dress were wringing wet from sweat, as I'd been so incredibly hot while I'd been standing next to the grave. The dress felt very tight now around my bust and also the sleeves. I couldn't remember if I'd put deodorant on in the morning and wanted to sniff my armpit, but couldn't do this in front of a stranger. I wished I could take my dress off but there was no way I could do this either in a room I had never been in before and in front of a woman I did not know.

'Where am I?' I asked the lady.

'The room for Beauty,' she replied but said no more.

I could see from the look on her face that she was concerned about me but she was not very good at speaking English, and she wouldn't have known I could understand Ndebele, so she didn't explain properly my predicament. But now that I was becoming more aware I could hear that there was still singing going on somewhere outside.

'I think I'll go back to the funeral then,' I said, and I started to get up from the bed. Isn't that the whole reason I was here anyway?

'No,' she said very quickly, shaking her head quite forcefully. 'You must stay here.' She poured some water from a plastic bottle into a tin mug and handed it to me.

I took a sip of the water. It was not cold but when I drank it I realised how thirsty I was, so I drank some more. Now that I thought about it, I recalled that I hadn't actually had anything to eat or drink all day. I had been so scared that I would bump into Sherry-Lee at the house before I set off for the compound, I'd snuck out early through the side door before she got up. No wonder I'd fainted. I looked at the old lady in the room with me and realised that the other people at the funeral probably didn't want me to go back either in case I fainted again. Talk about making a spectacle of myself and spoiling poor Gogo's funeral. Tears came into my eyes as I thought about this, but then I looked at the lady again and managed to control myself.

'You go back,' I said, pointing to the door. She hesitated but I nodded my head. 'It's alright, I'll be fine. You can go back to the funeral; I promise I'll be fine.'

With some reluctance she picked up her hat and opened the door.

'It's alright, it's alright,' I said quickly, as she hesitated in the doorway.

The bright sunshine from the opened door made me feel slightly giddy again and I decided that it was for the best after all if I rested up a bit longer in the dark of Beauty's room. The old lady closed the door behind her and I lay back again on Beauty's soft, lumpy bed but this did not stop me from looking around, because I'd never been into any of the Af's houses in the compound before. I quickly noticed that the room was chock-a-block full of all her belongings as if this was her bedroom, her sitting room and her dining room all in one, and it had strong smell of polish or something like that about it. A wardrobe was in one corner with lots of boxes and bags piled on top of it, a dresser on the opposite wall full of plastic dishes and containers and also some pots and pans. It had glass sliding doors at the back and I could see some glasses and plates inside. Next to the dresser was a Formica dining table with four chairs. In the middle of the room there were two small armchairs each with a cushion and pieces of material over the arms. I recognised the material from a dress Gogo had made me some years ago. She must've used the scraps to make these cushions and arm covers. There were many boxes and piles of things covered in pieces of material (most of which I recognised from various outfits Gogo had made for me over the years) but I wasn't about to start removing the material to see what was under these piles.

The room was extremely crowded but still very clean, but just as I was thinking this a large cockroach ran out from underneath the dresser, scurried across the shiny, polished floor and disappeared under one of the piles. This made me wonder how many other cockroaches there were lurking in the room.

I took another sip of water and decided that I was starting to get a bit bored. I could still hear the singing outside and wondered how much longer everyone would be at the funeral. I knew I could not leave the room until it was over, in case the mourners saw me sneaking off, and that really would be the biggest insult to Gogo. I was just starting to think about trying to go to sleep when the door opened again, letting in a shaft of bright light, so that for a moment I could not see who was entering. But the door closed quickly and as I peered in the direction of it I saw, to my amazement that a white woman had come into the room. This really surprised me, because I hadn't seen any other white people at the graveside and besides this, this was the mine compound where only the Afs live.

'Sabi Star?' this lady asked, before I could carry on wondering about these things, and this made me even more amazed, because she had used my special, private name. In fact I was so surprised that I didn't reply at first so she had to go on.

'Hi,' she said, 'my name is Clare and I was a friend of Dorca's for a while.'

2

Clare

IMAGINE this rather surreal scenario; a village on a gold mine in the middle of the African bush, miles away from any town. Small houses made out of concrete blocks, and mud huts dotted intermittently amongst patches of maize, grasses, weeds and trees, with rocky hills in the distance. Black men, women and children surrounding an open grave, crying and singing and praying, and in amongst all of this a young white girl, standing right next to the grave and almost falling into it.

For me, living now in America as I do, it was vibrant, exhilarating and exciting, despite the fact that it was a funeral, and therefore it was sad too. Initially, I had no idea that the white girl was there because I had stationed myself away from all of the activity, trying to blend as best I could into the background, unnoticed. But as I stood in the cool shade of a large tree, leaning against the trunk, I became uncomfortably aware of three small picanins, appearing from I'm not sure where and settling themselves on a nearby anthill to stare at me. At first, I smiled courteously at them and the one little girl smiled back, the second girl looked very embarrassed and the third child, a boy, didn't change the expression on his face at all. They continued staring at me until eventually I could resist the temptation no longer; I surreptitiously aimed the camera I was holding at them and took some photos. I'm a photographer by profession and therefore I always try to take advantage of any photo opportunity I come across; the image of these three children, with their black, smudgy skins, wide eyes, snotty noses and raggedy clothes, huddled on their anthill and staring blankly at me most definitely made an intriguing photo. I've been finding lots of photo opportunities since I arrived here in Zimbabwe; this aspect of my stay has been great so far. Unlike the western world, people here don't seem to get all het up about having their pictures taken; you give them some prints and they're usually delighted.

I've been back here for four weeks now, staying and 'working' on a wildlife conservancy belonging to my cousin, Rob Fenton and his wife, Leanne. I used to come here a lot when I lived in this country as a kid, and also when I was a teenager living in the United States, coming back every few years for holidays. The conservancy was a cattle ranch then, but Rob changed it to a conservancy about fourteen years ago, selling all his cattle and stocking it with wildlife. He named it the Ubejane Conservancy because Ubejane means rhino in the native language and they have a fair-sized rhino population in this conservancy, which is pretty impressive really, as rhino are badly poached in this part of the world. They have many other types of wild animals too, as well as a safari lodge for hunters to stay in during the hunting season and for tourists and other people during the off season, although it's never that busy then.

Rob's sister Janine and I were very close when we were young, maybe because we were the same age. I was pretty tight with Rob too, although he was two years younger than us. I used to crave my visits to Zimbabwe to stay with them on their ranch more than anything else in my life when I was a teenager. We used to camp down by the river, drive round the ranch in their beat up old Land Rovers, go horseback riding; all so different from the more sterile life I lead back in the States. Tragically, Janine was killed in a car accident when we were twenty two and I never came back to stay after that, although I have sort of kept in touch with Rob. However, he must've still been pretty surprised when I emailed him six weeks ago to ask if I could come and stay for a while, as I needed some 'time out' from my real life. I had never met his wife Leanne before and was not expecting someone like her. It's difficult to describe what I mean, but let me just say that I always feel slightly inadequate in her company. When Rob replied to my initial email he asked if I'd mind staying at their lodge, saying that it would be useful having me there, keeping an eye on things. When I got here I quickly decided that Leanne had probably thrown a bit of a wobbly at the prospect of having me staying in her house for an undetermined length of time, but had agreed to let me stay in the lodge as a compromise. I suppose it suits me pretty well as I need time on my own to sort myself out, and at least neither of them has asked me prying questions about why exactly I am here, even though I'm sure Leanne is itching to find out all the gory details. Anyways, I don't have a great deal to do at the camp when there are no guests so I spend most of my time taking photographs and working on them on my computer. When we do have guests, which has been on two weekends so far since I've been here, Leanne arrives a few days before with lists of instructions of things to do and things to buy and she usually sends me off to the nearest city, Bulawayo, to get supplies.

The reason I happened to be at this particular funeral is because Jabula Sibanda, son of the deceased lady, works as a waiter at the lodge. He had told me about his sick mother, and I, with nothing better to do and quite interested in exploring further afield in a quest to find new subjects to photograph, offered to drive him to visit her twice. When he told me his mother had died I asked Rob again if I could drive him to the funeral and he seemed pretty cool with this idea.

So I had gotten to meet the deceased and I certainly thought that she was a grand old lady. Even in her sick state she had great dignity and it saddened me to think that she had had no opportunity to do anything more with her life than clean and look after someone else's house. This house where she worked can be seen quite easily from the road to the mine compound. While the homes in the compound are small and scraggily, the main house looks very grand and gracious from the road; a big, rambling three storey place, surrounded by rolling green lawns and large trees. I'd love to take a peek inside. There's obviously no shortage of money there judging from the cars parked in the garage and the light aircraft on the airfield just down the road from the house. Jabula told me that the mine, and indeed the whole property, is owned by a family named Stirling and they made lots of money a long time ago from mining gold, but he has never elaborated on this.

And so, because he's never really told me much, I had no idea that there was a young girl living at the house and that she would be at the funeral. I didn't notice her for a while, so preoccupied was I with the picanins and their staring at me. I did notice however what must've been the hearse (it was really just a beaten up old pickup truck) drive through the compound and around a patch of mealies near to where the hole had been dug to bury the old lady. Jabula had told me on the way here that many, many mine workers and their families had been buried in this area near the mealie field and when I looked around from under my tree I could see this; quite a few crosses here and there obviously marking some graves, and then other graves marked with piles of stones. I noticed with interest that on some graves there were belongings which I guessed the dead person must've used when they were alive; a tin mug or plate or even an old shoe or other item of clothing. I wondered if anyone would put something on Jabula's mother's grave that she had used in her lifetime.

It was only when the little girl fainted and nearly fell into the grave that I realised that she was there. Even though I was fairly far away, leaning against the trunk of my nice shady tree, I couldn't help but notice the commotion this caused. The priest stopped droning on in his monotonous way and stood, completely stunned, looking over his bible with his large glasses perched on his nose as Jabula first caught her, then steadied her, probably unsure of what to do next, and then finally scooped her up and took her off to a nearby hut. I noticed that she was a very skinny little girl dressed in a dark blue dress that seemed way too small and tight fitting, as it rode up her thigh when Jabula carried her off. She had thick, dark hair tied in a tight plait, which fell across her face as her head lolled against Jabula's shoulder.

The service restarted when Jabula came back, the priest picking up where he'd left off with renewed vigour, but I was no longer remotely interested in any of this, wondering instead if I should do something to help the little girl. Strangely, I felt that as the only other white person there I had a responsibility to her and besides this, she had looked so pathetic and vulnerable when Jabula carried her off with her legs and knickers exposed in an undignified way. The priest eventually finished his monologue and the congregated mourners broke into another song, which I knew from the previous songs would be very slow, very long and very monotonous so I decided to take this opportunity to go and see how the girl was.

The three children were still sitting on the anthill, although they were no longer solely focused on me now, but I walked up to them and tried to ask them who the young white girl was. I wasn't sure if they understood me but the eldest girl blinked and said something that sounded like 'Sabi Star,' which confused me as I know that this is a strange looking indigenous bush which grows at the lodge. However, she escorted me to a hut a ways off from all the activity and when I entered and murmured rather hesitantly, 'Sabi Star' to the girl lying on the bed I could see from her reaction that this was indeed her name.

'My name is just Sabi,' she eventually explained after I had introduced myself.

*

When I was getting ready to leave, Jabula informed me that he had asked Rob if he could stay a few days at the mine to be with the rest of his family. I was surprised and slightly peeved when he told me this. If I'd known before I may not have been so keen to come, as it meant driving back in the bush alone and I hadn't driven any distance on my own in the middle of the bush. However, there was nothing for it but to set off, trying to cast aside my worries about getting lost or having a puncture or meeting a herd of elephant or something like that. I was able to rule out the prospect of meeting elephant when I remembered that they were usually on the other side of the conservancy to where I'd be driving, and I just had to hope like hell I wouldn't have a puncture.

As for getting lost, as soon as I started my journey I found that I recognised distinguishable trees and kopjies, making it fairly easy to know which direction to go. It takes about an hour to drive from the mine to the lodge, and once I'd overcome my initial worries I started to enjoy myself. When I first arrived in Zimbabwe at the end of October, the rains had not yet started and the bush was extremely brown and arid-looking, but now, just four weeks later and after a few extremely heavy rainstorms, the bush has turned thick and lush. It's wild and rough looking, so different to the countryside back home, which for the most part is manicured and tamed with lots of fences and everything in its place. Here the dusty, corrugated road was the only sign of any development for most of my journey. Obviously, closer to the lodge there are further signs of civilization, more roads, some fences and then finally tar on the section of the road that climbs steeply up the huge dwala, on which the camp is built.

*

I thought of Sabi as I drove home. Sabi Star. What a strange young girl with a strange sounding name, a wounded character I could tell, not quite sure how, but then I reminded myself cynically that one wounded person can easily recognise another. I'm speaking for myself, that is. She will have no inkling, I hope, of the deep wounds that I'm trying to heal; first because I'm so good at keeping them hidden and second because at just fourteen or fifteen she must surely be far too young to have such insight. Hopefully, she's still innocent enough and self absorbed enough to have many illusions of a better life to come one day.

*

I had expected to have the lodge to myself when I got back, so I was surprised to find Rob's Land Cruiser there as I roared up the steep hill and parked in the garage next to it. I found him in the lodge office and as soon as I saw his face I could see that something was wrong.

'Thank God you're back now,' he said as soon as he saw me. 'I was worried that you'd be delayed, and we need you because there are going to be people staying in the lodge tonight.

'Oh yes?' I asked.

'We had a rhino mother and calf culled in the early hours of this morning. Andre and the trackers have been out all day trying to catch the poachers. Fuck, I hope they get them this time.'

He looked at me angrily as he said this.

'Sorry about my language, but I'm really pissed off.'

'Hey, I don't blame you,' I said.

Poaching is a real problem in this part of the world and we have at least six rhino poached every year at Ubejane. Other animals are poached too, especially zebra, but rhino are of most concern because if the rate they are killed goes on as it is, they will be extinct in the not too distant future. The poachers kill them solely for their horns. I still find it hard to believe that these almost prehistoric animals are killed for no other reason than this. The horn is dug out or hacked off the face and the carcass is left to rot in the bush. Rob told me that there have been times when the horn is gouged from the rhino's face before the animal is even dead, but it dies later from infection. How terrible is that?

Andre is head of the anti-poaching operations here on Ubejane and he lives in a small house near the main homestead with someone called Wayne, who is his second-in-command. Apparently before they came to work here twenty to thirty rhino were being poached every year. Andre and Wayne are both in their early thirties, appearing to be quiet types who are completely at home in the bush; although I have noticed that they seem to take it in turns to go to Bulawayo on alternate weekends.

'I get doubly angry when a calf is killed,' Rob went on, 'and especially if it's a female as this one was. But at least we found the carcasses this time, just a few hours after the cull, they were still warm. We got the ground trackers out straight away and they seem to have picked up the poachers' tracks.'

'That sounds promising.'

'Yes. And just so that everyone knows we mean business, we managed to get the rhino dehorning guys to come today, too. In fact, they were coming sometime soon anyway but after what happened here this morning I radioed them and asked if they could get here asap. They'll arrive later and stay here tonight, and tomorrow they will go off in their helicopter and try and dart as many rhino as they can find. They remove as much of the horn as possible without injuring the animals, so making them less attractive to these thieving, poaching bastards. There will be three or four of them staying here I believe, and Andre and the two police officers who've been working with him will also probably want to eat here tonight.'

Fanwell, the lodge cook, had taken a few days leave as we hadn't been expecting visitors until the weekend and so I realised with a slightly sinking heart that I'd have to do all the cooking myself. Fanwell is an excellent cook and can serve up a delicious meal with little fuss or bother it seems, while I have no such skill, and especially not in the lodge kitchen, which is basic to say the least. And to make matters worse, I also knew that there wasn't much in the pantry as I'd be planning on going off to Bulawayo in a few days time to do a major restock. But of course I couldn't start divulging any of these worries to Rob right then, he looked stressed enough about everything as it was.

'By the way Clare,' Rob went on, 'Graham phoned our house this morning, wondering how you were getting on. I told him you were doing well.'

I stared at him for a moment, my mind racing as I tried to digest this information without showing any outward reaction. I made a great effort to look as normal as I could and I'm sure I managed this even though my smile felt very insincere to me.

'Oh great, and how is he?'

'Fine, it seems. I suggested he came out for Christmas, said we'd really like to see him, but he thinks he might be too busy still trying to finish off his work. Anyway, I'd better get going, lots to do trying to mop up the mess these bloody poachers have made. I'll see you later.'

He quickly left and I was glad that I could throw myself into all I had to do, preparing the lodge for the guests I'd have later. This was the first time Graham had made contact with me since I've been here. Of course, I could've contacted him, but things are very difficult right now and I've never thought it was my place to do so. Not making any contact has been very easy for me as there is no cellphone signal or any other means of outside communication, for that matter, at the lodge. The thought of his coming out here for Christmas filled me with both hope and apprehension, but thankfully there was no time to dwell on any of this right then. I had to make sure that everything was in order for when the visitors arrived later.

The lodge is built on a fairly high rock hill or dwala and the surrounding countryside is flat in comparison, so that you have a great feeling of elevation and there are amazing views from nearly everywhere. It comprises of thatched garages, kitchen and office blocks as you come in, and beyond these, over a small patch of lawn and around a big rock is a large sitting/dining lapa, as they call it, partly open and partly moulded very cleverly into the natural rock structure. In front of this is a wide stone deck with a fire pit and a barbeque where we congregate most nights when visitors are here. Steps lead upwards from this deck to the pool and bar area, which have been built around the rocks at the highest point on the dwala, so that there are three hundred and sixty degree views from every position up there. We often come up to this place to watch the sunsets or sunrises. The rest of the lodge consists of seven smallish thatched A-framed buildings dotted around, each with a little verandah out the front, French doors into a bedroom, which sleeps two, and a bathroom behind this. They are very comfortably decorated and Rob, quite the enterprising architect I've come to realise, had the ingenuity to design an outside shower/bath alongside every bedroom. I have spent many an hour luxuriating in my outside bath, most often with a glass of wine in hand, and watching a magnificent sunset, or a night sky alive with millions of stars, as I have pondered on the ridiculousness of my situation, situated here in this tiny little slice of supposed paradise, but knowing really that my life is a complete mess and at some stage I'm going to have to sort myself out.

3

Sabi

SOMETIMES I wonder if Dad isn't a bit promiscuous himself. He's had loads of girlfriends ever since I can remember, he really has. I've always hoped that he'd marry someone nice and that I'd have a loving stepmother, but this just has not happened. And this current girlfriend, Sherry-Lee (she always explains that it's Sherry-Lee with a double e as if this is supposed to make her special), is almost the worst of the lot, and that's saying something, because none of them have been particularly nice. She's a lot younger than Dad so that we'd be more like sisters than daughter/stepmother if he was to marry her, cross fingers and toes this never happens. She lives and works in Bulawayo, but when

Dad is around she drives down here to the mine every weekend and I just hate it. She makes me feel doubly uncomfortable in my own home. She's got this way of making me think I'm always doing something wrong. It's no wonder I've always spent as much time as I can away from her and with Gogo, but Dad has always frowned on me going down to the compound with her, so most of our time was spent in the kitchen.

One good thing about this is I've learnt to be a really good cook. I am actually the best in my cookery class at school and in some ways it's a shame I know how to do well in my tests and have been put in the A stream, because next term I won't be able to do cookery any more. Only the C and D streamers do cookery once we get to form four, which is the form I'll be in when I go back to school next term, I have to do Physics and Chemistry instead.

Sherry-Lee brought me back home from school yesterday. I really didn't want to drive all the way back here with her but what choice did I have? Dad had told the headmistress that she'd pick me up and I couldn't exactly start arguing about this when the headmistress summoned me to her office to tell me. But as it turned out Sherry-Lee switched her iPod on really loud so we didn't have to talk much after all. At first I'd glance at her every now and then and try to think of something to say but she basically ignored me and listened to her music so I soon didn't bother. In actual fact, she has quite good taste in music and I know my friends would think so too, but then the gap between our ages isn't that big; just nine years or so, as opposed to the twenty years between her and Dad.

*

She was her usual 'charming' self when I got back from Gogo's funeral, as was my dad.

'Where the hell have you been?' he yelled as soon as he saw me.

Oh boy, how I hate it when he yells like that, which happens a lot when You-Know-Who is around. They were standing on the back verandah so of course they noticed me the minute I walked through the little back gate. The back verandah has 'mile-a-minute' creeper growing up the pillars and as this is always thick and lush and cascading down over the beams like a curtain, I didn't see them standing out there. If I had, I would have snuck around to the front gate or otherwise I would have waited for them to go back inside. But now they'd caught me.

'I went to Gogo's funeral,' I replied, trying to sound like they would have approved.

'Jeez Digger, you really shouldn't let her fraternize with the Munts the way she does,' Sherry-Lee said. 'She'll end up being like them before you know it.'

She turned to me with distaste.

'You really shouldn't have gone to that funeral Sabi. It's not the place for a young white girl.'

I looked hard at her and wanted to tell her it wasn't her place to tell me what I should and should not do, but I bit my tongue and turned my attention to my feet instead.

'I gave Dorca's family two hundred dollars to pay for the funeral so that should have been fine for them, in fact more than enough,' my dad said.

I looked up at him, 'I'm sure it was, Dad, but I still wanted to go and pay my respects. I've known her all my life and I feel really sad that she's died.'

'Stupid,' Sherry-Lee said, turning to walk back into the house.

But this time I could not help myself.

'It's not. You don't know anything about it, because you have only known us for a short time.'

She stopped dead in her tracks and turned round.

'Long enough Sabi to…..'

Thankfully my dad butted in and interrupted her.

'Unfortunately Sabi, the Rawsons have invited us for tea and drinks so we've been looking for you for the last few hours to tell you to get ready.'

'You didn't tell me before.'

'I didn't know I had to, I didn't know you'd wander off to the compound on your own.'

Sherry-Lee yawned.

'Can't we go without her Digger?' She looked at her watch.

'There's still time, surely she doesn't have to come with us.'

I continued staring at my feet as I thought to myself that the last thing I wanted was to go to the Rawsons for tea, drinks, anything, for that matter, with her and my dad. I wished, as I have so many times before, that he wouldn't hang around with her. I can see that she is very pretty and that she had a good figure, but she just is not a nice person. Why can't he see this?

'Ok then, let's get going,' my dad said to her.

*

After they had gone, I went and lay on my bed and brooded about what Sherry-Lee with a double-e had said. It's really stupid that she should tell me that I shouldn't mix with the Afs on this mine when considering I've lived here virtually the entire fifteen years of my life. How can you live in a place for so long and just ignore most people that live there too? You can't, I say. Before we came here, Dad had been trying his luck at cattle ranching down in the Lowveld. He and my mother had been there for at least ten years but he came to the mine soon after I was born, which happens to coincide with when my mum died.

This mine belongs to Dad's family. It's a gold mine and they made a lot of money from it many years ago, so the story goes. I suppose by some people's standards we still have lots of money, although I don't really see it this way. I certainly don't get as much pocket money as most girls in my class, which is why I try finding other means to earn. The house we live in was built by my dad's grandparents and it's very big, three storeys with six bedrooms and five bathrooms. It's way too big for just Dad and me and, of course, Sherry-Lee doesn't count because when she comes to stay she always sleeps in Dad's room.

I think what happened was that after my mother died Dad didn't like living with just me on the cattle ranch in the Lowveld and so his mother persuaded him to come back here to the family mine and start reworking it. The gold price was very good then and with all the new techniques for removing ore from the ground and gold from the old dumps they decided that it would be worth their while again. And I think they were right. Dad has done pretty well from it and I'm sure this is why young girls like Sherry-Lee like being with him.

I can never make up my mind whether I like living on the mine or not. I certainly like my bedroom. It's really big and has an en suite bathroom and a balcony, which overlooks the garden. Not that I spend much time on the balcony. It's really hot in this part of the country for at least eight months of the year and I spend a lot of my time in my bedroom with the air conditioner on full blast. But I've got all my things in my bedroom and my gran, my dad's mother, helped me decorate it quite nicely and it really is my favourite place in the house.

What I don't like about living on the mine is that I spend so much of my time alone. It's always been like this. We live about one hundred kilometres from Bulawayo, where I go to school, and twenty kilometres from the nearest small town, Gwanda, so we really are pretty far away from things. I have been at boarding school in Bulawayo since I was five years old, so at least during the school term I've got lots of people around me, but when I get back here I'm pretty much on my own. I've never asked a friend to come and stay here before, mainly because Dad can sometimes be so rude, but I've decided it's time to change this and I asked Sarah if she'd like to come after New Year. I explained to her how Dad can sometimes be and she said, 'no worries,' which of course is fine for her to say as he's not her dad, but at least she will come prepared. Now I just need to put it to Dad and I'll do this when Sherry-Lee isn't around, otherwise she'll definitely shove her oar straight in and make it all the more difficult for me. I've decided that she's probably a bit jealous of me because even though my dad isn't very loving towards me, I do still belong to him and I think she probably wants him to belong to just her. I don't think she has too much in her life, judging from the car she drives and you'll probably find when she looks at this house of ours and the cars my dad drives and his aeroplane which he uses to fly himself from one mine to another, she'd like to have a share in all of this, too. Since she got here she's spent most of her time lying by the pool catching a tan, when she isn't in my dad's bedroom or having her meals. Talk about boring, and I just have to hope and pray my dad eventually realises this and stops letting her come and stay.

*

I had a lovely rest of the day at home without them. I haven't been home for the whole of the last term and since getting back I haven't had a chance to relax, what with the trauma of losing Gogo and having Sherry-Lee around, forever criticising me. But without her here, I was able to do what I like best, lie on the sofa and flick through all the television channels and watch exactly what I want. There weren't any interesting movies on but I discovered that Zimbabwe was playing Sri Lanka in a one-day cricket match in Bulawayo and so I spent quite a lot of time watching this, mainly to see who I knew when the cameras panned onto the crowds. Cricket matches are always the places to go to see and be seen if you're a kid my age, and sure enough I saw quite a few of my friends there. Most irritatingly, I saw Tracey dressed in a pair of jeans so tight she must've struggled to get them over her hips, and a small t shirt that showed a great deal of her tummy. She was obviously sitting quite close to a camera because it kept panning on her and I was not happy to see that she was sitting in a crowd that included Mike. She kept getting up and walking around, though, probably to attract the cameraman and to show off her abs, but Mike didn't seem to notice her comings and goings, well from what I could see by watching them in between the shots of the cricket. I felt a bit left out from time to time, alone in my sitting room while all my friends were socializing at the cricket match. That's the problem with being the daughter of a mine owner and living so far out of town on a mine.

I eventually got bored, lying around with nothing of interest to watch on TV except the cricket match and they were showing way too much of the actual game and not enough of the crowd to hold my attention, so I decided I'd go and see how my fort was doing. This fort is actually a large, fat baobab tree growing near the river. It works really well as a fort because the trunk must've split a bit when the tree was still small and this has made a hollow that is almost like a small cave. And you can climb up this and into the first fork between the branches and there is a little hole in the branches where I have always kept the things I like to play with at the fort. In the old days when I was little I used to keep the doll my gran gave me there, (Poppy was her name), along with her clothes and blankets.

Gogo used to come with me to the fort, but she couldn't fit through the gap into the hollow of the trunk let alone climb up and into the branches, so she used to sit on a rock nearby and wait for me. After a while, she used to get restless and start saying 'come now Sabi, it's time to go home.' I used to ignore her for as long as I could but in the last year or so I've actually preferred to go on my own. You see, I now go to the fort to practice my smoking and I keep my cigarettes and matches in the hole in the branches. I wondered if the packet of cigarettes I left last time would still be there. If I don't plug the hole really well with rocks and stuff the baboons come and find my possessions and steal them. That's what happened to poor Poppy I'm afraid to say. Once when I got there, I discovered that I didn't have any matches, and so I chain-smoked my way though a whole box of cigarettes. Well, that's exaggerating a bit, but I'm sure I had at least eight cigarettes and I did feel pretty lousy at the end of it, even though I thought it was quite funny to start off with.

When I got to the fort this time, I found that the hole had not been tampered with. I carefully plucked out the rocks and balanced them on the fork of a higher branch so that I could put them back when I was finished. I broke a twig off the end of a branch, and pushed it into the hole and poked it around. I always do this to make sure that there isn't anything nasty in the hole like a snake or a scorpion. I always sit slightly away from the hole when I do this, in case something comes rushing out, even though the worst thing I've ever found in that hole is a beetle. Anyway, when I was satisfied that the coast was clear, I put my hand in and found my cigarettes and matches. I opened the box and found that there were just eleven cigarettes left. I'd have to ask someone in the compound for more at some stage, especially if Sarah did come down to stay because I know she would also enjoy smoking in the tree. I lit a cigarette and started coughing violently. It tasted awful, worse than usual, although it always does take me some time to get used to it again when I've had a break during the school term. I looked at the cigarette carefully. It seemed fine so I had another draw and even though it still tasted awful and made me feel quite dizzy I persevered. I leaned up against the one branch, with my feet propped up on the opposite branch, and spent my time trying to devise a plan on how to get rid of Sherry-Lee. How could I make my dad see that she really was no good for either of us? Of course, the most obvious thing would be to find someone else for him to fall in love with and this made me think about Clare. Mmm. She seemed so nice, but I couldn't see her wanting to give up her life in America to come and live on a mine in the middle of nowhere. I wracked my brain trying to think of something else but nothing worthy of consideration came to mind.

I got home when it was nearly dark and was not surprised to find the house empty. My dad often doesn't come home until after I've gone to bed. Of course, I've had Gogo before to cook me something and stay with me until he got back, but I suppose I am old enough now to be at home alone. I was quite tired anyway and didn't mind an early night after all the trauma of the funeral and everything.

However, when I woke up the following morning and there was still no sign of them I was very surprised. I walked past my dad's bedroom door and saw that it was open which was not usual because Sherry-Lee usually stays in bed until very late when she is here, with the door closed so that no-one will disturb her. I went downstairs and noticed that all the lights were still on everywhere and that's when I realised that they hadn't come home at all. This was most definitely not usual. I went out to the back verandah where there is a good view of the road and even when you can't see anything on the actual road you can usually see the dust from cars that are driving up or down the road. There was no dust and no cars. I sat there waiting.

Patience eventually arrived for work at eight o'clock. I watched her come though the back gate and walk over the back lawn without even knowing that she was being watched. She got quite a fright when she stepped onto the verandah and I said 'Morning Patience.'

She jumped backwards and then started to laugh when she saw it was me.

'My wey, my wey, my wey,' she said, shaking her head.

'The boss hasn't come back and I'm wondering where he is,' I explained to her.

She looked surprised herself but just looked at her watch and said we should wait for him. She went into the house and came out again five minutes later with a cup of tea and toast and Bovril for me.

'You go and watch the television,' she suggested, but I really didn't feel like it at this time of the morning so continued sitting on the verandah and watching for dust.

Eventually, at nine o'clock, Patience said she'd go down to the manager, Mr. Potgieter's house and ask him if he'd heard from my dad. Funnily enough, I hadn't even thought of that before.

4

Clare

WE left Zimbabwe and went to live in America when I was twelve, just after I'd finished junior school. My father had been working as a geologist on the mine at Hwange and an American man, Jim Bishop, worked there for a while. He and my father became friends and when he went back to America he arranged a job for my father in Texas and that is pretty much the reason we left. Zimbabwe had been independent for eight years by then and my parents decided there was no future for white people here. Unfortunately, at twelve I didn't see things this way and I was very unhappy with their decision; something I have still not fully reconciled myself to, and as a result have spent most of my life wishing things hadn't gone the way they did. Obviously, everything is always that much rosier when you are a kid. I'm sure it wasn't that great in Zimbabwe then, but it is impossible to think of it differently when all memories are such happy ones. While other people may ponder on the war before independence and all the problems afterwards with white people still being abducted and killed, none of this really impinged on my little life. We had the Hwange game park nearby and we'd oftentimes go there, sometimes just for the day but on other occasions we'd camp at a water hole for the night and I can still remember the great excitement I felt as I zipped myself into my sleeping bag, listening to the elephant grumble and trumpet as they splashed and drank water just a short distance from our campsite. I didn't have siblings but this didn't bother me then as I had loads of friends and we always seemed to have so much to do; hacking on horseback in the bush, swimming at the club, hanging out in our tree fort, playing tennis, squash, and polo cross.

At first the idea of moving to America was fairly exciting, but I quickly changed my mind about this. In the first few weeks we were there, the kids at my new school were vaguely interested in me, mainly because my accent was different to theirs, but this soon wore off and from then onwards I found myself continually trying to fit in with a group of kids I had absolutely nothing in common with, and in a place that was completely foreign to me in every way. I missed the bush and my previous life so much it actually used to hurt, and I could never understand how my parents didn't miss it as much as me. I think now they probably did, but neither of them had the time to dwell on it too much. They were both always off working, or so it seemed. I think if I'd had siblings things would have been easier for me as I'd have had them for support, but I did not, and I went from being the confident, self assured, outgoing little girl I was in Zimbabwe to a shy, lonely, self absorbed and depressed teenager, except for the times when I used to come back and stay with my cousins.

When I've been for therapy, as I have in recent months, my therapist has agreed that the move to America would have had a profound effect on me, but at the same time she has made me see that I could have dealt with it differently, and not let it destroy me like it did. I wasn't so sure I liked being told this; I like having excuses for my inadequacies.

All I know, though, is that I felt like a misfit when I first got there, and after so many years of living there, I still don't feel I fit in properly.

But the interesting thing is that now I'm back in Zimbabwe after not having been here for over fifteen years I feel that I don't really fit in here either anymore. I look at life here and I observe it through the eyes of an outsider, making me continually question what I see and experience. I see that there is still a lot here that is magical, but there is so much that is a complete mess now, and I really struggle to get my head around this.

I look at the idiosyncrasy of Rob and Leanne's life for instance. Rob has lived in this part of the world all his life and never had any desire to live elsewhere. He has adapted and changed to make things work for him and on the whole has been pretty successful. It was very clever of him, for instance, to change their cattle ranch into a game conservancy, getting foreigners to invest, because when the first real rumblings of disgruntlement started about the whites having all the best farmland, he knew that if he kept it as a normal farm it would almost definitely be confiscated.

How right he was; all the ranches in the area have been taken from the white families who previously owned them while Rob and Leanne still have theirs, yet realise it may still be taken at any time. All it takes is some politician with the right connections deciding that he wants it, and it will be gone in a flash. But they appear to ignore this and just get on with things. They have a wonderful expanse of land, with their beautiful lodge and a comfortable home and hundreds of different species of animal; they have stunning bush with amazing trees, kopjies and waterways. On the face of it, it's paradise, yet once you've been here a while you see that, besides the fact that it could be taken away in an instant, they have endless other problems too; problems with animals continuously being poached, fences cut and stolen, trees felled for firewood and rivers being silted up by people illegally panning for gold.

*

The rhino guys, as I thought of them, arrived shortly before dusk and comprised of a team of four, Steve, Dave, Clive and Pete. They are based in Chiredzi, a small town in the south-west of the country and they work for the Rhino Conservation and Research Trust and one of their ongoing jobs is the dehorning of rhino. Apparently, if all the rhino were left with their horns, the poaching problem would be almost uncontrollable. Steve is the pilot of the helicopter they use to find and dart the rhino before dehorning, and Dave is a vet. I think Pete and Clive are like apprentices, they're both pretty young.

Before dinner (I managed to cook up a spaghetti bolognaise for this) I found myself sitting around the fire pit with Pete and Clive. We were having a drink while waiting for Andre and Wayne and the policemen who had been tracking the poachers to arrive. Junior, another of the lodge waiters arrived, with our drinks and a bowl of nuts and Clive immediately started up a conversation in fluent Ndebele with him. After Junior left, I commented on his excellent command of this language.

'Well, I was brought up on our family farm, that's where I learnt to speak it,' he said.

'Me too,' Pete said. 'My brothers and I used to play with the Abantu in the farm compound all the time when we were growing up. I think we spoke better Ndebele than English, and we really struggled when we got back to school and had to start speaking English again.'

'Well I'm impressed,' I said.

'Mm,' Clive murmured, 'and a fat lot of good it's done me, everything is fucked up now.' He took a swig of his beer. 'Everything's been taken from us you know, everything. Our home, all the buildings, the sheds, the pumps, engines, tractors, all our tools, irrigation pipes, every single thing they could get their hands on, all in the name of land reform.'

'Surely they couldn't take things like tractors and equipment,' I queried. 'I mean, you hear that land was confiscated but what right did they have to take equipment, as you had to have bought all of that. Surely they couldn't claim a right to it too.'

Clive gave me a sad look. 'Oh yes they could, they could and they did, because no one was going to stop them.' He paused as he took another swig of his beer. 'The police said there was nothing they could do because it was a 'political' issue.' He paused again. 'And of course, we haven't received a cent in compensation, not one cent.'

'It sounds like sanctioned robbery, then?'

'My family certainly see it like that, after all the money they put into developing our place, and it's all been destroyed now anyway.' Pete answered. 'Basically the white farmers were used as an excuse to intimidate.'

'But things have improved in recent years haven't they?' I queried, 'now that there's a unity government?'

'Marginally so, but the economy is still struggling. Agriculture was the mainstay of the economy and you can't just destroy it, turning it into small scale, barely subsistence farming, and expect everything else to be fine, and also, the intimidation on the farms is still really bad.'

I tried to imagine what it must be like, to have your home, your livelihood and basically your whole identity taken from you, and I realised that my experience of being made to go and live in America was actually nothing in comparison. I felt a moment of remorse, that I'd always made such a big deal of it.

I could see, though, that, despite everything, both Pete and Clive still have a great passion for their country. I've noticed this about a lot of the people I've met here; they don't keep questioning things like I do; only the people who want to leave or have left do this. Those that have decided to stay have this 'we'll just get on with it despite everything' attitude, with one of the favourite expressions being, 'we'll make a plan.' Leanne and Rob are again very good examples of this. I'm amazed at how they appear to take everything in their stride; they just don't let all the things I mentioned earlier get them down.

*

Rob and Leanne came to the lodge for dinner and to find out what had happened as far as catching the poachers was concerned. Leanne knew that we didn't have much in the way of vegetables at the lodge, so she brought lettuce, tomatoes, cucumbers and celery for a salad, to go with my spaghetti bolognaise. Like everything else she does, Leanne is a very competent gardener (with the help of three gardeners) and all this stuff for the salad was freshly picked from her vegetable patch. She didn't bring their two young children though; Polly and James were left at home with the maid. I've noticed that this is still the norm when people go out in the evenings in this country. Well, I suppose they can, as everyone seems to employ a maid, if not two or three. I have yet to meet anyone who does not.

Polly and James are the quietest children I've ever met, they're six and eight and so well-behaved you hardly know they are around, even when they are; I think Leanne does most of their talking for them.

They all live in Rob's parents' house which is about five kilometres from the lodge. They moved there after Rob's dad died and his mother went to live with her sister in South Africa. It's a big old rambling farmhouse, a house that has been built onto again and again over the years and as a result it's a bit confused, with two of the four bedrooms leading from the dining room and one of the bathrooms the other side of the kitchen. But it's comfortable enough and it's got a really beautiful garden, with rolling green lawns, huge indigenous trees and big flower beds full of shrubs and flowers. I can remember, even as a child, thinking what a beautiful garden it was.

Leanne marched into the kitchen with a big basket of stuff for the salad and put it on the kitchen table. She immediately sniffed the air and then walked to the stove, taking off the lid of the pot in which I had cooked the spaghetti meat.

'Mmm,' she said, trying a bit on a spoon. 'I think you need more salt and herbs in this. It's a bit bland right now. And maybe some more tomato puree too.'

It's this type of behaviour that always makes me feel inadequate. I don't think she means to, well hopefully she doesn't mean to, hopefully it's just her way. She's quite a bit younger than me, somewhere around thirty two I'd say, but because she's so incredibly organised and efficient, I can't help feeling intimidated by her.

'Do you need some help with the salad?' she asked.

'No, no, I'm sure I'll be fine,' I answered, wanting her to leave quickly.

'Well don't over cook the pasta whatever you do; there is nothing worse than overcooked spaghetti. I'll leave you then to concentrate,' she said, as she marched off down the path to join the others for a drink, the tight pants she was wearing doing nothing to hide her large bottom, I noticed gleefully.

*

Andre, Wayne and the two policemen arrived a bit later and the relative tranquillity of the lodge was soon to be shattered for the time being. I was still in the kitchen trying to make a salad that would meet Leanne's high standard, when I heard their vehicle roaring up the dwala. I looked out of the kitchen window and saw the four men go to the lodge office and Rob and Leanne soon joined them. There was quite a lot of talk going on and when I finished the salad I decided to go and see what had transpired.

'It is regrettable that you had to open fire on the poachers, Andre,' one of the policemen was saying as I neared the office, 'but I know that you had no alternative.

I will make this very clear in my report.'

'Yes,' Andre replied, 'they had no intention of handing themselves in.'

'I agree,' the policeman continued, 'they would have tried to kill you first, and that's because the ringleader was with them and he didn't want to be discovered. But I believe the situation here might improve now that he has been killed.'

'Damn shame it had to get to this,' Rob said, 'I would never have known he was up to this.'

Leanne was sitting in the chair looking quite shocked, I thought, and I wondered what had caused this. I slipped in through the door and as I did so I too was in for a shock when the policeman said, 'well unfortunately it usually is the one you least suspect who is the most guilty. I believe he has been your cook for a very long time.'

'He was my parents cook, Inspector Moyo,' Rob said, 'and then we moved him up here to be camp cook when my father died.'

'Who?' I spluttered.

Everyone turned to look at me as they had not known I was there. 'Fanwell,' Leanne said in a slightly resigned voice.

I was dumbfounded. 'No,' I gasped, 'not Fanwell.'

'I believe it is he that is the one, 'Inspector Moyo replied. 'We have been looking for the ringleader for some time, although before today we were not sure that it was actually him. Fanwell Dube is his name and he worked in conjunction with his son, Innocent Dube.'

'But how could he? He was always here cooking,' I

said rather stupidly.

'Huh,' Wayne interjected, 'in his spare time he was leaking information to the poachers. We've had our suspicions for a while that there was an insider informing the poachers about our activities, but like Inspector says, we didn't know until today that it was him.'

'Is he alright?' I asked.

'They are dead, both the father and the son,' said Inspector Moyo. 'I believe Innocent was his first born.'

*

When I woke early the following morning to make breakfast, I was still stunned by these revelations. I stood next to the stove, stirring the mealie meal porridge, as I'd watched Fanwell do on numerous occasions, his black brow often sweaty from the heat of the wood stove, his greying hair just visible underneath the chef's hat Leanne always made him wear. I'd always liked the way he called me 'Mummie', as opposed to most of the other workers who always call me 'Madam'. I gulped back my sadness as I remembered how he'd told me he wanted to take a few days off so that he could go and spend some time with his wife. I'd naively thought how nice this would be for him, and I wondered now why on earth he'd gotten embroiled in poaching activities, he must surely have known what the consequences could be.

The rhino guys went off for the day in their helicopter, apparently to dart and dehorn other rhino in the conservancy, but they'd asked if they could spend another night at our lodge. My mind raced slightly, as I wondered what I could give them for their dinner. There was very little of interest in our deepfreeze so I got into the Land Cruiser and drove to Rob and Leanne's house to see what I could scratch up there. As per usual, Leanne was able to come to the rescue with great ease. She had a freezer full of eland meat and she immediately pulled out two large fillets, looking at her watch as she handed them to me.

‘I usually like to defrost these at least a day before we eat them, ’ she said, ‘to make sure they are well matured, but if you leave them in the kitchen up at the lodge it should be warm enough in there with the wood stove. They should defrost pretty quickly and be fine for tonight.’

She was friendly enough when she was explaining all of this, but as usual, I felt slightly incompetent as she told me what I must do. I wished I could stop myself from feeling this way around her. We then marched down to her kitchen garden to collect some more lettuces, tomatoes and cucumbers for a salad to have with the eland fillets. She has a very high fence around the garden to make sure that no eland, or any other game, for that matter, come and help themselves to her lovely veggies. If they should dare, I thought to myself-I sure would not, with her guarding over them.

I spent the rest of the day sitting in the lapa with my laptop, going through my photographs. I was especially pleased with the ones I’d taken of the picanins on the anthill at the funeral. If I’d been in America I would have sent one or two off to friends and former colleagues, as I know they would’ve liked them, but here at the lodge in the middle of the African bush, this was not possible. I still find it strange that there is so little means of communication from the lodge, although with the way things are in my life right now, I do rather like it this way, it makes everything so much simpler.

As the day wore on, I started looking out for the return of the helicopter and eventually, as the afternoon shadows were beginning to lengthen, I could see it coming from far off, just a little black dot at first in the early evening sky. I was pleased about this, as it gave me time to drive down the dwala so that I could watch it come in to land. It's fascinating watching helicopters from such close proximity and I wanted to photograph every stage of its landing, hoping that I could somehow capture the excitement that is created. The whirring, burring and thumping it makes as it hovers for a moment above the ground before dropping down with a slight bump. The way the long bush grass is swished almost horizontal by the gush of wind created by the rotating propeller. The way the loose grass and leaves and sticks are blown furiously about as if they've suddenly been given life, before slowly losing this life again as they flutter to the ground as the propeller gradually slows down. The last time I'd watched helicopters, I recalled, I hadn't been able to get nearly so close. It was in Louisiana after Hurricane Katrina when they had flown over my home in their droves, flying towards the coast to search for and rescue survivors from that storm.

The helicopter's engine was not switched off as I expected, but instead Clive jumped out and ran across to me while the others continued to sit inside.

'Steve asked if you'd like to come for a short flip,' he yelled above the sound of the helicopter's engine.

'Gee, yes,' I said without hesitation, looking around quickly to make sure there wasn't anything of value in the vehicle.

'Don't worry, we'll only be a short while,' Clive shouted.

I grabbed my camera and jumped out of the cab, quickly locking the driver's door and putting the keys firmly into my pants pocket, before running across the short space between the helicopter and my vehicle.

'Thanks so much for inviting me,' I yelled as I climbed in.

'Only a pleasure,' Steve yelled back over the noise of the helicopter engine. 'Here, come and sit up front with me.'

Looking at the ground from the large rounded glass at the front of a helicopter was amazing. It's like looking down onto a model of the countryside, with rocks and trees casting long shadows onto the ground. And then suddenly the model comes alive when animals, obviously frightened by the noise of the helicopter, try to run away to safety. I took some great photos of wildebeest and zebra running across the plain just below the lodge as we flew over them.

'Sorry it can't be for longer,' Steve said as we turned back after what was a very short flight. 'It's pretty expensive flying these things.'

I wished it could have been longer.

'Yeah, I'm sure,' I answered, hiding my disappointment as best I could.

As we flew back towards the makeshift helicopter pad on the flat grasslands below the lodge I couldn't help but notice a beat up old Land Rover hurtling along the dust road towards the lodge. We came in to land and the vehicle slowed down and made towards where I had parked my pickup.

'Who is it?' Steve asked, obviously as curious as I.

'I'm not sure,' I replied hesitantly, and then I suddenly knew exactly who it was. 'What the heck?' I gasped.

Jabula was driving the vehicle with little Sabi Star sitting next to him in the passenger seat. She was the very last person I expected to see here.

5

Sabi

AS Clare stepped from the helicopter I forgot my troubles for a moment as I watched her. Oh boy, how I would love to be like her when I grow up properly. She looked really good in her khaki shorts and top and smart hiking boots and socks. No one here wears hiking boots and socks like that; most people just wear slops or tackies. The propeller was still turning, slower now than when it first landed, but she bent a little as she ran under it even though it was well above her head. Her hair blew back as she ran and I decided then and there that I was going to have my hair cut these holidays, even though it could never be like hers. She's got short, straight, hair, whereas mine is sort of curly and what I think of as mousy brown. I've always hated it and that's why I keep it tightly plaited and out of the way.

She came towards us, and as she did so, she tilted her head to one side as if she was asking what we were doing here and of course as soon as she got to us she did exactly this.

'What the heck? You're the last people I expected to see in this place. What on earth are you doing here?"

I was about to launch into the whole story, when Jabula said, 'Mr. Stirling had a car crash last night and has been taken to Bulawayo for treatment.'

Clare's face dropped. 'Is he.....?'

'He has broken his leg quite badly, but otherwise he's alright I think.'

'Phew, that's a relief.' She looked at me again. She must've been wondering why we had come all the way here.

'They suggested I went to the Rawsons but I didn't want to go there because they are also Sherry-Lee's friends.'

'Sherry-Lee?' Clare asked

I remembered I'd never mentioned her to Clare. 'She's my dad's girlfriend. She was driving the car.'

'Oh dear, is she ok?'

I blanched slightly, 'She's in a coma.'

'Oh dear, that doesn't sound good.'

'No.' I turned my attention to my feet, as I always do when I feel bad.

'Sabi wanted to stay here so, I said I'd drive her,' Jabula explained.

'Mr Potgieter, our manager said it would be ok,' I said quickly.

'Of course, that's absolutely fine.' I was very relieved that she didn't hesitate for a second when she said this and I looked up at her and smiled. 'Hey,' she continued, 'why don't you two carry on up to the lodge and we'll follow right behind you in the pickup. They had some rhino poached here yesterday morning and these guys are the rhino dehorning unit and this is their helicopter. I'll tell you all about it later.'

We drove up the steep hill, the engine revving loudly as the Land Rover struggled to get up. As soon as I saw the lodge, I loved it, I knew this despite my worries. The main thing I noticed when I first got there were the sabi star plants all over the place. At home we only have one plant which Gogo kept in a pot and it is small and stunted but here they are quite big, well at least up to my chest and they really do look like miniature baobab trees. At this time of the year they don't have their flowers but this didn't stop me from admiring them.

The others arrived shortly after we got there, lots of men although I noticed that some of them were quite young. There were some introductions, but it all went in one ear and out the other, as it always does with me.

'I think you should sleep in the bedroom next door to mine,' Clare said. 'Did you bring some things with you?'

Thankfully, I had packed some clothes; the trendy jeans that my gran gave me plus the tops from Sarah's mother and after that I didn't have much else, just some shorts and tops that are getting too small, but obviously Clare didn't know this. We walked down a stone path to a small thatched building. Clare opened the door and stepped in, pulling the curtain back to let in the evening light and I followed. The room had two large wooden beds, with a mosquito net over each and a bedside table in-between. There was a grass mat covering the floor and a dressing table and chair on the opposite side of the room to the beds. The curtains and bedspreads were made of khaki-coloured material with red edging. Clare showed me the bathroom through a door at the back of the room.

'Will you be ok here, do you think?'

'Oh yes.' I said quickly. 'I really like it.'

Clare stood leaning against the cupboard and pointed through the window to another thatched building a little way from mine. 'That's where I sleep. If you shout very loud I'll hear you if you need me in the night,' she said with a laugh, but then she came and sat on the bed opposite me and looked at me.

'You've been having a hard time haven't you, since we met, hey?'

'Yes,' I said, but I didn't want to go into details just yet.

'But your dad is going to be ok?'

'Yes.'

'Well that's the main thing.'

But this was the problem. Was it? There I had been just yesterday sitting in my fort and trying to devise a plan to get rid of Sherry-Lee, and now she had been seriously hurt in the crash. I felt pretty bad about this and couldn't help wondering if my negative thoughts had had something to do with it. At school, in the dorm at night, we sometimes talk about the power of the mind over matter and how it can attract positive or negative energy, and by doing this we can make things happen if we really think hard enough about them. I have never been sure if I believed any of this, even though Tracey says it really does work, but now I'm starting to think that maybe it does after all.

Clare broke my train of thought.

'Come; let me show you something outside.'

We stepped onto the small verandah at the front and walked around the side of the building and there she showed me an outside bathroom. The bath had been sort of grooved from the rock, and there was also a shower.

'What do you think of this? I've got the same outside my place and I love lying in the warm bath in the evenings and looking up at the sky. The stars are just amazing here, absolutely mind-blowing.'

I thought about this and decided that I'd really like it too and I nodded my head as I agreed.

'You are a funny little thing,' Clare said laughing softly, 'you are so quiet.'

'Am I?' I said, and then stopped. My head is always so full of thoughts; racing from one to another that I really didn't know this.

'Sorry.'

'It's ok, but it would be nice to hear what you're thinking some of the time.'

That was a change from my dad and Sherry-Lee who never really want to hear anything I have to say.

'But come; let me show you something else I think you'll like,' she continued.

I followed her back along the stone path to the main area of the lodge, passing other buildings the same as our bedrooms and then up some steep stairs which went round a rock to the top, where there was a thatched shelter and a swimming pool.

'Wow,' I said.

The water from the pool looked like it was going over the edge on the one side.

'Great hey? It's called an infinity pool.'

'Ah, ha.'

'And don't you just love the three sixty degree view you get from here,' Clare said, swivelling around as she said this. 'My cousin was really clever building the bar and pool right up here. We sometimes come here in the evenings when the sun is going down, like now, and swim in the pool as we watch it set.'

Clare glanced at her watch.

'Well, my friend of few words, unfortunately I can't do this now as I have to think about providing something for these men for dinner. Cooking is not my strong point and so it's never very easy for me. Unfortunately our cook is, um, is no more. Do you want to come to the kitchen with me?'

*

I felt very proud of myself later, because it was actually me who made the dinner, well most of it, anyway. I'm lucky that I've learnt to cook well, and when I saw that Clare didn't know what to give everyone other than some boring looking eland steaks that she'd defrosted, I said I'd help out. I ended up making a cheese soufflé as there didn't seem to be that much in the pantry. Gogo used to be a good soufflé maker and she taught me how to make them a while back. It really is very easy; it's just a matter of making a good white sauce, then adding the cheese (in this case), tasting it to make sure that there is enough salt and pepper, then adding egg yolks and finally folding in the stiffly beaten egg whites.

Clare was amazed that I could do all of this on my own. She made a salad, and after I'd put the soufflé in the oven I made pancakes for pudding. This was even easier than it ever was when Gogo and I used to make them at home because there was a packet saying 'pancake mix' in the pantry. All I had to do was add a cup of milk and two eggs to a cup of pancake mix, pour a tablespoon of this mixture in a frying pan, let it spread over the bottom of the pan and then toss, which I always enjoy doing. Clare was impressed that I could toss them so high without dropping them.

Everyone talked about rhino poaching during dinner and, as I know nothing about this, I didn't say anything. I just had my coke and ate my dinner and spent quite a lot of time analysing Clare, trying to work out how she made herself look so good with no effort. All she was wearing was jeans and a white shirt and when she first came from her room her hair was wet from her shower, but it just bounced back into its style without her having to do anything. Obviously, it is cut in a way that makes it like this and I wished then and there I could cut my hair the same.

I, on the other hand, didn't think that I looked good, even though I was wearing the trendy jeans my gran gave me, only now they didn't feel trendy compared to Clare's. Oh well, what could I do? I noticed that the leader of the unit, whose name I still hadn't picked up, seemed pretty keen on Clare. He had been very quick to help her braai the steaks on the fire, and now he was sitting next to her at the table and talking mainly to her all the time. The only two people whose names I've picked up are Clive's and Pete's. Out of the two of them, I decided Clive is the nicer. But I know he's too old for me, as he must be about nineteen or twenty and Tracey has told me that when boys get to that age they like to do all sorts of weird things. I looked at Clive and wondered what it would feel like. Some of the older girls Tracey hangs out with at school have talked about sucking penises, besides all the usual stuff boys and girls do. It sounds really weird but Tracey says they love it. You can do it anywhere without anyone really noticing if you are discreet – at the movies, in cars, even at cricket matches; I'm really not sure if I'll ever want to do such things! I wondered what Clive would have thought if he'd known what I was thinking about every time I looked at him. Obviously he didn't, but he talked a lot at the dinner table about other things; he seems to know a lot about rhino poaching too. I was just wondering how long he'd be around when the leader, Clare's admirer, said they'd be making an early start in the morning and that they'd be staying somewhere else tomorrow night. This disappointed me, as it would have been nice to have Clive and Pete around for a few more days. It would've made Tracey green with envy if I could've told her when we got back to school that I'd hung out with some nineteen-or twenty-year olds.

Clare and I ended up going to our rooms at the same time. She stopped outside my lodge to tell me her plans.

'I had intended all along on going to Bulawayo tomorrow,' she said, ' to do some shopping for the lodge, and now that you're here I think you should come too so that you can see your dad. I'm sure you must be very worried about him.'

In fact, since I'd been busy with cooking and then having supper my worries had practically gone away, but now they did come back, and, added to this, came a new one, was Clare planning on leaving me somewhere in town while she was there?

As if she could read my mind she went on, 'Is there someone in town you would like to stay with, rather, so that you can be close to your dad?'

There wasn't. I knew that Sarah had gone away and there wasn't anyone else I particularly wanted to stay with. I much preferred the idea of being here at the lodge, but I could hardly say this.

'Um.'

I stared blankly at my feet.

'Um.'

'I'm very happy if you want to come back here with me, especially as you're such an incredible cook, but obviously it's up to you if you'd prefer to be with your dad.'

'Well, um, I think he'll have to stay in hospital and I won't see too much of him anyway, so maybe it will be better to come back here and help with the cooking.'

'Good, I'm glad you said that, and hopefully your dad won't mind either.'

I couldn't see why he should.

6

Clare

I didn't wake Sabi early, as I knew I could cope with breakfast on my own, but I did think of her as I prepared it. It had been great to see her so proud of herself, making the soufflé and pancakes and then watching us all intently as we ate them. Of course the rhino guys would have probably been quite happy with just the eland steaks, but I would never tell her this. I figure she needs a confidence booster any which way she can get it.

I had to give the rhino guys pretty much what they'd had the previous morning for breakfast, mealie meal porridge, followed by boiled eggs and toast, but none of them seemed to mind this. It would be a relief to get more food into the lodge, plus another cook. Rob told me yesterday that he'd contacted a few of his friends in town about putting the word out for another cook. It's odd for me, being used to the way things happen in America, to look for prospective employees like this. Back there, we'd contact an employment agency, or put an ad in the local paper, but here it's the 'bush telegraph' that works best, apparently.

'You'd never know who you'd get otherwise,' Leanne told me.

I guess it's a pretty small community here, well the white community that is, with everyone seeming to know everyone else. I haven't got in touch with any of my childhood friends since I've been back, as I'm still feeling too vulnerable to have anything more than superficial contact with anyone, which is how it was with the people who've come to the camp for weekend stays. The first was a group of six and the second comprised of ten people and I can see that it must make a very pleasant break for them, lying by the pool, going on game drives, fishing, sitting around in the evenings, chatting and playing games.

When I go to Bulawayo on my shopping trips I stay in Rob and Leanne's house in a suburb called Hillside. It's a fairly small thatched house, but situated on a big, rocky property and has a very nice view of a small dam. They have a maid called Stella and a gardener called Tenacious and these two look after the place even when there is no one there, and it is always nothing short of immaculate.

*

Bulawayo is a fair sized town about two hundred kilometres from the Ubejane Conservancy. I find it fascinating comparing it to my hometown back in the States now that I can see it through adult eyes. Both towns have similar sized populations but while my home can be described as clean and well kept for the main part, Bulawayo most definitely cannot. I'm sure when I used to come here years ago it was an orderly place too, but in recent years it has become quite run down and dirty in most parts; potholes in the roads, street lights that don't work, burst sewers, litter and rubbish dumped everywhere. Leanne told me, well lots of people I've met have told me, that this is because the economy collapsed after the liberation party allowed their supporters to take over the white owned farms. Apparently inflation hit the trillions of percentages, with the local currency becoming meaningless, so that institutions like city councils could not cope under such conditions. In recent years, with the advent of a unity government the local currency has been dropped. Leanne told me that the reserve bank just used to print the local money like toilet paper, to hand out through all sorts of means to the ruling elite and their hangers on, and the only way this practice could be stopped was for the new government to simply do away with the currency, just like a naughty school child would have a privilege taken away because it was being abused. You would have thought the people who had been doing this would have been embarrassed by their behaviour, but apparently there has not been a bit of this, they made themselves too rich to care and now their main worry is that they no longer have access to such easy cash. How they would love to get their own currency back I'm sure, but in the mean time we all use United States dollars here, something that I find quite amazing.

*

We arrived in Bulawayo around midday and went straight to the house in Hillside. Stella and Tenacious had been told that we were coming, so windows had been opened, fresh sheets put on the beds, the drive and garage beautifully swept and there they were as we drove in, ready and waiting to meet and greet us. This is certainly one aspect of life in Zimbabwe that I could get very used to again. If I've been away from my home in the States for any length of time I usually get back to a dishwasher full of (hopefully clean) dishes that needs emptying, a drier full of clothes that need sorting, a bed that needs making and surfaces that need dusting. Here, it's like arriving at a hotel. Stella even puts vases of flowers in all the rooms when she knows that anyone is coming to stay.

I phoned the private hospital where I knew Mr. Stirling had been taken and was told that visiting hours were from eight to ten in the morning and from four to six in the afternoon. As we had time to kill, and I was only planning on tackling my very long shopping list the next day, I decided to use the time to do something that I had come to realise was a necessity with regard to Sabi; to sort out her wardrobe. I've noticed that she does not have any clothes that actually fit her properly. I mentioned earlier that the dress she wore to the funeral was way too small for her, well it turns out that she has been busting out of everything I've seen her in since, poor kid. I haven't said anything to her as I know how self-conscious a girl of fifteen can be, so I simply suggested, as casually as possible, that I needed to buy myself some new outfits and maybe she'd like to see if there was anything she'd like, too. Her face lit up at this suggestion, before going back to its usual slightly guarded expression.

'Why, what's wrong?' I asked.

'Um, well, I don't have any money.'

'Hey, it's ok, I discussed it with Leanne and she said that if you helped me out with the cooking at the lodge then she'd pay you for your work. You're already owed for one meal.' I hadn't really spoken to Leanne but decided then and there that I would, I'm sure she'd be quite happy to go along with it, she may be bossy but she's got a kind heart. And anyways, if Leanne is against the idea, I'd use my own money. It would be well worth it.

'Oh, wow.'

'Exactly, so where do you think we can go?'

'My friend Sarah usually goes to a place called The Unity Village during week days; it's a flea market.'

'That sounds good.'

'At the weekends Sarah goes to the Bend Over Bazaar where all the clothes are on the ground in piles.'

'Oh yes?'

'You have to dig into the piles to find anything.'

I've heard about this. Old clothes that people in the Western world put into charity boxes when they want to get rid of them.

'Sarah's found some real bargains,' she continued, 'but it's only on weekends.'

'Oh well. Let's try going to the Unity Village instead,' I said, silently thankful that we didn't have to start riffling through piles of discarded old clothes from my home country and elsewhere.

I parked the vehicle outside the Unity Village. As soon as we stopped, the car was surrounded by people trying to sell us a whole range of commodities, things I most certainly didn't want to buy, like rat poison, bulbs, knives, tomatoes, bananas, feather dusters and huge bags of monkey nuts, to name just a few.

‘No, thank you,’ Sabi said in a firmer voice than I’d ever heard her use before, completely ignoring the question I’ve noticed on previous occasions the vendors always ask, ‘Do you know how much?’ I’ve always found this a rather stupid question because of course there is no way anyone could possibly know how much they want for their commodities. But I’ve still been caught many times when I’ve answered them, saying ‘No I don’t know how much,’ and although I know this elicits a whole range of prices, I somehow have still not learnt how to deal with them. But Sabi showed me exactly what to do; she showed me that you politely ignore them. However we had no sooner safely negotiated our way through the vendors when we had to deal with the ‘vehicle attendants’, there is always a multitude of them, desperate to look after your vehicle every time you step out of it in town.

‘It’s alright,’ Sabi said to them, again in such an authoritative voice I was quite taken by surprise.

When we had gotten far enough away from them I said, ‘Hey well done, I usually have a whole gang of them waiting by my car, saying they have looked after it for me.’

‘That’s because of your American accent.’

‘Why so?’

‘They know you will let them stay.’

I thought about this as we walked into the Unity Village, let them stay, let them stay where? I glanced back at our vehicle and saw that there was no-one standing beside it, unlike all the previous times I’ve been shopping in Bulawayo.

'Well, thanks for showing me how to do it,' I said, realising how naïve I actually must seem now, when it comes to the ways of Africa. Fifteen years away is a long time and things change. I definitely can't remember then being harassed to such an extent by supposedly well-meaning people

I was expecting the same harassment in the Unity Village, but there was not a bit of it. I was quietly intrigued by the place. Row after row of stalls made up of plastic roof and sides, and all jam-packed with clothes of every colour, type and description. Admittedly most were cheap, Chinese junk, but at the same time the clothes were more or less up to date as far as fashion is concerned. I was amused that there was not a mirror or change room in the whole of the Unity Village it seemed, but by holding items of clothing up to ourselves and asking for the opinion of each other or anyone passing by, we were able to decide on quite a few outfits to buy. I bought myself two pairs of khaki pants and I bought Sabi a great deal more. Shorts, shirts, dresses, sandals; it was wonderful to see her so delighted by her new acquisitions. Most American kids of her age usually have so much, but it seems that she has been badly deprived in this area.

*

Mr. Stirling lay in his hospital bed looking distinctly uncomfortable when we arrived. It was hard to make out what he looked like because of the injuries to his face, but I could see that he had thick blond, straight hair which was just starting to turn grey. At first glance I could not see anything of Sabi in him, with her olive skin and darker, curly hair and wondered if she took more after her mother. He was in a private room which had just one bed in it, two chairs covered in red plastic and a television that looked like it had come out of the ark. The curtains were on the threadbare side and hung limply in the French window, which opened out onto a wide verandah with a waist high wall along the edge. The door and curtains were wide open and as his room was on the fourth floor I had a very good view of the hospital grounds and of the roofs of the houses in the neighbouring residential suburb, as I stood near his bed. Mr. Stirling would not have had this same view unless he pulled himself up, and it was very apparent that he would not be able to do this in the state he was in.

Sabi bit her bottom lip as soon as she walked into the room and saw him, and I can't say I blame her. We had neither of us expected to find him in such bad condition. We had bought a bag of grapes and some chocolate from the supermarket on our way to the hospital and she tentatively stepped forward and gave them to him. I was surprised at how reserved they were with each other, but put it down to the shock of her seeing him this way and he just feeling plain uncomfortable. It was his right leg that was broken and it must be a bad break because the cast went halfway up his thigh and his leg was slightly elevated in a sling type contraption that was rigged up over his bed. He also had some real bad grazes on his left arm, a nasty looking gash on his forehead and a black eye. He grimaced slightly whenever he made any movement.

'Wow Dad, are you alright?' Sabi asked.

He frowned as he looked at her, 'What do you think? Do I look alright?'

'I'm really sorry Dad.' She bit her lip again, looking at her feet and there was an uncomfortable silence in the room. 'Um, by the way, this is Clare Boucher and she works at the Ubejane Conservancy Dad,'

'Hi,' I said, trying to make my voice sound as friendly as possible, but he didn't respond so I went on, 'Sabi has been staying at the conservancy since your accident. One of our waiters happened to be at your mine at the time of the accident, as he was attending his mother's funeral, so he brought her back to us once he'd found out what had happened to you.'

'I thought I said you were to go to the Rawsons,' Mr. Stirling said, looking at Sabi and still ignoring me.

Sabi still looked at her feet.

'Um, I don't really like the Rawsons, Dad'

'It's got nothing to do with who you like and who you don't like. It's up to me.'

'Yes, Dad.'

'And where are you staying now?'

'Don't worry Mr. Stirling,' I butted in again, 'she's staying with me at my cousin's house in Hillside. I think you know him, Rob Fenton.'

'Of course I know him, but doesn't he live at Ubejane?'

'Yes, yes he does, but they have a house in town and I stay in it whenever I come to Bulawayo to stock up on provisions. I made a point of bringing Sabi to town as soon as I could so that you wouldn't be worried about her.'

At that moment the nurse arrived with her trolley, which at a glance seemed to carry thermometers in glasses of liquid, bowls of cotton wool and an array of medicine bottles. She appeared delighted to meet Sabi, 'And who are you my little girl?' she asked as soon as she entered the room.

'I'm…' Sabi started, looking very embarrassed.

'Ah, ha, Mr. Stirlings daughter?'

'Yes.'

'Come to see Daddy, have you? Such a good little daughter you have Mr. Stirling.'

She took the clipboard from the bottom of the bed as she spoke to him.

'And let me look at this,' she said as she slid her hands under the sheet.

'Let's leave you for a moment, shall we,' I said, making a move towards the French door onto the verandah, with Sabi following right behind me. The nurse closed the thin curtains behind us.

'Your poor father,' I said once we were standing next to the low wall, looking out at the view beyond, 'he must be in quite a lot of pain but he will soon be fine, I'm sure.'

Sabi bit her lip but continued to stare at the view.

'Try not to worry too much Sabi, it really looks worse than it is, I'm sure, but maybe we shouldn't stay too long now, as he is obviously very uncomfortable.' She looked quite relieved when I said this.

The nurse soon drew back the curtains and popped her head out of the door.

'All is well, you can come now,' she said.

She had already wheeled her trolley out of the room by the time we got back in.

'How did this happen, Dad?' Sabi asked, once we were again standing uncomfortably beside his bed.

'Sherry-Lee was driving. An impala leapt in front of the truck and she swerved to avoid it and we rolled.'

'Is she ok, Dad?'

'No, she has been flown down to South Africa as she has head injuries that can't be treated adequately here.'

He stared intently at her as he said this, his voice sounding strained and cold. It was obviously a very awkward situation for both of them and things seemed to get even worse when the door opened a moment later and an elderly man came in. It was apparent from the look on his face that he was very unhappy.

'You know what, Sabi. Leave us now,' Mr. Stirling said, as he turned his attention to his new visitor.

I was quite shocked by the offhand way he treated his daughter.

*

When we got back to the house in Hillside we discovered that the electricity was off. This is something else I find most fascinating and frustrating about life here in Zimbabwe these days, the endless, endless power cuts that everyone has to endure. How businesses can operate under such conditions is beyond me. Apparently, there is not enough power being produced or imported to supply all the country's needs, so areas are simply cut off for hours and hours at a time as a way of restricting consumption. According to Leanne, and many others for that matter, the power situation would be better if all the power stations had been run more efficiently, but apparently many of them have not been maintained properly over a very long period of time, and most especially in the last few years when the economy went into freefall. Anyways, whatever the reason, the reality is that everyone has to contend with many hours of no electricity almost every day of their lives. There is no way the average American would put up with this. It seems that if possible people have generators and invertors to give them enough power during the power cuts, but of course the average man in the street cannot afford these, they just have to accept their lot. Thankfully, at Rob and Leanne's house they do have a large generator and Tenacious went down the drive to the shed where it lives and switched it on as soon as the daylight started to fade. We could soon hear the muffled purr of the engine, and the lights flickered back to life.

'I am making you peri-peri chicken and chips for your dinner, Madam,' Stella said as she brought a tray with a jug of water, a bottle of wine, glasses and an ice bucket onto the verandah where I was sitting. 'I think the intombi, Sabi, she will like this,' she stated in her matter of fact way as she set the tray on the dresser.

'I'm sure she will, thanks Stella,' I said, Sabi not being with me on the verandah just then to confirm this.

I wish everyone would stop calling me 'Madam' all the time, I've asked Stella and Tenacious, as well as all the staff at the conservancy to call me 'Clare', but for some reason they will not, except for Jabula who doesn't mind at all. Leanne says I shouldn't encourage them to call me 'Clare' and that they don't mind 'Madam' at all, but it just seems so colonial to me after living in the States for so long.

Above the sound of the generator I could hear the low rumbling of thunder far away in the distance, and I hoped that we would have another storm in the night. There have been a few since I've been here and I've always been thrilled by them, with thunder and lightning clapping in quick succession as the rain pours heavily, yet softly sounding on the thatched roof of this house and of the lodge. These storms most usually stop as abruptly as they start, leaving the vegetation heavy and dripping and the ground saturated. Then in the morning it's like none of it ever happened, with not a trace of any of the water and the sky back to its cloudless, bright blue self. I poured myself a glass of wine and sat down again to watch the lightning flashing a ways off in the northern sky while I waited for Sabi to finish in the shower. I'd have to have mine quickly afterwards, as the geysers don't work with the generator.

*

We settled down to our peri-peri chicken and chips at a small round table on the verandah a while later, clean and comfortable after our showers, wet hair dripping around our shoulders. This was the first time I'd seen Sabi with her hair down, as she always has it in a tight plait. I decided it was a shame she didn't let it loose more often, she has thick, curly hair and cut properly it would be very pretty.

The lightning was still flashing in the distance but as she served the dinner, Stella said she doubted that it would rain here tonight. I decided I was not going to take her weather predictions as gospel; I have learnt on previous visits that she likes to think of herself as a weather lady, despite the fact that she is often wrong. I had a second glass of wine and Sabi had a glass of cordial orange and water and I was amazed when she immediately started opening up to me, as soon as Stella left us. She is usually pretty monosyllabic.

'You may have noticed that my dad doesn't like me,' she started in a very matter of fact way.

I looked up from my food, not knowing how to respond to such a comment, especially one that came from such a young person, who should not be having such negative thoughts.

'What do you mean? Of course he likes you. All fathers love their daughters.'

'Well, not him. And he has every right not to because it was my fault that my mother died. I can't really blame him.'

7

Sabi

I told Clare the whole story as I know it, and basically it goes like this.

My mother and father were married for seven years and thought they'd never have children, when suddenly my mum fell pregnant with me. This had at first seemed like a great blessing, but unfortunately things quickly went very wrong, because she died giving birth. I've hated the thought of this all my life, but unfortunately there is no getting away from this fact. Gogo told me all about it. I'll give Dad his due, he never actually told me that it was my fault, and of course Gogo didn't either but I'm forever going to think it is, in the knowledge that she died just hours after I was born. According to Gogo it was a freak of nature. She explained to me that I decided to come into this world four weeks before I was due, and it happened to be on the very day there had been a huge, huge rainstorm; five inches or so of rain falling in just a few hours. As a result, the river rose to such an extent that they couldn't cross the low level bridge to get her to the hospital. Isn't this unbelievable? So when I decided to make my entrance into the world my mother had no one but Gogo to guide me out, and after this happened she started to haemorrhage badly and there was nothing that poor Gogo could do to stop it.

Despite the way my dad has behaved towards me since then, I do feel sorry for him, stuck in the middle of the bush with a tiny new-born baby, who had managed to kill his wife while she was giving birth. No wonder he doesn't love me. I can hardly blame him.

Clare kept shaking her head as I told her about this.

'Honestly Sabi,' she said, 'I really think you've got it all wrong. There is no way your father can blame you for your mother's death, just because she died shortly after you were born. It was not your fault.'

'But he does Clare, honestly he does. In the whole of my life he's never shown me any love and he's more often than not angry with me. You saw how he was this afternoon.'

She shook her head again.

'Well, of course, he's in a lot of pain right now so it would be hard for him to be very demonstrative.'

I don't actually know what demonstrative means, but whatever it is, I know his injuries don't have anything to do with the way he treats me. He's never been injured before, but he always treats me the same. I didn't say this to Clare as she went on defending him.

'But what I did notice this afternoon,' she continued, 'is how concerned he is about your welfare. I can understand that he's worried about you staying with us when he doesn't know me at all. I'll have to sweet talk him a little more tomorrow, when I take you to see him again.'

I thought about this for a moment. He did seem worried about me staying with Clare, but I really can't believe that it's because he doesn't know her. I've stayed with loads of people over the years, that he's never ever met, and he's never shown any concern about this. I wondered if maybe he could tell that I really like Clare and he doesn't want me to be with someone who actually cares about me properly. No, surely that can't be the reason for his attitude.

*

Clare had to wake me up the morning after our long discussion. I felt very comfortable being with her and I was glad I had told her my darkest worries, even though she did not believe me. It rained very hard in the night, and whereas usually I always hate rainstorms, as they make me think about my mother dying after a very bad one, this time I actually enjoyed it as I snuggled deeply into my warm bed, feeling safe and secure. I slept very well and was dead to the world when she came into my room, somewhere around eight in the morning, with a nice cup of tea for me to drink in bed. No one has ever done that for me before.

'Hey Sweetie' (no one has ever called me that either), she said, as she opened the curtains, 'why don't we go to the hairdresser first thing this morning. My hair desperately needs a trim and maybe you'd like to have a cut too?'

How amazed I was that she should suggest this, when I've been wishing for this exact thing nonstop for the last few days. Maybe there is something to this business of the power of the mind after all. But then I thought of Sherry-Lee and what I had been wishing for her, and I decided that it wouldn't be a good thing to have such powers.

Clare went on, 'I phoned Leanne's hairdresser and she can take us at nine, so we can go straight from there to the hospital to see your dad afterwards. After that, I'll need to tackle my shopping list. Rob phoned this morning to give me a list of a whole lot more that needs to be bought, so I may end up staying in town an extra day, as I don't think I'll get it all done today.'

After she had left the room, I finished my tea, and then sat up in bed with the cupboard doors open as I tried to decide which outfit to wear. If I was at the mine or the lodge I'd probably wear shorts, but as we would be shopping maybe a dress would be better. I had three new ones to choose from and I like them all equally. It was so kind of Clare to take me to the Unity Village to buy all this gear; it's really cool stuff and I know Sarah is going to be green with envy. I tried phoning her to tell her I was in town but her phone was out of range; she must still be away. I didn't bother phoning Tracey, as she'd just snigger if I told her I'd bought my clothes at the Unity Village; she buys all her clothes in South Africa, she says you can only buy rubbish here in Zimbabwe. I don't agree with her but I'm not going to start an argument about it. I feel a bit bad that Clare spent so much money on me; it must've come to nearly a hundred dollars, but she kept saying I'd earn it back when I start helping her with the cooking at the lodge.

I eventually decided to wear the light green halter-neck dress and as soon as I put it on I noticed that it made my eyes look really nice. I've never actually noticed before, but my eyes are really quite an interesting colour, I've always thought that they are plain old brown but now I think they may be greener in colour. Once I'd finished checking this out in the mirror I turned my attention to shoes. Clare had bought me three pairs of sandals and after trying them all on with the dress I decided that the white slip-ons looked best with it.

*

I couldn't help but admire myself in the glass door of the hospital entrance as we walked in; I was so chuffed with my new hairstyle. It isn't exactly short, just much shorter than it has ever been before, than I can remember anyway. It's so nice to not have to wear it in that boring old plait and it curls really nicely around my face. The hairdresser's name was Treasure and she said I'd look good with a fringe, because my forehead is very wide and once she'd cut it I knew exactly what she meant. She explained that it would be a small fringe as my hair is so thick anyway and then she cut the rest of my hair sort of shoulder length, so unfortunately I will still have to put it up in elastics when I am at school. We can only wear our hair down if it just touches our collar; if it's any longer we have to put it in pigtails or a pony-tail. Once you get to form four, which I will be the year after next, you're allowed to use clips.

We got to Dad's room on the fourth floor and Clare suggested I went in first to show him my new style. I knocked gently and then popped my head in the door. I was surprised to find two other people in the room, an old man and an old lady. I didn't know who they were but they looked so unhappy I wanted to back out of the room again, but Dad noticed me and told me to come in. My heart sank as the look that crossed his face was not an approving one, although he didn't say anything. The two other people turned and looked at me too and I noticed that the lady had been crying. My heart sank further. There was an awkward silence for what seemed like a very long time until Dad said, 'this is my daughter Sabi.' Neither of them actually said anything in response so I said hello to them and then thought that maybe I should turn my attention to the view outside. But before I could do this, Dad spoke again, 'these are Sherry-Lee's parents Mr. and Mrs. Goosen.'

'Oh,' I managed to say.

'Unfortunately, they have come to talk to me about Sherry-Lee. She died yesterday morning in South Africa. I heard about it late last night.'

I bit my lip as many thoughts rushed through my head, the main one being that I had been wishing for something like this to happen. Oh jeez, now what had I gone and done?

'I'm very, um very sorry,' I managed to stammer and I noticed that Sherry-Lee's mother's eyes welled with tears again. The father put his arm around her shoulders. I felt so terrible about the way I had been thinking about Sherry-Lee recently that my eyes welled with tears too.

'I'm so sorry,' I said again, and I truly did mean it. Her dying hadn't been what I actually wanted to happen, just her not being in our lives any more.

'Thank you,' the mother said, 'you are a kind little girl.'

I couldn't believe she could say this to me. I'm not kind, I'm not kind, a voice in my head yelled but I stayed quiet.

'God dammed awful thing to happen,' the father said to Dad, 'there was nothing they could do for her and the doctor said that it's actually a blessing that she died. Would've been a vegetable if she'd lived, is what he told us.'

The mother started crying properly now and Dad looked extremely uncomfortable. I felt genuinely very sorry for all of them, in fact for all of us in the room. A moment later there was another tap at the door and Clare walked in tentatively. A look of shock crossed her face when she saw all of us standing around Dad's bed looking so unhappy, and I could see that she didn't know what to do.

'Maybe we should go, Dad,' I managed to say quickly. 'I'll come back and see you later.'

*

I didn't want to go shopping after hearing the bad news but Clare insisted that I did. She said I couldn't sit around the house moping all on my own.

'I'm sure this is very difficult for you but the best thing is to keep busy. I'm so sorry that you have had such bad news. You must've been very fond of her, poor girl.'

It shocked me when she said this, but then I realised I had never told Clare anything about Sherry-Lee.

*

We got back to the hospital late afternoon and this time Dad was alone but still looking very uncomfortable and unhappy.

I'm so sorry about your loss,' Clare started off, as soon as we were in the room. 'What a terrible thing to have happened.'

'Thank you,' was all my dad said back.

'If there is anything I can do to help please let me know.'

My dad looked at me.

'Thanks, I see that you have done a great deal already.'

He looked away from me and straight at Clare now.

'Would you mind leaving me alone with my daughter for a while?'

'Gee, yes, of course. I'll go and wait in the car downstairs, Sabi. Come and find me there when you've finished.'

As soon as the door closed behind her, Dad started up, 'What the hell has she been doing to you?'

'Umm, what do you mean, Dad?'

'Well, look at you, in that stupid little dress, and what on earth has happened to your hair?'

'All my clothes are too small for me, Dad. I promise, Dad, I can hardly fit into anything anymore; everything is too small so Clare said she'd buy me some more clothes. She didn't ask for any money or anything like that but it cost a hundred dollars and I said I'd pay her back.' I wasn't sure how to tell him about the money I'd earn by helping with the cooking.

'A hundred dollars for crap like that? You've got to be joking.'

'She bought me quite a lot of stuff, Dad, so that I have different things to wear.'

'Well, I hope that the rest of the stuff is more functional than what you've got on right now.'

'It's just fashionable, Dad.'

'You don't need to be wearing things like that. And your hair; is it supposed to be fashionable, too?

'The hairdresser said that a style like this would suit me better than keeping it in a plait all the time.'

'It's seems that Clare is trying to change my daughter without consulting me.'

I had been waiting for him to say something like this.

'She's not, Dad, it's me who wants to change and she's just helping me.'

'Bloody Americans, they think they are so superior and that they know more than anyone else. Well I think the sooner you get out of her company the better.'

I had been dreading something like this happening, the minute I saw the disapproving look on his face I knew that he'd say something like this.

'Ah no, Dad, please let me stay with her. You know her cousin, he's like us, and so is his wife. They are not in the least bit American. They all say I can stay at the conservancy, and there is even a job for me there helping out with the cooking, as their old cook turned out to be a rhino poacher and he was shot and now they don't have anyone to do the cooking at their lodge.'

I knew I was babbling but I didn't want my plans changed.

'You are far too young to have a job as a cook, for fucks sake. No, you don't need anything like that. I think we will go back to plan A. I will phone the Rawsons and say you will be going to stay with them after all. When can Miss Clare take you there?'

'Aah Dad, please don't make me go to the Rawsons. I don't really know them very well and I don't feel that comfortable with them.'

'But you feel comfortable with an American stranger?'

'It's just that she's been very kind to me and she's not completely American.'

Maybe this would change his mind.

'She was born here, and only went to America when she was little.'

'Whatever, I still think it's best for you to stay with the Rawsons. When can she drop you there, or should I phone them and ask them to come and collect you?'

'No Dad, Clare is planning on going back to the conservancy the tomorrow; she can drop me on the way.'

*

I didn't tell Clare how rude my dad had been about her and how he thought she was trying to change me. I felt too embarrassed to say anything like that so I just said that he would prefer me to be with people that he knew. But deep down I was very angry with him, and I was very unhappy with this change in plans. I think of the Rawsons, well, Mrs. Rawson, anyway as Sherry-Lee's friend as Mrs. Rawson and Sherry-Lee were at school together, although Sherry-Lee is, I mean was, a bit younger. And besides, in the times that I've seen the Rawsons since they've been married, and even more so since Sherry-Lee has been going out with my dad, I've always felt that Mrs. Rawson and Sherry-Lee share the same impression of me; I've always felt that they both see me as an irritating little girl.

And now, of course, I'm even more mixed up about Sherry-Lee. I think that maybe I actually am a bad omen in my dad's life. First my mother died because of me, and now his girlfriend has died, again because of me. Maybe I'll cause the death of someone important in his life every fifteen years or so. I don't like to think like this but maybe it is true. Maybe I'm just plain bad luck for him.

*

'What a shame you won't be able to help me with the cooking at the camp after all,' Clare interrupted my morbid train of thought, 'but we'll try to make a plan later. How long does your dad think he'll be in hospital?'

'I think two to three weeks.'

'Mmm, well I'll see what I can do.'

My heart soared with hope for a moment as I wondered what she was considering.

'But back to the present,' she said, before I could get too excited, 'Steve from the rhino dehorning unit has invited us out for dinner tonight. How does this sound to you?'

I thought about this and decided that it didn't sound very good at all. I had noticed that he seemed pretty keen on her and the last thing I wanted was to have to play gooseberry all night.

'I really could do with your company Sabi,' she continued, 'as I don't want to encourage Steve in anyway. I haven't mentioned this to you before, but I have a husband back home in the States, so I'm not really in a position to be going on dates with single men alone.'

I stared straight ahead of me as I digested this information, trying not to show any emotion. I don't know why, but it just hadn't occurred to me before that she would be married, even though she is fairly old, and so it shouldn't surprise me at all. I wondered why her husband wasn't with her and why she hardly talked about him and why she didn't even wear a ring on her wedding finger. But with all these questions floating around in my head all I could ask her was what his name was.

'Graham' she said. 'He's busy back home sorting out his life; otherwise it would be lovely to have him here. He's great fun; I know you'd like him a lot.'

8

Clare

IF my husband were to walk into the room right now I can almost guarantee he'd make an impression. I was surely impressed the first time I laid eyes on him, and I've noticed in the ten years since that most other people usually are. He's certainly a good-looking man, even though he's starting to go a bit bald now, but this does not take away from his inherent good looks. Two aspects of his appearance struck me the most when we first met, and those were his height and his skin, nothing unique I'm afraid. All I can say is that he's six foot four, but he accentuates this height by carrying himself very straight and tall, and he has the most beautiful, smooth olive skin, just a little lighter than Sabi's. When we first became lovers I used to spend hours stroking his arms and his back and his stomach as if he was a dog or a cat. He used to laugh at me for doing this, although I always noticed how he used to luxuriate in it. And even now, after all these years and everything that has happened, I still love the feel of his soft skin under my hands. But besides his striking looks he also has a charismatic character and this most times shows in his face, by the way he holds his mouth, by the way his eyes twinkle when he talks, by the way his nose crinkles when he laughs.

Yes, I'm sure most people are quite taken by him, whether they are male or female.

He's a writer and he certainly knows how to use words to great effect. How I've always wished I could speak and write like him, his turn of phrase, his quirky little comments, the often amusing way he describes something that is really quite mundane. He tells me that he taught himself to express his thoughts in as interesting a way as possible by always being in tune with the way others may write or speak. I've tried to do this too, since he told me it is learned, not inherent, but I have come to believe that he is wrong and that his is indeed a real gift. He is mainly a travel writer although recently (and unfortunately for me) he has started writing about more serious topics like wars and strife and coups and assassinations. I loved his travel writing days because more often than not I would join him on his trips to the countries he was assigned to write about, giving me endless opportunities to photograph interesting and different subjects myself.

Graham has a way about him that makes most people feel they can confide in him. Maybe he's only honed in his listening skills as a way of improving his writing, but whatever, when you first meet him you think that you can tell him anything, and he'll be understanding and sympathetic. When we first started going on our trips together we used to spend hours and hours at dinner every night, discussing all manner of topics, and it seemed that we were completely in tune with the way the other thought.

The therapist I was seeing before I came out here has explained to me that this is how romantic relationships usually do start. She gave me books to read and then we would discuss in our sessions how most people are attracted to those in whom they subconsciously recognise aspects of their parents' characters and this (again subconsciously) makes them feel how they felt when they were very, very young, when they felt completely loved, cherished and cared for. The therapist and I discussed over many hour-long sessions how this will make lovers look (unconsciously/subconsciously) to the other as a way of healing the hurts that life has inevitably meted out, and this other person, unaware of everything that has been projected onto them, and in turn having to deal with their own hurts and expectations, will inevitably fail to become a healer.

But ten years ago none of this was of any concern to me, and all I thought then was that I had met someone whose company I enjoyed immensely, who seemed to understand me better than anyone else and with whom I wanted to spend as much time as possible. It was as simple as that then and in some ways it still is, despite everything that has happened since. I don't think there has been one waking hour of one single day since I've been here in Zimbabwe that I haven't found myself stopping and wondering what he is doing that exact moment, that exact second and wishing more than anything that we were together still.

Oh yes, my life is in a mess, that I am here and not at home with him now.

I decided to start wearing my wedding ring again the day after Steve took Sabi and me out for dinner. I had been keeping it in my small travelling jewellery case ever since I arrived and I had not wanted to wear it before now. But after the surprised reaction I got from both Sabi and Steve when I mentioned that I had a husband back home, I decided that it was best to simply have it on and then I wouldn't have to start assuming a defensive stance if and when the topic came up.

*

It was very obvious to me that Sabi did not like the idea of going to stay with the Rawsons. What a shame her father would not let her come back to the camp with me, and help out with the cooking. It would have given her something to do and would also have made her feel useful, but for whatever reason he was against this idea. Before we left Bulawayo, I suggested that I approach him again about letting her come back to the camp with me, but she had looked quite stricken when I mentioned this and said I must not do it.

The Rawsons also live on a gold mine, quite close to the Stirling's place. I decided they seemed to be a pleasant enough couple when I got there to drop Sabi off. They were just starting their lunch when we arrived and we were invited to sit down at their dining room table and join them. Martin Rawson appears to be about the same age as Sabi's dad and I'd put his wife Vanessa at about ten years younger. She's very elegant and looks like she's just stepped out of a fashion magazine, quite strange really, when she's living in the middle of the Matabeleland bush. Our lunch was served by their maid, who afterwards went onto the verandah which adjoins the dining room, where their two infant girls were sitting at a low table on small plastic chairs, ostensibly eating their lunch. I noticed that the maid squashed her bottom into a spare plastic kids chair and tried her best to bring some order to their meal, while the girls in turn did their best to either ignore her, or alternatively be rude to her. Sabi had told me about these girls on the way down, and how badly behaved they always are, and certainly they were living up to this description of themselves during their lunch.

The main topic of conversation at our table was the death of poor Sherry-Lee. Understandably they were incredibly upset about this, especially as she had spent her last day with them at their house.

'I still can't believe it,' Vanessa said, 'I just can't get my head around it. She was a form one when I was a senior at school, so we weren't friends then but I've always seen her around and obviously I've got to know her well in the last year or so since she started going out with Digger. She was actually quite good fun to be with, once you got through her prickly exterior.'

I was surprised; I hadn't realised there had been a prickly exterior. They carried on talking about Sherry-Lee for a while and somewhere during the course of their conversation the very thing that I had secretly been wondering about, ever since I'd heard about the tragedy, leaked out; that Sherry-Lee had in fact had far too much to drink and that she shouldn't have been driving at all.

'She just kept on insisting,' Martin said, 'and when she jumped into the driver's seat and refused to get out, Digger didn't bother to stop her because he'd also had far too much to drink and was feeling pretty tired himself.'

'Oh God, we were all so stupid. They should have stayed the night here and driven back in the morning.'

Vanessa shook her head as she said this.

'So, so stupid of us to let them go home.'

I glanced at Sabi, who was sitting with her lips tightly pursed, in the way I have come to know she does when she is feeling bad. She stared straight in front of her and didn't say anything, but on the drive down she had told me that she felt responsible for the accident, because they were coming home to be with her, as she was alone. I had tried to tell her that she should not blame herself in any way and that they were entirely responsible for their actions, but I don't think she believed me, just as she didn't believe me when I told her that she was not responsible for her mother's death, either. Oh dear, to be so young and so full of guilt. I wish I could remove some of this from her.

We finished eating and I thought I'd better start thinking about going; I had a vehicle full of groceries that would need unpacking as soon as I got back to the conservancy. The kids had finished their lunch way before us and shot off to climb a nearby tree in the garden, while the maid tried to clean up the mayhem they had left behind.

'Thanks Regina,' Vanessa said as she got up from her chair, 'please bring some coffee onto the verandah for us. Are you sure you don't want some, Clare?'

I glanced at Sabi and when I saw the stricken look on her face I suddenly felt a great reluctance to leave her just then.

'Ok, let me have a quick cup and then I really will have to get on. How far is it to the lodge from here, do you know?'

'About sixty kilometres by road, I'd say. I'll get the map so that you can see which of the back roads you can take,' Martin replied.

Regina brought the tray of coffee while we settled ourselves in the wire verandah chairs and watched the children, who were now pretending that they were baboons in the tree.

'Careful, careful,' Vanessa fretted. 'The last thing we need is a broken limb.'

'Have you ever been to the Ubejane Conservancy?' I asked, having just come up with a brilliant idea.

'No, actually we haven't,' Martin replied, as he returned with the map, 'which is quite surprising really when you consider how close it is to where we live.'

'Why don't you come down next weekend, then? We haven't got a booking, as far as I know.'

For the first time since we'd arrived, Sabi looked interested in what was being discussed. She glanced quickly from Martin to Vanessa, who in turn looked questioningly at each other.

'Mmm, could be an idea,' Martin started.

'Oh yes, honey, let's do it. We haven't got anything else on.'

'OK, then, let's. What can we expect there?'

'Well I'd suggest,' I said quickly before they changed their minds, 'that you arrive on Friday afternoon and once you're settled we'll go on a game drive in the evening. They have a very nice pool at the lodge, which I'm sure the kids will want to spend a lot of time in on Saturday, if the weather remains as hot as it is now. We could also go fishing at the dam nearby, and maybe go on another game drive again Saturday evening. Have a late brunch on Sunday and then head home when you are ready after that. That seems to be the format for most people who come for the weekends. I think you'd enjoy it'

'Sounds good to me. Do we bring anything?'

'No, we provide everything, unless there is something special you want to drink. Otherwise, we supply all meals inclusive, but drinks are bought from the bar. The all-in tariff is sixty dollars per night per person, half price for kids.'

I was very pleased that I had come up with this idea, and that it had been so well received by the Rawsons, because Sabi immediately started to look way happier about everything. At least she now had something to look forward to in the midst of all the other traumas she was going through.

*

My therapist explained to me during the course of our many sessions that the heady, hazy days of romantic love will often come to a quick conclusion when the idea of 'commitment' comes into a relationship. Surprising this may seem at first, but apparently when a couple decides to commit all those subconscious illusions each has projected onto the other become that much more significant, now each has to live up to what the other unconsciously expects from them. Of course, they cannot do this, as they have no idea about the hurts the other has assumed they will magically heal, and therefore they inevitably fail in their partner's view.

Hence the romance ends and disillusionment starts.

Maybe this theory can be widened to encompass many other aspects of life too. For instance, myself here in Zimbabwe right now. I'm enjoying my life more than I have in a very long time, all things taken into consideration, and maybe this is partly because I'm not really committed to anything and I don't have any important responsibilities. Sure, if people come to stay in the camp and there is nothing for them to eat then I'll be held responsible, but hey, I'll manage to find something. It's been a very long time since I've just been able to 'exist' like this, without having to worry about endless responsibilities, and I'm enjoying it all immensely. If only it could go on like this forever, but of course I know it can't and in actuality I probably wouldn't really want it to, because then I'd start expecting more from my life here. Yeah, in the end, real life must take over again and I can almost guarantee that if this was my real life I wouldn't find it nearly as enjoyable as I do right now.

So therefore, while this limbo period lasts, I must just try to enjoy each day as it comes.

*

Rob asked me to drive to the neighbouring conservancy to collect the latest clients, a couple from America who wanted to come to our place on a short photographic safari. This place is called the Limpopo Conservancy, and it is situated right on the banks of the Limpopo River, the river which separates Zimbabwe from South Africa. I hadn't been to this area before, and while a few weeks ago I'd have been nervous to go on my own and would have asked if Jabula could come with me, this time I was real happy for the opportunity to drive along the dusty bush roads on my own, enjoying the surroundings and views, without having to worry about anyone else. And the scenery along this drive really is quite spectacular, reminding me in some ways of the parts of Utah and Arizona that I have driven through on my way to the Grand Canyon. I tried to work out what made me think this as I drove down the dust road, because on the face of it they are not really that similar, and I decided that it is because in both of these places it feels like being on another planet, with all the weird trees and strange-looking hill formations that make up the landscape. Both places are also semi-desert with bare, red earth and hills, so adding to their seeming quite similar.

Rob gave me a map showing me how to get there along the back roads, and I found myself having to stop fairly often to look at it carefully, or otherwise I would ask the locals walking or riding their bicycles or driving their donkey-drawn scotch carts along the road.

I arrived at the Limpopo Conservancy mid afternoon, knowing that I was expected to spend the night there before taking the clients back to Ubejane the next day. I noticed that as I got closer to the Limpopo River the bush became way more thick and lush with large trees and long grass. A couple by the name of John and Kate Manning own this place and they live in a large open plan house, built by themselves they told me, right on the banks of the Limpopo River and in the shade of huge fig trees. It's literally a stone's throw from the river. They explained to me that it gets very hot during the summer months, so they need their garden to be as shady as possible. I can understand this, coming from the southern states of America as I do, but I quickly decided that their heat is nothing like the heat we experience in the Deep South. Back home, our heat is debilitating, whereas here, on the banks of the Limpopo River, it is balmy when in a shady spot, and once a slight breeze gets up. They don't have the humidity we have back home, and I think this is what makes it more manageable.

We sat on their verandah in the evening to eat our supper, listening to the river running gently no more than twenty metres away from us with tree frogs (I was told that was what they were) squeaking in the trees above, and hippos grunting in the river beyond. We sprayed some insect repellent on our arms and legs and didn't have to worry about bugs any more, unlike back home, where we would've been carried away by mosquitoes and other midges if we'd been dining outdoors like we were then. The weather here in Zimbabwe is really quite exceptional, it's understandable in this respect why so many Europeans wanted to come and live here in times gone by.

The clients I had come to collect were an American couple from Atlanta so we found we had a lot of common ground. They had been staying at the Limpopo Conservancy to observe and photograph all the prehistoric relics that can be found in this area, things that I had not known before were here, like dinosaur fossils and even footprints stamped into the rock face millions of years ago. When I heard about this I wished I'd arrived earlier so that I could have taken a look at and photographed some of them, too, but when I made this comment I was immediately issued with an invitation to come back again any time. With my new freewheeling lifestyle I knew this would not be difficult to arrange.

I slept in a guesthouse consisting of a bedroom and bathroom some thirty metres from the main house. In the middle of the night I woke up dying of thirst and discovered to my dismay that I didn't have a glass in either the bathroom or the bedroom. I decided I'd walk across the lawns to the house to collect a glass, but when I stepped onto the verandah I got the fright of my life; the garden between the main house and me was full of buffalo. I don't know how many were there at the time, but there was no way I could go and fetch my glass with them grazing on the lawn. I sat at the window for a long while and watched them grazing quietly in the dappled light of the moon shining through the trees, some of them mooing every now and again, sounding similar to cows.

Eventually, they wandered off and then quite suddenly, were all gone but knowing that they could easily be lurking in the thick bush just beyond the garden I could not contemplate going off to the house to fetch a glass. Instead, I tried to drink from the tap with the palm of my hand, but had little success and woke in the morning feeling dehydrated and with a thumping head. My host and hostess laughed at my dilemma and gave little sympathy except to hand over two aspirin and say how lucky I was to see the buffalo. As the headache subsided, I realised how lucky indeed I had been, spending a beautiful, balmy night with two hundred or so buffalo on the banks of the Limpopo River.

My only regret was that I didn't have anyone there to share the experience; for me it's always so much more fun when I do.

9

Sabi

THE Rawsons' children are called Lottie and Jessica and they are real pains. If they are not tearing around being really noisy and knocking everything in their path over, then they are bugging me and being incredibly irritating.

'Watch me spin round, Sabi,' Lottie yells, moving her feet in tiny circles so that her dress flies out and she eventually falls down dizzy.

'Look at how I can do up my buttons Sabi,' Jessica shouts, undoing her buttons so that she has to do them up again (wrongly I might add) while I watch.

Talk about stupid!

'Run round the garden with me, Sabi.'

'Come and bath with us, Sabi.'

'Come and help us colour in, Sabi.'

'Please sit next to me at table, Sabi.'

'No, I want her to sit next to me, please let her sit next to me, Mom.'

They both made such a fuss that I eventually had to sit in between them at every meal.

I asked Vanessa if I could bake a cake and she said she'd be delighted if I did. She told me to ask Regina where everything was in the kitchen, but of course I'd only been in there for a few minutes when the two brats found me.

'What are you doing Sabi? Can we join in?'

They didn't even wait for an answer but I knew they would make a great fuss if I chased them away, so I found each of them their own stool to stand on, and gave them each their own mixing bowl and spoon and I put some of my mixture into their bowls. You would've thought this would have kept them happy but of course it did not.

'Jessie has more than me, Sabi,' Lottie said.

'No I have not.'

'Yes you have. I want some more.'

She stretched across the table to try and take some from my bowl and managed somehow to fall off her stool, pulling my bowl off the table as she fell. You can imagine the commotion she made after that. I tried my best to console her but thankfully Regina came back into the kitchen to see what the fuss was about and gave her a big scolding. She then cleverly scooped out what was left of the mixture in my bowl and put it into both of the brats' bowls and told them to go to the verandah to mix their cakes. I think they ate most of what they had because both bowls were pretty empty when I saw them later.

In the meantime, I had to start my cake all over again. What a waste of the six eggs and all the cocoa powder I'd used in the first mixture. Gogo would've been furious if she'd been there, as she hated anything going to waste. Anyway I finally got to make my cake; the Doubly Delicious Chocolate Chiffon Cake that I'd made for my Home Economics exam at the end of last term, and which the teacher, Mrs Nyathi, said was the best cake out of the whole class. It's such a shame I've had to give up Home Economics, but I suppose I'm lucky that I do well in my tests and stuff and am in the A stream. I felt very bad for Darlene when she was put into the C stream, because she was really upset about this; she will be doing Home Economics as well as Sewing but she says she hates both subjects. Sarah and I weren't surprised when she was moved to the C; she got something like ten percent for her Maths exam at the end of last term.

Vanessa is good at sewing. She has a little room next to the office and she spends a lot of her time sewing in there. She makes the girls most of their clothes, dresses that are the same, which I think is a bit naff, even though they are actually quite sweet. But she makes herself very nice clothes. I'd say she has really good style. She buys all the latest fashion magazines and copies the clothes she sees in them, and she can even do this without using patterns, which I think is pretty clever.

I showed her all the clothes that Clare bought me at the Unity Village and she seemed to like most of them a lot. She asked me if any of them needed altering and in fact there were some that did so she said she'd show me how. She ended up doing most of the altering herself, as I'm not much good at sewing, but I did manage to learn a thing or two, so maybe next time I'll be able to do it myself. She gave me a few suggestions as to how I could put some of the shorts and tops together in different ways so that they would seem like different outfits, and she gave me two scarves and a belt. I'm not sure if I'll wear the scarves but the belt will go really well with my new shorts and longs. She also went so far as to make me a few extra summer tops. She told me they were really easy to make and that she often makes them for herself if she has any leftover material. I can see that they are quite simple, as they just consist of a front and a back piece joined together with a high neckline and cutaway armholes, which make them look stylish when they are worn. After watching Vanessa doing all this sewing, I started to think that when I get home I'll take out the old machine Gogo used to use and have a go at making something myself. I told her this.

'Oh wow Sabi,' Vanessa said, looking really excited, 'I'm so glad you're interested in sewing. Let me give you your fist lesson right now.'

She opened the cupboard in her sewing room where she keeps all her pieces of material and went through them till she pulled out a piece. 'Here, what do you think of this?'

It had pin stripes in pastel colours.

'It's really nice, Vanessa.'

'Good. I'm going to teach you how to make a sun dress.'

It turned out really cool and I know that Sarah will be impressed when I tell her I made it myself. It has a straight bodice which comes just below the bust, with the stripes going horizontally and then the stripes of the skirt part go vertically. The skirt part consists of three pieces, one front and two back, with a zip going all the way down the back. I thought it would be hard putting in a zip, but in fact it was pretty easy. Vanessa insisted that we have pockets in the side seams and she showed me how to put these in, too. She also showed me how to gather the top of the skirt part by sewing big tacking stitches and then pulling them in so that the piece ends up the same size as the bodice. The dress has 'spaghetti string straps' as Vanessa called them, and she showed me how to sew them and then push a knitting needle through from the inside out to pull them the right way. I felt really pleased with myself when it was finished, although I'm sure Tracey will be critical of it when she sees it next term. But I like it and I'm going to try and make myself another one when I can get some more material. Vanessa says I will need about one and a half metres of material if it is 1.5 metres wide, or otherwise two metres if the material is 1.2 meters wide.

I thought that Vanessa would be like Sherry-Lee and spend most of her time ignoring me or making me feel unwelcome, but in fact she's not like this at all. It seems that she actually likes having me staying here and doing stuff with me. They've got a tennis court in their garden and some evenings she has asked me to play tennis with her. I'm not a bad tennis player; I played fourth couple in the Under Fifteen A team last term and I'll probably be in the Under Sixteen team next year. Vanessa says I give her a very good runabout and I'm hoping that I may be promoted to the third couple next term, after all this practice I've had these holidays.

*

I'd been staying there for nearly a week when I was told we'd all be going to Bulawayo the next day for Sherry-Lee's funeral. I'd been wondering about what was happening as far as this was concerned, but when it was finally mentioned my heart sank. I did not want to go to Sherry-Lee's funeral for a number of reasons. Firstly, even though I feel bad that she has died, there is nothing I can remember about her that can make me decide that she was a nice person, to me at any rate. Secondly, I still can't help but wonder if my strong wish for her to get out of our lives didn't have something to do with her actually dying. I really need to talk to Sarah about this whole business of 'the power of the mind' and find out what she thinks about it, but in the meantime I feel very uncomfortable with the way I'd been thinking about Sherry-Lee the very day before she died.

Vanessa woke me early on the day of the funeral. I'd made up my mind the night before what I'd do; I'd pretend that I was sick. They were only planning on going to Bulawayo for the day, anyway, so it would be fine for me to stay here and for Regina to look after me. So, when Vanessa came into the room, I rolled over and moaned slightly. I felt bad about lying, but I didn't know how else to get out of going to the funeral. I could hardly tell Vanessa my real feelings about Sherry-Lee, when I know they had been good friends and that she is very upset about what has happened.

'I threw up last night, Vanessa. I think it was something I ate.'

In fact, I was feeling a bit sick now, with worry, but I hadn't actually vomited or anything like that.

Vanessa looked concerned, 'Oh dear, are you all right now?'

'No, I still feel very nauseous.'

She came and stood next to the bed and felt my head.

'Well, I don't think you have a temperature but you are a bit clammy and you look a bit peaky. How strange, the rest of us are feeling fine. I wonder what it was that has not agreed with you.'

I didn't say anything but sat up and then quickly flopped back onto the pillow.

'Mm, I wonder if you should stay here, after all,' she continued. 'Would you mind if you didn't come to Bulawayo with us? It'll mean not seeing your dad, although he won't be at the funeral anyway, as he still isn't allowed out of hospital.'

'Can you give him the biscuits I made yesterday when you go to visit him? I think it will be best if I stay in bed here. The last funeral I went to I ended up fainting, and I don't want that to happen again.'

Vanessa probably thought I was exaggerating, but she just went on regardless.

'Ok then. I'll tell Regina to make some food for you during the day, although you probably don't want to eat anything just yet, but hopefully you'll start to feel better later.'

She stopped for a moment and then said something that got my pulse racing.

'Maybe we'll leave the girls here too, now that you are going to be around.'

I stared at the roof, trying to hide my horror at this idea, but thankfully she quickly changed her mind.

'No actually, my mother will be very disappointed if I don't take them to see her. No, we'd better take them after all.'

Phew, I thought.

It was actually quite nice having the place to myself for a change. I managed to fall back to sleep again after I heard them drive off, and didn't wake up again until after ten o'clock. I lay in bed for as long as I could after this, but eventually I just got too bored and decided to get up. Regina had finished cleaning the lounge when I went through, and she suggested I lie on the sofa and watch television while she brought me some tea and toast. I've hardly watched any TV since I've been staying with the Rawsons because, as you can imagine, when the brats are awake we have to watch what they want, which is always cartoons and then in the evenings I have to watch what Vanessa and Martin want to watch. But now I was able to make the most of having the remote to myself, and typically there was very little of interest so I ended up mainly watching the Food Network channel.

I also spent quite a bit of time looking at Vanessa's magazines, which I'd noticed she keeps in her sewing room. I love magazines, but unfortunately don't ever have much access to them. Sarah has some at her house and of course Tracey reads them all the time, but these are mainly for teenagers, while most of Vanessa's are geared for the more mature woman, I'd say. I read a fascinating article about the joys of masturbating, which I found a bit of an eye-opener (even Tracey would have learnt a thing or two) and another article on kinky things people like to do to each other. Again I thought of Tracey and wondered how shocked she'd be if she knew that some people like weeing on each other and having anal sex. I thought that was just what homosexuals, did, but according to this article, this is not so. I can't wait to tell

Tracey all about it next term and see what her reaction is. I'm sure even she will be surprised when she hears this. But it was the 'agony aunt pages' of the magazines that I enjoyed reading the most. In the one magazine people write to someone called 'Doris' and in another to 'Dr Ellen', asking them for advice on a whole range of problems, which I found fascinating.

*

When the family eventually came home in the early evening it was my turn to get the shock of my life. They had Vanessa's brother with them and it turns out that Vanessa's brother is none other than Mr. Norris, my PE teacher from school. I nearly fell over when he got out of the car along with the rest of the family.

'You'll know my brother, Sabi,' Vanessa said, smiling happily to me. I'm afraid there was nothing I could think of to say back, but I did wonder what she'd think if she knew how Mr. Norris had joked with me. She certainly wouldn't be pleased, I'm sure. I hadn't even known before that she had a brother and I definitely would never have put her and Mr. Norris together as brother and sister. Mr. Norris is so strong and sporty-looking whereas Vanessa is small and fragile.

'Don't look so shocked, Sabi,' she carried on saying, 'poor Neville has been getting bored in Bulawayo during the holidays, so I suggested he came down here for a few days so that he can come to Ubejane with us this weekend.'

So Neville is his name. I tried to pretend that having him there was no big deal, but in fact I felt incredibly self-conscious having him around. I wondered what on earth Sarah and Tracey would think if they knew and of course all the other girls at school too. He was his usual friendly self, but this didn't stop me from feeling very uncomfortable. Teachers are supposed to be for school, not for having around during the holidays. We were planning on going to Ubejane the day after next and I decided that if I could get through tomorrow, I'd be fine afterwards because when we got to the lodge I could hang around with Clare in the kitchen or whatever.

*

After breakfast, I managed to get Vanessa alone and I asked her if the driver could take me back to my home to collect a suitcase for me. You see Clare had lent me one of her cousin's suitcases after she had bought me all my new clothes and I wanted to give this one back when we got to Ubejane. I thought this was an excellent idea. It would also give me the opportunity to spend a bit of time at home, and maybe go down to my fort to collect my cigarettes. But guess what? Vanessa happened to tell Mr. Norris what I wanted to do and he offered to take me himself. I couldn't believe how my plan had back-fired, and I couldn't think of any reason why I should suddenly change my mind, except to have another vomiting attack, which would look very suspicious when I'd told them all I was much better the day before.

So mid-morning I got into the pickup truck Mr. Norris borrowed from Martin, feeling really embarrassed, as we set off to my home. Of course, I worried that he'd make one of his stupid jokes again and I didn't know how I'd react, just him and me alone in the truck for a twenty minute drive to my house and a twenty minute drive back. But, amazingly, he didn't make any such jokes, and in fact was just really, really nice. I, on the other hand was still feeling so self-conscious that I could do little else than stare out of the window all the way to my house, even though he kept commenting on things he saw along the road. When we got to my house we found

Beauty there and I took her aside and told her not to say anything about me to him, but to give him some tea in the lounge. I told him I needed to go to the farm compound to see someone there about an important matter and that I'd be at least an hour. He didn't seem to mind this, and so I was able to escape and go off to my fort. It was lovely to be able to relax there for a while and to have a cigarette, but I didn't dare take the packet back to the house with him there. When I got back I saw him snooping around the garden, so I went out to tell him that we could go back now as Beauty had found an old suitcase for me and put it in the back of the truck.

During the trip back Mr. Norris kept up his prattle, telling me quite a few interesting things about the teachers at school. I actually started to relax a little in his company and when we were nearing the Rawons' house he asked me if anyone had ever shown me how to drive, and when I said 'no' he said he'd be happy to give me a lesson. I thought, 'what is there to lose, why not,' so while he walked around the bonnet to get in the passenger side I slid across the seat to the driver's side. He had to show me how to push the seat forward as I'm quite a bit shorter than he is and then he gave me a lecture about the gears and the pedals and about letting the clutch out slowly with my left foot while I gradually pushed my right foot down on the accelerator pedal. I found it very difficult at first and kept stalling the engine, but Mr. Norris only laughed at me and said everyone always finds it difficult at first. After seven times I eventually managed to get it and we crept along the road in first gear, with me realising that steering isn't as easy as I'd thought it was either. He made me stop and then start and again I managed to stall the engine but got it right the third time. He then let me go from first gear to second, but kept telling me to keep my right foot ready to move quickly from the accelerator to the brake pedal, when necessary, and to go very slowly. He told me I must not keep my left foot on the clutch as it's called 'riding the clutch' and it's really bad to do this. We stopped and started another few times and then we were near the Rawson's garden gate and he told me he didn't want to risk me driving through it in case I banged it.

He got back into the driver's seat and I said I'd walk to the house, and while I did I wondered what the girls at school will think when I tell them that Mr. Norris gave me my first driving lesson, and I decided they'll all be green with envy.

10

Clare

VANESSA and Martin are so lucky to have those two darling girls of theirs. They're such little characters, once you get to know them, especially the younger one, Lottie. She really made me laugh when they first arrived. What happened was that I heard the revving of their vehicle as they drove up the steep driveway to the lodge, so I quickly went round to the parking area to greet them. There was the usual commotion as everyone got out of the car, gathering their things and greeting me; 'Hi Clare, hi girls, hi Clare, hi Sabi,' and so on and so forth. Regina, the maid was the last to get out of the car and when she greeted me with 'hello Madam,' little Lottie, who happened to be standing next to her looked up at her stunned.

'Madam, why are you calling her Madam, Regina?' she asked suspiciously. 'I thought her name was Clare,'

Oh how we laughed, I don't think there are many three year olds back home who would get confused about whether someone's name is Clare or Madam. Back home too, most of the people I mix with don't have childminders to take with them on weekend jaunts. However, I can't say I really blame Vanessa for wanting to bring Regina. She had sent an email the day before, asking if she could bring her as I'd told her that the lodge, being built on a huge dwala, had many sheer drops, and she didn't want to spend her whole weekend watching her girls' every move.

*

I should have a child more or less Lottie's age now too, a little boy of somewhere around three years old. Graham and I decided to try for a baby after we'd been married for two years but found it harder to conceive than we'd ever envisaged. It's weird how this so often happens, after spending most of one's fertile years trying not to have a baby, when one finally decides that it's time, it's extremely difficult to do so, if not impossible. At the time, I was thirty-two years old and so definitely defined, in reproductive years, as past my prime. Yet I did not feel this way, thinking I was no different from when I was in my mid twenties, making me extremely frustrated that it was so difficult to conceive. But finally after over two years, and just when it was starting to become a real issue for me, as much as I tried to tell myself that it was not, I fell pregnant.

How happy we were that it had finally happened, despite my experiencing extreme morning sickness during my first trimester. A small price to pay I decided. Midterm through my pregnancy I decided to give up my job in the photography shop where I worked, ostensibly so that I could prepare properly for the baby. I wanted to take my role as a mother very seriously, but also, we'd bought a lovely six acre plot a few years back and I'd never had the time, working the hours I did, to do all the things we'd planned to do when we first acquired it. Our property is a few miles out of town, very close to the Mississippi River, so that the levee that runs alongside the river forms one of our boundaries. There is a main house on the property, plus a barn and some sheds. All needed work done on them, and with a few months to go before the arrival of the baby, I was desperately keen to tackle some of the things we had planned. It's amazing how that nesting instinct kicks in when you are going to have a baby.

One morning, a morning when Graham happened to be away, lecturing at a travel writer's workshop in Aspen, I decided to hang the new blinds I'd bought for the baby's bedroom. It was a fairly innocuous chore, but it resulted in an incident that changed our lives forever. It was so stupid of me, so incredibly stupid. Ever since that day, I've gone over and over in my mind the event, and I still can't understand why I allowed myself to be so irresponsible. Instead of going down the stairs, out of the kitchen door and to the garden shed to fetch the ladder, I pulled up a wooden washbox on which I climbed so that I could reach the top of the window. And when I did this and saw that I was still not quite high enough to reach easily I looked around the nursery and saw a small wooden stool, which I perched on top of the wash box and climbed back up again. Whenever I've thought back on what happened next, it seems like it was in slow motion. One second I was trying to push a hook into the wooden rod above the window, on which the blind was going to hang, and the next I was falling. I tried to stop myself, to steady myself on the stool, to grab at the wall next to me, but the stool slid out from under my feet and fell on the floor and I tumbled right down on top of it. I lay for a moment, trying to determine if I was injured or not and thanking my lucky stars that I had not broken my neck, and as I lay there I gradually became aware of a warm wetness between my legs and a sharp aching in the bottom of my stomach, as if I was experiencing a very bad period pain.

We lost the baby at twenty-four weeks. Such a terrible tragedy, and made that much worse when I had to have a hysterectomy a year later, so putting paid to any ideas we still had of ever having a child of our own. Graham never blamed me for what had happened, but I blamed myself, and when I knew that I would never be able to give him a child it made me feel less adequate as a wife, as much as I tried to tell myself that lots of couples never have children and they cope just fine.

Graham started to change subtly after my accident. Whereas before he had always enjoyed the light-heartedness of working as a travel writer, afterwards he started to question the relevance of this, and he began to search for more serious issues to write about. He wanted to be taken more seriously and decided he could do this by writing about issues that he thought were more significant than just what all the different holiday destinations in the world were like. Six months after my hysterectomy he left for Afghanistan for a month. He wanted to try to find a different perspective on which to write about the conflict there, and I suppose he was pretty successful, because his articles were snapped up by various publications in the States. A few months later he travelled to Gaza, at the time when the Israelis were trying to blockade supplies getting in there, in retaliation for the Palestinians kidnapping one of their soldiers, and again Graham wrote some thought provoking articles on what was happening on both sides of the conflict. This was just the beginning of his new-found career.

As a result of his relative success, he started to feel a greater sense of purpose in his writing, which was great for him, but unfortunately not good for us. Whereas before I most often joined him on his trips, now it was usually impossible to do so. He certainly did not want me with him, getting in his way and I had no desire to go to all the conflict-torn zones of the world.

*

I was quietly warmed when I saw how well Sabi got on with little Jessica and Lottie. They certainly seemed to be very taken with her, and there was often quite a lot of squabbling between them as to which of them could be as close as possible to her. When we went on our game drive on Friday evening they insisted on sitting either side of her on the back bench of the Land Cruiser we use for safaris. She didn't appear to mind this at all, even though they must've been a little irritating, leaning on her legs and trying to copy her every move. Vanessa's rather attractive brother, Neville, sat the other side of Jessica but all three girls seemed to be rather in awe of him.

On Saturday, Rob said he would take us all to the dam to fish. Rob had this dam made fourteen years ago, so he told us, by building a wall across one of the seasonal rivers that run through the conservancy. It's probably four or five kilometres long and a kilometre wide at its widest part, so it's a fair stretch of water, especially for this part of the world, which could almost be described as semi-desert. The water rose very quickly after the wall was finished, and the dam makers didn't have enough time to remove many of the trees in the catchment area, so because of this they are still there today, only dead and bare now. However, it makes for a rather attractive feature and the trees are also very useful to tie up the pontoon from which we use to fish. The dam has hippos and crocodiles in it which made me feel a little nervous at first. I'm not worried about the crocodiles, as I'm used to the alligators we have in the bayou back home, which Graham and I fish in from time to time, but I sure am not used to large, fat hippopotami anymore, and I became especially wary of them when Rob started going on about how they are responsible for more deaths in Africa than any other wild animal.

However, I finally convinced myself that the pontoon was a very sturdy vessel and any hippo or crocodile that tried to attack it would most definitely regret their decision. I've also noticed that most animals do their best to get away, whenever we come anywhere near them. But Martin still had to lecture the two little girls severely about not putting their hands near the water. He told them a story about how someone he knew nearly had his hand bitten off when a crocodile appeared from nowhere and snapped at him as he was washing his hands. That had the little girls looking pretty worried, for a while, anyways. Thankfully Martin appears to be a very keen fisherman and he seemed determined to instil this keenness in his daughters, showing them how to push the hooks through their worms, 'Aah, that's so gross Dad,' as well as how to cast off the side of the pontoon, 'now careful girls that you don't accidently hook someone in the eye.'

Polly and James were with us this time, as quiet and well behaved as possible. They'd obviously done a lot of fishing before; neither of them had to ask anyone to help them as they sat next to their mother, who also seems to be pretty nifty with a fishing rod.

Neither Vanessa or I had any interest in learning how to catch the bream in Rob's dam, so we sat in the shade of the awning at the back of the deck watching everyone else's antics. Vanessa is definitely one of the most elegant women I've met in Zimbabwe so far, she should really be living in New York or London or Paris, where she can dress herself up as elegantly as she does for people who will actually appreciate the way she looks. She does seem rather out of place, always in some amazing outfit and in the middle of nowhere, with just us to admire her. She doesn't seem to mind though, well that's the impression I've got on the two occasions I've met her so far. Maybe she just likes to look good for herself. Leanne, on the other hand, cannot be called a fashion icon. She's short and a little dumpy and has absolutely no fashion sense whatsoever, always wearing her khaki 'uniform'.

I was a little worried to see that Sabi was more subdued than usual, and I vowed to have a word with her when we got back to the camp. Even though Rob had now hired another cook, I've still been trying to encourage her to help me in the kitchen, because I believe it makes her feel useful and good about herself. So, for instance, on their first morning I singled her out after breakfast and asked her to give me some advice on what to pack in the cooler boxes for our fishing expedition. She seemed very pleased with this and I could see that she was delighted when I raved about the chicken and lettuce mayonnaise rolls that she helped me make, but once we got onto the pontoon with everyone else she went back into her shell again.

I didn't have a chance to talk to her after the fishing trip and then, when we got back to the lodge after our evening game drive, I went to look for her, but she'd disappeared. I decided instead to have a luxuriant soak in the outdoor bathtub that adjoins my lodge but the weirdest thing happened while I was there. It was a beautiful still evening, with one of those long, golden sunsets that they get so often in this part of the world. While we get lovely sunsets back home too, it's usually too hot to stay out of doors to appreciate them, or otherwise you are carried away by midges if you do. But here, it's not too hot and the flying bugs are manageable, so I went up to the bar, poured myself a glass of white wine with lots of ice and then went down to my outdoor bathroom to soak in a warm bubbly tub while enjoying the amazing view of the sun setting slowly below the horizon. As usual these days, when I'm in a situation like this I think about Graham and the problems we've been having and I try to think of a way I can make things better again. I lay in the rock bath for what seemed like ages, so that it was almost dark before I noticed the time. I got up from the now cool soapy water, stark naked, obviously, and as I reached forward to retrieve my robe from the rock next to me I realised that Neville was standing a distance away from me, just beyond another big rock, and it seemed like he was staring at me. I jumped with fright when I saw him but he quickly bumbled on,

'Ah, oh, I'm sorry; I must've taken a wrong turn.' He sort of turned away as he said this while I grabbed my robe and shoved myself into it. 'Damn,' he carried on, 'I'm never really sure where I am in this lodge.'

I don't know why, but I just didn't believe him, and suddenly it occurred to me that he had actually been standing there for ages spying on me. But of course there was nothing I could say or do about this, I was hardly going to accuse one of our paying camp guests of being a peeping Tom and the last thing I wanted to do was upset Vanessa by telling her my suspicions about her brother.

*

I managed to get Sabi by herself later.

'You seem a bit quiet,' I started. 'Well a bit quieter than usual, because as you know I think you are one of my quietest friends as it is,' I joked.

'I don't mean to be,' she replied, smiling. 'I just don't know what to say.'

'Is it ok at the Rawsons?'

'Vanessa is very nice. She's been teaching me how to sew and all that.'

'That sounds like fun. And it seems like Vanessa knows a lot about clothes.'

'Yes, she's been showing me fashion magazines and all of that. She likes my hair a lot too.'

'Great.'

'Her brother, Mr. Norris, is our PE teacher at school, so it's a bit weird staying in the same house as him.'

'Is he a nice teacher?'

'Everyone at school thinks he's really cool.'

'But not you?'

'He's a really good coach, tennis, hockey, swimming. It's just a bit odd having him around during the holidays, even though he's always really nice to me. I never knew before that he was related to Vanessa but still, he's given me a driving lesson and he says he'll give me more. I suppose it's not so bad having him around, just a bit weird as he's my teacher.'

I couldn't help but think that there was more to it than this, but trying to get information out of Sabi is like trying to get blood out of a stone, so I didn't try to press her further.

11

Sabi

I was very sad when we left the lodge at the end of the weekend. I'd been looking forward to it, ever since I'd got to the Rawsons, and now it was over and we'd had such a great time, too. Besides this, I helped out a lot in the kitchen and Clare told me she'd get money from Leanne to pay me for all my hard work. They've got a new cook called Lovemore, who seems to be good but he's still learning the ropes so Clare kept asking me to check on things. On Saturday evening when we got back from fishing I went with Lovemore to gut the fish we'd caught; I'd caught two medium-sized bream, Martin had caught one a bit bigger than mine plus a huge barbel, that got the girls extremely excited, until he threw it back in the water, but the most amazing thing was that Mr. Norris caught the biggest bream of us all. Anyway, Lovemore and I gutted them and filleted them and then deep-fried them in piping hot oil after rolling them in flour and spices. I made a tartar sauce, the way Gogo used to, out of mayonnaise, gherkins and finely chopped spring onions and we served them as snacks before supper. Everyone raved about them, except for the girls, who said theirs had bones that got stuck in their throats, so there was a lot of spitting from them until I told them they couldn't have any more if that's the way they were going to behave.

I felt very flat and depressed when we got back to the Rawsons house but after tea Martin suggested we all went for a swim, as it was such a hot afternoon. They have quite an interesting pool because it is completely round. Martin says it was made the same way reservoirs are made with a tin frame and so it is not very deep and the same depth all over. Anyway what's nice about it is that you can work up a current if everyone in the pool walks quite fast in the same direction. So Martin, Vanessa, Mr. Norris and I did just this while the girls bobbed around uselessly in the middle with their water wings, and before we knew it we had such a good current going that we could float on our backs and carry on going round and round without having to kick or anything. Obviously, the current would start to weaken so we would all put our feet down again and walk fast until it was strong enough to float round and round again. It was really good fun and we did it for ages until Vanessa said she wanted to go inside to wash her hair and blow dry it.

In the evening Martin made a fire in the braai area and we cooked some deliciously tender sirloin steaks out there. By now, Vanessa had come to realise that I'm quite a good cook, so she asked me if I knew how to make the steaks more interesting. I mixed up my usual marinade with tomato sauce, vinegar, brown sugar, Worcestershire sauce and mustard and marinated the steaks in it while we waited for the fire to be ready. Regina made a potato salad and I helped her with a green salad.

By the end of the evening I was starting to decide that it wasn't so bad being back at the Rawsons' after all, although I knew I would still have much preferred to be at the lodge.

The next day I was woken by the sound of yelling. I find it very hard to wake up early in the school holidays and usually manage to sleep until mid morning, but this morning it was not to be. I got up to see what the commotion was about and thankfully I was the last to arrive at the scene of the disaster; at the big tree near the verandah in which Jessica and Lottie insist on playing baboons all the time. Well, this time Jessica had fallen out and hurt her arm and she was making sure that we all knew how sore it was. Regina tried to hold her still while Mr. Norris, squatting down on his haunches next to her, tried to assess the damage. Vanessa stood next to them, saying she had always known something like this would happen.

'I'm afraid it's broken,' he eventually said. 'Quite badly so, I think.'

'Oh God, I've been waiting for this to happen, ever since they started playing like baboons in this bloody tree.' Vanessa answered.

'You're going to have to get her to a doctor to have it set properly. There is no way we can try to do it here.'

'I'll radio Martin and tell him to get back here as soon as possible. Hopefully, if we leave soon we can get to Bulawayo and be back before it gets dark.'

An hour later they were packed up in their twin cab and driving down the drive. Jessica had been given two large teaspoons of Stopain, which had made her a bit drowsy, but she had still whimpered and moaned up to the moment they left. It was decided that Mr. Norris and I would stay behind, as there wasn't a lot of room in the car with Jessica needing to lie down on the back seat. I wasn't too upset about this as I knew Jessica would carry on fussing all the way to Bulawayo and I didn't much fancy this, but at the same time I wasn't sure I wanted to spend the whole day with Mr. Norris, either. I knew he was trying to be really nice to me, but for some reason this just made me feel very uncomfortable. I resolved to keep as far away from him as possible. I didn't know exactly how to do this, until I eventually decided that the only real alternative to being in the house with him was to be in the bush alone. I don't mind this, as I've always spent quite a bit of time exploring the bush at home, so I went into the kitchen and made myself some polony sandwiches and a bottle of juice and then I set off. I told Regina that I was going for a picnic but asked her not to tell Mr. Norris. The last thing I wanted was him following me.

It was fun exploring a different place. There are some hills about two kilometres from their house and I decided to make for these. About halfway up the nearest hill there is an old mine shaft, which I thought would be disused, but when I got to it I was surprised to find three or four people at various levels digging away like crazy. They were just as surprised to see me, well, in actual fact more so because once I saw them I knew that they were gold panners, just like we have at home. We have so many panners at home that sometimes it seems that the hills around our house are alive with people scratching in them for gold, especially at night, when you can see their fires twinkling here, there and everywhere.

Anyway, once they'd got over their initial surprise of seeing me they didn't seem at all perturbed at having me around, so I climbed to the top of the hill where I had a very good view of the countryside all around. I always enjoy being in the bush except for one thing; in summer I'm always worried that I will come across a nasty black mamba. Apparently, they are a very aggressive type of snake, while most other snakes will try to get away if they hear you coming. Dad has told me a story about how one actually chased him and tried to bite him when he was farming down in the Lowveld before I was born. No one wants to be bitten by a black mamba; I have been told you will be dead within half an hour. All of this always comes to mind whenever I'm walking through thick bush, and when it came to mind this time I decided I'd prefer to climb a big tree at the top of the hill and spend the rest of the day up there rather than risk meeting a black mamba in the bush.

When I eventually got back to the house mid afternoon I had the distinct impression that Mr. Norris had been waiting for me. He was in the sitting room watching rugby on television, but must've seen me through the window as soon as I came up the drive.

'Sabi, Sabi, Sabi, I've been worried about you. Where on earth have you been?' he said, as soon as I walked into the house.

'I decided to go for a picnic in the bush.'

'Oh, if only you'd have told me, I'd have come with you to look after you.'

Jeez like, thank goodness I didn't, I thought to myself. 'Um, don't worry, I was fine.'

'But so much nicer to have company hey?'

Well that's questionable, I thought, but obviously I didn't say it. 'Anyway girl, come and have a cup of tea and then I'll take you for another driving lesson. You'd like that wouldn't you?'

Well I would actually, but I didn't want to sound enthusiastic. 'I'm not sure. Regina may need help with the supper.'

'Nonsense. Now come, let me pour you a cup of tea, I've got an empty cup here ready for you.'

After tea we went to the garage to get the truck for my second driving lesson. I was way better at it this time, only stalling the engine three times altogether. It's amazing how easy it is to learn how to combine the clutch being released with the accelerator being pressed. When I'd done it a few days earlier and kept stalling the car I thought I'd never get the hang of it, but now it just seemed so easy. We spent nearly an hour driving around all the roads in the area and I really enjoyed myself, but when we got back to the house we were met with bad news. Bad news for me, at any rate. Vanessa had phoned to say that they were going to stay the night in town. They had had to give Jessica an anaesthetic to set her arm properly, and she was staying in hospital overnight. This was the last thing I wanted to hear; now I'd have to stay the entire night in the house alone with Mr.Norris.

He was his usual over-friendly self, but I tried to discourage him by being as surly as I possibly could. When he wanted to eat his supper at the dining room table I said my favourite TV programme was on and I really couldn't miss it. Of course, this was not the case and I didn't even know what was on, but not wanting to be caught lying I just quickly flicked the television onto the entertainment channel and then proceeded to pretend that I couldn't miss an episode of 'The F Word'. In actual fact, I think it's a really pathetic programme and I've never watched a full episode, but I didn't want to start changing channels in front of Mr. Norris. Eventually it ended and 'How to Look Ten Years Younger' started and then he took over the controls and said with a rather pathetic laugh that I didn't need to watch programmes like that, 'you're so lovely and young anyway'! He flicked onto the History Channel and I tried to watch an incredibly boring documentary about Stalin until eventually I gave up and said I was tired after such an early start and I needed to go to bed.

And that was when things changed.

I'd been in bed for a while and in a deep sleep I think, when I awoke abruptly with the sound of my bedroom door being opened. The Rawsons house is such that all the bedrooms are in one wing with a passage running along the side. Vanessa and Martin have their bedroom at the one end of the wing with an en suite bathroom, the girl's bedroom is next to theirs, then there is another bathroom which I've been sharing with them and there is my bedroom and finally at the end of the wing there is another bedroom with another en suite bathroom, in which Mr. Norris was staying. So Mr. Norris's room and mine are right next door to each other. From the first day he arrived I wanted to lock my door but there had never been a key in the lock and even on this night when I went to bed I considered pushing a chest of drawers across the door and then trying to lodge it there with a chair, but decided this would look pathetic and would not keep anyone out if they wanted to come in.

Anyway, he came in and before I knew it he was pulling the bedclothes back and climbing in with me. I nearly died of fright but a little voice right inside me warned me not to over-react. He'd obviously just had a shower because he smelt of soap and he seemed to be a bit damp. It was dark, so I couldn't actually see him, but I think he was only wearing a dressing gown. I was wearing my pyjamas with long pants and a t-shirt top but the top had ridden up a bit while I was sleeping and I could soon feel his hands on my back. But more horrifying, I could feel what I thought could only be his large penis pressing against my leg, and he kept pushing it into my leg a bit harder by moving his hips towards me. I've never actually felt anyone's penis before but Tracey always talks about them and of course I've read things, so I know that they become big and hard when a man wants sex. Mr. Norris tried to put his mouth over mine, thankfully he'd cleaned his teeth, but I could still smell the wine he'd been drinking at dinner over the smell of toothpaste. I turned my face away so he ended up kissing my neck, which was just so gross, but better than my mouth.

'Sabi, Sabi, I've always thought you are the most beautiful girl at school. I've always thought you had the most beautiful breasts.'

As he said this, his hand slipped round to my front and he started to feel my nipple. I had to use every ounce of control I have in my body not to do anything stupid like start screaming or trying to slap him. Having been brought up by a man like my dad, and having to deal with people like Sherry-Lee all my life, I have learnt that usually the best way to react is not to react at all, but to try and make a plan instead.

I had to think very fast this time though.

'Mr. Norris,' I started.

'Neville, please call me Neville my darling little girl.'

I think I may have shuddered then but I moved myself a bit to try to disguise this.

'Neville, umm,'

He stroked my hair and pushed his hips into me again, 'Yes my lovely,'

'Neville, this bed is too small for us. I'm feeling very hot.'

He tried to kick the bedclothes off with his foot.

'Neville, you've got a nice big double bed in your bedroom, let's go in there rather.'

'You clever little thing, yes, let's do that. Come.' He started to pull the mosquito net back.

'Let me just go to the toilet first. I'm really bursting,' I said.

I didn't know if he'd try to follow me to the toilet or not, but it was the only chance I had to try and get away from him. He climbed out of the bed and started towards the door, while I pretended to be getting up too, and thankfully I heard him walking down the passage towards his bedroom. I scrabbled around on the floor, trying to find my slops, which I knew were there somewhere. Thank goodness I found them fairly easily and slowly tightened my hand around them, and then I also made for the door. I knew I didn't have very long to get away, he'd soon notice that I wasn't coming to his bed. It was very dark but I knew my way around quite well. I slipped down the passage, quickly feeling my way into the bathroom to turn on a tap to try and muffle any noises I'd make and then I carried on down the passage, feeling for the door that I knew led into the hall, opening it as quietly as possible, moving across the hall to the front door, unlocking it without making a sound and then I slipped outside. I was shaking uncontrollably by then, never sure whether he would come up behind me and pounce. Once

I was outside I put my slops on and rushed towards the gate. There is a high security fence around the whole garden, about thirty or so metres from the house. When I got to the main gate I discovered that it was locked with a large, fat padlock. I wanted to cry with terror but then I told myself that at least I had lots of bushes and flowerbeds to hide in, in the garden and it would take a long time for him to find me. Maybe long enough until Regina came to work in the morning.

And then I heard his voice.

'Sabi, where are you?' As if I was going to tell him.

'Sabi, you're being stupid. Come back.'

I crouched in a bush, desperate to make a run for it, but of course I could not.

The moon was half full so I was able to see a little, but not enough to know where he was. However, luckily for me, he obviously went into the house to look for a torch, because the next minute I could see the beam flashing around.

'Come now, Sabi. Everyone is going to think you are a fool, hiding in the garden all night. Come back now.'

The torch flashed around a bit and then I could see it moving in my direction. He was still a fair distance away from me and I knew I had to make a move before he got too close, because then he would hear me. I ran from where I was in the bushes next to the front gate to the garage, and crept behind it. But I felt trapped there, between the garage wall and the fence, so I carried on moving behind the garage until I got to the other side. I then remembered the pedestrian gate that Regina and the gardeners used, and so I made my way slowly to it. I couldn't see the torch light, as I was now in the back garden and Mr. Norris wasn't calling anymore either, so for all I knew he was making for the pedestrian gate too. I got to it and saw that it was closed. At first I thought it was also locked, but as I pulled at the lock in my terror and frustration I realised that it had not been pushed closed. I pulled it off the latch, wrenched this back with a loud clanging noise but I didn't care about noises any more. Lucky about this, because the gate squeaked loudly as I opened it, but I rushed through and pulled it closed behind me just as I saw Mr. Norris running down the back path towards me.

'Hey, Sabi, come here,' he shouted.

I slammed the gate closed, rammed the latch back into the gate post and shoved the lock back into its slot just as Mr. Norris got to me and tried to push my hand away. But I was lucky, I clamped my hand as hard as I could on the lock and I heard it click closed. He'd have to go and look for the key if he wanted to get out.

'You stupid little girl, 'Mr. Norris hissed at me, but I didn't stay to listen to any more, or make conversation with him. I took off down the path and into the bush as quickly as my legs would carry me.

'I'll get you, Sabi, don't think that I won't get you because I will. I'll make you pay for this, just you understand this.'

I ran until I couldn't hear the sound of his voice any more.

12

Clare

I lay in bed thinking of the busy day ahead of me and I was glad of this. I know that if I don't have much to do I start to think about my life and it becomes ever more apparent to me what a terrible mess it is in right now, as I do little more than drift aimlessly from one day to the next (if I am honest with myself). I try telling myself that I'm having 'time out' while I get myself back on track, and in most ways I'm enjoying my life here, but none of it is 'real', and of course I can't go on like this forever. At some stage I'm going to have to face up to reality again, and then what?

My room here at the lodge is very pleasant. I like it especially when the mosquito net is down and floating gently around the bed. Back home in the States we never use mosquito nets because, with the exception of a very few months of the year, we most usually have artificially temperate air blowing through the house. In the summer we have the air conditioning on all day, every day and on the few occasions when the power has been disrupted by something like a hurricane, as it was after Hurricane Katrina a few years ago, I think I will go mad trying to cope with the heat. And then, of course, in the winter we have the heating on, so most usually the house is closed up against the elements, a distinct unit existing outside of nature. Here, on the other hand, nature is very much a part of human habitation. There are spiders and large soft, white geckos on the walls of my bedroom, running up and down occasionally, but otherwise seemingly pretty motionless and when I lie in my bed and look into the wooden rafters and the thatched roof above, I can see all sorts of tiny living creatures going about their daily business. Leanne says that the spiders and geckos are good to have on the walls as they eat the smaller creatures, and that I mustn't try to kill them otherwise I'll upset the balance of nature.

As I lie in my bed I can also hear all sorts of outside noises, like rustling leaves when the wind blows, and the most amazing array of bird noises. Tweeting, rattling, calling, chirping, squawking; when I stop and analyse all the individual sounds from all the different birds, as I do from time to time I'm always amazed by them all. In America I am used to hearing nothing but the quiet humming of the artificial air units. And whenever I listen to all of this, I think how much Graham would enjoy it, and how great it would be to share it all with him, and this makes my heart wrench uncomfortably as I realise yet again how much I miss him and how bad I feel about everything. Since I've been here I've only contacted him the once, when I emailed him to tell him that I had arrived safely. The only time I've heard from him is when Rob told me he said he might come out for Christmas, a thought that still leaves me feeling both excited and apprehensive.

At the lodge there is no cellphone signal or any other way of communicating with the outside world except for a radio, to get hold of Rob and Leanne in the case of an emergency. I've actually really enjoyed this, being so incommunicative. Back home we have our phones practically surgically attached to our bodies, and we spend half our lives on them, calling and texting and skyping and emailing and checking to see if we've had any calls, texts, emails and skypes. It's been a real pleasant change living with none of this. But Rob and Leanne have a very high aerial at their house, which gives them a cellphone signal, and they also have satellite internet coverage, so there has been no need for me to be so cut off from the outside world. I've just wanted it this way.

*

When I got to Rob and Leanne's house I found a very anxious looking Leanne.

'Oh God,' she said as soon as she saw me, 'I've just had the most worrying phone call from my sister in Bulawayo.'

'Bad news?' I asked.

'Yes, I'm afraid so. They're having real hassles with a group of people who call themselves the Indigenisation Committee. You've heard about this whole indigenisation business that is being talked about these days haven't you?'

I have, it surely can't be doing business morale, or investor confidence any good. A proposal has been passed through parliament making it law that if a company owned by local white people has assets worth more than five hundred thousand dollars, then fifty-one percent of it has to be given to black people. I certainly find it quite amazing, that a company which a white Zimbabwean may have sacrificed much and toiled hard to create over the course of his life time, has to simply be handed over to black Zimbabweans, just because his skin is the wrong colour. Surely you can't just give people something for nothing and expect them to have the know how and motivation to be successful at it, too. It certainly doesn't appear to have worked with the farms, if what you see is anything to go by. There are acres and acres of land lying idle or only semi-productive almost everywhere you look. Once-prolific farms are now derelict, with the people who have been put on these farms living in squalor, chopping down the trees, overgrazing the bush and growing pathetic crops that will often times not even bring in enough to feed themselves. It's not as if they even own the pieces of land they are trying to eke out a living on, and if they ever criticise the liberation party that put them there, they will be thrown off. Not knowing any better though, they struggle on, below even subsistence living for many. Anyways, now that this has been done, a new election ploy has had to be found, and it's called indigenisation.

'Mmm,' Leanne said, as if she could read my mind, 'it is easy to destroy what you have not built up, hey?'

I thought about this for a moment and was impressed by her profound comment. 'Yes,' I answered. 'How right you are.'

'So easy to destroy,' she repeated. 'You see destruction everywhere in this country.'

'Yes,' I agreed again. 'I have certainly noticed this.' I hesitated for a moment. 'But, going back to your sister, I thought theirs was just a small family business?'

'That's exactly what it is, but you know how people are. They will jump on a band wagon, if there is a band wagon to jump on to.'

'Well hopefully it'll blow over,' I said, but I was thinking yet again how challenging life in Zimbabwe really can be. As much as you try to ignore the politics, sometimes you just can't help it when it has the potential to disrupt your life so badly.

'Anyway,' Leanne moved on, in her ever efficient way, not letting anything get her down for too long, 'let's discuss the cycle challenge that we will be involved with in the next few days. It is a challenge for the riders as well as for us, providing the food and accommodation for them all, believe you me. We've been doing it for the last four years, as part of a rhino conservation awareness programme, and although it's good fun and good for rhino awareness it's a lot of hard work too.'

We were sitting in her office and she went to the wall on which there is a large map of Zimbabwe.

'Ok,' she said, 'let me show you the route. They are starting here in Bulawayo today and riding south about sixty kilometres through the Matobo Hills and spending their first night here.'

She pointed to an arbitrary place on the map.

'There's a very pleasant camp there, where they'll all stay and the owners of this camp will provide them with both dinner and breakfast and will also do the water points for today's ride, as well as their ride tomorrow to the Mshabezi Dam here.'

She pointed to a dam on the map.

'It's about ninety kilometres from where they will have spent the night and there's not much there accommodation-wise, just A-framed shelters under which the cyclists will sleep if it rains. There will be back-up vehicles, by the way, taking all the riders' personal and sleeping gear from one place to the next. The owners of the camp in the Matobo hills will sort out the dinner and breakfast again for the night they stay at Mshabezi Dam, but then we take over the next day. You following what I'm saying?'

'I think it's clear so far,' I answered.

'We will need to set up a water point here,' she said, pointing to another arbitrary place on the map, 'a second water point here,' bang went her finger again on the map, 'and they will finally arrive at our tented camp here,' and so her finger shifted again. 'They will spend Thursday night at our tented camp and then cycle across the Conservancy on Friday and stay Friday night at the lodge. We'll have two water points along the way from the tented camp to the lodge on Friday. As you can imagine it's quite a task, providing dinners and breakfasts as well as all the food and drinks they need at the water points.'

I think I must've been looking very confused at this stage because she laughed at me as she glanced at my face, 'Don't worry, it's not that bad. It'll all be pretty simple food; just lots of it will be needed.'

'I can imagine. They must be very hungry after all their cycling.'

'Exactly. Anyway, let me finish off their route as far as affects us. After spending Friday night at our lodge, they cycle down this way,' she outlined a route with her finger on the map, 'towards the Limpopo Conservancy and the Mannings will take over from there onwards until they cross the Limpopo River here,' her finger shifted again, 'and into South Africa.'

'It must be pretty exciting for them, especially in areas where they could easily run into herds of elephants and such like.'

'Well, yes, when they are in areas where there are dangerous animals like parts of our conservancy they have to stay on the roads and keep together, with back up vehicles travelling both in front and behind them. When they are in areas where there is no such threat, they can cycle in groups of three of four through the bush.'

'How many people will there be?'

'I believe there are thirty cyclists this year, and then there will be the drivers of the back-up vehicles and a few other arbitrary people so we're looking at having to feed about thirty five or so people for the whole of Thursday and Friday and then Saturday breakfast.'

'Wow.'

'Yes, we're going to have to buy in a whole lot more food. I've got lists here,' she handed me three pages of efficiently written lists. I glanced at them. 30 loaves bread, 10 boxes lasagna; I stopped reading and looked up at Leanne as she stated; 'you will have to go to Bulawayo tomorrow to do this shopping.'

'Sure,' I said, not feeling quite as confident as I sounded.

'Great, and what we need to do now is go off to the tented camp to see how everything is there. That place hasn't been used in months, and if I go on previous experience, the baboons will have probably moved in big time. We'll need to get rid of them and clean the place up.'

'I told all the maids and gardeners from the lodge to be ready at the compound gate after their tea this morning.'

We have a gaggle of gardeners and a multitude of maids working at the lodge. I'm still not used to having all these people around all the time, sweeping and cleaning, washing and polishing, clipping and mowing and weeding, but I do have to admit, they sure make life a whole lot easier, especially when we are busy, as we'll be over the next few days.

*

The tented camp is on the banks of the Mshabezi River (the same river that is dammed way up north) and is situated under large acacia trees. The tents are erected under A-frame thatched shelters which have cement floors and small bathrooms built behind them, so it's really quite luxurious as far as tented accommodation goes. The tents had all been zipped up since the last time the camp was used, so the baboons were not able to get into them, but as soon as we arrived I saw what Leanne meant about them taking over the rest of the camp. There is a large central thatched lapa where guests obviously congregate for meals and such like, and although all the furniture had been taken out and stored in the zipped-up tents, or locked-up storerooms, the baboons had certainly made themselves at home in this shelter. There was baboon crap all over the place and obviously in times of boredom the baboons had tried to take the thatching grass out of the roof. Thank goodness we had all the workers to help clean up the mess. First, all the baboons were sent packing, much to their indignation it seems, judging from the barking and screeching that ensued as they scampered into the bush. Then we all knuckled down and got cleaning, sweeping up all the thatched grass lying in and around the shelter, removing all the droppings, a massive job, as most were very old and crusty, and finally, polishing the floors. Once this had been done, we had to carry all the heavy teak chairs and tables from the tents and storerooms and arrange them in the lapa. I discovered that Leanne really is an amazing worker, and while she had everyone bustling around and being useful all day, she also got in there and made herself just as busy, if not busier than anyone else. I was very impressed and knew that without her bossiness, the whole job would've taken a great deal longer.

She had the gardeners slashing the grass, sweeping the paths and cutting wood for the boilers, while the maids dusted the furniture and cleaned the surfaces. We stopped for a break at lunchtime. Leanne had brought sandwiches for her and me, while one of the workers had peeled off sometime during the course of the morning and built a fire to cook sadza and relish for all of them. By mid-afternoon the camp was looking way better than it had when we first got there and all we had to do then was tackle the kitchen area. This too is a thatched, semi-open shelter but it has a closed in storeroom at the back in which all the crockery, cutlery, pots and pans are locked away. While some maids dusted, swept and polished the kitchen, others cleaned all these utensils and Leanne and I went for a walk around the camp to make sure that all the toilets flushed, the taps had water running out of them when they were switched on and basically we checked on all the minor things that it is taken for granted work, but it turns out they don't when a place has been sitting idle for a long time.

It was after five, when the sun was beginning to sink in the sky and the light was dimming to a more yellowish glow, that we were ready to leave the camp. Two gardeners were left behind to guard the place against the baboons, Leanne and I got into the cab of the Land Cruiser while all the others climbed into the back and we were ready to drive the thirty odd kilometres back to the homestead along the dusty bush roads. The journey should've taken a little less than an hour but it took longer because at one stage we found ourselves amongst a huge herd of buffalo and we had to drive very slowly as we manoeuvred our way through them. I was glad Leanne was driving, because if it had been me we would still be there, politely waiting for them to get out of the way, which it turns out they are not very good at doing. Leanne, on the other hand, hooted at them and banged her hand on the side of the cab and this usually made them jump indignantly to the side, sometimes mooing at us.

'Aren't they very dangerous?' I asked nervously at one stage.

'They would be if we were on foot but they are not going to attack this truck, I can assure you.'

We eventually got back to Leanne's house at nearly eight, after dropping all the workers off at the compound on our way past. Rob must've heard us coming because he was at the garage waiting to meet us.

'God, I've been wondering when you'd get back,' he started, even while we were gathering our stuff from the vehicle. 'I had a very worried Vanessa on the phone at about five this evening. Apparently Sabi has disappeared, she isn't with you by any chance, is she?'

Leanne and I looked at each other in surprise. 'Disappeared, what do you mean by disappeared?' Leanne asked.

'Gone, Leanne. She was supposed to be at the Rawsons' and she's not there, she's gone without a trace.'

'Wow, how weird,' she said.

'Vanessa hoped she might have come here.'

'God no, how on earth would she have got here?'

'Surely she must be somewhere there,' I said. 'I wonder why Vanessa would think she'd come back here.'

'She was probably just hoping, but one of you had better call her as soon as possible and tell her that she's not here, so that they can send out a search party.'

'What a strange thing to happen,' I said, 'I can't believe she's just disappeared.'

'Yes, I agree it seems odd, but you go into the office and call Vanessa and I'll bring you a glass of wine there. I bet you need it after your hectic day. And stay for supper before you go back up to the lodge, there's lots in the oven.'

Vanessa was not happy when I told her that Sabi was not with us. 'Oh Jeez,' she said, 'I was so hoping that she had come down to you.'

'Afraid not. When did she disappear?'

'We're not really sure, actually. What happened was that Jessie broke her arm when she fell out of a tree yesterday morning and we had to rush her into Bulawayo to have it set. We hoped to get back yesterday evening but the doctor wanted to keep her in the hospital overnight. Neville was here, of course, and Sabi stayed behind too and apparently she just wasn't here when he got up this morning. He's frantic with worry, as you can imagine. He feels responsible, as she was under his guardianship at the time.'

'Yes, I can imagine.'

'He even drove to the Stirlings' mine this morning to see if she had gone there but of course there was no sign of her, and of course he's helping the police as much as possible. Oh Jeez, why on earth would she disappear like this?'

'I don't know what to say,' I replied. 'She seemed quite happy when she was here for the weekend, maybe a little quiet, but that's how she often is. She told me she was enjoying staying at your place and how good you were being to her.'

'Did she say that? Sweet little thing.'

'What about her father? Does he know where she could be?'

'No, nothing. I felt terrible telling him that she'd disappeared. He doesn't need any more stress in his life right now. He said nothing like this has ever happened before, it's not as if she's ever run away or anything like that.'

'And her friends in Bulawayo? Sarah, Tracey?'

'I phoned them too, nothing to tell me I'm afraid.'

'This is just so weird. How could she just disappear from your house in the middle of nowhere in the middle of the night?'

'That's exactly what I've been thinking. I cannot imagine what could have happened. The house was locked, the security fence was locked and Neville was here all the time and he heard nothing, apparently.'

Later, when I got back to the camp I lay awake for a very long time, unable to sleep properly, so worried was I about Sabi. I just couldn't understand it.

13

Sabi

I was woken very early by the peeping alarm of a clock. At first I was disorientated, not knowing for a moment where on earth I was, until I started to become conscious of familiar noises, the far-away kadunct, kadunct, kadunct of the stamp mill, the persistent crowing of cockerels. Then I remembered; I was safe in my own bed in my bedroom at my home on the mine. I lay in bed for some minutes listening to the comforting sound of the mill grinding ore as it has done all day, every day ever since I can remember, trying to convince myself that I would be safe now. I came to my house at about eight last night, when I knew that there would be no one else about, and I was so tired then that all I could really do was have a shower and flop into bed. I did remember to set my alarm though; I knew that I would have to be up and out of the house before dawn if I didn't want anyone to find me. So even though all I really wanted to do was cosy on up in my bed and go to sleep again till mid morning, I forced myself instead to get up and get going. But first I had to find something to wear that still fitted me. All my new clothes are at the Rawson's place and my old clothes are fast becoming too small. I wasn't planning on seeing anyone today but at the same time I didn't particularly want to spend the day naked. I eventually found a pair of pink shorts that Gogo had made me at least three years ago and a green t-shirt that my gran gave me a few Christmases ago, that still fitted, sort of. I also grabbed one of my baby blankets that I still keep in my cupboard and flung it over my shoulders. I carefully folded up the pyjamas I had been wearing the whole of yesterday and put them amongst my other clothes at the back of my cupboard where I was sure that no one would notice them if they looked. I then went to the bathroom to wash and clean my teeth and I was very careful to dry the toothbrush thoroughly and mop up any water that had splashed the night before when I was showering. I tied up the mosquito net and made my bed and made sure that everything looked exactly as it had when I arrived.

Then I went down to the kitchen where I found a plastic bottle in which I mixed some Mazoe Orange juice and water. I went to the freezer where I knew there are always frozen loaves of sliced bread and I managed to break myself off a couple of slices. As I did this I told myself that when I returned to the house tonight I must remember to take some bread out of the freezer so that it would be thawed in the morning and I could make myself a couple of decent sandwiches. I went into the pantry to see what else I could take and decided on a packet of chips. That would have to do for today, but it did occur to me that I could not do this for very long before Beauty started to notice that food was disappearing. I would worry about this later. But for now I went up to my dad's room where I knew he always had a secret stash of cigarettes and found some easily in his bedside drawer. It did not escape my notice that he had a packet of condoms in there, too.

After one last look about to make sure I had covered all my tracks I slipped out of the kitchen door, locked it and hid the key on the post underneath the mile a minute creeper where I knew Beauty or Patience would look for it when they came to work later, I went through the back gate and into the bush towards my fort. I got there in plenty of time, at least half an hour before dawn broke and people started to get up and get going on the mine. The only sounds I could hear were the birds, always very noisy at this time of the morning, and the thumping of the stamp mill, but I knew that in a short while I'd hear people shouting and talking as they set off for work. I was glad I'd brought one of my baby blankets along too because it was quite chilly before the sun came up.

This is where I had been this time yesterday too, except that yesterday I hadn't had a good night's sleep in my bed or a nice shower, or a wash, even.

When I first made my escape from Mr. Norris I had no idea where on earth to go and I had walked aimlessly through the bush for at least half an hour before I devised my plan to come home. Our place is only about eight kilometres or so from the Rawsons so I was able to walk here easily during the night, although I was certainly very grateful that I had managed to grab my slops before I left, because I would not have been able to walk that far through the bush barefooted. At first I had been very scared, walking through the bush in the dark, what with snakes and leopards and the like so I made my way to the road where I felt much safer, especially when I found myself a nice stick to use if a leopard decided to attack me. It may sound stupid, I know, but every now and then a leopard does attack a human being and it would just be my luck if it happened to me. It was way easier walking along the road in the semi-dark, so much easier to see the way ahead by moonlight than it had been when I was tripping through the bush. I decided that if anyone or any vehicles came along the road I would duck into the bush, but this never happened and I met absolutely nothing or no one on my way home.

I got there in the early hours of the morning, somewhere around four o'clock I think and I knew it was too late to stay at the house so all I did then was get the kitchen door key from the post and sneak into the kitchen to find something to eat. Just as I had today, I made myself a bottle of Mazoe Orange juice and water and found some snacks in the pantry and then I made my way to my fort where I know no one will ever be able to find me. I spent the whole of yesterday sitting in my fort, mainly thinking about Nerdy Neville, as I've decided to call him from now onwards, and how lucky I had been to have managed to escape from him. Before yesterday I had thought of him as a pretty harmless although charming type, but now I thought of him as positively repulsive. It was like I could still almost feel the way he had pushed his hard penis into my thigh and the thought of it made me feel nothing but relief that I had managed to get away from him before he pushed that nasty thing anywhere else. I wondered if anyone else would believe me if I told them what he had done, and decided that most would probably think I was making it up. I think even Sarah and Tracey would think I was pulling their legs if I told them that he had got into my bed and started rubbing himself up against me. I have to admit; when I thought about it later I even started to wonder if I had imagined the whole thing. But then I told myself, surely not, I wouldn't have spent the whole night walking along dusty roads through the bush, worried that I would stand on a slithery snake or be attacked by a marauding leopard just because I had imagined that Mr. Norris had got into my bed. No, it had definitely happened, it was very real. But would anyone else really believe this?

*

So what does a girl do all day sitting in a tree waiting for darkness to come so that she can go home? Not much, is the short answer. On the first day I was too stunned by what had happened and too tired after my long walk through the bush to really want to do much more than just relax. However, on the second day I felt much more active after my good night's sleep and I found it hard not being able to climb down from my fort and go and do what I wanted. But I was too scared that someone would see me and report me, and that people would then come and get me, so I was very good and sat in my tree fort all day. I had the packet of cigarettes from my dad's drawer so I smoked three or four of these during the course of the day to while away the time.

When even this became boring, I challenged myself to climb up the tree as far as possible. Up until then the highest I'd ever climbed was to my fort, but now that I had time on my hands I decided I'd find out exactly how high I could really go. This is easier said than done. Although a baobab tree has a thick trunk, which should be helpful for climbing purposes, it has quite slippery bark that can make the going pretty tough. After I had made my decision to climb as high as I could I decided to work out my route first. I lay on my back in the fork of the tree, looking into the branches above me and trying to decide on the best way up. I was mainly looking for holes in the branches in which I could put my feet, and areas where there were lots of branches on which I could stand or hold on to. I eventually decided I knew exactly how I'd do it and so I started my upwards climb (or ascent, as our Geography teacher, Mr Nyoka would say).

I did pretty well, actually. I got so high that if I'd gone any further the branches would have actually broken because they became just too thin to be able to take my weight. The view from up there is great and made the climb worth it. I could see some of the houses in the compound, I could see one of our mineshafts, I could see the cyanide ponds and I could even see our house, although it was just the roof that I had a view of. I sat there for ages and ages just looking out at it all. It's always interesting to look at something from a different viewpoint. Besides the usual sounds near me like insects buzzing and birds twittering I could also hear the tinkling of bells from the Afs' cows that my dad allows to be kept on a certain section of the property. I could obviously still hear the thumping of the stamp mill and the odd call as one person talked to another. I could hear the pling, pling, pling from the panners' pick axes as they dug in the hills beyond the river and then suddenly I could hear the sound of a car. This made me look towards the area where I knew the road is, and sure enough I saw dust rising as the car moved along the road. I scanned the bush, hoping for a glimpse of the car and finally I did see it fleetingly, and to my horror I saw that it was the Rawson's truck. I felt the hair on the back of my neck go up and goose bumps rise on my arms and legs as I realised who was most probably in that car. Nerdy Neville. I sat, hardly daring to move in my tree, straining my ears and eyes for any sign of him, where he was or what he was up to, even. It was horrible, and especially when I tried to imagine what I'd do if he actually did come this way and find me. I had to keep telling myself that there was no way this would ever happen. No one knew about my fort and this had always been a very isolated part of the property. No one ever comes here except for me. Eventually, I heard the sound of a car again. I stared at the place in the bush where I'd glimpsed the truck before and I hardly blinked until I saw it going back in the direction it had come from. I was so relieved when I did see it that I felt rather shaky afterwards, and I had to wait a while until I felt stronger before I could even consider climbing down the tree again.

My nights became a lot more interesting than my days. By five o'clock in the evening I was usually desperate to get out of my fort and back to the house, but I had to steel myself to be as patient as possible and wait until dark when I knew for sure that no one would see me, especially now that I knew that Nerdy Neville had been sniffing around, and had probably told Beauty to call him if ever I did turn up. So it was usually after eight before I would get to the back verandah, find the key on the pillar under the mile a minute creeper and let myself back into the house. Of course I could not switch on any lights but I did have the head torch my gran gave me for Christmas a few years ago, and I would walk around with this on my head. As I got into this new routine of spending the days in the tree and the nights at the house I found my appetite growing and the first thing I would want to do every evening when I got back to the house was find something to eat.

Thankfully, the pantry was well stocked with things like tins of spaghetti bolognaise and baked beans, and I would usually open the can, pour it into a bowl and heat it up in the microwave, if there wasn't a power cut, that is. If there was a power cut I'd have to have it cold. I would then take it into the sitting room, close all the curtains and sit and watch television while I ate my dinner. At first I thought it was great, that I could watch exactly what I wanted but most usually I found very little that interested me, and so I found myself thinking instead of my nice bed and being safe and secure under my mosquito net. But it was always a real palaver before I could go there, having to wash and dry my bowl and put it back in the cupboard, and then dry the area around the sink, put the tin that I'd opened next to the back door so that I would remember to take it with me the next day (can you imagine what Beauty would have thought if she discovered a new empty tin every day in the kitchen, or even the dustbin), open the curtains in the sitting room again, and plump up the cushions. Gogo had always accused me of being useless at housework. She would've been amazed if she could have seen how good I had become now at tidying up after myself. Only when I'd finished all of this, would I be able to go upstairs and have my shower. When I did this I would rinse out the pink shorts and green top and thankfully, it being hot at this time of the year, they were usually dry enough in the morning for me to be able to wear again. I had tried on some of my other shorts but they really were way too small and would probably have split when I tried to climb up the tree in them. I did find some other t-shirts that still fitted, thank goodness, so at least I didn't have to wear the same green one every day. I also found a jersey I'd forgotten I had, screwed up in a small ball at the bottom of my cupboard, and so I would take this with me every day when it was still cool in the mornings. I left my baby blanket at the fort, in the hole that I've mentioned before so that I could throw it over my legs to cosy things up when I first got there in the morning.

By the third morning, I was starting to get very tired of my routine. It was tedious having to get out of bed so early and then stay away all day while I waited until it was safe to go back. I started to feel sorry for myself, asking myself why it is that life is always so difficult for me, while everyone else has such an easy time. As I so often do when I'm feeling down, I thought about my mother and the tragedy of her death. How different my life would have been if she had not died. I'm sure if she was alive I wouldn't have stupid pervy teachers chasing after me, and then nowhere to go when I needed to get away from them. She wouldn't have allowed any of this to happen to me. She would have made sure I had lovely clothes always, nicely cut hair, she would have told me to invite friends around all the time so that I didn't get lonely.

I got out of my bed with great difficulty on the third morning. When I opened my bedroom curtains I discovered that my bleak mood matched the bleakness of the weather. During the night a cold, wet front had come up from the south (this is where the cold weather fronts always come from) and even though it was still dark I could see that the sky was full of clouds. It was windy and there was dampness in the air and of course this made me worry that it might rain. So besides all my usual early morning chores, covering my tracks so that no one would know I was staying at my house, I also had to dig around in the hall cupboard for something in case it did rain. I eventually settled on a windcheater that belongs to my dad. I put it on and noticed that it came down below my pink shorts and that it had a Springbok Rugby emblem on the left front side. I knew that I must look a sorry sight in it but as I wouldn't be seeing anyone it didn't really matter.

The day was miserable. It rained quite hard at dawn, but instead of blowing over and warming up it stayed cold and guti for the whole day. The windcheater wasn't properly waterproof and so I was wet, after the rain, and I remained damp the whole day. While it's usually pleasant sitting in my tree fort when the weather is warm, in cold, damp weather it's just plain uncomfortable. How I wished I hadn't come here at all today and had hidden in the house instead. I decided that if the weather was no better tomorrow I most definitely would not come, and I spent some time thinking about where I could hide myself in the house. I eventually decided that I'd climb up to the third floor of our house. No one has been up to this floor in years and it's really only used as a storeroom now. There is no way that Beauty would ever go up there.

Because it was such a horrible day it got dark earlier, so I was able to leave the fort at seven as opposed to my usual time of near eight o'clock. I was frozen solid by then and the first thing I did when I got back to my house was have a hot, hot shower. I only started to feel normal again once I'd stood under it for a very long time and thawed out properly. I went into my dad's room and found a pair of his tracksuit longs and a sweatshirt, and I put these on. They were way too big for me but I was glad of this because at least they kept me warm. I couldn't believe the weather had turned so cold for this time of the year. It's usually very hot here in December and even though there are rainstorms, they usually blow over quickly and then it's hot again. This cold guti weather is very unusual, it really is.

14

Clare

THURSDAY morning, our day for taking over responsibilities for the bicycle race and the weather was utterly dismal. Yesterday it was clear and hot, even a bit on the humid side, but nothing like it can be in Louisiana in the summer, and on the whole I would've described it as very pleasant weather. But sometime during the night a cold front blew in and I woke on Friday morning to a howling wind and drizzly skies. Certainly not the sort of weather for cycling long distances through the African bush, or for standing in the African bush waiting for the cyclists to come by for food and drink, as was my chore for the day. I put a sweater on over my shirt and longs, and, still feeling chilled when I stepped out of my bedroom, I decided to grab the thick jacket I'd brought with me from the States. It's fairly waterproof, but I decided I'd have to spend most of the day sitting in the car, only getting out when the cyclists actually arrived, if I wanted to stay as dry as possible. However, Leanne, ever the consummate organiser, had some tent-type gazebos which she had one of the gardeners haul out from a storeroom. She gave one to me and one to Jabula and told us to erect them at each of our water points so at least we would have some shelter, albeit scanty. The plan was that I would set up and 'man' the water point that was the furthest away, and therefore the one that the cyclists would get to first, while Jabula and the camp cook would set up the second one and be ready to receive the fastest riders while I was still waiting for the stragglers. Then once everyone had been through my water point I would pack up and head for the tented camp, where Leanne and her cook would have been for most of the day preparing snacks and dinner for when the cyclists started arriving.

Rob and Andre were cycling in the challenge; apparently they do it every year. Leanne also told me that Steve and some of the other rhino guys would also be coming through on their bicycles.

The gardener picked up my gazebo, boxes of food and drinks from Leanne's kitchen and once the car was packed he and I set off for my water point early. We must've been on the road by six. The last thing I wanted was to be unprepared when the front runners arrived. My water point was about thirty kilometres from the Mshabezi Dam so I had a fairly long drive to get there. First I had to drive to Gwanda, then turn off there and head up what is known as the Old Gwanda Road to Antelope Mine, where I had to turn off again, this time down a gravel road, which I was instructed by Leanne I must travel up for ten kilometres and then I should find a suitable site for my water point.

As I drove along the main road towards Gwanda, I thought a great deal about little Sabi. It was three days now since she'd disappeared without a trace and everyone was getting extremely anxious about it. Neville had driven the police all over the district speaking to people and trying to find some clues, but nothing had materialised from any of this it would appear, absolutely nothing. The police in this country most often do not have their own transport, so if you want them to do their job you have to provide the transportation. Vanessa told me how lucky they were that Neville was free and available to do this for them, because it would've been very difficult for her, what with a child with a broken arm at home and Martin unable to give up the time either. With Christmas coming there were all sorts of loose ends that had to be tied up on the mine before the end of year shut down.

The whole thing worried me immensely. I still couldn't even start to imagine how or why she had disappeared like this. I went to see her father while I was on my shopping trip in Bulawayo and even though he tried not to show it, I could see that he was quite shaken by this turn of events. He appeared a lot more disposed to seeing me this time and we discussed at length many different reasons as to why she may have disappeared, but none of them seemed in the least bit realistic. I could sense his frustration at being stuck in a hospital bed, and unable to do anything useful about trying to find his missing daughter. After seeing him this way I knew for sure that Sabi was wrong when she said that her father did not care about her. He obviously struggles to show his emotions in the normal way, but judging from his reaction to her disappearance I could see that he most definitely does have a huge amount of affection for her. I felt frustrated too, that I was so busy right now and couldn't spend some time trying to find the girl although admittedly, I have no idea where I'd start to search even if I did have time on my hands.

Leanne had insisted I bring another one of the gardeners, Phinias with me, to help erect the gazebo and carry the heavy boxes. Unlike Jabula, Phinias is a man of few words. I tried to make small talk with him but he could only answer yes or no and he was even really uncomfortable doing this, so I soon stopped trying to converse with him. However, I was very pleased he was with me when we had eventually driven the prescribed ten kilometres from the turn off after Antelope Mine. I found what seemed to be a fairly sheltered place to set up the water point, but by now the drizzle was pretty heavy and it was extremely windy so once I stopped the car I realised it was far from sheltered, after all. Definitely not the sort of weather to be doing what we were doing, but obviously we couldn't get out of it now. I sat for a few moments in the driver's seat surveying the bleak scenery outside; I'm sure in good weather it must be really lovely with big flat rock-type hills both to the right and left of the road and the road winding gently down into a valley beyond. The view would probably be wonderful on a clear day but today all I could really see was low cloud.

There were a few goats wandering around the area, some with bells tied to bits of leather around their necks. The tinkling sound of these bells I have come to realise is synonymous with rural Zimbabwe. The rain did not seem to perturb them, they moved from thorn bush to thorn bush browsing, and sometimes finding something on the ground to eat, too. Lucky goats to be so contented, I heaved a big sigh of resignation, got out of the truck and ran to the back to get the gazebo out. The sooner we got it up, the sooner we would have some shelter of sorts. It's a fairly easy contraption to erect but with the wind billowing around us this proved to be a lot more difficult than it would normally have been. When we opened up the roof part and tried to push the poles into the slots a gust of wind nearly took it straight off down the road. Eventually, we managed to get the poles in place and I hung onto it and tried to steady it while Phinias rushed around with a hammer, hammering the pegs into the ground. Finally, we had it up and Phinias then fetched the folding tables out of the truck, while I heaved the first box out and started to unpack the food that I had brought. I reckoned in this weather most of the riders would be more hungry than they were thirsty.

Phinias and I had been ready and waiting under our gazebo for over half an hour before the first riders arrived, saying nothing to each other as had become our habit, just listening to the rain gently pattering and watching the drops drip slowly from the roof of our shelter. I was interested to see that Steve was in the leading group of riders. I hadn't been aware before that he was that fit. He and the other three riders in his group were covered in mud and soaking wet. I laughed out loud when I saw them. Talk about the epitome of 'drowned rats'. Steve got off his bike and gave me a great bear hug before I even knew what he was doing, leaving me with a wet and muddy jacket afterwards.

'That'll get you,' he said jokingly. 'God Almighty, this weather is unbelievable, couldn't be more crappy if it tried.'

'That's for sure, definitely not bike riding weather,' I replied. 'Not water point manning weather either to be honest.'

He laughed. 'I can see it must be pretty dreary sitting under this gazebo. By the way this is so and so, and so and so,' their names went in one ear and out the other, as always seems to be the case with me these days.

'Hi,' I said, 'you must all be starving. Help yourselves.'

We had lots of high carb food like doughnuts, sausage rolls and biscuits as well as energy bars and dried fruit. They shovelled food into their mouths and replenished their stocks in their backpacks as fast as they could.

'Jeez,' Steve said in between mouthfuls, 'some of the rivers are pretty swollen, we've had to carry our bikes through them and at one stage the water was right up to my chest. I'm going to be so chaffed by the time I finish this evening, having to ride and walk in these soaking cycling pants for the rest of the day.'

'And what about the wet rocks,' said one of the other riders. 'Some of them are so slippery; my front wheel has actually slipped from underneath me twice.'

'Hell, yes,' said the third, 'I nearly came a cropper just now; I'm pushing my bike down the really steep parts now.

The morning wore on in much the same vein, with the riders arriving in groups of four or five every fifteen minutes to half an hour. Thankfully, around eleven o'clock the rain stopped and a watery sun started to show itself sporadically in small gaps in the clouds. As if on cue, the obligatory group of picanins arrived on the scene, and proceeded to find themselves a spot from which to watch us. I smiled to myself as I looked at them, remembering the last bunch that had observed me at the funeral and comparing them to this lot, huddled under a still wet thorn bush, just staring. Obviously they did not have very much to do with their day. I went back to the truck, grabbed my camera and took some snaps of them, both individual and in a group. I don't think they knew what a camera was because they did not react in any way, just carried on sitting and staring, only moving to shoo away a goat or looking elsewhere if a noise distracted them. I thought about showing them the photos I had taken, in some ways I did not want to as it would take away their innocence and the next time someone pointed a camera at them they may start posing, but then I decided it was only right to show them in case they wanted me to change something (highly unlikely I know but I still felt I had better).

I called them over to the gazebo and, acting very coy and shy now, they came across to us. I showed them the screen on my camera and as I slowly went from one photograph to the next the looks on their faces changed from being amazed to being incredulous to being downright amused. There were howls of laughter from all of them as they looked at themselves on my camera screen. One little boy dressed in shorts and shirt that were so torn they were barely worth wearing, ran ten metres or so across the stony ground, his bare feet kicking at the stones as he went, so excited was he by what he saw, and then he ran back again, hooting with joy. I decided I wanted to print some of the photos for these kids and bring them back, imagining their delight at having them to stick on their hut wall. I was struck by just how different they are to children in the first world and how lovely it is they are so innocent and delighted by such simple things, and yet how sad that they have so little and so few prospects.

I had been counting the riders as they came through and if my calculations were correct I believed that two more groups still had to arrive at my water point.

Realising that I still had plenty of food and drink for the cyclists I decided to give each picanin a doughnut, a small packet of biscuits and an energy bar. Well they were so delighted by their spoils you would have thought that it was Christmas Day and I was Father Christmas. But Phinias was obviously getting a little tired of all my magnanimity I think, because he shooed them all away once I'd given them the food.

'They will beg for more, Madam. They will always beg for more now.'

Of course, he was right, and I realised that every time they see a white person in the area from now onwards there is a good chance they will expect to be given something from them. Maybe I shouldn't have done it.

The next group of riders arrived on the scene shortly afterwards, and the monotony of hanging around at the water point came to an abrupt end. Rob was in this group of riders and as he skidded up to my gazebo he started telling to me about what had happened.

'Hey Clare, you're going to have to change your plans for the day. Jamie Peters fell off his bike a few kilometres from here and we think he's broken his collar-bone.'

I gawked at him, surprised. 'Hey,' I said, 'that doesn't sound good.'

'Yeah, he obviously can't ride anymore, so you are going to have to go and fetch him and take him back to Bulawayo. I'm afraid he's in a pretty bad way, not life threatening or anything, just in a great deal of pain.'

I don't know Jamie Peters but I did not like the idea of someone lying around in the bush in the middle of nowhere and very far from anywhere and in a great deal of pain. 'How did it happen?' I asked.

'Well, as you can imagine these rocks are pretty slippery with all of this rain, and he was going downhill a bit too fast and basically just lost his grip. He tried to right himself and his front wheel went into a small gully and he went over the handlebars, landing on the hard rock he'd been riding down.'

I winced at the thought.

'So you and Phinias need to get this gazebo down as quickly as possible and go back and get him. The last two riders have stayed with him until you get there, so give them food and drink and then get Jamie off to hospital in Bulawayo as quickly as you can.'

I glanced for a moment down the road. The cloud was high enough now that I could see down into the valley but I wondered how on earth I was going to find Jamie and the other two. As if reading my mind, Rob unclipped his GPS from his bicycle handlebars and handed it to me.

'Here, this is the spot where they are.'

He pointed to the map on the screen.

'Take this so you can find the place they are at. I'm afraid they were off road when the accident happened so you are going to have to do a bit of bush bashing.'

Bush bashing my hat. I'm sure even Lou Strauss would've struggled with the route I had to take to get to Jamie Peters. Thank goodness the truck had four-wheel drive otherwise Phinias and I would still be stranded in the middle of nowhere ourselves, instead of the saviours, the knights in shining armour that we were supposed to be. I found it positively nerve wracking, the truck sometimes leaning way too far over for my liking, as I manoeuvred my way up and down huge rock hills to the place the accident had occurred. It must've been around midday by the time we found the small group, Jamie sitting down and leaning against a boulder, holding his arm in a protective way while the other two meandered around anxiously, obviously unable to relax while they waited for us. Their relief when they saw us was palpable.

'Thank God,' said one stranger. 'You seemed to take a long time.'

'Sorry, we had to pack up the food and the gazebo and then the going was pretty tough getting here.' I turned to Jamie, 'Sorry this has happened to you,' I said. He looked terrible. His shoulder was set at a very strange angle; his face was white with pain and covered with sweat, despite it being a cool day. I dreaded the idea of taking him all the way back to Bulawayo in this state, but obviously there was nothing else that could be done.

'Thanks,' he said.

'I've got some painkillers, so let me give you a couple now. I'm afraid the journey back to town is going to be very uncomfortable.'

I went to the back of the truck and took out the box I'd put aside especially for these three cyclists, so that I wouldn't have to dig around in the back of the truck trying to find them food and drink.

'Here, this is for you to stock up on,' I said to the other two cyclists.

As soon as we could, we packed up the box again and then struggled to get Jamie's bicycle into the back of the truck along with the gazebo and boxes of food. The journey into Bulawayo was as uncomfortable as I had predicted, especially the first part, when we had to drive back over the rocks and through the bush, until we got to the dirt road. Thankfully, we were in a twin cab and Jamie lay on the back seat. I'm sure he must've felt every bump and corrugation and I'm afraid to say there were many. The road we took back to Bulawayo was dirt all the way and like many rural roads in Zimbabwe now, has not seen a grader in many a long year. When we got to the very bad parts in the road, when even my teeth seemed to rattle as I drove over the corrugations, I tried going very slowly, but I'm not sure this made any significant difference. And to make matters worse, the sky blackened again and the rain started pouring down. The truck was splattered with mud as we drove through puddle after puddle and there were a few moments again when I thanked God I had four-wheel drive, as we would definitely have gotten stuck in some of those puddles if we had not. All in all, it was a very stressful journey and obviously the more so for poor Jamie. I was very relieved when I started noticing litter dumped all along the sides of the road, because I knew that this meant that we were nearing the town. I usually hate this litter, it is absolutely disgusting and I can never understand how anyone can just dump their rubbish as they seem to do all over this country, but on this occasion I was pleased to see it. I looked at my watch as we drove through the hospital gates and saw that it was after four in the afternoon. Jamie had phoned his wife as soon as we had gotten into cell phone range, and she was at the casualty department when we got there. I heaved a sigh of relief as I handed him into her care and the care of the hospital staff.

I decided that it was too late now to set off back to Ubejane and that Phinias and I would have to spend the night in Bulawayo. Leanne would just have to cope with everyone by herself tonight. I knew that she would be more than capable of doing this, thankfully, as there was no way I wanted to drive on that road at night. I learnt very quickly when I first arrived in this country that it is insane to drive at night on the open roads. There are stray animals (mainly cows and goats) everywhere and the lights on the cars you come across are often beyond a joke. The highway patrol back in the States would be blown away by the way many motorists operate here. I drove back to Ubejane at night with Rob just a few weeks after I arrived and I was a nervous wreck by the time we got there. At one time on this journey we came over a rise in the road and there was a scotch cart pulled by four donkeys right in front of us, trotting in the middle of the road with not a light or a reflector on either the cart or the people in it. Thankfully, we saw them in time to swerve out of their way, only because the donkeys were pale in colour and the driver was waving his whip, otherwise there is a good chance we would have rammed into the back of them. And then, later on that same journey, we passed a car that had no working lights whatsoever, the driver must've been seeing his way by the light of the half full moon. Whenever a car approached, someone in the passenger seat flashed a torch on and off to alert the nearing vehicle of their presence. Again, it was a close call that we didn't smack right into them, as we didn't notice the flashing torch until we were practically on top of them. So, having had this experience before, and not being in the least used to such craziness on the roads, there is no way on earth that I was going to try it on my own. I decided instead that I would go upstairs and see how Digger Stirling was getting along, and then Phinias and I would go back to Leanne and Rob's comfortable house where we'd spend the night before heading off early in the morning. I really wanted to find out from Digger if there had been any news of Sabi so Phinias waited in the car while I went to see him.

Digger's face was bleak and angry when he saw me. 'That stupid little girl,' he said. 'I had a visit from Neville Norris yesterday, you know, Vanessa's brother who also happens to be a teacher at her school. He confided in me about what happened the night she disappeared.'

'Oh yes?' I said.

'My stupid fucking daughter tried to make a pass at him, apparently.'

'No!'

'Oh yes, they were alone at the Rawsons' as their daughter had broken her arm. Apparently, Sabi crept into his room after he had gone to bed and tried to climb into his bed.'

'No!'

'He felt very bad telling me this, but at least I know now why she's disappeared. Stupid little girl.'

'I can't believe she'd do something like that.'

'Why not? All women have the potential to be sluttish.'

I blanched as he said this.

'Anyway,' he carried on, 'keep this information to yourself for the time being. I'll make her regret her behaviour when I next see her, don't you worry.'

'But I just don't believe it, Digger.'

'Why not?' he repeated.

'There is just something about Neville Norris that I'm not sure about,' I said, ignoring his previous jibe. 'One or two things have happened that make me wonder about him. I don't really want to go into it now. I know he's charming, but I can't take him at face value. Sorry, I know the Rawsons are good friends of yours, but just hold off on any judgements just yet, and I'll do the same.'

15

Sabi

I woke very early as usual and even though it was still dark I knew that the weather had not improved from the day before. Well, there was no way I was going to risk spending another cold, damp, horrible day up that tree. No way. No way. As I was not going to leave the house at all this day I decided not to bother changing out of my dad's old tracksuit bottoms and sweatshirt. I intended keeping myself as warm as possible, so all I did was roll the trouser legs up enough so that I wasn't dragging them along the floor and I did the same with the sleeves of the sweatshirt. Then I did all my usual chores; tying up the mosquito net, making the bed, wiping down the surfaces in the bathroom after washing my face and brushing my teeth, going down to the kitchen to find something to eat and something to prepare for later. In some ways I thought I may be wasting my time; with the house empty I sometimes wondered if Beauty and Patience were coming in to work every day. However, I couldn't be sure.

Until either of them arrived though, I could lounge around in the sitting room and watch television, which would at least make my day way more interesting than it has been of late. I very cleverly devised a plan so that I would hear them well before they actually came in, if they did, giving me enough time to grab my food, plump up the cushions and scuttle upstairs to the third floor before they had a chance to find me. What I did was I opened the side door of our house which has a Yale lock on it, and then I went back through the kitchen and out of the kitchen door, locking it behind me and putting the key on the pillar where it usually goes, only pushing it further back this time so that it would be harder for them to reach. I had found a glass jar from the pantry and I put this on the pillar in front of the key so that when they reached up to try to feel for it they would knock the glass jar over, which of course I would hear. I realised that they may wonder how on earth a glass jar got to be on the pillar, but I decided that they would be so shocked by it falling down and crashing all around them that they wouldn't spend too much time trying to work that one out. I then dashed around to the side door of the house and back inside, pulling it locked behind me.

I was able to watch television until nine o clock before I heard the jar crashing down. In actual fact, I was quite happy when I did hear it because I soon discovered that there really isn't that much on television to watch so early in the morning. If I had been a youngster I'd have probably enjoyed the cartoon channels, but I grew out of these many years ago and there is definitely not much of interest to watch so early, on the channels I usually watch. I was also pleased to hear the jar crashing because it made me realise how well my plan had worked. I decided I've become pretty clever at leading a secret life. As I crept out of the sitting room and through the hall to the stairs I glanced quickly through one of the windows, and as I was ducking below it I saw Beauty outside on the back verandah, picking up pieces of broken glass.

I quietly closed the door leading onto the third floor and turned the key in the lock; so that Beauty would not be able to enter, in the highly unlikely event that she would try. If she did, then I decided that it would just be one more mystery that she would have to solve. I smiled to myself as I thought of her becoming more and more confused as she came across more and odder things in the house.

In the olden days when my grandparents lived here at the mine, the third floor of our house was used as guest bedrooms, my gran told me, but ever since my dad and I have lived here it's been shut up and has just been used as a dumping place for junk. When I was a kid I often used to come up here and make a fort for myself amongst the abandoned furniture and boxes. Poor old Gogo used to sit on the top stair waiting patiently for me while I pushed furniture here and there and balanced cushions and blankets on top of the furniture to make passages and caves to crawl in and out of. I used to do this for hours and now that I think about it, I realise it must've been really boring for Gogo, as I used to keep calling for her to come and help me, and of course she was way too old to be able to climb over the furniture or crawl down the tunnels to wherever I was. Anyway, someone at some stage must've come up here since then and put everything back in a fairly orderly way because as I looked around now I could find no trace of my long-forgotten forts. It's been so many years since I've actually come up here, I can't even remember the last time I did. Anyway, at least there's a bathroom, so I can go to the loo when I need to.

I decided to sit by the window for a while to see when Beauty left the house. I thought she probably wouldn't stay that long, what with no one supposedly here and all that. However, I soon discovered that I could not have been more wrong. I'd only been sitting at the window for twenty minutes or so when I saw a black man opening the back gate and coming up the garden towards the kitchen. I lost sight of him when he walked onto the back verandah and disappeared under the mile a minute creeper. This was certainly not what I'd been expecting, but I sat on the window ledge for quite a while longer expecting both he and Beauty to make an appearance at any time. But I waited and waited and nothing happened, and I eventually started to wonder if I'd just missed them; maybe I'd lost concentration for a while and they had gone off during that time. I couldn't remember losing concentration, but I never know, sometimes I do, and I don't even realise it. I was so bored now, just sitting and staring out of the window that I decided I'd go and investigate. I had to walk very slowly across the room for fear of a floorboard squeaking (all the floors in our house are made of teak and they can squeak very loudly in places). I got to the door, turned the key as quietly as I could and then opened the door. It opens out onto the top of the stairwell so you cannot see anything from there until you climb down the stairs, but I didn't want to do this, so I just stood there and listened. Well, imagine my surprise when I heard the sound of the television; that was the last thing I'd expected. I strained my ears to try and hear more. It sounded like they were watching a movie, but they kept talking to each other too. Wow, what would my dad think if he knew that Beauty was bringing her boyfriend to our house to watch our television? Then I started to wonder what else they might get up to in our house, my mind stated to race with ideas of them doing ‘it’ in my dad’s bed and then lolling in his bath afterwards. Jeez, he’d have a hairy canary if any of this was happening (I decided it most probably was) and he found out.

Whatever, this had really spoilt my plans for the day; they were obviously not planning on leaving the house for a while yet, so I would not be free to relax in my house as I thought I would. I closed and locked the door again and walked slowly back into the main room and sat on one of the sofas in there, after pushing away some of the junk that was piled on it. In the olden days this was probably the guest sitting room and there were two bedrooms and the bathroom leading off from it. My gran used to tell me that they had people coming and staying with them all the time and they used to have big dinner parties when people came. I always thought that it sounded like they had a very exciting life, unlike us, unfortunately, who hardly ever have people staying except for boring girlfriends of my dad’s. I quickly moved on from this thought though, as I’m still feeling very uncomfortable about Sherry-Lee’s death. From my possie on the sofa I could see that there was nothing of interest in this sitting room and as I had hours to kill I decided to have a squizz around the bedrooms. I actually can’t remember ever going into either of these rooms ever before. They can’t really be described as bedrooms any more. Ok, they do still have beds in them, but these can hardly be seen under all the other junk, mainly old furniture, curtains and stuff and they have that old, musty smell that rooms have when they haven’t been opened up in many years. There were quite a few boxes, but all of them just seemed to have things like old blankets, curtains, pillows and that sort of thing in them. I slowly threaded my way through the boxes and furniture of the first bedroom until I got to the wardrobe along the back wall of the room but when I tried to open it I found it was locked. How weird, I thought and of course there was only one thing I wanted to do now, and that was to open it to see what was inside.

I looked around, hoping the key would be somewhere about, stupid I know when it has obviously been locked for decades, but you never know. Luck wasn't on my side, however, and there were no keys anywhere, not even hanging in the bedroom door. I tried to force the door open but it was jammed tight. I wondered how easy it would be to break it open, but I quickly decided that this would be very difficult, without making a great deal of noise. It is one of those really solid, old fashioned wardrobes that were made to last, and the only way I would be able to break it open would be to take an axe to it and chop a hole in the door. Well I didn't have an axe and Beauty would most definitely hear me if I started doing that anyway, so that idea was quickly shelved. By now though, my frustration levels had risen by one hundred percent as I really wanted to look inside. I crept back into the sitting room and went to the window seat in the hopes that I'd see Beauty and her boyfriend leaving. No luck here again, so in frustration I opened my packet of sandwiches and ate them all in one go. I was now feeling very irritated with stupid Beauty.

The weather was still dull, not as bad as yesterday but still overcast and drizzly. It had rained earlier and it would probably rain again but for now it was fairly dry. As I sat there pondering the weather I suddenly had a recollection of having seen a bunch of keys that looked like they were for old fashioned-furniture in the drawer in my dad's bedside table when I had been looking in there a few days ago. Stupid Beauty, I thought to myself, I'd have to wait heaven only knows how long still till I could go and get them. I sat for quite a while longer trying to control my patience, and then it finally ran out on me, I decided I'd go and get the keys, and if Beauty heard me then so be it, I knew her secret now and I'd swear her to silence about me being here otherwise I'd tell my dad what she did when the house is supposedly empty. I didn't really want to start making threats like this though, so I unlocked and opened the door as quietly as possible and crept down the stairs like a mouse. My dad's bedroom is on the second floor and thankfully quite close to the stairwell so it didn't take too long before I was in there. I could hear the television blaring downstairs and my heart was beating really fast as I opened my dad's bedside drawer and reached for the bunch of keys. I half expected Beauty to come in at any moment and catch me, but luck was on my side this time and she did not. I was able to creep back up the stairs, all the time hearing the television blaring away in the sitting room on the ground floor but no sound of the dreaded footsteps of someone coming up the stairs to catch me. By the time I got back into the sitting room on the third floor, and closed and locked the door behind me I felt quite shaky with worry.

But at least I had the bunch of keys now. I crept back to the first bedroom and to the wardrobe. There were many keys on the key ring, and as always seems to happen in such cases (Sod's law) I had to try almost every key on the ring before one slipped into the lock and slid round as I turned it. 'Voila!' as our French teacher, Monsieur Zulu, would say.

I didn't know what I expected to find in the wardrobe, and I wasn't that surprised when I discovered that it was full of woman's clothes. But as I stood looking at them it gradually started to dawn on me whose clothes they probably were; my mother's, and I grew cold at the thought of this. I reached out and tentatively touched some of them, as they hung limply and lifelessly from their hangers. Like the room, they had an old, musty smell to them, which I realised was to be expected when they'd been here practically my whole life probably, all fifteen years of it. There was nothing of my mother around our house, no photos or anything else to remind us of her, and yet now I had come across a whole wardrobe full of her. I took out a dress and held it up to me. The dress went down to below my calf, it hung in one straight piece and was really quite plain, but it was made from light soft material and I decided that anyone who wore it would have to have had a good figure. Ok, so my mother had a good figure, it seems that she was a bit taller and fatter than me but not by much. How interesting. Obviously, the fashions were slightly different fifteen years ago, to what they are now, but despite this I decided that most of the clothes in the cupboard were actually quite nice. If I had them washed I'd actually not mind wearing most of them one little bit.

The wardrobe consisted of a hanging part on one side and shelves and drawers the other side. There were a few jerseys and tops on the shelves as well as a couple of pairs of shorts and trousers. I thought to try on a pair of shorts but then I saw that they had a high waist and of course we never wear anything with a high waist these days, as they must've done then. But then I spied a denim skirt that I liked the look of and I took my dad's big, baggy tracksuit bottoms off, unzipped the zip and stepped in to it. It felt really good on, it settled on my hips nicely just as I like skirts to do, as I'm obviously a little smaller than my mother was. I flipped through the tops and found a t-shirt that would go nicely with it and quickly whipped off my dad's old sweatshirt and put it on. I then found a pullover and tossed it over my shoulders and decided that I'd be quite happy to wear this outfit anywhere. I wondered what my dad would have to say if he noticed I was wearing my mother's clothing, but then I decided I didn't actually care. Somewhere deep inside me, I resented my dad for not showing me any of this before, for hardly ever telling me anything about my mother, for almost acting as if she'd never existed.

I then started to open the drawers, there were two of them and each contained various bits of paper, but then my heart quickened when I discovered a few photos of my mother. To be quite honest, I can't remember the last time I saw a picture of her, as I said before we haven't got any around our house, but I do know I've been shown what she looked like from my gran and other people, but this was all a long time ago and the photos were usually pretty small. But here was a big photo of her, a head and shoulders shot of her and I stared in wonder at her face, at her straight blond hair with a fringe across her forehead, her wide-apart eyes and her smiling mouth and I could see that she had been really pretty. I decided I'd keep the photo and my dad would just have to accept it if he ever found out. I flipped through the papers and picked one out to read it. I could see that it was an email that had been printed. On the top of the piece of paper was the name Caroline Stirling, my mother's name and the date, 20th July 1997. She must've been pregnant with me at the time, as I was born in November 1997.

I noticed that the email had been sent to 'hunterman@acaciasamara.co.zw'.

'My love,' I read with a quickening heart, 'how thankful I am that at least I am able to communicate with you this way. Unfortunately, I can only do it when I am alone in the house and I long for these moments more than anything else in my day. I find that as long as I can tell you how much I love you then I can deal with all else that comes my way. But how, how, how I miss you; often throughout the day I find myself wondering what you are doing or thinking at that exact moment, and last night I thought I would perish without a way to snuggle down safe inside your arms- I yearn so badly for it.' Wow, I thought to myself, squirming slightly with embarrassment, my mum must've really loved my dad. I wondered where he was at that time, that they weren't able to be together and that he should've had such a weird email address. Maybe he used to be a hunter and that's why he thought of himself as 'hunterman'. How weird that he's never told me this. I read on about what she had been doing since she'd last written, it didn't sound like she had been doing that much, to be honest, and then the letter ended, 'All my love in the most passionate way, my thoughts will be far away from here and instead with the most wonderful man in the world as he goes to bed tonight in his house on the Enterprise Road.' The only Enterprise Road I know of is the one in Harare; my dad must've been staying there before and after his hunts. I was truly amazed by this letter, I'd never really thought much about my parents' relationship, but I hadn't expected all of this. I suddenly felt very sad for my dad, that he had never been able to find someone to love him again like she had, and that she had died when I was born. No wonder he resented me so much. I picked out another page, again an email with my mother's name on the top and this time the date was the 10th September 1997 but on the top of this page I was shocked to read, '*Did you really have to do this today, you stupid selfish bitch, can you not even respect my fucking birthday!*' I recognised the handwriting as my dad's and it's true, the 10th September is his birthday. Why on earth would he write something like that? I quickly read the email with interest.

'My love,' it started again. 'How tantalising it was to speak with you today; so wonderful after not having heard your beautiful voice in three whole weeks. Perhaps it is because it is soon now, before my life changes so drastically, that the moments when I find myself stopped and missing you are that much more poignant.' I realised that she must be talking about my imminent birth, but again I found myself wondering why my dad wasn't with her when she was so heavily pregnant with me. He must've been off hunting again. She went on to tell him about the preparations for my arrival into this world and I found myself with a lump in my throat, knowing how everything had eventually turned out. She ended by telling him how sorry she was she couldn't phone him more often and how passionate her feelings were for him. I almost cringed as I read, 'I imagine your face across the pillow from me every night, and the way your shoulders curve above your chest. God, I wish you were here but always remember I love you in the most passionate, passionate way.' Amazing stuff, but there were rings and exclamation and question marks around all of this and, '*how can you betray me like this, you disgusting, revolting slut*,' in my dad's handwriting. I was completely taken aback by this. How could he be so nasty to her? And yet it didn't really surprise me that much, he's been pretty mean to me over the years, too.

But the shock I had then was nothing like the shock I was to get very soon afterwards. After looking at another couple of pages of stuff that didn't seem particularly interesting or relevant, I came across another sheet of paper that I slowly and reluctantly recognised as my mother's death certificate. My heart sank as I read,

Name of deceased: Caroline Jane Stirling

Date of death: 8th November 1997

Place of death: Crocodile Creek Farm, Nuanetsi, Zimbabwe

Reason for death: Suicide by drowning

Underneath this were a doctor's signature and stamp and then a policeman's signature and stamp.

I looked at this and looked at this as I tried to comprehend what I was reading. Surely there was something wrong here, something completely and utterly wrong. My poor mother had died in childbirth, she had died having me. What was this 'suicide by drowning' business that had been printed so officially here? I found a tiny space on the bed to sit down, as I tried to register this. Why on earth would anyone have put this when it was so untrue? Slowly, slowly, slowly, however, like a tortoise walking along a path, it gradually became clear to me that it wasn't actually wrong, and what was wrong in fact, was what I had been told. I thought about this for a long time and as I did it gradually dawned on me that my dad had never actually discussed my mother's death with me, just like he'd rarely discussed my mother with me at all. It was Gogo who'd told me the story about the river swelling its banks on the night I'd been born, so that they had been unable to get my mother to a hospital. She had obviously told me this story to try to make it seem better, because the thought of my mother actually drowning herself is so difficult to try and get my head around. And the reason my dad has never told me what happened is because he is responsible for her doing it, she was so terribly unhappy with him, being so mean to her all the time, that he obviously drove her to drown herself. As I came to this realisation I felt a surge of hatred for my father that I never thought I would ever be capable of. Ok, I have always been disappointed that he has never been able to show me any love, but I have always hoped that eventually he would, maybe once I've proved myself at school and gone on and found a successful career. I've always thought that he'd then be proud to have me as a daughter, and this has motivated me to try hard at school and sport all the time. But now, now that I know the truth I don't want him to ever be nice to me, I actually don't want him to ever lay eyes on me again. I wondered how easy it would be to 'undaughter' myself from him, the opposite of being adopted by someone, if you know what I mean.

Now, all I wanted to do was to get as far away from this house as possible. Before I thought of it as his house, as my house, as our house, but now that I knew the truth, I didn't want it as my house any more. Let him rot here by himself for the rest of his life. I looked around to see if there was a bag or suitcase I could put some stuff in, and thankfully there was. It was full of faded, half broken Christmas decorations, including a very mangled-looking tree. I took them out and carried the bag back to the cupboard. I wanted to fill it with as many of my mother's possessions as possible and then I was going to leave forever. I carefully put the photographs, the death certificate and the printed emails into the side pocket, and then I packed the bag with my mother's dresses, jerseys, skirts and tops. I didn't want to leave anything behind, but there was too much stuff for just the one bag, so I reluctantly had to. I zipped the bag closed and dragged it across the room towards the door.

Beauty was going to be in for a real shock when I suddenly materialised from nowhere.

16

Clare

OTHER than Steve, Andre and Rob, I can't say I got to know any of the other cyclists at all, except on a pretty superficial level. I'm sure if I'd been at the tented camp on Thursday night as was originally planned, I would have felt more in with the gang, but this was not to be and as it was, the way things turned out I ended up being even more out of sync with them all than ever. What happened was I got up at five the morning after taking Jamie to the hospital so that Phinias and I could get back to Ubejane in good time to still 'man' my water point for the cycle challenge, but when we got to the lodge I discovered that everything had changed.

'The cyclists, they are not bicycling today, Madam,' Lovemore informed me as I walked into the kitchen to collect the food and drink.

I looked at him, surprised. 'Sorry?'

'The cyclists. They are not bicycling today, as they have gone to look for the picanini missus.

'Picanini missus?' I enquired, for a moment at a loss.

'The one who has disappeared. The cyclists, and the boss and madam, and everyone else, they have gone to look down mineshafts for her.'

'No,' I gasped. 'What do you mean? Why? Where?' As I started to fire these mono syllabic questions at him I saw his face cloud over in confusion. I stopped and took a deep breath, trying to calm my racing heart. 'Why have they gone to look for her down mineshafts Lovemore?'

'The police, they have said this is where they need to look. They have gone to help the police because there are so many mineshafts in this area. There are big mineshafts and small mineshafts and there are many gold panners living down these shafts looking for gold.'

Yes, but did they find something to make them think they need to look down mineshafts?'

'I am sure they will have found many panners Madam and they maybe arrest those that don't have permits.

'But did they find anything in connection with the girl?'

'I am not sure.'

I realised at this point that Lovemore had no idea if there were any further developments. Maybe he knew where everyone had gone though, so I asked him.

He shook his head solemnly. ‘No, I do not know where. There are mineshafts all over the place. Many of them, and there are many, many panners looking for gold down them.’

I thought I’d scream if he mentioned gold panners again, so I quickly retreated and went to the garage. The only way I could find out anything was to drive the five or so kilometres back to Rob and Leanne’s house, where I would get cellphone signal. All the way there my head raced with one ‘scenario’ after another, none of which were pleasant to consider.

My phone was in the glove box of the twin cab where I’d left it when I drove back from Bulawayo. I leaned forward to retrieve it as soon as I had parked the vehicle in their drive and rushed into the office to plug it in to the aerial. I tried Leanne’s phone first and got the recorded message, ‘The number you have called is presently unavailable. Please try again later.’ I tried Rob’s phone and got the same message. I felt a ripple of irritation, where on earth were they? I then phoned the Rawsons’ house phone. The phone rang and rang and just as I was about to give up it was answered.

‘Hello,’ said a cheery-sounding female voice.

‘Regina is that you? It’s Clare. Is Mrs Rawson there?’

‘Oh hello Madam, how are you?’ came a high-pitched, sing song reply.

‘Fine, fine, thanks. But I wanted to talk to Mrs Rawson, is she there.’

‘Ah no Madam, the madam has gone into the bush with the boss.’

‘Do you know where they have gone, Regina?’

'No, I'm not sure where they are. They are in the bush and I am here looking after the girls. I'm sure the madam and the boss will come back soon.'

'Has the young girl been found Regina?'

'I'm not sure Madam, maybe. Maybe they have found her now.'

'Maybe, what do you mean by maybe? Has there been something new found?'

'Maybe Madam, I'm not sure. Maybe.'

I realised at this point that Regina too was still completely in the dark.

'Oh dear Regina, it's so worrying.'

'Ah yes, but I'm sure they will find her soon.

I put the phone down again and tried to decide whether to phone Digger or not. It might just make him more stressed than he already was. After some contemplation, I decided that other than satisfying my own anxiety to a certain degree it would do no good phoning him, so I reluctantly got back into the twin cab and drove back to the lodge to wait for news.

I couldn't concentrate on anything much except to make sure that all the bedrooms were ready for our guests later. All the time I thought about Sabi and her quirky little ways; the pleasure she got whenever she did any cooking for others, her excitement with the new clothes we had bought together, and her delight with her new hair-style. I felt sick to the pit of my stomach with worry that she had disappeared like this without a trace. When I finally heard the engine of a vehicle roaring up the steep drive mid-afternoon I literally ran to the garage to accost whoever it was who had arrived. It was Rob, with some of the cyclists who I did not know, all looking hot and dusty. The weather had cleared significantly during the course of the day. I looked at Rob searchingly as he got out of his Land Cruiser.

'And?'

'Ah, nothing. It's like looking for a needle in a haystack.'

'Why are the police so keen to look down mineshafts now? Has there been some information?

'No, no, they just don't know what to think at this stage.'

I breathed a sigh of relief, this sounded much better, that they were just hoping to find something, some clues.

Rob and the others had come back to the lodge early because they needed to go back to the tented camp to fetch the bicycles. Everyone had made off from there this morning in vehicles but as they were going to continue with their cycle challenge the next day the bicycles had to be collected. Apparently, they had a long trailer at the camp on which most of the bicycles would fit. The rest would have to go in the back of Rob's Land Cruiser pick-up. I offered to go with them to help but Rob said I should rather go back to their house to fetch some tents and mattresses as there wouldn't be enough beds for everyone at the lodge that night. He said I should look for Gladys as she'd have the key to the storeroom and she could help me load them into the twin cab.

*

By eight o'clock Saturday morning all the cyclists and helpers had had their breakfast, packed up their kit, sorted out their bicycles and vehicles and left the lodge. As soon as they were gone I went straight to my room to lie down, suddenly overcome with fatigue. I immediately fell into a deep sleep so was quite confused later when I was woken with a tapping at my door followed by, 'Madam, Madam, come quickly.' It was Lovemore, beckoning me from outside.

'What is it?' I called out, as I rolled onto my back, forcing myself out of my deep sleep.

'Come quick,' was all he answered.

I hastily pushed my feet into the sandals next to my bed, opened the door and when I found he was no longer there, I walked down the path towards the kitchen to find out what was going on. I came round the big rock at the end of the path and was surprised to see a scotch cart and three donkeys standing in the driveway next to the garage. It was a sight that was so incongruous with the setting that I stopped dead in my tracks and just stared at it. For a moment I didn't recognise the woman sitting on the front bench of the scotch cart. I knew I knew the face, but it was out of place here and I couldn't think who she was. But then it came to me; it was Beauty, Jabula's sister. There was a man sitting next to her, holding the reins. The donkeys, all rather raggedy-looking, I noticed, stood patiently in front of the cart; their only movement being the swish of a tail or flick of an ear.

'Beauty,' I said eventually, 'what on earth are you doing here?'

She glanced behind her into the back of the scotch cart and as she did this a curly brown head popped up. 'Hi,' Sabi said, and this time I'm sure my mouth must've dropped open with surprise.

'What on earth…' I repeated.

Sabi looked about. 'Is anyone else here?' she asked tentatively.

'Just the staff, cleaning the camp.' By this time I had walked right up to the scotch cart and I could see that she had been covering herself in a blanket in the back of it. 'Goodness Sabi, we have all been worried sick about you. Where on earth have you been?'

'At my house, the house on the mine.'

'But the police went there, they went to look for you there at least three times and they didn't find any trace of you.'

'It's a very long story.'

That was surely the understatement of the century. I could not help but give her a long, questioning stare, but she just looked down and avoided eye contact.

'Well, anyways,' I said, trying to sound calm and unflustered, 'it's very good to see that you are safe and sound, everyone has been terribly worried about you, you know. Hop out of there and we'll get you freshened up, and afterwards we'll go down to the house and let everyone know that you're fine.'

As I finished my sentence I was shocked to notice a look of horror cross her face at this suggestion. This silenced me for a moment, but then I continued, 'What's the matter Sabi? We have to tell everyone that you're here, so that they can call off the search party, we really do have to you know.'

Unfortunately this did nothing to reassure her. She still looked very worried, and she bit her lip in the way I've noticed she does when she wants to say something but doesn't know how.

'Come now,' I said as light-heartedly as possible, 'hop out at least and let's get something for you to eat and drink, it'll all be ok, it really will.' But I could see that she was not so sure. I turned to Beauty, 'what time did you leave the mine, have you had breakfast?'

'No Clare, we left at about five o'clock, just when it was starting to get light.'

'Well at least the weather has improved and you didn't have to go through any rain on your way here.'

She glanced at the sky and then looked at me.

'The weather was good.'

I couldn't help but think what an inane exchange this was when there were so many more pertinent issues to discuss.

'Anyways, you go to the kitchen and ask Lovemore to make you something to eat and drink. I'll take Sabi to her room, so can you ask him to bring some tea and toast for her and me there.'

But even as I spoke, I could see Lovemore standing at the kitchen window, watching and listening to everything, making me think that I could well have just asked him straight-up. I have come to realise that there are always eyes and ears here in Africa, noticing every little thing that ever happens, making it all the more extraordinary that Sabi had managed to disappear so thoroughly for so long.

I turned back to her.

'Come now Sabi, let's go to your room.' I held out my hand to help her out of the back of the scotch cart. She looked pale and dishevelled. 'Are you feeling ok?'

'Not really. I think I'm getting a cold. My throat is very sore when I swallow,' she said, standing up.

As she did so, I was surprised to see that she was wearing a rather old-fashioned looking skirt; a short, denim pencil skirt with a zip and small pleats in the front and pockets in the side seams. I'd had one fairly similar many years ago. This one seemed way too big for her and hung loosely on her hips. She had on a black t-shirt that also looked a couple of sizes too large for her. I wondered where she'd gotten these clothes, even though I had known all along that she'd left all the new clothes I'd bought for her at the Rawsons'. Vanessa had told me this right away, a fact that had added to the mystery surrounding her disappearance.

We walked down the path to our rooms. I put her in the same one she'd had last time, next door to mine. Thankfully, the maids had had time to change the sheets and sweep and clean while I had been asleep.

'Do you want to have a bath or shower, after your long ride in the back of that scotch cart? It must've been pretty dusty and hot.'

'No, I'm fine thank you.' She sat down heavily on the bed as she said this, looking around her.

'The lodge was completely full last night; we had thirty five cyclists and their helpers staying here, they are doing a cycle challenge from Bulawayo to the Limpopo River to raise rhino awareness and the problem of poaching.'

'Ah, ha.'

Of course, she wasn't interested in any of this, but I didn't want to launch too quickly into trying to find out what had happened to her these past few days. I could see she was fragile and didn't need to be interrogated, and I certainly wasn't going to tell her what her dad had told me. Thankfully, Lovemore arrived that very moment with a tray of tea and toast. She was obviously hungry and ate two slices back to back, although I could see that she had difficulty swallowing. I leaned forward and felt her forehead.

'Gee, you're burning up. You must be feeling awful.'

'I am.'

'You haven't got any pyjamas here or anything?'

'No.'

'Ok, well let me go and get you something to wear, plus some aspirin and, I think the best thing is for you to get right into bed and sleep.'

She looked greatly relieved at this suggestion. I got her tucked up in bed with the curtains drawn but as I was about to leave she sat up in bed and said, 'please, please don't tell anyone that I'm here yet. I need to talk to you about everything first. There is an envelope in my bag there, with letters and things in it that I want you to read so you can help me try to work out what happened.'

'What happened…..?'

'Something terrible happened. I'm very confused. Please read it so you can help me, but I can't think about it right now. Just don't tell anyone I'm here yet. Please.'

With a sense of dread, I took the envelope back to my room. I sat down in the chair on the front verandah and opened it. There were quite a few pieces of paper inside; at first I just noticed printed emails. I glanced at the date of the first, 1997, and then I began to read, and as I read, my hands started to sweat, my heart started to pound and

I started to feel weak and nauseous. It was like a déjà vu, it was like I'd read these letters before. The emotions being expressed in the letters, the outrage being scribbled in the margins, I could relate to it all. I eventually finished reading the letters, and then I sifted through the pile of papers. I found photos of an attractive looking woman, blonde and frail-looking. I guessed she might be Sabi's mother, although the only resemblance was the wide-apart, greenish-coloured eyes. I finally got to the death certificate; I read it with horror, 'Suicide by drowning'.

I closed my eyes, and took a deep breath, trying to control my emotions. All of this was utterly, utterly sickening.

17

Sabi

I must've slept for the whole day, because the light through the crack in the curtains was yellow and glowing, as it is in the evenings, when I eventually woke up. Clare had left a glass of water next to the bed and I sat up to take a sip. My throat was really sore when I swallowed, but it felt a bit better when I had the water in my mouth. I hate, hate, hate getting colds, especially when they first start and the area at the back of my mouth, where my nasal passage joins my throat, is so sore I can hardly bear to swallow. And of course, when this happens, I want to swallow all the more. It's so horrid. As I was thinking these things, Clare came in with some lozenges and more aspirin. She also had a cup of tea and a biscuit, which she said I must eat before I had the aspirin as it is bad to have aspirin on an empty stomach. She felt my forehead as I sat up in bed eating the biscuit.

'Oh dear, you're still very hot. Unfortunately there isn't a thermometer here so I can't take your temperature, but I'm sure you must have one.'

I felt my forehead too. Yes, it was definitely hot.

'Anyways,' she continued, 'the aspirin should help to get it down a bit, and I think that when you've finished your tea you should have a luke-warm bath. That should make you feel a bit better.'

I thought about this and agreed with her, I've always noticed that a bath makes me feel better when I'm sick.

'Lovemore has made you some nice chicken soup for your supper,' she continued. 'I'll come back a bit later with it and we can have it together, before I settle you down to go to sleep again.'

'What's the time?' I asked.

She glanced at her watch, 'six fifteen. You must've been really tired as you slept for ages. I put my head through the door a few times to check on you and you didn't even stir once.'

She went into the bathroom to run my bath, and when it was ready she left me to soak on my own. Clare is always so kind and thoughtful to me. She had put bubble bath in the water and as I sank into the warm, bubbly water I felt all comfortable and safe again. It made me realise just how ill at ease I'd been feeling this whole week, even though I thought I was fine at the time. I lay in the bath for a long time, sometimes sliding right down in the water so that I covered my whole head with bubbles. It felt very good and I almost forgot my sore throat. Eventually, when my skin was starting to look like prunes I got out, dried my body and hair vigorously and then got back into the pyjamas Clare had brought for me earlier. Well, they weren't actually pyjamas, just shorts made out of soft t shirting material and a short-sleeved t-shirt. I realised they must be Clare's, as they were a bit big for me, although Clare isn't that much bigger than me really.

I was back in bed when she returned. The cook was right behind her, carrying a tray and he put it on the wooden trunk at the bottom of my bed.

'Sakubona missus,' he said.

'Yebo,' I replied. I noticed that on the tray there was a pot and two bowls as well as a basket full of rolls. On seeing them, I realised that I was really hungry again. There was also a butter dish and two glasses of milk. Clare started ladling the soup into the bowls and after handing me one she buttered some rolls, put two on a plate and put it next to my bed. I took one of the rolls and dipped it into my soup, making the bread all soggy, just as I like it.

'Good, hey?' she said as she took a sip of her soup.

'Yes, thank you.'

Clare was sitting at the chair next to the dressing table.

'Now Sabi, I have to tell you, one of the staff must've informed Leanne and Rob that you had pitched up here, because she came racing over to find out earlier this afternoon.'

My heart dropped. 'Oh no,' I said.

'I'm afraid so, I did ask everyone to keep it to themselves but, well you know how it is, there were too many people here, for everyone to keep silent.'

'So what did you say?'

'I told her you were sick and you wanted to discuss some things with me first, but I'm afraid to say she phoned Vanessa and your dad to tell them you were here, even before she came to see me.'

My heart dropped further. 'Oh no!' I thought for a moment, 'are they coming over now? Am I going to be taken away again?'

'No, no, I made it very clear to Leanne that you are far too unwell to go anywhere else at this moment in time.'

'I can't go back to Vanessa's again, I just can't' I blurted out, 'and I never want to see my father again. Never!'

Clare looked slightly surprised when I said this.

'Why ever not? He's been worried sick about you. He really has Sabi.'

'Did you read the things in the envelope?'

'Yes, yes I did. It must've been a terrible shock for you, finding all that stuff. I assume you had never seen it before.'

'No. I found it in a cupboard on the third floor of our house. The cupboard was locked. It had all my mother's stuff in it.'

'Oh wow, how awful for you.'

'But can't you see, Clare, I don't want to see my dad again, it's because of him that my mother killed herself.'

Clare stared at me. She had stopped eating her soup.

'Why do you think that, Sabi?'

'Well, I know my dad, I've always known he isn't exactly the nicest man in the world and there she was, trying to be loving and kind to him writing him all those emails while he was away, and he just treated her like dirt. Didn't you notice all those terrible things he wrote about her? It was horrible, calling her all those names and everything.'

Clare looked distinctly uncomfortable.

'I don't think it was actually like that I'm afraid to say.'

I was confused by this and didn't really know what she meant. 'I think you may have got the wrong end of the stick,' she said.

'What do you mean?'

'I don't really want to say too much, as I obviously don't know any of the facts, but to be quite honest, I don't think your dad is the bad guy you think he is. I don't believe the situation was as simple as your mother writing your father love letters, which he threw back into her face, so to speak.

'What is it then?'

'You know what, Sabi, maybe I should go into Bulawayo in the next few days and talk to him about it all. I'll show him what you found and say that you are very confused and worried about everything.'

'I told you that my gogo told me that my mother died giving birth to me. I've always believed that story.'

'Yes, you told me.'

'So to now find out that she actually drowned herself......'

'You must've got a terrible shock. It is a great pity that no one told you the truth before, but maybe the truth was just too difficult to tell a small child.'

'Anyway, that's why I had to leave my house. When I realised that there are all these deep, dark, horrible secrets lurking around there, I had to get as far away from the place as soon as I could.'

'Well I'm very glad that you came to me. You may be surprised to hear, this but I understand about deep, dark secrets, and because of this I will do everything I can to try to help you.'

'But I don't think my dad will want to talk to you.'

'I will do everything I possibly can to encourage him to do so. We have actually become better friends since you disappeared. I went to see him in hospital last weekend and I believe he was very pleased to see me, and to discuss things with him. He was very worried.'

After Clare had gone, I lay awake for a long time wondering what other story there could be. It had all looked so obvious to me, but now she was trying to tell me that it was not so. It's horrible being a child and never having control over your own life and when adults keep trying to 'protect' you; meantime they are doing no such thing.

*

And I thought I was in for a great, big, fat taste of it again in the morning, before I had even had a chance to get my thoughts together, when guess who arrived at the lodge? Vanessa and her brother, Mr. Norris.

Clare had come to my room earlier to have breakfast with me, mealie meal porridge this time, which felt very soothing on my throat, and she told me that she wouldn't go to Bulawayo until I felt much better. She hoped that this would be the next day, as she really did want to try to get to the bottom of things with my dad as soon as possible. She said that when she did go, I'd have to move in with Leanne and Rob, as I couldn't stay at the lodge on my own. I wasn't entirely happy with this suggestion, as Leanne can be a bit bossy, but at the same time I realised there wasn't an alternative. Anyway, after we'd discussed this she left me to sleep again, as I still had a temperature and all of that, and I was just nodding off again when there was a tap at my door and she was back, telling me that Vanessa and Mr. Norris had rolled up.

'They're desperate to see you, Sabi. They feel so responsible after you disappeared from their house.'

I sighed and rolled over to face the wall.

'Hey, Sabi, they're waiting to see you,' she said.

'I can't see Mr. Norris like this Clare, in bed and stuff.'

She gave me a long, questioning look.

'You think so, hey? I think you look perfectly presentable.'

'No,' I said, so loudly she sort of got a fright and looked at me a bit strangely. If she but knew what had happened, she'd act quite differently, but the problem now was that I was not entirely sure I knew exactly what had happened myself, maybe I'd got it all wrong too, just as she told me I got the other story wrong.

'Ok, well let me tell Vanessa to come in. Is that ok?'

I nodded.

'I'll be back in a mo.'

Vanessa came up to me as soon as she entered the room and gave me a huge hug.

'Sabi, darling, we have all been beside ourselves with worry about you.'

I felt quite bad when I saw the look on her face. I know that she's actually a nice person, and I would never have run away from her.

'Oh my dear,' she carried on, 'look at you, all pale and sick-looking.'

I answered by giving a very loud sneeze, and it was at that moment that my cold broke. I had to jump out of bed and run to the bathroom to grab some loo paper for my nose, which was now streaming. I blew and blew and then pulled a whole lot off the roll to take back to bed with me.

'Let me bring you a box of tissues.' Clare said. 'I've got one in my room.' She shot off to get them and I braced myself for fifty questions, but nothing of the sort happened. Instead, Vanessa pulled forward my suitcase and said she'd brought all my clothes from her house.

'Shall I unpack them and hang them in the cupboard,' she asked instead.

My relief was huge, because I knew what this must mean, that she wasn't about to haul me back to her house.

'Yes please, that would be great,' I answered quickly.

She started unpacking, while I lay in the bed sniffing and wiping my nose. It was lovely to see all my lovely new clothes again.

'Here you are,' Clare said, returning with the box of tissues plus a tin of Vicks. 'Do you want me to rub some on your chest and back? It should open your airways a bit and make it easier for you to breathe.'

'Don't worry. I'll do it thanks,' I said, feeling embarrassed just at the thought of Clare rubbing anything into my chest and back. 'I'll do it just now,' I continued, knowing that I'd have to pull the t shirt up to do this and I didn't really want to expose myself to them, as much as I liked them. I still waited for questions about where I'd been, and couldn't believe it when there were none. Instead, they talked about what I should do in the next few days.

'Clare tells me she is going to go to Bulawayo to see your dad as soon as you're feeling better. He's so relieved that you are safe and sound,' Vanessa said, but I felt so mixed up about him I had no idea how to respond. 'And another thing, he got out of hospital yesterday and your gran has come out from England to look after him until he can walk around properly again.'

I've always liked my gran, she's good fun and loves playing cards with me. We have one special game that we play all the time when we are together, although I'm going to have to wrack my brain to try and remember it, as she hasn't been here for over two years now and I haven't played it with anyone else.

'That's great that Gran has come out. When did she arrive?'

'Yesterday. They're going to stay at the house in Bulawayo for a while as your dad won't be able to get about at the mine house just yet, what with the plaster right up to his thigh and all of the stairs you've got there.'

Gran used to live here in Zim, but she left during what she calls the Holocaust, which was the time we had a few years ago when the country was in such a bad way you couldn't buy anything in the shops, or anywhere else for that matter. She said she couldn't cope with no food, no fuel, no electricity and no everything, and so she went off to live In England. The rest of us in Zim used to have to go to Botswana or South Africa to buy everything we needed, but Gran said she was too old to be having to go to the neighbouring countries to buy the basics. I don't really blame her. There were times when the border was so bad we had to stand in queues for hours and hours, just to get out of the country and to come back with our shopping. If I was Gran's age I wouldn't have wanted to do that either. Anyway, she left Memory, her maid and Bigboy, her gardener, at the house to look after it and Dad used to stay there from time to time when he had business to do in town. It's actually a really nice house in Suburbs, quite close to my school. I sometimes had ideas of living in that house when I got older.

'Anyway,' Vanessa continued, hanging the last dress in the cupboard and then closing and zipping up the suitcase, 'Clare and I think that after your ordeal it may be an idea if your friend Sarah came down here for a week or so, to keep you company while you get over it. Would you like that?'

I couldn't believe what I was hearing. No fifty questions, no scolding, no bossing me around and trying to make me do what I didn't want to do.

'I'd love it if Sarah could come.'

'Good, I thought you would. I know how it is, when you've had a difficult time there is nothing like a girlfriend to chat to, to put everything back into perspective, don't you agree Clare?'

'Oh, yeah.'

'I actually took the liberty of phoning her mother last night to see if she was free, which she is, so I will phone back tonight and we'll try to make a plan as to how we can get her down here.'

After that they left me to rest up again. I lay in my bed staring up at the gumpoles in the thatched roof thinking about having Sarah here and how great it would be. Obviously, we'd have to stay at Rob and bossy Leanne's, which was a bit of a pity, but that's life for you. At least Sarah would be here. If there is anyone in this world who will believe my story about Mr. Norris it will be her, even though I know she is going to be completely shocked by it.

18

Clare

FOR the whole of the drive to Bulawayo, all two hours of it, I felt nervous and shaky. The last thing I wanted to do was go and see Digger Stirling, and confess all my dark secrets to him, yet I believed that it would help him, him and Sabi if he heard my story. After reading all those letters and documents Sabi had brought back in that envelope, I knew for sure now that their relationship was in a complete tangle and always had been because of an adulterous association that had occurred even before she had been born. Unfortunately, I have learnt the hard way about adultery, and the terrible harm it will bring, the terrible hurt it will cause and I hope, in fact I believe, that

Digger Stirling could be able to come to terms a little better with his experience if he hears about mine.

Maybe I'm being too much of a busy body; in fact I know I definitely am. I know that what happened in their family years ago doesn't actually have anything to do with me, yet every time I meet Sabi and see the mess her life is in I find myself wanting more and more to be of help to her, and on more than just a superficial level. Of course, there is a flip side to all of this too. My life is also in a complete tangle, I also need to talk to someone who has some understanding of how damaging adultery is, and maybe, hopefully when I have done this I will be able to find a way to sort myself out.

As I drove to Bulawayo I thought about how I could broach the subject with Digger Stirling. How do I do this, especially with a man like him, who has lived with the hurt for so long, he has become closed up and hardened by it? One of the first things I will try to make clear, I think, is that the two people committing adultery don't necessarily start off intending to do so; well this was certainly true in my experience. I believe it happened because communication broke down between Graham and me, he wanted to do one thing and I wanted to do something else, and every time we tried to discuss how we could reach a compromise, we ended up arguing about it. With us, everything unravelled totally when he decided to go to Palestine in January, to observe again the unrest there. I accepted and understood this, but unfortunately after that particular uprising had been quashed, he decided he wanted to stay in that part of the world and experience and report on the Syrian situation. So what was supposed to be a six week trip away from home ended up being three months, and three months of not being together, not understanding what the other is going through, not supporting one another's endeavours, is just too long. When I look back on it all now, of course I know that I should simply have gotten on a plane and gone over there, gone to join him, but at the time there just seemed to be too many reasons why I did not. Certainly there was one main reason; I cringe now when I think about this.

*

I arrived in Bulawayo around noon and went straight to Rob and Leanne's house in Hillside to drop off my bag. As always the house was immaculate with Stella and Tenacious waiting for me to arrive, fresh flowers cut and arranged in vases in my bedroom and in the sitting room, a jug of cold water and an ice bucket full of ice, placed on the sideboard on the verandah alongside a bottle of orange squash. I thought again about how great an aspect of life in Africa this is, having everything ready and prepared as if one has just arrived at a hotel. Stella said there was bread and cheese in the freezer and she could make me a toasted cheese sandwich if I liked, as there was electricity for a change and Tenacious wouldn't have to switch on the generator. I decided to take up this offer, and poured myself an orange and water and flicked through the television news channels while I waited for her to prepare it. I hoped the power wouldn't go off later, as Tenacious had told me they only had a small amount of diesel left for the generator. I then decided that I should go and buy some more diesel, as well as something to eat for tonight, before I went to old Mrs. Stirling's house. She had told me to come for tea at three thirty. Leanne had given me a list of provisions that needed to be bought for the lodge, but I decided I'd do all the shopping tomorrow. I was feeling way too uneasy to tackle any grocery shopping now.

Mrs. Stirling has a lovely, old-fashioned house in a suburb of Bulawayo called Suburbs. The house is big and square, with a tin roof painted green, and is set in a large garden with two well-established oak trees, beds full of flowers and rolling green lawns. I was amazed, when the electric gate opened and I drove slowly up the brick drive, to find such an immaculate-looking place, she having been in England for the last couple of years. She obviously has an excellent gardener, too.

Mrs. Stirling walked onto the front verandah, even before I got out of my vehicle. She stood and watched me as I climbed out, adjusted my skirt and came towards her, all the while feeling very self-conscious.

'Hello my dear, you must be Clare,' she said, holding out her hand to shake mine.

I noticed that she had a very English accent, which was certainly in keeping with her English looking garden with the oak trees and English flowers.

'Mrs. Stirling?' I replied.

She must be in her late sixties I decided, slim and elegant looking with short grey hair and piercing blue eyes, like her son's.

'Exactly. So nice to meet you. Come in, do.'

She walked back into the house and I followed, noticing as we walked through the dining and living rooms (she called it a drawing room I found out later), the antique furniture, the large gild-framed paintings on the walls, the vases filled with huge flower arrangements. It was like a beautiful English country house, similar to some that Graham and I used to stay in sometimes, when we were in England and he was doing his travel writing. After walking through a second living room (study to her), we stepped out onto a verandah full of cane furniture, large pots with palm trees in them and a pool along the far end. It was so colonial it seemed for a moment as if I'd gone back sixty years or so.

Digger was sitting in one of the cane armchairs with his leg resting on a cane stool in front of him.

'Hi,' he said. 'Can't get up still, as you can see.'

He was wearing a pair of shorts and a t-shirt and I realised it was the first time I'd seen him not in his pyjamas and dressing gown. He looked quite youthful.

'Hi, don't worry please. Good to see you out of hospital finally.'

'Thank God, that place was really getting to me.'

'I can imagine.'

A maid dressed in a brightly coloured ethnic looking uniform, except that it had lots of frills and lace too, stepped onto the verandah carrying a tea tray.

'Thank you Memory,' Mrs. Stirling said as she put it on the cane coffee table in front of her. 'Would you prefer coffee Clare? I know you Americans don't drink tea like we do.'

'No, tea is good for me thanks.' There was a plate with what looked like home made shortbread on it, and she offered it to me, as she put a delicate fine bone china teacup and saucer on the small table next to my chair. I can't remember the last time I've drunk tea out of a fine bone china cup with a saucer.

'I'm not actually American,' I said. 'I was born here and only went to live there with my parents when I was twelve.'

'Oh, really?' She paused. 'So tell me, what was your maiden name then?'

'Frazer,' I replied. 'My dad was a geologist in Hwange.'

'Well, I never. So what has brought you back here after all this time?'

I swallowed hard.

'Well, that's what I've come to talk to Digger about, actually.' Digger gave me a penetrating look, but said nothing. I could feel my palms starting to sweat.

'I'm afraid to say it's in relation to what Sabi found when she was staying alone at your house last week.'

'Thank goodness that girl has pitched up again,' Mrs. Stirling interrupted. 'We were all so worried about her. Even the police were starting to think it may be something more serious. "Suspicious" is the word they were beginning to use. Thank goodness it turned out not to be so. Has she said anything to you about why she ran away like that?'

'I'm afraid not. She's been pretty sick these last few days and we haven't wanted to press her. But her friend Sarah arrived at the conservancy today, I met her off the bus before I drove up here, and maybe Sabi will confide in her.'

'So, what did Sabi find?'

Digger's voice was flat as he asked me this.

There was nothing I could do but get on with it.

'A whole lot of printed emails your late wife wrote, plus some documents, one of them being her death certificate.'

There was silence.

Eventually Mrs. Stirling coughed, and took a sip of her tea.

'Oh dear,' she said.

'Have you got these things here?' Digger asked. 'It's a very long time since I read that crap.'

I scratched in my bag and handed the envelope to him. He opened it up, took out the papers and started reading them, his face closed up and strained as he did so. Eventually he threw them on the coffee table and shook his head.

'Fuck,' he said.

Mrs. Stirling took another sip of her tea. 'More tea?' she asked.

'I don't like talking about any of this,' Digger said. 'What the fuck has it got to do with you, anyway? Why don't you just get out of our lives?'

'Please Digger, let her continue. She has come here because she wants to talk to you, so at least try to be civil, won't you. And do mind your language, please dear.'

'It hasn't got anything to do with me of course,' I said. 'It's just that Sabi came to me, pretty battered and bruised emotionally, after discovering all of that and expecting me to resolve things for her.

'Oh for fuck's sake, what crap.'

'Digger, please,' implored Mrs. Stirling.

'The problem is,' I continued, ' Sabi thinks that your late wife wrote these emails to you, and that you basically blew her off, and that's why she killed herself.'

'What?'

'When she read those emails she thought they were from your late wife to you, and she could not understand why you retaliated so viciously with all those comments you wrote in the margins.'

Digger picked up the pile of papers again and reread them for a bit, paging through them furiously as he read a bit from one and then a bit from another.

'She thinks that your angry behaviour caused your wife to take her own life. She blames you and is very upset with you.'

'Me? Well that's a fine how do you do, after everything I've been through.'

'Yes, I know. I told her that there is more than likely another side to the whole story, a side that I obviously don't know about, but that I would come and see you and tell you of her misunderstanding and of her need to know the truth.'

'And why are you so sure that she is wrong, why are you so sure that these aren't from my late wife to me?'

'Because I recognise cheating when I see it. You asked me why I'm here in Zimbabwe, Mrs. Stirling. The reason is because I cheated on my husband, and when he could no longer tolerate my betrayal, he kicked me out of the house.'

Mrs. Stirling gawked at me, not knowing how to respond to this revelation. Digger grunted and stared at me, but said nothing.

'So, although I have no knowledge of the exact circumstances of your situation,' I continued, 'I do understand how hurt you must've been and I can see what havoc it has played in your life, and in Sabi's life.'

There was still no response so I went on.

'When I read what you wrote in the margins of those emails, I recognised the hurt I know my husband felt when he found out about my cheating on him. He also found emails I'd written, expressing similar emotions, and it caused him a huge amount of harm when he read them.'

'So why did you cheat on him, then? Did you no longer love him, is that why you treated him so badly? Tell me.'

'Of course, I can make excuses for myself, even though I know all the time that they are meaningless in the face of how I behaved. My husband had been away for a few months, I felt angry with him that he was not there. I decided it was a kind of rejection of me, and as I began to develop these negative thoughts about him, so I became aware of someone else who showed anything but rejection of me, someone who was showing a great deal of interest in me, someone who knew how to make me feel good.'

Digger grimaced.

'God, it's pathetic. This world is full of shitheads willing to screw others into feeling good about themselves, regardless of the consequences, isn't it?'

'Digger, please,' implored Mrs Stirling.

But it was my turn to grimace now. I had come to this painful realisation too, once I'd been caught, once my betrayal had been discovered, but I'm afraid to say it was only then that I saw things this way. Up until then, I'd lived in a fantasy world like some love-sick teenager, forgetting about everything that really mattered in my life. And what made the whole thing even more sordid in my case, was that the man in question, Mitch Garry, is married too. He was cheating on his wife; I was cheating on my husband and really, for no other reason than to make ourselves feel good about ourselves.

'Yes, it is pathetic,' I answered. 'Pathetic. Now that I look back on it I can see he was just having a good time. He had a wife he had grown bored of, he felt frustrated with his life at that point, and I was a means to a bit of excitement, he was simply having fun.'

Digger shuddered. 'My wife's lover was married, too. He's still with his wife I believe.' He hesitated before continuing. 'So why did you end it? I assume you did?'

I looked down at my hands, clasped in my lap. I glanced at my wedding ring on the third finger of my left hand.

'As most often happens in these situations, we were caught. He had gone away with his wife and child to Florida on a holiday, but every morning he would sneak off to the beach to phone me. One morning he was late in doing this, and I, cocky and self absorbed as I had become by then, texted him some stupid message telling him how much he turned me on and such like, and his wife read it.'

Digger smiled at me, a hard, cynical smile. I felt I could see the disgust in his eyes.

'Serves you right.'

'Yes, the next thing I knew I got a reply which, when I received it, I thought at first was from him, but when I read it I nearly died.'

'Ah ha. And.....'

'It said, 'Keep away from my husband you stupid, selfish, self-serving worm. You are just one of the many women he has fucked in his life.'

'Phew! Well done her. So how did that make you feel?'

'Like she said. Like a stupid self-serving worm. I'd wormed myself into their marriage without a care about how it would damage her. I was mortified when I read her text, but I knew I deserved every word of it, and way more besides.'

'Well, at least you admit this, even if it's only this. My wife never admitted anything. She just killed herself.' The words hung in the air like a poisonous gas. What could anyone say that would make this sound better?

'Yes, I've just had to live with the knowledge that she cheated on me, that she made a complete fool of me, and she never even had the courtesy to tell me why.'

He sounded very bitter when he said this, and who could possibly blame him.

'You know what,' Mrs. Stirling butted in, 'I think we could all do with a stiff gin and tonic. It's nearly five o'clock and I believe we need one after all these revelations.'

It was actually only a little past four, but I wasn't going to argue with her.

She disappeared through the door into her study to find the drinks, leaving Digger and me struggling to know where to go on from here.

'So what was it like, screwing another man and your husband at the same time?' he eventually asked. 'I've often wondered how my wife managed this, without me suspecting anything.'

I cringed at the harshness of his voice.

'Thankfully, I didn't have to deal with this. My husband was still away when Mitch and his family left for Florida. But I want to tell you that when I was having this affair it was all like a fantasy to me, when I look back on it now, I realise that, because I knew in my heart of hearts it was so wrong, it became so much more intense and passionate. I had to see it as this incredible love affair to justify what I was doing.'

'And when you look back now, was it really so amazing?'

'No, now when I think about it I can see just how sordid and sneaky and nasty it all was. And, to be honest with you, when I think about him, I know how badly he behaved too. A few hours after I got the text from his wife, he phoned me. He'd obviously snuck out of the house again after spending some time trying to appease her. I asked him if they were going to separate and he said no, he couldn't leave her or their child. I said that it would then only be fair on her if we had absolutely nothing whatsoever to do with each other ever again. He agreed, yet afterwards he kept phoning me until a few days later I told him he had to stop. He couldn't bear rejection of any kind and carried on. Then I got an email from his wife. I'll never forget it.

She wrote, "If ever again you decide to commit adultery, try to think beyond your base carnal cravings and at the incredible damage you are going to cause. I am a real person with real feelings and I have done nothing to deserve being treated with so little respect by you. From now onwards, when you think about my husband, do not ponder on your lustful thoughts, that turn you on in the way you described yourself in your text, but focus instead on the indescribable pain that your selfish, self-serving behaviour has caused." '

Digger sniggered. 'That must've made you feel good. I wish I'd been able to do something like that, but I was too busy burying my wife and coming to terms with her suicide.'

I looked at him.

'How terrible for you.'

'Yes, it was. And tell me, how did you react to the poor, cuckolded wife?'

Mrs. Stirling returned with a silver tray on which three glasses of gin and tonic were set, ice chinking as she set the tray down. I accepted mine gratefully and took a large sip.

'Well, of course, I wanted to respond to the wife by defending myself, by saying how it wasn't just me, how it takes two to tango, how he'd come onto me etcetera, etcetera, but she probably knew all that too, she didn't need me trying to justify myself in any way. So I simply replied to her email and said I would never have anything whatsoever to do with her husband in any way ever again.'

'And have you?'

'No. He carried on trying to get hold of me, phoning, texting, skyping, messaging me on Facebook, but I didn't answer, ever. I unfriended him on Facebook, I got a new sim card with a new phone number, and I basically deleted him from my life. When I confessed everything to my husband on his return a couple of weeks later, and I can assure you that was a horrific ordeal, it was made a little easier by my being able to tell him this. It made him feel a bit better about trying to patch things up and we tried really hard to do this.'

'So why did he kick you out of the house, then?'

'Two months later he came across my old sim card in my dressing table drawer and he put it into his phone. The first thing that popped up when he switched it on was a text Mitch had sent me just a few days before, begging me to meet up with him again. I hadn't seen this text as I wasn't using the sim card any more, but my husband didn't believe this, and he told me to leave then and there and he never wanted to see me again.'

'Can't say I blame him.'

'No, I can't either.'

'So what do you think of all this, mother?' he said, turning to Mrs. Stirling.

'All terribly sad and unnecessary. As you well know, Digger, I've always wished that you were able to have it out with Caroline, to talk to her about the affair, to try to gain some perspective on it all. She had her reasons, you were responsible in other ways too, but it is a tragedy that you were never able to talk about any of it with her.'

Digger turned back to me.

'So guess how I found out that my wife had cheated on me?'

'Um, letters, emails, maybe you overheard a phone call?'

'No, none of the above, I'm afraid to say. How I knew she'd had an affair was when I looked at the child she had just given birth to, and saw that it was the spitting image of some Goffel hunter chap who used to stop over for the night every now and then on his way to the hunting concession.'

I gaped at him. 'Sorry….?'

'Imagine my surprise when I was expecting to see a fair-haired, pink-skinned baby like my wife and I, and lo and behold, instead I see an olive skinned, woolly haired child who bears absolutely no resemblance to me, to anyone in my family or anyone in my wife's family. Has it never occurred to you that Sabi looks completely different to me?'

'Um…' I was at a complete loss for words.

'Uh uh, I'm sure it has, I'm sure it has to most people, but they politely say nothing. Well, the reason is because she is the progeny of a man by the name of Mr. Dennis Masterson. I very kindly offered him accommodation from time to time when he needed it, and that's how he repaid my hospitality. He used to delay his stay sometimes, needing to service his vehicles in my workshop but obviously he was servicing more than just these.'

'Digger, please,' Mrs. Stirling interjected. 'Try not to be so coarse.'

'I believe he ended it before Sabi was born; although I don't think he made this clear to my wife. I knew nothing until the day of Sabi's birth, and when I made my discovery, my wife didn't even have the courtesy to explain anything to me. She just went off and topped herself the minute my back was turned.'

After all these years I could see that he was still being eaten up with rage. I felt desperately sorry for him.

'We've been through all this before, Digger,' Mrs. Stirling interrupted, 'we decided that she thought Sabi was yours, and the shock of discovering that she was not, just sent her over the edge, especially after the trauma of giving birth and everything.'

'Damn her to hell. I discovered all the emails and other crap afterwards, when I was trying to sort out all her things.'

'It must've been terrible for you.'

'It was.' He calmed down a bit after this and took a sip of his gin. 'At least you now know why I am such a hard arsed bastard. That woman spoilt my life.'

19

Sabi

'SO, did you do your disappearing act because of Mike and Tracey?' Sarah asked as we walked into my room with her suitcase.

My heart skipped a beat. 'What about Mike and Tracey?

'Well, you know, them being an item and all that.'

'Since when? I don't know anything.'

'Since the beginning of the school holidays. You know James Carey had that party to celebrate the end of the school term? Most of the kids in Bulawayo were there. That's when she got off with him.'

'How am I supposed to know any of this, being stuck in the bush like I am most of the time?'

'She posted it on her wall on Facebook the day before you disappeared. For her status she wrote "in a relationship with Mike Carpenter". I thought you'd seen this, and that's why you disappeared.'

'No.'

I was suddenly overcome with jealousy at the thought of Mike and Tracey together.

'I know you liked him and he likes you too.'

'Nothing has ever happened between us.'

'I know, but Tracey also knows you like him, so I thought it was a bit mean of her.'

'Mmm.'

'Apparently, they both got really drunk at James' party and snuck off behind the swimming pool house, and she let him go all the way.'

'How do you know this?' I could feel my jealousy levels rising by the minute.

'She told Darlene and Darlene told me. In fact, I think Darlene has told the whole of Bulawayo.'

'Oh well.'

'Yeah, Tracey has done it with at least three people I know already. You and I are way behind her on that front.'

'There is no one else that I am interested in.'

Unfortunately, this was the truth. I really like Mike, with his brown curly hair and big blue eyes, he's really nice. He's also a really good water polo player and the wing in the first team rugby at his school, which is quite an achievement, as he was only in the Lower sixth this year. Sometimes I've even fantasised about him giving me his rugby jersey at the end of the rugby season next year. That's what the players do when they come to the end of their last season at school; they give their jersey to their girlfriend.

'I actually think Brad Van der Westhuizen is quite cute,' Sarah said.

'Do you?'

I thought about him for a moment. Mmm, maybe. He's a good hockey player and did really well in the interhouse athletics competition at his school in the first term. Sarah's mother had taken us out to the school for the day to watch the athletics.

'I remember he won the open hundred metre race,' I said.

I also remember Mike came second, but I didn't mention this.

'Yes, that's when I first noticed him properly.'

'So you're telling me you've liked him all this time and you've never told me before?'

'Well, there has never been anything between us, until he sent me a text asking me to go to his party, and when I said I couldn't, he sent me another text saying how disappointed he was.'

'Really?'

'And since then we've been texting each other all the time. In fact, have you got signal here, as he'll probably be expecting something from me?'

She took her phone out of her pocket to check how many bars there were.

'No bars,' she said, struggling to hide her disappointment.

'No, I'm afraid there's no signal here.'

'Oh dear, he's going to wonder why I'm not texting him all of a sudden.'

'Why were you texting him anyway, when he's home from school now. Haven't you met up?'

'No, he's gone to Harare to play in a cricket festival. He'll only be back just before Christmas.'

I'd forgotten he was a good cricketer too.

'Well we can go down to Leanne and Rob's house for you to text him, as they have an aerial there.'

'Jeez, but that's miles away.'

I had thought I was being very clever when I talked Leanne into letting us stay at the lodge, even though there are no grownups around. We were initially going to stay at their house, and I was really just chancing my arm when I asked Leanne if we could rather stay here. I had expected her to say no, but instead she said she thought it was a great idea, as long as Gladys her maid and Lovemore the cook were here she couldn't see why not. Now all Sarah wants is to be close to cellphone signal. It seems as if I just can't win.

'Why don't we go and have a swim and I'll show you around the rest of the lodge.'

The weather has really warmed up again after that cold front we got last week, and the temperature of the water is great. It's three days now since I arrived at the lodge and my cold has completely gone, thank goodness. The only way I can tell that I even have had a cold is that the sides of my nose are a bit chaffed looking.

Sarah scratched in her bag for her bikini while I went into the bathroom to collect my school costume, which I'd hung in there to dry after swimming yesterday afternoon.

'I've actually brought two bikinis, 'Sarah said, 'if you want to borrow one. Maybe we should spend some time working on our tans, not that you ever really need to with that lovely brown skin of yours. I wish I had a darker skin like you. I'm forever having to slap on sunblock and if I ever forget it my mother gets really irritated with me.'

Sarah has a very fair skin and light reddish hair, but she is still very pretty I think, even though she has railway tracks on her teeth right now. But they will come off in six months time. I'm quite lucky; my teeth came out pretty straight on their own.

'Can I borrow your other cozzie please? I do tan, and I love having bikini marks on my body.'

Sarah was very impressed by the pool area of the lodge, the infinity pool, the three hundred and sixty degree view from any place up there, the thatched bar area with the smooth wooded counter and fridges behind it. She went up to the bar and tapped on it.

'Service please, service please.'

I laughed at her.

'Two Malawi Shandies please with lots of ice,' she continued in a loud voice as if there was a waiter behind the bar.

I went behind the bar to make these. I didn't know what they were but Sarah gave me instructions.

'Orange juice, ginger ale and lemonade,' she said, with great authority

'Mm, that's good,' I said taking a swig of mine.

It was actually really sweet but after another sip I started to get used to this.

We sat on the love seats at opposite ends of the pool, sipping our drinks and enjoying the tepid water. Sarah finished her Malawi Shandy before me, put her glass on the paving next to her, slipped off her love seat and swam the whole length of the pool and back again under water.

'Can you do that?' she gasped when she came up, wiping the water from her eyes, her braces flashing as she spoke.

The pool is pretty small so I knew I could, it's just that I don't like opening my eyes under water, as the chlorine hurts my eyes.

'Aren't your eyes burning from the chlorine?'

'I didn't actually open them.'

'What, but didn't you bang into the side of the pool then, under water?'

'No, I just felt with my hands. Try it; it's as easy as anything.'

It was, and we both did it quite a few more times before, settling on our love seats again.

'Well, this is the life,' Sarah said, enjoying herself now.

I wondered if she was still hankering after a cellphone signal.

'So tell me, if it wasn't because of Mike and Tracey that you ran away, then why did you?'

'You really want to know?'

'Of course, I was just as worried as everyone else when I heard you'd disappeared. It's a bit of a weird thing to do, you know.'

'Yes, I wouldn't have done it except that something scary happened.'

'What.'

'You know I was staying with Vanessa and Martin Rawson, my dad insisted I stayed with them.'

'Ah ha.'

'Well, Vanessa's brother is Mr. Norris.'

'Mr. Norris from school? Mr. Norris the swimming teacher, who half the girls have a crush on?'

'Yes, that one, although he's actually a bit weird I think. His name is Neville, by the way.'

'Neville Norris, that sounds quite funny.'

'Anyway, Vanessa's little girl fell out of a tree and broke her arm, and they had to take her to Bulawayo, and I stayed at their mine with Mr. Norris. They didn't come back that night and when I went to bed Mr. Norris tried to get in with me.'

Sarah stared at me.

'You're joking,' she eventually spluttered.

'I don't think I am, although sometimes I wonder if I am imagining it now, yet it was all so real at the time. I remember that I was lying in my bed about to doze off when my door opened, and he came in, wearing his dressing gown. He took it off and got into the bed and started rubbing his penis along my thigh.'

Sarah sat on her love seat, her mouth literally dropped open with surprise.

'You are making this up. I can't believe it.'

'I told you, I don't trust myself anymore either but I really do think it happened. I can remember the feel of that penis on my leg and as that's never happened to me before I can't believe my imagination would play such tricks on me.'

'What did it feel like?'

'Hard and rubbery.'

'Did you actually see it?'

'No. It was dark in my room.'

I hesitated.

'The thing is, Sarah, if it didn't happen and I was imagining it, first of all why would I have such a good memory of it, and second, surely I wouldn't have trekked through the African bush in the middle of the night, running away from him. It wasn't exactly fun, you know. I was really scared I'd stand on a snake or something.'

'But why on earth would he do something like that?'

'How am I supposed to know?'

'Mmm, people do weird things at times. So was it big?'

'What?'

'His penis?'

'It felt pretty big, but as I've said, I've never felt one before, so I've nothing to compare it with.'

'Neither have I. Tracey would be a better judge than us.'

'Anyway, my main worry now is that I don't know how to tell anyone. I mean, look at how you reacted, and so imagine how grownups would react. My father would definitely think I'd made it all up, especially as he's such good friends with Vanessa, he'd definitely take Mr. Norris's side, as he is Vanessa's brother.'

'Yes, Mr. Norris can be a bit strict at times, so I don't think anyone could imagine him in bed with one of his students, rubbing himself up and down her leg. He sounds like that randy little Staffordshire bull terrier I used to have, Butch. Do you remember how he used to try and hump people's legs all the time?'

When she said this I started to laugh, and then she started to laugh and the next thing we knew, we both couldn't stop laughing at the thought of Mr. Norris behaving like her staffie, Butch. We slipped off our love seats and rolled around in the water, and laughed and laughed and laughed until our sides were sore and we'd choked on some of the pool water. Eventually, we managed to control ourselves and we scrambled back onto our love seats again.

'The thing is, what am I going to say to my dad and everyone else? I can't just say I ran away because I felt like it. I have to think up a story.'

'Some of the girls at school would be green with envy if they knew what had happened.'

'Surely not, it was really scary. They'd just think I was lying. And that's what I also worry about; some girls may be cross with me if I told on him, they'd maybe think I was just trying to cause trouble for him.'

'Yes, maybe you're right. We'll have to think about this one.'

*

Clare came back the next afternoon and I was really happy, because she brought my gran with her. I hadn't been expecting this, as I knew she'd come out from England especially to look after my dad.

Gran hugged me and hugged me when she first got out of the car.

'Darling, darling, look at you, so grown up and elegant now.'

I was actually wearing the new shorts and halter-neck top, which I do think look pretty good on me.

'And look at your hair, such a lovely style.'

Well my hair is always pretty difficult to control but yes, it is looking better than it's ever looked before, thanks to Clare's hairdresser.

Gran eventually stopped hugging me. 'And you must be Sarah,' she said, holding out her hands towards her. Gran has always been a really friendly person. It's such a pity her son didn't take after her. It was as if she was reading my thoughts. 'You will want to know how your father is, Sabi, dearest,' she said.

I didn't really, but couldn't exactly say so. 'He's so much better than when you saw him last I'm sure. Of course he's still got the cast right up to his thigh, so he's pretty immobile, but he's so much happier now that he is out of hospital. Memory and Bigboy are looking after him while I'm here seeing you.'

'So what have you girls been up to?' Clare asked.

‘Swimming, tanning, reading magazines,’ I said.

‘Chatting,’ Sarah continued.

‘Well, I’ve bought some of the latest magazines from England so at least you can get up-to-date on all the latest scandal and fashions,’ Gran said.

After unpacking all the stuff in the car that was for the camp, Clare said she would take Leanne’s shopping to her house right away.

‘Save us the bother of unpacking it out of the car then packing it up again,’ she said. ‘Why don’t you come with me Sarah?’

I wasn’t in the least bit surprised when Sarah jumped at this offer, what with her need to text Brad and all of that. I followed Gran to her room and sat on the bed while she unpacked her small suitcase. She always brings me nice things and this time was no exception. She gave me two really yummy-smelling lip-glosses, a pair of sunglasses and a bikini.

‘I was going to give you the sunglasses and bikini for Christmas but thought that you may like to use them while you’re staying at this lodge. I’ve got one or two more treats for you for then, anyway,’ she said, winking at me. ‘Now why don’t you show me around the place and then we’ll find somewhere to have a nice cup of tea. I’ll be parched by then.’

We eventually decided to have our tea sitting on the sun loungers next to the pool. Gran was amazed at the view and said it was the best place in the lodge to be. Lovemore brought the tea tray and Gran produced a packet of Oreos, which she knew I had always liked.

‘Brought out especially for you, dearest,’ she said.

'Thanks so much, but you know you can get them here now.'

'Goodness I know, how things have changed since I've been away. When I was here last you couldn't even buy bread, let alone biscuits. I couldn't believe the shops when Clare took me around them this morning. I can remember just empty shelves before. When I tell my friends in England about how it was they think I'm making it up, they cannot imagine shops with nothing in them.'

'It is better now, yes.'

'But your father says things are still pretty bad as far as the economy is concerned. I'm afraid there is still no investor confidence in this country and there won't be while the old guard continues to have so little respect for property rights. Your father was telling me that they are now trying to grab the mines….'

Maybe she saw a look cross my face at the mention of my father; I tried not to show any emotion, but she stopped in her tracks, took my hand and said, 'Oh dear Sabi, we have to talk about your father, I realise there has been a huge misunderstanding.'

'It's ok Gran.'

'No, I'm afraid it's not.' She let my hand go, and took a sip of her tea.

'I want you to know, Sabi that we all love you very much, certainly I do, and I know your father does too, even though he has a very difficult time showing it.'

I didn't say anything, so she continued.

'He had a bad time when you were born, dearest, and I'm afraid it has left him scarred. Yesterday when Clare came to see us she told us that you thought he was responsible for your mother's death.'

'I read her letters and emails to him.'

'Clare told us, she brought them for your father to read again, as he hasn't laid eyes on them for such a long time. He has, rightly or wrongly, tried to forget about them, and everything connected to them, but of course he can't and maybe he should have told you earlier the whole story, maybe I should have, it's just that neither of us knew how to tell you and when you would be old enough to understand.'

I was now a bit scared by her words. What on earth was she talking about? 'What, Gran?'

She paused. I could see that she was very uncomfortable.

'Well, you see, dearest, over fifteen years ago, before you were even born your mother became friendly with a hunter who used to come and stay on the ranch. She became so friendly that she thought she was in love with him. Those letters you read were letters she had written to him.'

'They weren't to Dad?'

'No.'

'But she was married to Dad. Why was she writing letters like that to someone else?'

'Your father didn't know she was writing those letters to someone else and she never told him about it. He only found them later, once she had died.'

'Killed herself, you mean.'

'Yes.'

'Where were you at the time Gran?'

'Well, I was living in my house in Bulawayo, but I used to go to the ranch to stay with them from time to time. I had no idea either that she was writing letters like that to someone else. I thought your parents loved each other and cared for each other very much.'

'So why was she doing it, then?'

'I have no idea. Maybe she was lonely; your dad was out a lot, checking on the cattle and stuff, maybe she was bored. I will never know.'

I stopped dead in my tracks as I suddenly recalled that she had said that the letters were written by a hunter.

'Gran was he a black man?'

'No my dear, he was a coloured man.' I tried to digest this. I thought of all the coloured girls at school. Most were ok, but we still usually stick to our own race groups.

'Did you ever meet him?'

'I believe I did. He was very friendly and once offered to service my car for me. He left before you were born though. He had a wife and children in Harare.

'So why was she writing letters like that to him, if he was married to someone else?'

'Again, I cannot say. But there is something I do need to tell you, something that is very important.'

'What Gran?'

'That man is actually your father.'

I stared at her, thinking I must've misunderstood what she was saying.

'Sorry?'

She leant forward and took my hand, but, I grabbed it away as I jumped up and ran, ran down the stairs as fast as I could. I couldn't face being with her now. I couldn't face being with anyone.

20

Clare

‘I’M afraid she married my Digger because she thought he had lots of money,’ Mrs. Stirling said, putting her wine glass on the table next to her chair.

We had finished our dinner and gone outside to the fire pit, where we settled ourselves in two of the chairs surrounding it. One of the gardeners lights a fire in the pit on the deck outside the living area every night when there are guests at the lodge. It makes a pleasant place to relax and sit before and after dinner; there is always something so mesmerising about a fire. We had not sat there before dinner tonight, so taken up were we with having to tell Sabi the truth about her parentage, and then trying to calm things down afterwards. Poor little thing, she rushed off to her room after Mrs. Stirling tried to tell her what had happened all those years ago, and then refused to come out or see any of us afterwards. Initially, Mrs. Stirling went after her, but Sabi locked her door and she would not open it to her so she came and asked me to go and try appeasing her, but Sabi wouldn't let me in, either. I could hear her sobs coming from inside, but she just kept telling me to go away. Poor Sarah, she must have been totally confused by everything that was going on, and sat in the sitting room trying to flip through a magazine, wishing I'm sure, that she was safely tucked up in her own home. Eventually, Mrs. Stirling came and found Sarah and told her, as concisely as possible, what she had told Sabi earlier. She said that now that 'the cat was out of the bag' it was pointless trying to cover anything up. Sarah's eyes nearly popped out of her head when she heard the story, despite trying to look cool about it all. During dinner we avoided discussing it, knowing that Sarah didn't need to hear any more than the basics, but after dinner she said that she would try to go and talk to Sabi. After she'd gone I noticed that the fire in the pit was lit and suggested to Mrs. Stirling that we take our wine glasses and go and sit by the fire. She jumped at this suggestion so I decided to bring the remains of the bottle with me.

'His real name is actually Philip,' she continued. 'My husband started calling him Digger when he was a tiny baby and I'm afraid it just stuck.'

'Well it is appropriate,' I said.

'Oh yes, definitely,' she agreed. 'Anyway, I believe that young Caroline was as impressed with our lovely houses and the cars we drove and the overseas holidays we took, as much as she was with my Digger, and she thought she could have all of that if she was his wife.

Unfortunately, though, what she did not understand was that none of it was Digger's at that stage, it was all ours, and my husband was a hard taskmaster and expected Digger to prove himself before he was handed anything on a silver platter. We owned a hundred thousand acre ranch in the Lowveld for decades, but it had not been efficiently managed for a very long time so my husband handed the management over to Digger when he was twenty five and told him to turn things around.'

She took a sip of her wine and when she put her glass down I leaned forward and poured some more into her glass, and then into mine too.

'Thank you my dear, I'm afraid I need this after all that's been going on today,' she said.

'Yes, me too,' I answered, also having another sip. I held my glass up towards the fire, looking at the flames through the redness of the liquid. 'So what had Digger been doing before he went to work on the ranch in the Lowveld?' I asked absentmindedly.

'Actually he'd been living in Australia, working as a ranch hand in New South Wales,' she replied. 'He realised when he was there that he would never make the money in Australia to buy a property like the place he worked at, yet in Zimbabwe he could have all of it once he'd proved himself to his father, and that's why he decided to come back and show his father his mettle.'

'Makes sense,' I said.

'Oh yes, I was very approving at the time, we really wanted him to take over all that we had. Anyway, he met Caroline in the weeks after he came back from Australia and before he moved down to the ranch, when he had time to spare and money to spend, and I'm sure he gave her a grand old time. For a year afterwards he lived on the ranch while she worked as a secretary in Bulawayo and whenever he came to town they always had fun together, going out to dinner all the time and on trips to the Victoria Falls and Johannesburg. Her life must've been so much more exciting when he was around as she wouldn't have been able to afford that sort of lifestyle on the salary she was making as a secretary.'

'I suppose not.'

Mrs. Stirling looked at me. 'So you can't really blame her for wanting to marry him, can you?'

'No,' I answered.

'Only problem was,' she continued, 'things changed when they married and she went off to live on the ranch. Poor Caroline wouldn't have been used to the isolated lifestyle of living on a huge ranch miles away from civilisation. If she had been a different type of character I'm sure she could have got into the ranching lifestyle and found things to do to fill her days. Goodness in the early years of my marriage I led a very solitary life on the mine, rarely seeing anyone other than my husband and the staff. I took up sewing and knitting, cooking and gardening as well as painting, and I filled my days very well. But poor Caroline, she did not have a creative streak and she struggled to entertain herself, so I can understand that she must've become extremely frustrated with her lot.'

'After my debacle,' I said, leaning forward and pouring another splash of wine into her glass, 'I went for some counselling and my therapist told me how common it is in marriage for each party to expect their spouse to transform their lives into what they would like it to be. Instead of taking responsibility for their own happiness, they expect their partner to make them happy, and when this does not happen they fall out of what is often termed as 'romantic love' with that person.'

'Yes, of course-no one person can make another person happy, year after year, after year.'

I picked up another log from the pile near my chair and put it on the fire.

'My therapist told me that it is at this point in a marriage that it can fail, if one of the partners tries to find someone else who they think can make them happy. Only problem of course is that the next person will also not live up to your expectations for ever.'

'Exactly my dear, exactly. No one can fulfil the expectations of another. My own husband and I had to work extremely hard at our marriage, it certainly wasn't easy, but I do miss him now that he is gone. He died when Digger and Caroline had been married for three or four years, and afterwards I used to go down to the ranch fairly often to stay with them. To be honest, I never noticed any conflict between them, although I could see that Digger was away from the house all day, every day, dealing with ranching issues, while Caroline was left at home without much to do herself.'

'I haven't told anyone else about my business, not even my cousin and his wife. Certainly not his wife, I can't see her tolerating a 'fallen woman.'', I confided.

'Sad that you think of yourself as this now,' she said softly, 'but what is going to happen with your marriage? I get the impression you are in a state of limbo right now.'

'Yes, I am, I'm afraid. My husband threw me out of the house, remember. Not that I blame him.'

'Well, you cannot carry on like this forever. Is there any chance you can try to resolve things? Do you want to, in fact?'

'I really, really wish I could, but I just do not know how.'

'Well, you definitely aren't going to be able to do this with you here and him there, my dear. Have you tried to do anything about this?'

'He was so angry with me when I left; I've been too scared to make any contact with him.'

'From the way you told it before, he was angry because he thought you were still in contact with the other man. Have you told him that you were not?'

'I did at the time, but not again.'

'Well, I think that you should try again. You've both had time to let the dust settle, tell him again how much you regret your actions and tell him again that you have no desire to ever have anything to do with that other man again. If your marriage means enough to him, he may listen to you now.'

'Do you think so?'

'Well, hopefully he married you with the initial intention of thinking it would be forever, and if this is so, then hopefully he won't want to give up on it so easily. Yes, I'd definitely contact him again if I were you, and I'd also definitely continue with your policy of keeping what happened to yourself, if you can to resolve things. Other people will just start making their own judgements and having their opinions, and that will make it that much harder for both you and your husband.'

'Did Digger ever tell anyone about Caroline?'

'Only me.'

I looked at her as she stared at the fire, lost in thought for a moment.

'Oh deary me,' she eventually continued, 'it was all so appalling; we just didn't know how to handle it. Can you imagine how it was, having the baby, finding out about the adultery, dealing with the suicide?'

'Surely people must've known she'd committed suicide, what with the death certificate and all?'

'I'm sure everyone had their suspicions, but we just kept quiet about it all and just mumbled about the river flooding and such. I think most people would have put it down to post-natal depression, but poor Digger, he was so shattered at the time by everything else, he just couldn't bring himself to explain to anyone what had really happened. And then it became too late, it just seemed easier to keep it to ourselves.'

'So up until now everyone thinks that Digger is Sabi's biological father?'

'Again, there may have been a few raised eyebrows, at her olive skin and thick, curly hair, but he's never discussed it with anyone.'

'No wonder he's so hard, then, to have been hurt like that and then kept it to himself all these years.'

'Oh yes, it's been difficult for me also, to watch how he's changed over the years. I think one of the worst things for him is that Caroline killed herself as soon as she knew the baby wasn't his. She must have been so ashamed of herself, she couldn't face the consequences, but ironically, if she hadn't killed herself I'm sure he would have been able to find it in himself to forgive her, it's just that she never gave him the chance. That's why it was so good for him to hear your story; it was such a relief for him to hear what you had to say, and to vent his anger.'

'To be honest, that's why I decided to come and talk to him, I knew he would need to talk about it, to someone who would understand.'

She smiled at me as I leaned forward again to splash a little more wine into her glass, before pouring the remains of the bottle into my own.

'Good, so that's you dealt with,' she said, 'but what about Sabi? When I look at it all now, I can see how stupid it was that Digger and I didn't find a way to tell her that he was not her biological father. And now she's had this terrible shock.'

'Yes, but I can understand that it is not an easy thing to tell a small child. But at least she may have understood better why he has always been so distant towards her. She kept telling me that he does not love her.'

'He does love her; it's just that he's afraid to show a soft side in case he's hurt like he was hurt before. But now my dear,' she said, finishing her wine, 'I think we should both retire, maybe things will look a little clearer in the morning.'

*

I couldn't sleep, maybe from too much wine, but my head was spinning as I thought about poor Sabi, and also about my own situation. I kept wondering how I could make things better, if indeed I could, and what I would do if Graham refused to give me another chance. I think that's why I haven't contacted him before. I am scared that he will reject me outright; it's easier to keep things in limbo as I've been doing up till now, so that I can say to myself that maybe there is still a chance of reconciliation. But now crunch time is coming. I can't carry on like this forever.

I got up at five thirty the next morning, feeling stodgy and hung-over, but I made myself a cup of coffee and went and sat next to the pool so that I could watch the sun come up as I drank it. How beautiful it was, the sky was almost clear, but the colour changed gradually from a dim blue, with shafts of whitish, yellowish light shining through before the sunrise, to a brighter and more turquoise colour as the sun first peeped over the horizon, before pushing its way into full view. The birds had been making their usual morning racket earlier, but they seemed to stop for a moment, just before and after sunrise, as if they too were mesmerised by the spectacle of the sun rising, something that happens every single day and yet that is so often ignored by us human beings.

Surely Graham, with his appetite for life and different experiences, would love to watch something like this. Yes, I'm sure he'd love to spend a bit of time in this country, soaking up the natural beauty and freedom. I'm sure, also that he'd be intrigued by the ambiguities of the place, how many of the citizens have a great deal and yet most have practically nothing, how the 'haves' lead interesting lives and yet the 'have nots' can take it away at the whim of any politician who can use them, how there is so little racial integration, yet so much racial sensitiveness. Zimbabwe is not a country at war, yet in some respects it is. Yes, I'm sure Graham would be fascinated by all of this.

I finished my coffee and then set off in the Land Cruiser to Rob and Leannes' house to email him. I didn't want to put it off a moment longer and I knew that Rob unlocked the house very early every morning, before setting off on his rounds. Thankfully, no one was around when I got there; I certainly didn't want to have to make early morning small talk with Leanne. The verandah door was open, so I let myself in and went straight to the office, switching on the computer even before sitting down at the desk.

As soon as I got onto my email account I quickly scanned the In Box for a message from Graham. There was nothing, but this wasn't going to make me change my mind.

'Dearest Graham,' I wrote. 'It has been seven weeks now since I left and I hope that it is enough time for you to be a little less angry with me. Please, please believe me when I tell you that I did not make any attempt to contact Mitch ever again, after I had told you that I would not. I have never had any desire to contact him and I will regret to my dying day that I was involved with him in any way. I know that it was all ego and vanity-driven and that by doing what I did, I am a lesser person as a result of it. But if you can find it in your heart to try to forgive me, I will do everything possible to make things right for us again.

I think you would find it very interesting here. I think you'd be fascinated by all the new issues that have developed in this country in recent years, and the lives the people live, having to cope with a myriad of problems that no one in the States would ever dream of. I would love it more than anything if you would come and join me here for a while.

Dearest Graham, I am so, so sorry for the hurt I have caused you.'

I read the email through again, and then pressed the send button before I had a chance to change anything. I then looked more carefully through my emails in the In Box. There were a few messages from friends and clients back home, which I quickly scanned through, but didn't feel the need to reply to any. But then, as I was flicking through the many messages from Facebook I saw a notification that turned me cold, especially in the face of the email I'd just sent my husband; Mitch Garry, requesting to be my friend. I had 'unfriended' him ages ago, as soon as I had promised his wife I would have nothing whatsoever to do with him. I stared at it in horror, and as I did so I suddenly thought, 'wow, you are a complete jerk'. When I had told his wife I'd drop all contact with him she had emailed back, cc-ing it to him (so he certainly knew what her sentiments were). In her reply she said, 'Good, you are despicable and I cannot bear the thought of any member of my family having any contact with you whatsoever.' That was her final slap in my face, but here he was now, obviously wanting to re-establish some sort of contact, having no respect for the sentiments his wife had made so clear. What sort of man was he, that he should still have so little respect for her wishes? I cringed as I thought of how I had been so taken in by his charm and sexuality. I opened my Facebook account and I unsubscribed myself. That would stop him from trying to re-establish contact that way. All my other friends would wonder why I had done this, but so be it.

When I got back to the lodge, I found Mrs. Stirling sitting next to the pool nursing a cup of tea and a hangover. She smiled sheepishly when she saw me. 'Oh dear, I've got such a headache, my goodness I'm not used to drinking so much wine, haven't you got a headache too? I've taken two aspirin and hopefully my head will start to ease soon.'

'I wasn't feeling too good when I first woke up,' I confessed. The girls appeared at that moment, dressed in their swimming costumes and carrying towels over their shoulders. Mrs. Stirling and I looked at them apprehensively as they approached.

'Good morning both,' she said, maybe a little too cheerily.

Sarah smiled hesitantly and Sabi came over to her gran and gave her a hug. The look of relief on Mrs. Stirling's face was palpable.

'Oh Darling, how are you this morning?' she asked.

'Still very shocked, Gran. But Sarah and I have had a very long talk about it all and we've decided that for me to feel less confused about my identity I need to meet my real dad. I need to know what he's like.'

Mrs. Stirling's face dropped like a lead balloon.

'Oh dear, I'm not so sure if that's a good idea.'

'I'm not so sure either Gran, but I still need to do it. Does he even know that I exist?'

I was expecting Mrs. Stirling to say no, as she'd told me last night they'd told no one, so I was surprised when she said yes.

'Your father told him when you were first born.'

'And he didn't want me either hey?'

Sabi's voice sounded hard, way too hard for such a young child.

'Well, it wasn't that simple, I'm afraid. He is married, remember, with a wife and other children…'

'Wow, brothers and sisters,' Sabi said contemptuously.

'Sabi dear,' Mrs. Stirling persisted, 'you must understand and I will say this again and again until you believe me, it was never a question of your father, of Digger, not wanting you. You are his daughter, as far as he is concerned. His name is on your birth certificate. He never wanted it any other way.'

'He's struggled to show it, Gran.'

'That's only because he was so shocked by what happened and he was so hurt by it. But he has never not wanted you. I promise you that.'

'Well, I'm not so sure about that and because of this I'm not so sure that I want him as my dad anymore.'

Mrs. Stirling glanced at me, needing help and not sure how to proceed.

'Oh Darling, don't say something like that.'

'He should have told me the truth, Gran. He should have let me know.'

'He always thought you were too young to be told the truth. He never knew how to tell you…..' her voice trailed off hopelessly.

'You know what,' I interrupted. 'Why don't I take you to see this man, Sabi, your biological father? Where does he live Mrs. Stirling, do you know?'

'I believe in Harare. Digger will know. Yes, maybe that's not such a bad idea, if you really do want to see him, Sabi.'

'Well, maybe we should sort it out as soon as possible.' I said. 'It's less than two weeks till Christmas and I'm sure it would be better to deal with it before Christmas than after. Let's try and make the relevant plans today,'

We had our breakfast and afterwards set off for Rob and Leannes' house again, this time all of us. Sabi told me that Sarah was keen to send a few texts to some boy she liked, Mrs. Stirling was going to talk to Digger on the phone about setting up a meeting with Sabi's father (I could tell that she was pretty apprehensive about this) and I was interested in seeing if I had a reply to my email. Unfortunately, I had not, but I quickly consoled myself with the realisation that the time in Louisiana would have been after eleven at night when I sent it, so it would have been unlikely if he'd replied then anyway.

21

Sabi

SO here I am now, having to re-evaluate everything I've ever thought about who I am and where I come from, and when I say everything, I mean absolutely everything. Talk about confusion, all my life I've been thinking that my mother was this amazing saintly woman, her life coming to a tragic end with my difficult birth, and now I discover that this is all a load of rubbish, a total load of complete and utter bullshit (as Tracey would put it). Wow, what a difficult thing to get my head around. And here I've been thinking my whole life that my dad is my dad, not a particularly kind or loving dad, but still my dad and now I find out that he isn't at all. Jeez, no wonder he's struggled to be kind or loving; he must cringe every time he looks at me, knowing what happened to make me!

This is how my thoughts were going on our way up to Harare to meet my real dad, well, hopefully, anyway. It turns out he doesn't want to meet me (surprise, surprise). My dad, I mean Digger, got hold of him yesterday to say I wanted to meet him and apparently he started making all sorts of excuses as to why this would not be a good idea. Dad, I mean Digger, told Clare that we must go anyway and that he would try to sort it out. He said it would be harder for him to get out of it if we were actually in Harare.

It was difficult seeing Dad on our way through. I really did not want to, feeling as confused as I am, but it was impossible to avoid this, as we had to drop Gran off. We couldn't exactly leave her at the end of the street and make her walk home, pulling her suitcase behind her. And of course, when we did drop her at the house I couldn't very well sit in the car while Clare went in to discuss stuff with him. That would have been way too obvious. So I had no alternative but to go in and say hello. He was sitting on the verandah with his broken leg on a stool, and when he saw me he beckoned me over and pulled me close to him, and I think he almost started crying. That actually freaked me out a bit as he's never shown any emotion around me; it's weird that he should do so now. He didn't say much else but he didn't look like his usual self.

Clare didn't talk much to start with on our way up to Harare, maybe she knew that I wanted to think about things in silence. But then, as we went through the towns on the way she started pointing out things that I had never really noticed before. Like the litter everywhere. I'd never been that aware of it, but as we entered Gweru and she started muttering about it, I noticed how bad it really is, and then I noticed it in all the other towns too. She told me that in the States there would never be litter lying all over the place as there is here, people get fined for littering there, apparently. It was really funny when she was telling me this because we were travelling behind a bus at the time and as if on cue, every time she said how bad the littering is in this country someone would throw something out of the bus; tin cans, plastic bags, mealie cobs (not so bad, as they are bio-degradable), all sorts of things were flying out of that bus window. I couldn't help laughing and neither could she, even though we knew it's not really a laughing matter. The other thing she pointed out, which I'd never actually been consciously aware of before, is all the cultivating that goes on all over the towns. She asked what on earth it was that everyone was planting and I said it had to be mealies. This surprised her, she said that in the States people would be fined if they started digging up the parks and what she called 'green belts' to grow a few stalks of maize.

I was able to point out some interesting things to her too. One thing was something us girls always notice when we travel to Harare on the school bus to play tennis and other sports. I pointed out the huge, sprawling cemetery outside of Harare that we always take note of every time we pass it, mainly because it gets bigger and more sprawling every time we pass it. This time, as we drove by we counted four funerals going on. We girls have decided that the reason this cemetery has grown so big in such a short time is because of AIDS, so many people are still dying because of this virus. Clare told me that very few people die of it in the States anymore because they have easy access to anti-retroviral drugs. Clare told me that apparently Gogo took these drugs for a while, but then the hospital in Gwanda ran out of them and so she had to stop. Once you stop you can't really start again as they lose their potency. Poor Gogo, I hadn't known this before but apparently Jabula told Clare.

Another thing I pointed out to her were the newspaper billboards. My friends and I love to look at them when we're travelling around town because some of them are so funny. It didn't take me long to find a weird one, posted on a billboard next to a traffic light. This one read, 'Man claims donkey backed up to him'.

'I wonder what that story is about,' I said.

'Mm, I wonder,' Clare replied.

We saw a few more funny ones as we drove towards the place we were going to stay. 'Woman gives birth to four frogs' was one that caught my eye and then we both got a real shock when we read, 'Man dies as sexual organ grows to knee-length'. Clare said that the billboards in the States don't have nearly such interesting headlines on them.

*

Clare had booked us into a B & B in Borrowdale that Leanne told her about. At first Leanne had suggested that we stay with her sister and family but Clare disagreed, suggesting the trip could be a bit traumatic for me and I might struggle being amongst strangers. I think this is partly true. I am very nervous at the prospect of meeting Mr. Masterson, even though I feel I must, as I do not want to go through the rest of my life wondering what he is like. But I think that Clare may have had another reason for wanting to stay at the B & B, I think she did not wanted to risk staying with Leanne's sister in case she's as bossy as Leanne.

The B & B is really nice, very upmarket, I'd say, not that I've ever stayed in one before. I commented on the cost but apparently my dad, Digger, had insisted on giving Clare the money to pay for it. We are sharing a room but it has two double beds and is very big with a bathroom, en suite so it should be fine. It overlooks the pool and Clare suggested I went and had a swim while she checked her emails. The weather wasn't that hot so I didn't spend much time in the water, and when I came back to the room I found Clare sitting cross-legged on her bed staring at her computer and looking sad. I asked her if she was alright and she said that there wasn't anything from my dad about "The Meeting" so she would phone him in the evening.

The lady who runs the B & B's name is Mrs. Van Heerden, an old lady about the same age as my gran I'd say. She told us about a sushi bar nearby where we could go for dinner if we wanted. Clare was amazed when I said I'd never eaten sushi before, and so that's where we headed for our supper. It was in the Borrowdale Village, the name for the shopping centre near where we were staying and all the Christmas decorations and lights were up and lit, it was the first time I've felt even remotely festive this whole holiday. The sushi was OK, but didn't really fill me up, so we ordered a plate of fried calamari rings and chips also. I think I prefer fried calamari rings.

When we got back to the B & B Clare checked her email again and said there was still nothing from my dad so she phoned him. She was on the phone with him the whole time I was in the bathroom showering and cleaning my teeth and when I eventually came through she said goodbye to him and put the phone down. I wondered if she didn't want to talk to him while I was in the room, but when I got into bed she said that Mr. Masterson had finally agreed to meet us the following day at noon. My heart skipped a beat when she told me this. I messaged Sarah to tell her and she replied, 'cool!'

*

As we sat on the verandah of the B & B waiting for Mr. Masterson to arrive I felt so nervous I could hardly drink the strawberry milkshake Clare had ordered me. I'd been fine earlier. First, I'd had a huge breakfast of cereal and fruit and then two poached eggs, bacon, sausage, fried potatoes, toast and muffins, while Clare just had a cup of coffee and a bowl of branflakes. Afterwards, we decided to go back to Borrowdale Village to look around the shops. This is the first time Clare's been to Harare and she wanted to take a look around, but as she only knew about the Borrowdale Village, this is where we went again. It was busy and bustling, what with it being so close to Christmas, and I saw all sorts of things in the shops that I would have liked to buy. Clare must've realised this because she said I could choose something I wanted as a Christmas present from her. There was one shop which had really cool clothes, and after quite a lot of trying on I eventually decided on a mini skirt and matching top made out of a soft cream material. The top crosses over at the back and each crossover section is buttoned at the shoulder but it leaves a sort of open v shape in the small of my back, so it will be nice to wear on hot days. It's the sort of outfit I can imagine Vanessa making and looking really good in but I know Tracey won't approve. She likes to wear tiny shorts or tight jeans all the time with small tops that always show off her tummy, not her back.

All this clothes shopping was a good distraction, but now crunch time had come and I felt shaky and weak with worry.

'I wonder what he'll be like,' I said to Clare.

'I'm sure he'll be perfectly normal, perfectly nice.' she replied.

'You know,' I continued, 'I was just thinking last night as I was going to sleep that this man ruined my mother's life.'

Clare looked at me; I could see she was trying to decide how to respond to this.

'In a way, maybe, but on the other hand your mother didn't have to do what she did, to take her own life.'

'I wonder why she did. Do you think it's because he's a coloured? Do you think it was just too embarrassing for her?'

'No, I don't think that was the reason. Often times when a married person has an affair they are trying to run away from reality, they want to live in a fantasy world, a world of make believe, so the worst thing possible for them is for their affair to be found out, because it shatters the fantasy. I'm sure that's the main reason she did what she did.'

'You think so? You know, at our school although there are many different races in our classes we usually stick to our own race. I'm wondering how it'll be with my friends now that I'm coloured, not white. It worries me that, that I'll have to mix with the coloured crowd now and although I don't mind them, there is no one there I think I'll be that comfortable with, not like I am with Sarah and the others in my gang.'

'Did Sarah say something?'

'No.'

'And I'd be surprised if she did. I'm sure your friends won't treat you any differently; you'll still be their friend. The reason most people mix mainly with their own race is because they have more in common with them, they have the same values, the same way of looking at life.

Just because it turns out your biological father is a coloured man doesn't mean you're different now, you're still the same person you've always been. I'm sure your gang won't think you're any different.'

'I hope not, because I don't much feel like having to make a whole bunch of new friends.'

'Well, hopefully you'll continue making new friends all your life, but as I said before, you will become friends with people mainly because you share the same interests, not because of the colour of their skin. What I've noticed about people here in Zimbabwe is that the cultural and social differences between the races are still very, very great. It's going to take many generations till it narrows I think.'

She looked at her watch and glanced towards the drive.

'I wonder where Mr. Masterson is. Your father said he'd meet us at noon, and it's now quarter past.'

We continued to sit and wait. We waited till after one o'clock and when he still had not arrived Clare suggested we had something for lunch. I had a toasted chicken and mayonnaise sandwich and coke, and Clare had a Greek salad and water. We ate on the verandah so we wouldn't miss Mr. Masterson when he finally arrived. When we'd finished eating, Clare ordered herself another tray of coffee and I had a vanilla milkshake and then, when we'd finished these and he still hadn't arrived, Clare said she'd go and phone my dad, I mean Digger. She went to the bedroom and I continued to sit on the verandah. I decided to text Sarah to tell her what had happened, or maybe I should say what hadn't happened.

'Bummer,' was her reply.

'Typical,' I responded.

'But hey,' she texted back, 'the dentist phoned 2 say he had a cancellation and he cud c me 2 titen my braces. We r driving 2 Hre now. Any space at ur place 4 us 2nite?'

'How many?' I asked back.

'Mom and me.'

'I'll ask and get back 2 u.'

'gr8.'

Well, that made me feel a bit better, just when I was about to feel really, really despondent because Mr. Masterson had stood me up (so to speak). I went to the bedroom and found Clare sitting on the bed checking her emails again.

'Ah,' she said when I walked in, closing her computer with a solid click, 'I've spoken to your dad. He said he'd phone Mr. Masterson and get back to me. Hopefully, we'll hear something soon.'

'Ok, and guess what,' I said, very relieved now at the prospect of Sarah coming, 'Sarah texted me. You know how she has braces, well the orthodontist is here in Harare and she has to keep coming up here to have them tightened. She's got an appointment and they're on their way now, her and her mother. She wanted to know if they could stay here, too.'

'Gee.' Clare thought for a moment, 'I suppose I can go and ask Mrs. Van Heerden.' She looked at her watch. 'Let's go now.

But then we were distracted by my dad phoning. I could hear him talking loudly on the phone to Clare although I couldn't hear every word he was saying, just things like ‘stupid bastard’ and ‘fucking shithead’ and I assumed he must be referring to Mr. Masterson. Clare wasn’t saying that much back, just ‘oh well,’ and ‘no one can say we didn’t try’ and ‘I suppose he’s got his reasons’ and other stuff like that, which obviously meant that Mr. Masterson wasn’t going to come. I felt very, very upset about this, but at least I had Sarah to focus on.

*

They arrived at about six thirty, Sarah and her mother. Mrs. Van Heerden said there was plenty of room for them and she ended up putting them in a room right next door to ours, also sharing. I was so pleased to have them there. Sarah’s mother, Mrs. Langdon, has always been really nice to me over the years, always making me feel very welcome whenever I’ve stayed with them, which is many, many times. Mrs. Van Heerden said she could provide us with dinner if we wanted, for fifteen dollars a head, main course and a pudding. We decided this would be best as Sarah and Mrs. Langdon were feeling tired after their long drive and we’d been out the night before to a restaurant, anyway.

Sarah was in my room when I came out of the shower. ‘Where’s Clare?’ I asked.

‘She’s talking to my Mom. Mom told me to come here.’

‘Oh’

‘It’s about Mr. Norris.’

‘What do you mean?’

‘I told my Mom, on the way up here, she kept quizzing me about why you’d disappeared like you did. She thought it was because you’d discovered this business about your mother and the other man.’

'Jeez like, Sarah, what did you say?'

'Just what you told me, that he'd tried to get into bed with you and you'd run away.'

'Jeez like, Sarah. Did she think I was making up stories?'

'Well, she was a bit surprised. Everyone thinks he's such a nice teacher. But of course she didn't think you'd tell a whole long story like that if wasn't true. She's talking to Clare about it now.'

'Oh boy, I wonder if I should go and have my say now.'

'No, don't, they won't be able to talk properly if you're there.'

'Yes, I suppose they can discuss it more freely without us there. If we're there they'd keep trying to hold back, not wanting to say anything that may be too upsetting for our delicate ears.'

Sarah laughed.

'I know, they think we're so innocent, don't they? But hey listen, Brad is still here playing cricket. He sent me a text just now to say that tomorrow is their last match. Why don't we go and watch when I've finished with my dentist appointment?'

'Doesn't your mother need to get back?'

'She said she would spend tomorrow doing some Christmas shopping and stuff. She only wants to go back the next day.'

'I'll ask Clare, she might want to leave tomorrow now that the whole reason for us coming has turned out to be a complete waste of time.'

The door opened and Clare came in.

'What do you want to ask me?'

I looked at her, bewildered.

'Um, Sarah wants to go and watch cricket tomorrow after her appointment but I wondered if you wanted to get back, now that we're not going to see Mr. Masterson.'

'I can spend another day here. Joanne said she'd like to show me around other shops here. She says Harare has so much more to offer than Bulawayo and it would be interesting for me to see it.'

(Joanne is Mrs. Langdon).

'Brill,' Sarah said.

'Sabi,' Clare went on, 'Joanne told me what you'd told Sarah.'

'Yes?'

'Sweetie, why didn't you tell me or your gran before now?'

'I've had other things on my mind.'

'Yes, I suppose. Gee yes, you've been having such a bad time of late, haven't you?'

'I also didn't know if anyone would believe me, if I told a story like that, Mr. Norris being such a popular teacher, and Vanessa's brother, and all of that.'

'I believe you. Something happened that made me believe every word of it.'

'Oh yes.'

'When you were all staying at the lodge I found him spying on me when I was having a soak in my outside tub.'

Sarah started to giggle.

'Wow,' she said.

'He tried to make out he'd lost his way,' Clare continued, 'but even then I was a little suspicious. So I was not that surprised when Joanne told me, not at all in fact.'

I felt very pleased about this; thank goodness he hadn't just misbehaved around me. 'And as soon as we get back to Bulawayo I'll sit down again with your dad and tell him and he can take it up from there. Men like that shouldn't be teachers.'

'But so many of the girls really like him. He's so good at sport and coaching. I'm sure some of the girls will be really irritated with me for telling on him.'

'Sabi, you have to understand, there are some things that just can't be ignored, and this is one of them. We won't shout what happened from the rooftops, but the headmistress of your school has to be told, the police have to be told. All those girls who really like him will get over it, don't you worry.'

Jeez, I wasn't so sure. I'm sure she wouldn't have said that if she was the one having to deal with all these issues.

22

Clare

WELL, at least all these constant twists and turns in Sabi's life are a distraction from my own worries. I've been checking my email at least twice a day since I wrote to Graham, and with each day that goes by and there's no reply, I know that I can't even use the differences in time zones as an excuse any more. I had hoped so much that he'd respond to my plea, but I certainly cannot blame him for not doing so. Why should he? He's the one who's been so abused by my selfish behaviour.

It was terrible, telling him what I'd done. I had over a week after my final communication with Mitch's wife and before he came back from the Middle East to think long and hard about things. During this time, Mitch kept trying to get hold of me, and in many ways this worked in my favour, because with each attempt it became ever more apparent to me what a jerk he was. And then, when Graham got back, and I went to the airport to collect him, all the old feelings I had for him came flooding back, making the reality of how I'd behaved even more distasteful. I felt so bad by then, I broke down almost the minute we got back to the house, and he sank into one of the chairs at our kitchen table, stunned.

Eventually he got up, simply saying, 'And there I've been these last few weeks, so excited at seeing you again,' and with that he opened the kitchen door and walked out, letting the screen slam behind him. I heard his car starting up, and saw him screeching down the drive, and then he was gone. I quickly became frantic, worrying where on earth he'd gone and what he was going to do. I felt absolute repugnance with myself. After three or four hours he came back; it looked like he'd been crying, which of course made me feel even worse. He sat down heavily at the kitchen table again after collecting himself a beer from the fridge. His face was tight, and bitter.

'Do you want me to go?' I asked.

'Yes, no, I don't know,' he replied.

'I am so, so sorry,' I said, 'if I could turn the clock back six months and live through this time again, I promise I'd do it all so differently. I cannot tell you how much I regret my behaviour. I know sorry isn't enough, but I don't know what else to say or do.'

He took a swig of his beer and sat staring at the bottle in his hands.

'I feel like I've been violated,' he eventually said. 'I feel like my life has been invaded by this other person. I cannot bear the thought of him.'

'I promise I will never, ever have anything to do with him again, please believe this,' I said quickly. 'Whatever happens to us, I know I crossed a line that I should never have crossed, and I know my behaviour was abhorrent. I will always regret it. If only, if only you could forgive me.'

He looked long and hard at me and eventually he said, 'I will try, for the sake of everything we have done together and for everything we have together, I will try.'

I reached out to touch his hand but he pulled it away in disgust. 'You need to go for counselling, Clare, go and sort yourself out so that you never, ever hurt anyone again like you've hurt me.'

Things went pretty well, all things considered, until he found that other text. If it hadn't been for that, I would still be there, and maybe things would even be better still. It's like my adultery forced me to take a good, long look at myself and I didn't like what I saw. I was determined to become a better person for him. At the same time, I started appreciating him that much more, so that all I really wanted was to make him happy again. However, in this modern world and with the advent of the internet, it is so easy to cheat now, all you need is access to the internet and you can cheat any time you want, as long as you keep remembering to delete what you've been doing, and change your pass words. I swear Mitch Garry was doing this, even with his wife in the room, judging from all the many ways he kept trying to get hold of me. I lived in terror that Graham would find something some time, even though I changed my email address, my skype address, my sim card, and I unfriended him on Facebook and My Space. It's no wonder I have such dislike for phones and the internet now. It was really only a matter of time before Graham found something, and after that he didn't want to know my case anymore.

And, of course, when I look back on it all now I know that it was really just one big ego trip for me. I was just having fun, because I thought life had dealt me a bum hand. I was feeling sad and lonely and it was just so easy to look towards someone else to liven things up. How I cringe now when I think about it all. Mitch Garry, charming, good looking, interesting, a real fun person to be around, that's what I thought at the time. He owns a bicycle shop in my home town and is a real good cyclist, one of the best in Louisiana. This impressed me. He took a spinning class at my gym and that's where I first saw him. I couldn't help but notice the way his bright eyes seemed to rest on me a little longer and brighten a little more as they darted around the class while he told us to push ourselves harder, increase our resistance more and pedal faster. Of course, I could have ignored those brightening eyes and that athletic body as he pushed himself harder, increased his resistance more, and pedalled faster, but I did not, I chose not to. I could have thought about the wife and child someone mentioned he had, and the husband who I had, but hey, it was much more fun not to. I was bored, I was lonely, and my husband was not behaving the way I wanted him to. I checked the notice board at the gym that gives details about the instructors, I noted the address of his cycle shop, and I chose to go there, telling myself all along that I really did need a new bicycle. He was there to serve me, surprised a little at first, as we'd never actually introduced ourselves, but this was quickly rectified and he became the consummate salesperson. I could have taken a good, hard look at what I was doing then, but I chose not to, I was only too happy for him to show so much interest in me, checking the height of the saddle, the angle of the handle bars, the size of the wheels that would most suit my cycling style. It could have ended there, with my leaving the shop with a new bike, but as it so happened the (incredibly expensive) bike that we both decided would be best for me wasn't in stock, he only had one in the shop as a sample. He said he'd get hold of me as soon as his stock was replenished so I gave him my address and phone number, telling him how excited I was at the prospect of having this new bike.

Mitch, ever the helpful and charming salesperson chose to bring the bike round to my house a few days later. He pitched up at my front door one evening, wearing extra tight cycling pants and a very small vest, and he had my new bike in his truck along with his own. He'd also been thoughtful enough to bring me a new pair of cycling pants as a present, 'Because you're such an incredible customer', he said, and he offered to personally come on a ride with me so that I could be extra, extra sure that I wanted the bike before I committed myself. I could have taken a very good look at myself then and asked, hey, what the heck are you doing, but I chose not to, I chose instead to go upstairs, pull on the new cycling shorts, find a little top to go with them, and then run back downstairs to join him. We cycled on the levee near our house, probably just five miles down then five miles back, sometimes going slowly while we discussed the bike, other times going fast as he impressed me with his cycling prowess. We got back home; we were both dripping with sweat, it being July in Louisiana and therefore incredibly hot, I could have said thank you very much and given him a cheque as he drove out of my drive, but instead I suggested we cool off in the swimming pool. I chose to do this. I playfully ran around the house to the pool with him following close behind, I dived into the deep end fully clothed and he came right in after me. I splashed down, covering my head with water and as I came up again he grabbed me and pulled me into his arms.

I cringe every time I think about the way I acted then, and continued to act until his wife found my text message, and I cannot help but wonder what reason Graham would ever have for wanting me back again. I know now that I behaved with the moral integrity of a rat. Life is all about making choices. I had made mine, to my enduring regret, and now it seems that Graham has made his.

*

Sabi and Sarah went to watch some boy by the name of Brad playing cricket at one of the schools in Harare on our last day there. What a godsend it was that Sarah had pitched up as she did, otherwise I think Sabi may have felt incredibly low after the anticlimax of Mr. Masterson first promising to meet her and then deciding against it. As it was, they spent what seemed like ages getting dressed to go to the cricket match and then happily sauntered off, without even a backward glance or wave the minute we dropped them in the school car park. Joanne then took me on a more expansive shopping tour of the city. It turns out she employs people in Bulawayo to make handmade crafts that she sells in Harare. The boot of her car was filled with boxes of these crafts, mainly carved out of wood, and we went to various shops who sell this stuff for her. She told me that most people in Harare have so much more money than anywhere else in the country; she can only really sell her wares there, and it didn't take me long to understand what she meant. Graham has always commented on how, in what he calls "those tin pot African countries" everything is centralised around the capital city, while the rest of the country suffers as a result, and it appears that Zimbabwe is not an exception. Malls, shopping centres, lovely restaurants everywhere, the latest model car on the roads, in many ways it is like being in a different country in Harare to the rest of Zimbabwe. However, underneath all of this there is still the general sense of decay that is so apparent throughout the rest of the country, piles of litter everywhere, roads with raggedy edges, potholes and no markings, traffic lights that don't work, people growing pathetic little patches of maize in what should be designated green belts, weeds and long grass in the green belts that are not being cultivated, it's just a little less obvious in Harare.

Our guesthouse was a different story, though. Beautifully manicured lawns under large Masasa trees, a sparkling swimming pool, wide verandahs furnished luxuriously with deep armchairs, cushion-filled sofas and beautifully carved lamps and sumptuously decorated bedrooms and bathrooms. It was a real treat staying there and all for the same price as it would've cost me to stay at a Super 8 Motel in Atlanta or somewhere like that. However, around the perimeter of our guesthouse, there was the same high brick wall with an electric fence and an electric gate that all the 'haves' in Zimbabwe must erect to keep the 'have nots' out, so that the little haven away from reality can be enjoyed.

*

We arrived back in Bulawayo and went straight to Mrs. Stirling's old house in the Suburbs. Sabi was going to stay there now. She felt very nervous about telling her father about Mr. Norris. On the journey down from Harare she kept saying that her father would not believe her story and would blame her instead for the incident. I didn't dare tell her that Mr. Norris had done just this, but said instead that I'd do most of the talking.

Mrs. Stirling was standing on her front verandah, ready and waiting to welcome us when I parked the vehicle in her parking area.

'Darling,' she said to Sabi, holding out her arms to her as we walked up the steps. 'How was your journey?'

'Fine thanks, Gran.'

We followed her through the house to the side verandah next to the pool, where Digger was still marooned, poor man.

'Hi Dad,' Sabi said, hesitating slightly before she went over to him.

'Sorry that things didn't turn out the way you wanted. I could have told you that that man was a creep, and saved you all the trouble.'

She looked a little taken aback by this comment. 'Well, I did want to see what he was like for myself, but I guess I now know.'

Memory arrived with the tea tray. 'Salibonani,' she said, smiling brightly at Sabi and I.

'Hello Memory,' Sabi answered.

'Pass the shortbread round, will you, dear,' said Mrs. Stirling as she poured the tea.

Once I had my teacup safely in my hands, a piece of shortbread balanced carefully on the china saucer, I took a deep breath and then said, 'There's something Sabi and I need to tell you, Digger.'

'Oh god, now what,' he said with a groan.

Sabi blanched and stared at her feet. 'It's to do with why she disappeared,' I said, and then launched into the story about Mr. Norris. I noticed out of the corner of my eye that Sabi kept her eyes focused on her feet, just glancing at her father every now and again, to see the reaction on his face.

'Yes,' he said finally, 'I had my suspicions. Fucking pervert.'

Sabi looked more intently at her father then, a look of incredulity mixed with relief passing over her face.

'Well it's true,' he continued. 'I've had a lot of time to think about it, sitting here with nothing else to do, and I realised that there is no way in hell that Sabi here would've made a pass at that man. No way in hell. That's why I first became suspicious, that he made such a point of coming here to tell me about her.'

'It's true, Dad, I would never do anything like that.'

She glanced at Mrs. Stirling.

'I wouldn't, Gran, even when he kept teasing me at school; I just tried to pretend it was a joke.'

'Well, I'm going to ask the headmistress to come tomorrow, so I can tell her exactly what happened,' Digger said. 'That man needs to be fucking fired on the spot. I can guarantee Sabi isn't the only one he's been trying to have his way with. Fucking pervert.'

'Digger, dear, language, not in front of Sabi,' appealed Mrs. Stirling.

But Sabi did not mind his language one bit; the relief on her face was palpable. Obviously, a huge weight had been lifted off her shoulders. She got up and bounded across the verandah to Mrs. Stirling, giving her a huge hug.

'And then we need to tell the police,' Digger went on. 'Hopefully they'll string him up by his balls.'

Sabi gasped in astonishment.

'Digger, please,' Mrs Stirling hissed at him. 'It's only a turn of phrase, Sabi dear. Of course the police won't do that.'

A look of relief flooded over Sabi's face again while she said she'd go to her room and unpack. I hadn't seen her behave so jauntily around her father before.

'Well, thank you for taking her to Harare, Clare,' Mrs. Stirling said when she had gone.

'Yeah, that man is a shit, and it didn't surprise me one bit that he didn't bother to pitch,' Digger said. 'It was hard enough trying to speak to him on the phone. He kept cutting me off, slimy son of a bitch that he is, but I did eventually manage to extradite a promise from him. However he showed us he's not as good as his word didn't he? Fucking bastard.'

'Digger, please.' Mrs. Stirling implored yet again.

'Why? It's true. To my dying day I will never understand what Caroline saw in him, because I just cannot find anything. She fucking ruined my life because of that bastard, and never even had the courtesy to tell me why.'

'I can imagine it's hard for you,' I said. 'At least I've been able to tell my husband how regretful I am. Even if he can't forgive me, at least he knows how bad I feel.'

'Heard from him?' Mrs. Stirling asked.

'Nothing.'

'Serves you right,' Digger said with a sly grin, but I knew he was trying to make a joke of it.

*

I went back to Rob and Leannes' house in Hillside where I intended staying overnight, before tackling the massive shopping list Leanne had emailed. Stella and Tenacious had everything perfectly prepared for my arrival, as per usual. Thankfully, the power was on and Stella said she'd take a pork chop out of the freezer for my dinner. Tenacious said he's cut some spinach, butternut and beans from their vegetable garden for me to have with my pork chop. Talk about being looked after.

I poured myself a glass of water and went to sit on the verandah with my computer. I needed to run through Leanne's shopping list again. I'd been using a dongle to connect to the internet on my travels when there was no wi-fi and I plugged it in resignedly now and connected, and not expecting anything more than the shopping list in my inbox, it was almost in a blur that I saw that I had a message from 'Graham Boucher'. It had finally come. My heart skipped a beat as I looked at it for a moment, almost too scared to open it, in case it was an out and out rejection. Finally I did, and my heart soared with relief as I read, 'Arriving in Bulawayo 12.15 on 24th December, South African Airways flight from Johannesburg. I want to spend a few months checking out that country of your birth again, plus the surrounding region, so be ready for lots of travelling.'

That was all he said, but I leant back in my chair and took a huge sip of my water. I clicked the reply button. 'Thank you,' I wrote. 'I can't wait.'

23

Sabi

MY name is Sabi Stirling but recently I've been thinking that it's a shame it's not Sabi Star Starling instead, because then my first name would be a flower and my surname a bird. This would suit me just fine, because I'm very in touch with nature, well much more than any of my friends, at any rate. I think this is probably because I was brought up in the bush, on our mine near Gwanda. At the mine we have many different varieties of birds and these include birds called Glossy Starlings; I often see them in our garden. They are dark, almost black, but when the sun shines on them they're actually not in the least bit black, but in fact a glossy bluish green. When looking at them you realise how amazing it is that things can seem one way and then something happens and suddenly they're different. I've been noticing this a lot recently, and thankfully I'm a really resilient character and have coped well with the way some things have seemingly changed so much. My gran says I've been incredible.

But, thankfully, the end result of all of this is that things have improved significantly in my life. I've decided that it is Gogo who is responsible for a lot of this. I've decided that she has been looking after me from wherever she is, where people go to when they die. She told me once that in the African culture the dead will always take care of the living, and that's why it's so important to respect the dead. Well, I have certainly always respected her; both alive and dead, but now that she is dead I can definitely feel her helping hand in so many ways. For instance, if I hadn't gone to her funeral I would never have met Clare, and it was after that, that things started to turn around, not that I'll ever forget the bad periods I had to go through, too. I mustn't say anything negative about Sherry-Lee any more, as she is dead, and one must not speak ill of the dead (whatever they were like during their lives), but Dad is a changed person since she is no longer around, although I think this may also have something to do with me knowing now what happened with my mother, too. It must've been very hard for him, living with that secret all these years. And now that everyone knows, no one has been in the least bit perturbed by it. Even Tracey seemed intrigued when I told her; I think she may even be a little bit envious, because my background is suddenly so fascinating, whereas hers is rather uninteresting. Her father is just an accountant and her mother just plays bridge.

Not that there is anything wrong with playing bridge, when you get really old like my gran. Another great thing that has happened recently is that Gran has decided to come back and live here in Zimbabwe again, she'll just spend a few months of the year in her flat in England. She told me that one of the things that made her decide on this is bridge, all the old ducks that she used to play bridge with a few years ago are still desperate to play with her and the phone never stops ringing with them planning 'bridge fours' all the time. She had a 'bridge four' round at the house the other day. They ate a lot of cake and cucumber sandwiches, and drank a lot of tea, and then when they'd finished playing they all drank gin.

*

Leanne phoned to ask us if we wanted to go to the lodge at Ubejane for the holiday season. We hadn't made any other arrangements, so after first discussing how Dad would cope with this, we said yes. Leanne said they'd make his bedroom in a corner of the lounge area so he wouldn't have a problem getting about. She said she'd invited the Langdons, too, and I was very excited to hear this, even though it would mean having Sarah's rather boring twin brothers around also. They are ten years old and spend their whole time batting and bowling to each other; it's like they have no interest in anything other than cricket. Leanne apologised for the invitation being so last minute, but she said she only decided to have a big Christmas gathering when Clare's husband suddenly said he'd be coming to Zimbabwe for Christmas. This was just as much of a surprise to me, because Clare did not say a word about her husband visiting when we were in Harare. Leanne told Gran she wanted to show him a good old Zimbabwean time.

When we arrived at the lodge, Gran driving our Land Cruiser station wagon, with me in the front passenger seat and Dad on the back seat with his leg up, I discovered that Leanne had also invited Vanessa and Martin and their horrors. My heart sank when I saw their car, as I'm still very embarrassed that Mr. Norris is Vanessa's brother. But then I realised that she must've been feeling just as embarrassed, because she came rushing up to me, even before I'd got out of our car properly, and hugged me and apologised so many times you'd have thought it was her who'd tried to get into my bed instead of her brother. I told her that it was all 'water under the bridge', a phrase that Gran has used a lot recently.

Clare and her husband were there to welcome us, too, when we got there, even though they had just arrived from Bulawayo themselves, Clare having picked her husband up from the airport. They helped us move Dad from the car to his specially-made quarters in the lounge area, which wasn't exactly easy, what with his cast coming half way up his thigh and all. I was shy to meet Clare's husband, but he quickly made me feel like we'd known each other our whole lives. He's a really cool person, tall and good-looking even though he's getting a bit old now. Vanessa's horrors were nowhere about when we first arrived; I'd expected them to come rushing up to me and continue with their bugging ways, but then I discovered them on the front lawn, trying their best to get in the way of Sarah's brothers' cricket practice. They hardly even noticed me as I went down the path to my old bedroom.

Sarah was sharing the room with me again. She was lying on the bed flicking through one of the magazines my gran had brought last time.

'Hey,' she said when I walked in to the room. 'I didn't even hear you arrive.'

'We just got here now. Clare and her husband are helping Dad hobble to his place and Gran has gone off to her bedroom.'

'We got here before lunch. Jeez, those little girls are a pain; I see exactly what you mean. The one with the broken arm fussed the whole way through lunch because all she wanted to do was swim and her mother said she could not and so she carried on performing until the maid took her away.'

'Well, they've latched onto your brothers now. They're trying to play cricket with them.'

Sarah laughed.

'Brilliant, that should keep them all well occupied. Hey, I wonder if there is any chance of us going down to the house later, I want to text Brad.'

I hesitated.

'Maybe, I'm not sure actually.'

'Since I saw you the other day we've started going out by the way,' she said as nonchalantly as possible.

'Sarah, no!' I gasped. 'When?'

'He came round to my house two days ago, when I was alone there,' she said. I wondered for a moment if this meant they'd done 'it' and if that's what had changed their status. As if reading my mind she quickly said, 'hey, of course it's not like that you know. I'm not like Tracey.'

'Probably for the best though, hey.'

'Ja.'

'What a shame Leanne couldn't ask him too.'

'Well he's gone on a houseboat trip on Kariba for Christmas. His uncle is here from Australia.'

'So, how would you text him then, if he's in the middle of the lake.'

'He said there's a signal at various places when they come in to moor, so if I text he gets them when they come in.'

'I guess.'

I was a little disappointed to hear this. The last thing I wanted was to have to keep finding someone to take us down the hill to Leanne's house so that Sarah could keep sending text messages to Brad, on the off-chance that his house boat was moored fairly close to one of the few (I'm guessing) cellphone towers dotted over the vast area that Lake Kariba takes up. I decided then and there that this business of being in love is all rather tedious and I'd put it off for as long as possible.

*

As it turned out, we didn't go down to Leanne's house much to text Brad. We were way too busy at the lodge. Firstly, Clare asked us to help Lovemore out in the kitchen. She said that with so many people staying he'd need all the help he could get, and she said Leanne had offered to pay us for our work. Sarah isn't as good a cook as I am, but she still enjoys it, so every morning we'd spend a few hours in the kitchen making cakes and puddings for the day. It was fun thinking of different things to make every day and we even tried a few experiments. We also most often helped Lovemore with the salads for lunch, and then we'd go off to the pool to work on our tans. Of course, this isn't too difficult for me, but I still like having tan marks on my tummy.

Gran decided that we all needed to learn how to play bridge, everyone fifteen years or older, that is, so at least the horrors, the boring twins and Leanne's two kids were excluded. She said you mustn't wait until you are old to learn the game otherwise you'd be dead before you'd learnt all the 'intricacies' as she put it, she said you had to learn to play when you were young so that you had something to do when you were old. So every evening after dinner she'd set up two tables of four, and she'd move between the two tables, teaching us about trumps, and the value of each suit, and how to make a call. At first it was all just gibberish, but after the first night we started to understand a little and it was actually quite fun. I was glad Tracey wasn't with us, though; she would've hated it, I'm sure. Graham was definitely the best student; he picked up the game so quickly Sarah and I wondered if he'd played it before and was just pretending he hadn't. He promised he'd never played before, so we decided he must just be very clever then. In fact, he's funny, as well as clever, he was always making Sarah and me laugh with all the funny stories he kept telling us.

*

The Langdons were planning on going to the Victoria Falls to celebrate the New Year and they invited me to join them. Sarah says it's the coolest place to go for New Year, with half the population of Zimbabwe and neighbouring countries being there; well mainly the white populations that is. (I do realise now that it doesn't matter if I'm actually not white afterall.) The Langdons asked Clare and Graham if they wanted to come, but they said they'd prefer to have a quiet New Year at the lodge on their own, as they had a lot of catching up to do.

We got back to Bulawayo from the lodge just a day before I was due to set off for the Victoria Falls. Gran said it was a shame I was going away as she was going to organise another 'bridge four' at her house for New Year's Eve and she could have done with my help in the kitchen. I was actually very pleased that I would be away.

There was a letter waiting for me on the hall table when we got back. I was surprised when I saw it as I never get letters. I took it into the lounge to read; and sat down abruptly on the sofa when I glanced at the bottom of the first page and saw the name 'Dennis Masterson' written there. Jeez, what a shock this gave me. It was a handwritten letter, spidery, untidy-looking writing which was very hard to read so it took me a while to get through it.

'Dear Sabi,' I read.

'I am sorry I did not come to meet you when you came up to Harare. I did not want to upset my wife and family by bringing up something that happened a long time ago and that I have tried ever since to forget. Please do not think of me as your father, I have enclosed a letter from your mother, sent to me just before you were born. You will see that she would not have wanted this.

You are very lucky to have a man like Digger Stirling as your father. He is a good man.

With Regards

Denis Masterson.'

Gran was hovering, so I gave it to her to read. She walked to the window where she stood, fiddling with her glasses while I took out the second letter in the envelope. This time the writing was smooth flowing and easy to read, and I realised as I glanced at the bottom of the page that this was the first time I'd ever seen my mother's handwriting. I noticed that it was dated 1st November

1997, just a week before I was born, although she wouldn't have known that, as I was early, remember.

'My Dearest Dennis,' I read this time.

'I'm not sure where to begin but I know I must write now before the baby arrives. I have had plenty of solitude recently to think things through, and I have been back and forth with myself on how to tell you what I want, without causing more hurt. The feelings that have pervaded my consciousness in these last weeks are horror, distress, dismay, panic, appall, and guilt at what we have done and I take full responsibility for my part in what has happened between us, as well as for the incredible guilt I will now always carry. Digger is a very good man and should never have been treated with so little respect by me and I'm sure the same can be said for your wife. I know now that all I really want is to have his baby and to get on with the rest of my life and try and put behind me forever what happened between us. I never, ever want Digger to find out about what we did, because I know it would destroy a significant part of him and I would hate to be responsible for this. So please can this be the last time we ever communicate.

As I began, I'm now not sure how to end a letter like this, so I will simply say,

Wishing you all of the best always,

Caroline.'

I stared at it and blinked. Gran came over to the sofa and sat down. She fumbled with her glasses again while I handed her the letter, not knowing what to think of any of it. She read it very slowly and then she leant back into the sofa as she covered my brown, tanned hand with her soft, white one, sighing deeply.

'You know what Sabi,' she said. 'It will help your father so much when he reads this letter.'

'Really, why?' I asked.

'Because it will show him how sorry she was for what she did. He never knew this before and it's been hard for him thinking she didn't care.'

'Didn't she ever tell him?'

'No, I'm afraid she died before she had a chance to do this. But at least he'll know now that she meant to do the right things by him.'

I leaned back against Gran's soft arm as I thought about this. Jeepers, I decided, people can make their lives so complicated, especially when it comes to relationships between girls and boys. It is definitely much easier to stay unattached.

Just then I heard my cellphone go ba-beep, from where I'd left it on the hall table. Of course I wanted to go immediately and see who my text was from. Imagine my amazement when I saw Mike's name on the screen.

'Howzit Sabi,' I read. 'We r at the Falls. R u coming up?'

I stared at it for a good minute, re reading it before I answered.

'Yup, tomorrow.' I wrote.

'Cool. Text when u get here and we can hang out.'

Now that really confused me. What about Tracey? I rushed to my gran's study and switched on her computer. I opened Mike's Facebook page and looked at his status.

'Single,' I read.

I then clicked on to Tracey's Facebook page.

'Single,' I read again.

I looked at my watch. I needed to speak to Sarah. She'd be able to find out all the details, if she didn't know them already, but she was at the hairdresser having her hair trimmed.

Oh well, I thought, what the heck? I picked up my phone again.

'Sure,' I replied to Mike's text.

GLOSSARY

Abantu – people

Dube - zebra

Gogo - grandmother

Hamba Kahle - go carefully (often used in relation to a person who has died)

Intombi - young girl of marriageable age.

Nyathi - buffalo

Ndebele – refers to the language spoken by the people of Matabeleland in Zimbabwe (isiNdebele) or the actual people (amaNdebele)

Ngwenya – crocodile

Nyoka - snake

Sakubona – hello (when talking to one person)

Salibonani – hello (when talking to more than one person)

Ubejane – rhino

Umntanamu – my child.

Yebo – yes

Afs – a slang word for black Africans

Braai – barbeque

Chuffed - pleased

Coloured – the word used to describe someone of mixed race

Dwala –a big hill formed mainly from a large rock, or rocks.

Goffel – a derogatory word referring to a person of mixed race

Guti- damp, cold weather

Kopjies - smaller hills

Lapa – a thatched gazebo

Lowveld – refers to the lower, hotter areas of Zimbabwe

Mealies – maize

Munt – a derogatory word referring to a black person (derived from the Ndebele word Umuntu)

Penny cool – a small plastic sleeve containing sugary drink

Tackies- trainers or tennis shoes

Sadza- a thick porridge made from ground maize

These concepts didn't exist in Darwin's theory. It is correct to say that Darwin's ideas imply competition, but our current understanding of evolution does not imply a "battle royale" of everyone against everyone else. That's true for most living species, and in particular, humans are selected mostly for their capability to get along well with their fellow humans, providing help and being helped when they need it.

Unfortunately, the idea of evolution as a bloody affair, "nature red in tooth and claw," as Tennyson said, soon spilled over to speculations about whether some human races were "fitter" than others. Typically, that led to a pseudo-scientific hierarchy that saw Whites, or "Aryans," being at the top, with the "Darker Races" at the bottom, just a little above monkeys and apes. Of course, Darwin never said anything like that, and, besides, the idea of the inferiority of non-European races was characteristic of European colonial expansion well before Darwin. Nevertheless, this misinterpretation of Darwin's ideas provided a further justification for the colonial practices of slavery and segregation.

These concepts gradually percolated into the human sphere of beliefs, and by the late 19th and early 20th centuries, they led to the development of a set of ideas that went under the name of "Social Darwinism." In a crooked sequence of logic, some people understood that their survival in the fight for existence implied that they should enslave or exterminate other humans, preferably those who didn't belong to their ethnic and linguistic group. Social Darwinism was the first step toward the development and implementation of "eugenics" ("good generation"). The idea was to improve the genetic composition of human beings by selective breeding. In particular, the idea was to remove those components of humankind that were regarded as inferior.

The eugenics movement was influenced by the works of Francis Galton (1822-1911), a cousin of Charles Darwin. He hadn't really understood his cousin's theories, but he used his partial

understanding to coin the term eugenics in 1883. His ideas were further popularized by figures like Charles Davenport (1866-1944), who established the Eugenics Record Office in the United States in 1910. This organization collected data on family histories to identify hereditary traits and advocated for policies such as sterilization and immigration restrictions to prevent the spread of "undesirable" genes. Another proponent of social Darwinism was William Graham Sumner (1840 – 1910), a sociologist at Yale. He argued that social hierarchies were natural and that attempts to improve the conditions of the lower classes were futile. Benjamin K. Hays (1887-1918) attempted to use a form of Social Darwinism to rank human races, suggesting that some were more evolved than others.

These ideas were popular in the United States even before Darwin proposed his theory, but they went by different names. A typical one was the concept of "Manifest Destiny," which stated that the expansion of the Whites across the continent was inevitable and divinely ordained. This belief was combined with a sense of cultural and racial superiority among white settlers. It was used to justify the displacement and the extermination of the Native Americans of the continent.

In the United States, these beliefs went in parallel with anti-miscegenation laws that prohibited interracial marriage. These laws were in place for over three centuries, dating back to the colonial period. The first case of a law forbidding mixed-race marriages was enacted in Maryland in 1661, and Virginia followed suit soon after. By the time of the Civil War, many states had such laws that continued to proliferate in the late 19th and early 20th centuries. The motivations behind these laws varied but were deeply rooted in maintaining a racial hierarchy and upholding white supremacy. Some argued that interracial marriage was against the "laws of nature" or that it would lead to social and moral degradation. The laws often extended beyond black-white unions to include other racial groups, such as Native Americans, Chinese, and Japanese.

Stronger eugenic measures began to be practiced in the US around the beginning of the 20th century. Psychologists and researchers were involved in efforts such as the Committee to Study and Report on the Best Practical Means of Cutting Off the Defective Germ-Plasm in the American Population. In 1914, the committee recommended segregation and sterilization to preserve the blood of the American people.

The first eugenic sterilization law in the US was enacted in Indiana in 1907. It allowed for the sterilization of individuals deemed unfit to reproduce, such as criminals, the mentally disabled, and others confined to state institutions. Following Indiana's lead, other states began to pass similar laws. By 1927, 24 states had implemented eugenic sterilization laws, which targeted people with mental illnesses, disabilities, and those considered feeble-minded. The Supreme Court upheld the constitutionality of these laws in the case of Buck v. Bell in 1927, with Justice Oliver Wendell Holmes famously stating, "Three generations of imbeciles are enough." Eugenics became a rationale for sterilization laws, immigration restrictions, and other policies aimed at "improving the human stock," often targeting marginalized groups. By 1930, over 35,000 individuals were forcibly sterilized under eugenics laws. The number reached 60,000 in the 1970s.

Gradually, these ideas lost momentum. The last people to be condemned on the basis of anti-miscegenation laws in the United States were Richard and Mildred Loving. In 1958, Richard Loving, a white man, and Mildred Jeter, a woman of mixed African American and Native American ancestry, were married in Washington, D.C., to avoid Virginia's anti-miscegenation laws. Upon returning to Virginia, they were arrested and charged with violating the state's Racial Integrity Act of 1924. The Lovings were convicted in January 1959 and sentenced to one year in prison, with the sentence suspended on the condition that they leave Virginia and not return together for 25 years. They moved to Washington, D.C., but later sought to have their

convictions and sentences vacated, arguing that the law was unconstitutional. Their case eventually reached the U.S. Supreme Court, which in 1967 unanimously ruled that anti-miscegenation laws were unconstitutional under the Equal Protection and Due Process Clauses of the Fourteenth Amendment. The Supreme Court's decision in Loving v. Virginia effectively ended all race-based legal restrictions on marriage in the United States.

About eugenics, in 1942, the Supreme Court ruled that the involuntary sterilization of certain inmates violated the equal protection clause of the 14th Amendment. However, this ruling did not affect those living in state-run mental health facilities. In the 1960s and 1970s, the civil rights movement and increased awareness of human rights led to growing opposition to eugenic sterilization laws. Public opinion shifted, and many states began to repeal or stop enforcing these laws. In 1974, Virginia repealed its Sterilization Act, and other states followed suit. In the 1990s and 2000s, several states formally apologized for their role in eugenic sterilization programs and provided compensation to victims.

Other countries besides the US got involved in social Darwinism and eugenic policies. Some provinces in Canada, such as Alberta and British Columbia, enacted eugenic sterilization laws, leading to the forced sterilization of thousands of individuals. In Europe, countries like Sweden, Norway, Denmark, and Finland implemented eugenic policies that included forced sterilization. In Sweden, for example, over 60,000 people were sterilized between 1935 and 1975. The UK had a strong eugenic movement, with influential figures and organizations promoting the idea of selective breeding to "improve" the population. While forced sterilization was not as widespread as in some other countries, there were significant efforts to discourage reproduction among those deemed unfit. Switzerland, too, implemented eugenic policies, including forced sterilization, targeting individuals with mental illnesses and disabilities.

The Soviet Union had some peculiarities in this area. The originators of Communism, Karl Marx and Frederick Engels, were enthusiastic followers of Darwin's ideas, and they saw parallels between the theory of evolution and their theory of historical materialism. Both saw class struggle as an embodiment of natural selection within society, and Marx saw Darwin's work as providing a naturalistic basis for understanding social change. However, both Marx and Engels wrote scathingly about "bourgeois Darwinians" who tried to justify social inequalities using Darwinian concepts. Engels argued that human society is shaped by social and economic factors, not just biological ones. In the Soviet Union, these ideas led to the prospect of creating a "New Soviet Man," partly based on eugenics but more focused on ideological and social conditioning rather than biological selection. But this idea never took hold in practice, and it doesn't appear that the Soviet Union ever applied eugenic policies in its history.

It was in the Fascist countries during the 20th century, Italy and Germany, that eugenics was most popular. Italy was more moderate. Italian eugenicists, influenced by Catholic teachings, focused on positive eugenics, which emphasized better prenatal care, education, and social welfare rather than coercive measures, so forced sterilization was never enacted in Italy. Nevertheless, the Italian fascists adopted racism as an official truth, and they acted according to the idea that Italians were no less Aryan than their German neighbors. Hence, the state forbade marriage with certain foreigners, including Jews, even though they were Italian citizens. Nevertheless, Italy never implemented the extermination measures that Germany carried out against the Jews and other ethnic groups. Still, the Italian government collaborated with the German government by sending Italian Jews to German extermination camps.

The Fascist attitude also implied that Italians had the right and the duty to dominate the dark races. The concept of a *Posto al Sole* (a place in the sun) in Africa was the exact equivalent of the German

Lebensraum (vital space) in Europe. This idea led to the invasion of Ethiopia in 1935, justified by the racial superiority of Italians over those dark people who happened to occupy a land that, for some unexplained reasons, really belonged to Italy. The Italian conquest of Ethiopia involved the extermination of a large number of Ethiopians, but, at least, their complete eradication didn't seem to have ever been planned, at least for the short period (five years) in which Ethiopia was a colony of Italy.

Nazi Germany, of course, was the country of eugenics. With World War I, the Germans were not only defeated on the battlefield but also starved by the Allies in a deliberately murderous food embargo that continued well after the end of the war. Shocked, impoverished, and humiliated, the Germans reacted the way human societies do when they are under heavy stress. They looked for a scapegoat, and they found it in the *Untermenschen*, the "inferior humans." They were supposed to be mainly non-German groups in Germany and the neighboring regions, but also German citizens who suffered from disabilities or who belonged to different ethnic groups, primarily the Jews.

The Nazi government implemented some of the most extreme eugenic policies in history, including the "Law for the Prevention of Genetically Diseased Offspring," enacted in 1933. It led to the forced sterilization of hundreds of thousands of people. The Nazi regime also used eugenic principles to justify the Holocaust, the systematic extermination of millions of Jews, Romani people, disabled individuals, and others deemed inferior and a threat to the state. Even ethnic Germans were targeted. Many of them were not only sterilized but physically eliminated because the very fact of being alive made them a burden to the state.

During the same period, Japan may not have been classified as a truly "Fascist" country, but its government had several characteristics in common with the Italian and German governments. In Japan, eugenics was connected with the diffuse perception of

"racial purity." Nevertheless, the state intervened in the matter only after the end of World War II with the Eugenic Protection Law (EPL), in force from 1948 to 1996. It aimed to "prevent the birth of inferior descendants from the eugenic point of view and to protect the life and health of the mother." The law permitted the forced sterilization of individuals with intellectual or mental disabilities and those with certain hereditary diseases. Over 25,000 people were sterilized under this law, with around 16,500 of them not consenting to the procedure. In July 2024, Japan's Supreme Court ruled that the Eugenic Protection Law was unconstitutional and ordered the government to compensate the victims.

The misuse of Darwin's ideas was a tragedy of modern times, a result of the socio-political context in which his ideas were interpreted. In some quarters, it led to the demonization of the very concept of evolution by natural selection, and of Darwin himself, who never would have wanted to have anything to do with this distortion of his ideas. For the time being, fortunately, the ideas that were fashionable one century ago seem to have been abandoned, but you never know what the future can bring.

Contraception and Birth Control

In the Book of Genesis of the Bible, we can read the fascinating story of the young widow Tamar, who claimed her rights against all odds and succeeded in obtaining justice for herself and for her children. The story involves the actions of Onan, Tamar's second husband, who "spilled his seed on the ground" to avoid impregnating his wife. Today, we call that "Onanism", but that is more correctly described as *coitus interruptus*. It is one of the first mentions of contraception in history.

It would be long to explain why Onan did what he did, and why God then punished him with death. For what we are interested here, the story tells us that when Genesis was written, possibly as early as the 10th century BCE, people knew perfectly well that pregnancy was the result of full intercourse between a man and a woman, and that it could be avoided by refraining from performing or completing the act. Even earlier references to similar contraception methods can be read in some Egyptian papyri.

So, contraception is an old idea, but how old, exactly? Did it exist before written records? Were our hominin ancestors practicing it millions of years ago? We can be reasonably sure that most non-human creatures cannot link events spaced months apart and, probably, our remote ancestors couldn't do that, either. But, at some point in history, one of them must have experienced a "ha-ha!" moment: *that's* how children are born!

We can't know when that happened, but surely it was long ago. You can sometimes read that Australian Indigenous peoples did not connect pregnancy to sexual intercourse. It is a legend; a misunderstanding derived from some 19th-century reports. It is true, however, that some aboriginal groups interpreted human reproduction in terms of the combined effects of human sexual activity and spiritual or totemic forces. But that's nothing special. The concept that a God, or several Gods, intervene in causing the birth of a child is, after all, a common myth in many religions, including the Christian one.

Whenever the connection of sex to pregnancy may have been discovered, it opened up the possibility of conscious control of birth rates, and hence of population. Of course, the contraceptive methods available in ancient times were limited and sometimes dangerous. Abstinence was surely the most effective, but it was never popular. But a series of rules and social customs were often sufficient to keep boys and girls of reproductive age from having a chance to frolic together. One way was to forbid sex before marriage. A case in point

is how Ireland managed to slash the country's fertility rate after the Great Famine of 1846 by developing social customs that encouraged late marriage.

In addition, there were several "soft" contraceptive tricks. Onan's coitus interruptus had the advantage that it required no special equipment. Another soft option was to refrain from sex only during a woman's ovulation period. This method is known today as the Ogino-Knaus method, from the names of its modern developers, Kyusaku Ogino (Japan) and Hermann Knaus (Austria). The problem with the Ogino-Knaus method is that human females do not provide signals to males that they are ovulating; a characteristic called "concealed ovulation." It is a reproductive trait that humans share with a few other species: dolphins, mice, and some birds. Bonobo females also partly conceal their ovulation. For the species that show this trait, sex is not just a feature of the reproductive mechanism, but a cultural and social behavior. As such, it can be used as a social communication tool. Bonobo females, for instance, use sex during their non-fertile period as a tool to control males. Human females can play the same game, but they can't easily detect their fertile period, even though they may have hints from various body signals that males cannot perceive. It means that the Ogino-Knaus method is not very reliable as a contraceptive method.

When soft methods failed, individual women and families had the option of abortion and infanticide. Both have a long history. In ancient times, abortion was very dangerous for the mother, and it seems that it was rarely practiced as a contraceptive method. Infanticide, instead, may have been more common. In some versions, it had an especially perverse ring, such as when, in Ancient Greece, weak or deformed newborns in Sparta were exposed on hillsides like Mount Taygetus. Another perverse form of infanticide was, and remains, the selective killing of baby girls. It is reported to be done to create a surplus of young males who have little chance of finding a mate except by killing the competition in war. In modern times,

selective abortion or the killing of newborn females is reported to have become a problem in several regions of the world, when prenatal echography allows the early detection of the sex of a fetus.

A 2019 study[70] estimated 23 million "missing women" globally due to sex-selective practices, mainly abortion. Of these, China and India account for approximately 10 million each. In absolute terms, these are large numbers, but compared to the world's total population of 8 billion people, they represent less than a 0.3% difference. In evaluating these data, you also have to take into account that the natural ratio of females to males at birth is roughly 105 males to 100 females. It may be an evolutionary factor generated by the fact that males have a higher mortality rate than females. Not taking this factor into account leads to some exaggerated estimates, such as some newspaper articles that reported 63 million missing women in India, alone. [71] It is a number that simply makes no sense. Note also that the female/male ratio tends to decrease with time due to the longer lifespan of women. Hence, many countries have an excess of females in their population. For instance, Italy's population had a ratio of 95 males per 100 females in 2021. Nevertheless, Italy has a natural ratio of 105 males to 100 females at birth.

In extreme cases, society could react to a perceived unsustainable population excess by killing adults. We have evidence that killing the elderly was commonly practiced in the past and also in some contemporary societies. It even has a specific name among anthropologists: "gerontocide" or "senicide." The elderly were a favorite target for sacrificial rituals, and the usage may have been one of the factors that led to the legends about witches, often described as gaunt elderly women. Witches and witch hunts are characteristic of agricultural societies, and they still exist today and are practiced during famines. [72]

In our times, senicide is correctly seen as an abomination, but it may be closer to our world than we may imagine. During World War II, it was practiced in Germany when the government distributed

cyanide pills to the elderly in order to press them to commit suicide to leave food available for those who could fight (I describe this practice in my book *Exterminations,* 2024). In some cases, societies may also target adults in their prime, and in this case, these killings have the aspect of ritual human sacrifices. Several wars, including modern ones, can be understood as "delayed infanticides," where large numbers of young men were directed to kill each other and cease to be a burden for society.

All these methods are unreliable, sometimes violent, and often traumatic. Modern contraceptive techniques are a much better option, and their development goes back centuries. Condoms are reported to have started being used during the 16th century, made with sheep intestines. In the 19th century, they started being made using natural rubber. In the 20th century, synthetic rubber was used, greatly reducing prices and making condoms one of the most common contraceptive devices in the world, with the added advantage that it provided a certain degree of protection against venereal diseases.

Intrauterine devices (IUDs) emerged in primitive forms also in the 19th century, and then they became much more effective and sophisticated during the 20th century. In 1960, the FDA approved the first oral contraceptive pill, Enovid, developed by Gregory Pincus, John Rock, and others. It combined estrogen and progestin to prevent ovulation, revolutionizing family planning. At present, many variants of contraceptive methods are available. Long-acting reversible contraceptives (LARCs), implants (e.g., Nexplanon), and improved IUDs have become popular for their convenience and efficacy. These methods provide reliable and effective ways to avoid undesired pregnancies.

Voluntary male and female sterilization appeared at the beginning of the 20th century but became relatively common in the mid-20th century. Data from the National Survey of Family Growth indicates that by the late 1970s, about 25-30% of contracepting women in the U.S. relied on female sterilization, while vasectomy accounted

for roughly 10-15% of males' contraception. Globally, sterilization gained traction in countries like India and China, though often with government incentives that blurred the distance between voluntary and coerced.

Are contraceptive technologies part of the problem of the rapid fertility decline in some countries? It is possible, but, as always, it is difficult to analyze the behavior of complex systems when more than one factor acts to push the system in the same direction. Contraceptives make family planning easy, but, paraphrasing a well-known NRA slogan, "contraceptives don't prevent pregnancies, people prevent pregnancies." People who really don't want children can always find alternatives to rubber things, pills, and the like.

Nevertheless, contraceptives remain part of an ongoing cultural debate. Public sentiment toward contraception in 2025 varies globally. In some religions, contraceptives are seen as things that go against the will of God and hence are forbidden. Catholicism opposes contraception, but U.S. Catholic women often use it. Most Protestant groups support contraception, though some evangelicals debate its morality. Islamic scholars permit contraception within marriage, although there remain cultural stigmas in conservative areas (e.g., Pakistan). Hinduism and Buddhism have a generally permissive attitude. Traditional societies (e.g., rural Africa) may resist the concept of contraception due to beliefs in large families or spiritual concerns, or because they see it as disrupting fertility traditions.

In general, the question of contraception is strictly linked to the perception of population trends. When rulers needed a large number of young men to be used as cannon fodder (or pike fodder, or the like), contraception was abhorred and often forbidden by law. With the decline of the role of infantry in war, that ceased to be a priority, so that contraception became commonplace, not sanctioned, and even encouraged. With the current fertility decline, it may be possible that governments will backtrack and return to viewing contraception in a bad light, even forbidding it.

As always, the future is a labyrinth of bifurcating paths. We'll have to see where the many possibilities we have to control births at the individual level will lead us.

The Great Overpopulation Scare

Throughout history, overpopulation was a problem that ordinary people could perceive mainly from their empty stomachs. As a consequence, they would sometimes take the matter of reproduction into their own hands and quietly avoid providing rulers with the cannon fodder they required. That is, they would limit the size of their families by using whatever contraceptive methods were available.

For the rulers, instead, the idea that the commoners could decide by themselves whether to have children or not was anathema. The concept was considered both absurd and subversive. For them, there was a more straightforward way to solve the overpopulation problem: enlist the excess in the infantry and send them charging artillery and machine guns.

To see the concept of "overpopulation" appear as a societal problem, we have to wait for recent times. By the mid-20th century, data became available for the total world population. It was growing at a rate that seemed to be exponential. Many people saw the Malthusian tragedy in front of them: famines, wars, and new rounds of ethnic exterminations. It was a remarkable moment in human history; never before had the idea that there were too many people on Earth been a common worry and a subject of debate.

The overpopulation scare appeared as a typical dystopian theme of science fiction starting from the 1950s, reflecting the societal anxieties of the time. The stories tended to portray overpopulation through urban settings: endless city blocks and people packed into

tiny living spaces. One of the first novels of this kind that reached the general public was Harry Harrison's *Make Room! Make Room!* (1966). It was later adapted into the film *Soylent Green* (1973), which depicted a dystopian 1999 New York City with 35 million inhabitants living in squalid conditions. There followed novels such as William F. Nolan and George Clayton Johnson's *Logan's Run* (1967), which explored the theme of a society that obtained population control by eliminating people as soon as they reached 21 years of age. In 1968, John Brunner published his novel *Stand on Zanzibar*, with the title being based on the idea that the whole population of the time could fit standing shoulder-to-shoulder on the island of Zanzibar. Perhaps the most impressive story of this period was Robert Silverberg's *The World Inside* (1972), which depicted a dystopian world where people had given up all their rights except one: that of having sex and reproducing at will. Billions and billions of people lived in densely populated, gigantic skyscrapers, where all dissent was punished with immediate death, but where sex was completely free for everyone as desired.

Overpopulation fiction was merely a reflection of a theme that was also explored in scientific terms by individual researchers and research institutions. In the 1950s, the Rockefeller Foundation funded research on population growth and its implications. John D. Rockefeller III was a prominent advocate for population control. In 1952, he stated: "Population growth is the most serious problem facing mankind today." In the 1960s, the United Nations began to address population growth as a global issue. A 1963 UN report[73] stated: "The rapid growth of the world population is one of the most serious problems facing humanity, with profound implications for economic development, resource use, and environmental sustainability."

Among individual researchers, William Vogt's 1948 book *Road to Survival* was one of the first works to explore the modern concept of population growth and the probable outstripping of the available resources. He wrote that "we are already far beyond the Earth's carrying capacity." And "The day of reckoning is close at hand. The

human race is caught in a dilemma of its own making." His ideas remained influential in the 1950s and 1960s as fears of resource depletion grew.

Fairfield Osborn's 1953 book *The Limits of the Earth* argued that population growth would lead to environmental degradation and resource scarcity. In 1954, Hugh Moore published a pamphlet titled *The Population Bomb*, which later inspired Paul Ehrlich's more famous 1968 book with the same title. Ehrlich predicted widespread famines in the 1970s and 1980s. He wrote, "The battle to feed all of humanity is over... hundreds of millions of people will starve to death." Isaac Asimov, the well-known science fiction and science popularization author, wrote several essays on overpopulation. In 1988, in an interview with Bill Moyers, he said, "Democracy cannot survive overpopulation. Human dignity cannot survive it. Convenience and decency cannot survive it. As you put more and more people into the world, the value of life not only declines, but it disappears." Eventually, all the worries of this period could be seen as a revival of Malthus' ideas, and the proponents were sometimes described as "neo-Malthusians." But this modern version was based on a concept that Malthus didn't consider and that, probably, he couldn't even conceive: overexploitation, or, with the same meaning, "overshoot."

The idea of overexploitation is a cornerstone of biological population models. It implies that a population grows proportionally to its current size and, at the same time, to the amount of available resources. At some point, the population size may exceed the capability of the resource stock to replenish itself. At this point, the stock starts dwindling; nevertheless, the population growth can continue for a while, entering the condition called "overshoot." Eventually, the resource stock becomes unable to sustain the growing population, and the result is collapse.

The concept was implicitly expressed in the biological models independently developed in the 1920s by Alfred Lotka and Vito Volterra, sometimes defined as the "Rabbits and Foxes" model.

Imagine an island inhabited only by foxes and rabbits. The fox population tends to grow in proportion to their food source, the rabbit population. Unfortunately for the foxes (and also for the rabbits), the number of foxes tends to become large. The result is that they will kill off nearly all the rabbits. At that point, the foxes will be in full overshoot. Having destroyed their food source, they will necessarily starve and die. The Lotka-Volterra model assumes that with the foxes nearly gone, the few surviving rabbits will be free to reproduce and the cycle will restart. In actual ecosystems, a population crash may lead to extinction. Human beings are not immune to this destiny, as discussed in William Catton's book, *Overshoot* (1982)

Probably, the most influential and most discussed population study in this period was *The Limits to Growth*, published in 1972 and created by a group of MIT scientists. It was the first to attempt a quantitative evaluation of the world's economic system, taking into account an ensemble of parameters that included population. The study sketched various possible methods to stave off the economic collapse envisioned for the first decades of the 21st century, keeping the system at a moderate level of activity that was presumed to be possible to maintain for at least the whole 21st century and probably much longer, while avoiding a population collapse. You can find more details on the study in the appendix of this book.

Of these proposals, those that involved putting a cap on economic growth and consumption were rejected almost immediately by politicians and economists. The standard view in economics was (and remains today) that economic growth is always good and always to be pursued. Doing otherwise looked heretical, strange, and unspeakable. No politician could ever be elected by promising people to reduce their consumption, and hence their wealth. The idea fell flat, even though a small group of heretics supported (and still support) consciously choosing "degrowth" as a way to manage the economy.

Conversely, the idea of acting on the population by birth control looked easier and more palatable. It seemed logical that fewer

people would mean more resources per person, and that would make voters happy. At the same time, it would reduce the strain on depleting resources. Hence, economic growth could be maintained, at least in terms of GDP per person. Unfortunately, this idea didn't agree with the results of the Limits to Growth study. The model could be used to calculate the future of the economy for a situation in which the global population was kept constant at the 1972 levels. The result was not encouraging. If population control was coupled with policies aimed at reducing consumption, then the economic system could be stabilized. But if population was the only parameter that was kept stable, the model showed that collapse would occur anyway. True, the consumption per capita would increase to much higher levels than in the run without population control. Still, the strain on resources and the pollution problem would scarcely change, and collapse would occur anyway. The difference was that people would be much richer at the start of the collapse, but just as poor once they reached the bottom.

Nevertheless, the idea of solving complex problems with simple solutions is always attractive to decision-makers and the public alike. So, starting in the 1950s, the idea that population control was a magic pill to cure civilization's ills started being discussed and proposed by several pressure groups and associations. In most cases, the concept of "population control" was carefully framed in terms of "birth control," supposed to be painless, non-violent, and a choice, not an obligation. Considerable efforts were spent to distance these efforts from the earlier abominable methods used by the German Nazis. In time, the term "birth control" was almost universally replaced with the less threatening one of "family planning."

Initially the campaign for birth control/family planning affected countries that had high population density and a recent history of famines. In 1952, India became the first country to launch a national family planning program. The government promoted various contraceptive methods to reduce fertility rates, including male

sterilization. The program was resisted in rural areas where men saw it as a threat to their masculinity, while it was more successful in urbanized regions. In any case, the average total fertility rate in India declined from nearly six children per woman in the 1950s to the current value of about 1.9, below the population replacement rate. This result may not be due to the government's efforts, but rather to the population transition that appears to occur everywhere, regardless of what the government does or doesn't do.

Other countries faced similar problems. China was the one that implemented the most drastic measures to reduce natality by forbidding families from having more than one child. This story is discussed in a special section on China in this book. Other countries implemented family planning initiatives based on contraceptives, sterilization, and the legalization of abortion. The list would be long, but some notable cases are Indonesia and Bangladesh, which adopted measures similar to those adopted in India. In Africa, memories of the European colonial invasions made governments wary of acting to reduce population, an idea they saw as an invitation to be invaded again. Nevertheless, efforts to control population growth are being made in Kenya, Ethiopia, Rwanda, and Senegal. Still, the results have not been very successful, and Africa remains one of the few regions of the world where the human population continues to grow rapidly.

In Latin America, the efforts have often involved contraceptives, and some regions have an exceptionally high rate of use. For example, countries like Colombia, Peru, and Paraguay have achieved high levels of modern contraceptive use, ranging between 51% and 70%. In Latin America, the Mexican President, Luis Echeverría (1970-1976), implemented some policies to reduce the number of children, at the time an average of 8/10 per woman. Apparently, this was done as a direct result of the work by Victor Urquidi, an economist, academic, and member of the Club of Rome. In this case, and likely only in this case, the Club of Rome directly influenced a major country's population policies. In Europe, not many

countries adopted specific family planning actions, and the idea was abandoned as soon as they realized that they were facing a serious problem of fertility decline.

In the US, before World War II, the state encouraged people to have large families. Contraceptives were prohibited by law at various points in history. For example, the Comstock Act of 1873 banned the distribution of "obscene" materials through the mail, including contraceptives. It wasn't until the landmark Supreme Court case, Griswold v. Connecticut, in 1965, that the ban on contraceptives was overturned, at least for married couples. This decision was extended to unmarried individuals in the 1972 case Eisenstadt v. Baird, which established that the right to privacy includes the right of individuals to use contraception. The use of the contraceptive pill was approved in 1960, and in 1965, the Supreme Court declared unconstitutional state laws prohibiting contraceptive use by married couples. In 1973, the Supreme Court case Roe v. Wade legalized abortion.

But it was a brief moment. Birth rates rapidly declined in all areas that were called the "First World" (the West) and the "Second World" (the Soviet bloc and China). This trend was known as the "demographic transition" and didn't require draconian government measures to occur. As a result, family planning was rapidly losing momentum, while a strong new push for natalism appeared. The last hurrah of the anti-natalists may have been the 1992 declaration of the "Union of Concerned Scientists."

> "We, the undersigned, senior members of the world's scientific community, hereby warn all humanity of what lies ahead. A significant change in our stewardship of the Earth and the life on it is required, if vast human misery is to be avoided and our global home on this planet is not to be irretrievably mutilated."[74]

The declaration is still online, but the changing perception of the issue led the UCS to precede this document with a recent preface that defines it as "deeply problematic."

The Return of Natalism

At present, the perception of overpopulation as a problem remains diffuse. It is a correct stance considering that humankind has passed the 8 billion mark and is still growing. On the other hand, this perception has never been shared by everybody. The modern clash between the natalist and the anti-natalist positions became clear with the World Population Conference organized by the United Nations in Bucharest in 1974. It was supposed to be a milestone in which contraceptives and population control were to be diffused and promoted everywhere in the world. Instead, the representatives of Third World countries completely rejected the idea.

At that time, the concept of "Population Transition," that is an impending decline of the human population, was not yet evident from the available data. But a fertility decline had already been noted in many countries. So, a key slogan that emerged from the conference was "Development is the best contraceptive." This position argued that the key to addressing population growth was not through coercive family planning or birth control programs, but rather through socio-economic development. The proposers believed that by improving living standards, education, healthcare, and women's status, population growth would guarantee maximum prosperity for everybody.

The position of the Third World nations soon had the upper hand in the debate, with the proponents of population control accused of planning dark and dire things such as exterminations and genocides. Still today, the term "population control" has a ring of evil

attached to it that seems to be impossible to remove. Note, however, that a few years after the conference, China took a completely different position, favorable to birth control. The case of China will be discussed in a specific chapter in this book.

The debate went on, and the clash of natalism and anti-natalism continues to this day. It is mainly a political debate, and, as with all political debates, it follows the rules of politics, the main one being that the way to win is to demonize your adversary. One of the first targets of demonization was Thomas Malthus and his *Essay on Population*. Malthus had already been heavily criticized in his time, accused of undermining faith in divine providence, arguing that his ideas painted God as a harsh taskmaster rather than a benevolent creator. But the modern campaign turned the term "Malthusian" into an insult. Just as an example, Matthew Simmons, an expert in petroleum economics, reported that he gave a talk in 1994 in which he mentioned *The Limits to Growth* as not being obviously wrong, and that afterward, one of the attendees told him that he was "obviously a Malthusian" and, for that reason, wrong[75].

If you have some experience with giving public talks about these subjects, you know how easily it is to hear a simple (and wrong) syllogism that goes as, "Since what you say sounds like what Malthus said, and since Malthus was wrong, then you are wrong, too." We might refer to this approach as "Hitler's vegetarianism fallacy." That is, "Since Hitler was vegetarian, and since Hitler was evil, then vegetarianism is evil." But this is the way things go in the political debate. Anything you say can be twisted out of context and turned into something that condemns you to shame among men.

Here is a typical example of how Malthus was attacked using rhetorical tricks and distortions. Joel Mokyr, in his book titled *Why Ireland Starved* (1983), reports this sentence from a letter that Malthus wrote to his friend David Ricardo,

> The land in Ireland is infinitely more peopled than in England; and to give full effect to the natural resources of the country, a great part of the population should be swept from the soil.

This sentence gives the impression that Malthus was advocating the extermination of the Irish. But the actual sentence that Malthus wrote reads:

> The land in Ireland is infinitely more peopled than in England; and to give full effect to the natural resources of the country, a great part of the population should be swept from the soil into large manufacturing and commercial Towns.

Clearly, Malthus wasn't proposing to kill anyone; rather, he proposed the industrialization of Ireland to create prosperity in the country. Nevertheless, legends spread quickly on the web. You can see the truncated sentence by Malthus repeated over and over in other papers and on the Web to demonstrate that Malthus was an evil person who proposed the extermination of the poor. You can even read that this sentence demonstrates that the Irish famine was Malthus' personal fault. Too bad that at the time of the famine, Malthus had been dead for more than 10 years.

A similar treatment was reserved for the 1972 study *The Limits to Growth,* which was accused of being ideologically bent toward exterminating the dark races and having made "wrong predictions." You can read the details in my 2011 book *The Limits to Growth Revisited*. In time, the thesis and the data of The Limits to Growth seemed to fade from people's minds. However, there remained plenty of legends accusing various persons and groups of plotting a global culling of humankind or some specific ethnic group. The ancestor of these theories is *The Protocols of the Elders of Zion,* a forged document which surfaced in Russia in 1903. It described a secret Jewish cabal plotting

world domination, including the destruction of the Christian civilization, explicitly framed as an extermination. But these early legends pale in comparison with the hyperactive theorists engaged in finding extermination plots everywhere.

Despite multiple debunkings, the idea that culling plans are being prepared against humankind by evil secret societies remains very much alive. As culprits, various existing organizations are commonly listed: the World Economic Forum, the Club of Rome, the United Nations, HAARP, the Federal Reserve, the Bilderberg Group, and more. Others are creations of pure fantasy: The Gnomes of Zurich, the Reptilians, the Illuminati, and more. Even some individuals are often accused of covertly planning to cull most of humankind. The most often targeted one is probably Bill Gates, but the chairman of WEF, Klaus Schwab, is probably well placed in the second position. Currently, Elon Musk is gaining popularity as a would-be humankind exterminator. Yet, he is also known for his many statements about the need for women to have more children.

This binary attitude is diffuse throughout the debate and is likely to become a major stumbling block in all attempts to manage a demographic situation, which, as with everything that has to do with Earth's ecosystem, would need a nuanced approach, avoiding extremes such as terrorizing people because of overpopulation, or, for the reverse effect, extinction.

At present, the "natalist" position seems to have gained the upper hand, and most governments are making efforts to increase birth rates by supporting families with financial and other kinds of help. These efforts, so far, are failing, but perhaps more effective methods will be developed. Yet, all that's done in this field is based on the idea that low birth rates are the result of sociological factors only. The possibility that they are instead caused by pollution is almost never mentioned. That's probably because, if it turned out to be the main factor, or even just an important one, very little could be done to restore women's fertility, at least in the short run.

In the end, our future will depend on how we can avoid radical reactions to a situation that is rapidly evolving. There are plenty of mistakes that can be made in the attempt to control birth rates, and it doesn't matter much in which direction. Mistakes have been made in the past, and will probably be made again in the future. But this is how the human mind works, and whatever happens to us in the future will be, in large part, a result of our actions.

6. Case Studies

The faces of these people were subdued with hunger; pale, or rather of a ghostly yellow, indicative of the utmost destitution. They are starving. We hurried with horror from these frightful visitations, which are permitted by Providence for his own wise ends, sick at heart. (Marquis of Waterford, April 1846)

Figure 15 - Bridget O'Donnel and her two children at the time of Ireland's great famine. Wikipedia, Public Domain.

This section describes some historical cases that showed interesting population trends, either in terms of rapid decline, stability, or growth. It is not supposed to be a complete listing of all known cases. Still, it provides several examples that may be useful as an illustration of the considerations developed in the previous sections of the book.

Ancient Rome: metal poisoning

The ancient Romans had many things in common with us, but they never had a problem of overpopulation. Just consider that at the height of the Empire, ca. 1st-2nd century CE, the population of Western Europe is estimated to have been 20–30 million. Today, it is more than 10 times larger, with over 300 million people. From our viewpoint, Europe would have looked empty: a land of forests and small towns, crisscrossed by the network of Roman roads which had more of a military purpose than a commercial one. During Imperial times, overcrowding problems were mostly unknown, even though the capital city, Rome, had become large enough that it had traffic jams. Yet, the agricultural production of the time was more than sufficient to provide food for Rome and for all the cities of the Empire. It was the result of a sophisticated maritime transportation system that delivered food from the fertile regions of North Africa and the Middle East all the way to the coastal cities. The system remained in function up to the mid-5th century CE, as long as the Empire existed, securing food for the Roman citizens.

If anything, the ancient Romans had a problem of underpopulation, and they understood that perfectly well. With the start of the economic decline of the Empire, during the 1st-2nd century CE, natality plummeted, and it became more and more difficult to find enough manpower for the legions and the state apparatus. Several emperors enacted laws that encouraged couples to have children through financial incentives and tax breaks. Augustus (1st century BCE) was probably the first ruler to develop the concept of "giving sons to the country," a concept amply exploited by later rulers who saw themselves as extreme cases of alpha males, "fathers of the country." However, despite the emperors' efforts and the attempt to raid as many slaves as possible from neighboring countries, the Roman population started declining in Imperial times.

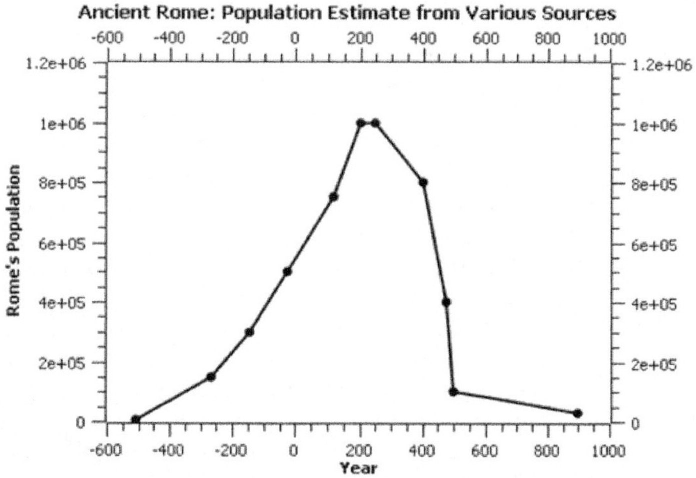

Figure 16 -- An approximate reconstruction of the population of ancient Rome. Data from various sources

In the figure, you can see a graph of the population of Rome. Take it as no more than an illustration: the data on the Roman population are highly uncertain and intensely debated among specialists. Nevertheless, the results are consistent with other reconstructions. The Roman population grew together with the extension, wealth, and power of the Empire. Then, it went down rapidly. It was a clear example of a trend that the Roman philosopher Lucius Seneca had identified during the peak of the Empire's power: that fortune grows slowly, but ruin is rapid. I called it the "Seneca Effect."

Eventually, lack of manpower made it impossible for the Romans to defend and maintain their provinces, and they had to abandon most of them. Finally, they were invaded by Germanic populations, who were not necessarily hostile but replaced the vacuum left by the Roman demographic decline. During the 5th century CE, the Western Empire faded away forever. Afterward, the European population is said to have been reduced to as few as 18 million people.

The collapse of the Roman Empire has puzzled historians for a long time, and hundreds of "explanations" have been proposed for an event that looked improbable, or even impossible. The mighty Roman legions were powerful and nearly invincible for almost a millennium. Then, in the 3rd century of our era, they started losing one battle after another, and in a couple of centuries, they had disappeared. The old Empire left only ruins and mentions in history books.

Most of the proposed reasons for the collapse were based on qualitative arguments and the whim of the historians who proposed them. "Loss of moral fiber," "influence of oriental religions," or "immigration," and many more. Only some proposals were based on real-world data. Of course, we lack detailed statistics about how the Roman economy evolved, but we can use proxy data. For instance, we can gather information on the productivity of the mining of precious metals from the fraction of silver in the Roman denarius coin. These data indicate that silver production collapsed with the great crisis of the 3rd century. A reasonable explanation is that the exhaustion of the Roman mines reduced the supply of gold and silver to the Imperial coffers. That made the Empire weaker and cracked the very fabric of the Roman society, which was based on monetary exchanges, as well as on the capability of paying fighters with hard cash. Not for nothing, the modern term "soldier" derives from the ancient Roman term "Solidus" for a gold coin of the late Empire.

The demise of complex systems, such as human societies, is rarely generated by a single factor. So, the depletion of the Roman precious metal mines surely played a role, but it may not have been the only cause of the collapse. An interesting peculiarity of the Roman collapse is that it may be the only case in history of a pollution-generated population decline for which we have quantitative data. We know that the Ancient Romans suffered from poisoning by heavy metals, in particular lead and mercury. The idea that the Romans weakened themselves because of lead poisoning was a remarkable intuition by a German scholar named Rudolf Kobert in 1909. He

lacked the tools to prove his ideas, and his theory was mostly ignored. Later, it was reproposed by S. C. Gilfillan in 1965.[76] Today, historians still debate this matter, but there is no doubt that heavy metal poisoning was a feature of the late Roman Empire. The Roman economy was one of the most successful mining-based economies in ancient history. They mined all sorts of metals, and their wealth was based on their production of gold and silver. But they also mined non-precious metals, including poisonous ones: lead and mercury.

Lead was widely used in Roman times for many practical purposes. Easy to smelt and workable at room temperature, lead could be used for pipes and vessels of all kinds. In Imperial times, drinking wine from lead cups became fashionable. The slight corrosion of the lead by the wine generated dissolved lead salts, giving the wine an extra sweet flavor that the Romans appreciated, but it also poisoned them. They may have understood that lead had harmful effects on human health, but they seem to have associated it only with the people who smelted lead. These workers were often affected by a mental degradation called "Saturnism," from the association of lead with the Saturn planet and the divinity Saturn. It doesn't appear that the Romans ever understood that their fancy wine goblets were making them sick. And that was not the only problem they had with lead. It was extensively used for pipes, vessels, and kitchen tools, and that generated a further source of lead that poisoned the Romans. It was also released into the air when used to smelt silver and gold from the rocks in which they were stored.

We know about lead poisoning in Roman times because lead is a systemic poison that accumulates in the bones. Its chemical properties are similar to those of calcium, a normal component of bones (it is termed a "calcium analog"). Nowadays, we can measure the lead content in bones by examining ancient Roman skeletons, and in this way, we can have some idea of how bad the problem was. [77] The result is that the Romans had enough lead in their bones to cause serious problems such as anemia, high blood pressure, kidney

disease, and fertility problems. High levels of lead are also associated with brain damage. Considering these effects, we may conclude that lead poisoning had a significant effect on the health of the Romans, and some historians speculated that the erratic behavior among Roman elites and emperors might have been due to lead poisoning. Did Caligula make his horse a senator because he drank too much wine in lead goblets? We will never know for sure, but we cannot exclude it.

Mercury was another poisonous metal that the Romans extracted, although not in large quantities. They used it in pigments, in particular as a cosmetic powder in the form of cinnabar (mercury sulfide). They also used it for gold extraction using the "amalgam" process, and for ceremonial purposes. Mercury is a fascinating substance: the only metal that is liquid at room temperature, but it is also a serious systemic poison for the human body. The Romans were aware, at least in part, of the toxic effects of mercury. The warders of mercury mines knew that the slaves engaged in mining would likely succumb to a mysterious sickness. The symptoms were tremors, extreme mood changes, and eventually loss of hearing and restricted vision, and the people affected were defined as having a "mercurial" behavior. Archaeologists have found significant traces of mercury poisoning in ancient Roman skeletons.[78] Again, mercury may have been an important factor in sickening them and causing the demise of the Empire.

The similarities with our society are, at the same time, numerous and worrisome. We are producing and spreading over the ecosystem a multitude of substances whose effects on the human body are scarcely known or even totally unknown. How about rare metals such as platinum, palladium, rhodium, and several others? They are so rare that humans have never been in contact with them. And, right now, we are spreading them in the environment as a result of the degradation of catalytic converters used to abate other poisonous substances in car exhaust. There are many more substances

released in the ecosystem whose effects are scarcely known, just as their combined effects. Yet, it doesn't seem that the authorities or the public are overly worried about the problem. Just like the ancient Romans, we are poisoning ourselves without even realizing what we are doing.

Could some astute Roman philosophers have noted that the Romans were killing their own population by their smelting activities? Could they have tried to alert the authorities about the problem that was risking the destruction of their world? If someone did, we may imagine that they were the target of a demonization campaign by the lead and mercury smelting lobby that succeeded in presenting them as slightly feebleminded catastrophists, whom nobody should listen to. Of course, that means using some fantasy to fill the missing historical records. Still, it is also true that the Romans had developed methods for "perception management" (aka "propaganda"), which may not be as refined as our modern ones but were nevertheless effective. And this is another worrisome element of similarity with our modern world. Are we going to be killed by propaganda telling us that some things are harmless, while we should know they are not?

Medieval Europe: Plagues and Famines

The COVID-19 pandemic that struck the world in 2020 was an exceptional event in human history. Never before had the entire world reacted to an epidemic so strongly and with such extreme measures. Never before had people accepted being locked inside their homes, forced to wear face masks all the time, to avoid getting close to other people, to be tracked, examined, tested, and provided with "passes" to be able to perform their normal activities. But many of them were

genuinely terrified by a virus that, at the beginning, was described as an existential threat to humankind.

The wave of terror that swept the world in 2020 century may have been a reflection of the great scare that originated from the disasters that struck Europe during the 14th century. First, there came the Great Famine of 1315–1317, then, 30 years later, the epidemic termed "Black Death." Both took their toll on the European population, estimated to have fallen from roughly 75 million in 1300 to 25–35 million by 1400, representing a 60–70% total decline over the course of the 14th century. These numbers are uncertain and may be exaggerated, but the disaster had truly apocalyptic proportions.

Figure 17 - Totentanz," the dance of death (1493) by Michael Wolgemut. Public Domain

The famine not only impacted the European population, but also the way of thinking of Europeans. It was at that time that painters started producing images of the Totentanz, the dance of death, with animated skeletons shown as armed with swords and pikes, overwhelming the puny efforts of living humans to stop them. It was

at that time that it became fashionable to have tombs where the image of the buried person appeared as a cadaver. For a few centuries, European thought seemed to be focused on death and the decay of the body. It was the time when the concept of *memento mori* (Latin words for "remember that you must die") became commonplace.

What happened that caused this huge disaster? We tend to see the Middle Ages in Europe as a "dark age" of superstitions and barbarism, but reality was very different. After the collapse of the Roman Empire in the 5th century CE, Europe had rebounded to create new social structures, a new economy, and a new culture based on Christianity. With the discovery of new silver mines in Eastern Europe, the economy could be "re-monetized" after the collapse of the Roman currency, and that generated a new phase of rapid economic growth. The population was growing, too, and, with the turn of the first millennium, it was clear that Europe had an excess of young men willing to fight for money and glory. That was the origin of the Crusades, when Europeans found no better way to get rid of the marauding bands of knights than sending them to fight in the Levant. That phase of history began in 1095 with the first military expedition attacking the Holy Land, marked by the cry, *Deus Vult*, meaning "God wills it."

The age of the Crusades lasted about two and a half centuries. It ended in 1291, when the last European stronghold in the Middle East, the city of Acre, was abandoned. It was an unmitigated disaster for Europe. Its economy had been wrecked by the war effort, and its forests had been destroyed to make ships and weapons. Now, the exhausted soil couldn't produce sufficient food. The Great Famine struck in 1315.

The great famine is not usually attributed to overexploitation but, rather, to climate effects. The chroniclers of the time noted how, from 1315 to 1317, heavy rains flooded fields, rotting seeds before they could sprout. The pattern was repeated, although less severely, in the subsequent year, and the famine didn't completely subside until 1324.

This series of events is well known, but is it true that the famine was caused by a change in weather patterns, as it is normally interpreted?

Of course, in those times, rainfall measurements were not performed, so the chroniclers could only discuss local effects and qualitative narrations. Today, we can do much better, and the data obtained from dendrochronology (the study of tree rings) does not show significant changes in rainfall before or during the famine.[79] It is more likely that the effects attributed by the chroniclers to higher-than-normal rainfall effects were instead due to soil degradation, in turn, caused by deforestation. Indeed, deforestation is clearly detectable in the dendrochronological data.

Apparently, in the 14th century, Europe was in a condition not unlike the current one, where the effects of normal rainfall are enhanced by the impermeabilization of the soil caused by deforestation and buildings.[80] The results may be disastrous floods and landslides, today as in ancient times. In a certain sense, the Europeans themselves had created the disaster that struck them in the form of the Great Famine.

The Famine was bad enough, but it was the origin of an even worse catastrophe: the later epidemic called Black Death. It is known that when a population is weakened by a lack of food, it is easy prey for all kinds of pathogens. Among many examples in history, this happened after World War I, when most of Continental Europe had been suffering under the effects of the Allied sanctions, preventing the import of food from overseas. The weakened population was struck by the Spanish Flu, which killed millions, starting in 1919.

In the case of the Medieval European Famine, malnutrition persisted for several years after the date chosen by historians to mark its end. Skeletal evidence reveals that people born during and shortly after the famine suffered from stunted stature and compromised health.[81] Hence, they may have been ill-equipped to resist the pestilence that hit them. The changes in the landscape, too, may have facilitated the spread of the epidemic. Depleted herds, fallow fields,

and disrupted trade slowed recovery and forced peasants to flood into towns, which became overcrowded and hence a probable focal point for the spreading of pathogens. This correlation may explain why the pestilence hit so hard, despite having been endemic in Eurasia for at least one millennium before.

So, it happened that, in 1347, a ship coming from the Middle East docked at Messina, Sicily, its crew afflicted with fever and grotesque swellings. It was the start of the epidemic that was later called the Black Death. The infected people persons suffered fevers, chills, and painful buboes. These symptoms were followed by hemorrhagic coughing or the blackened decay of gangrene. Few survived beyond days. Within four years, by 1351, the plague had swept all over Europe, claiming an estimated 25 to 50 million lives. Entire settlements vanished; large cities saw the loss of a large fraction of their inhabitants, so many that unburied corpses littered the streets. The chroniclers report of deserted villages, fields overtaken by weeds, and wolves roaming where herds once stood.

To contemporaries, the plague was no mere illness but a retribution for people's sins coming directly from the Lord. Clerics like John of Reading deemed it the prophesied end of the world. Flagellants scourged themselves in penance; others accused Jewish communities, inciting massacres across Europe, amplifying a trend of pogroms that had already started during the First Crusade. Physicians speculated on miasmatic vapors or planetary conjunctions, advocating bleeding as a cure, often hastening death.

Attributing the Black Death to God's wrath was no more accurate on the part of the chroniclers of the time than attributing the Great Famine to excessive rain. Modern science identified the culprit of the plague: a bacterium, the Yersinia Pestis, whose origins were likely in Asia's steppes. Its name comes from Alexandre Yersin, a Swiss/French physician who discovered it in 1894. The bacterium can affect fleas, which attack rats or other rodents. From the rat, it can spread to humans through the bite of infected fleas. When that was

discovered, rats gained a bad reputation that persists to this day. But, in practice, the bacterium can spread to humans much better in its airborne form as respiratory droplets than by the rare event of a rat biting a human being. Besides, rats can't travel as fast and far as human beings do. God, and even rats, had little to do with the Black Death, but the disaster surely had biblical proportions.

The Great Famine and the Black Plague are examples of how a population can collapse continent-wide. It was the result of several coupled factors, but one of them was overpopulation. Of course, Europe in the 14th century had a much smaller population than it has now. However, overpopulation is a term that depends on circumstances. For the capability that people had to manage their territory at that time, 80 million people were too many. It was not a Malthusian collapse directly caused by the limits of food production. We may see it more appropriately as a pollution-related collapse, with the term "pollution" intended to refer to the degradation of the ecosystem caused by human activities, such as deforestation.

It is sobering to think that we now have about 750 million inhabitants in Europe, intended as the geographic region that reaches all the way to the Urals, almost ten times more than in the 14th century. We have much better technologies that are supposed to help us cope with epidemics, but would it be possible to see a new outbreak of a major plague? It looks unlikely, at least in the current situation. Consider that the Black Death killed 20–50% of Europe's population. Compare to the COVID-19 toll: 0.09% of the global population. The fame of a global scourge of the modern pandemic was much exaggerated.

Today, we seem to be able to resist pathogens much better than our ancestors because of a combination of better nutrition, better hygiene, better medical care, and vaccines (even though the last category has fallen in disrepute with many people nowadays). In addition, the habit of long-range traveling in modern times has exposed people to contact with populations that were historically

separated. It means that our immune system is continuously exposed and tuned to new microorganisms coming from far away. That gives us time to develop immunity.

So, maybe we don't have to worry too much about a new black plague, at least as long as we can have a good standard of living, allowing us to remain healthy. Even the famed "bioweapons," object of so many worries at the time of the invasion of Iraq in 2003, may have been an overhyped threat. So far, the only case of a biological weapon having caused victims is that of the spreading of anthrax pathogens in the US in 2001, after the 9/11 attack on the World Trade Center. To this date, we don't know who was behind the attack, but we know that it resulted in a grand total of five victims. Consider also that the COVID-19 virus was said to be a bioweapon escaped from a research lab. If it was so, it was no better than a high-tech rubber band launcher. Things may change, though, in the hypothesis of a societal and economic collapse, which would leave people defenseless against normally not worrisome germs. It would be part of the "feedback" concentration effect that dynamic models see as a possible cause of a rapid population decline. The future is, as always, uncertain.

Ancient Europe: Inheritance and Population

Fertility and wealth are two strictly related factors in human populations. Wealth is accumulated over time, but it is well known that you can't take it with you when you start your path toward the Elysian Fields. So, if wealth is divided equally among many heirs, it would be gradually fragmented and dispersed, especially in times of high natality. One measure to counter this dispersion was the idea of "primogeniture," that is, the concept that a single heir, typically male, would take over the whole of the family's wealth. This use was

diffused all over the world, but it was especially important in Ancient Europe, from Medieval times to relatively recent ones.

Primogeniture was a nearly perfect "zero-sum" game: the family's wealth remained within the family. Playing this game, however, was difficult for various reasons; the main one being that the disinherited sons and daughters of a rich family were not happy about the idea, understandably so. That could have been solved by having just one male heir, but that was impossible in times when contraceptive techniques were ineffective and dangerous, and child mortality was high. A wealthy family aiming at just one heir could see him die before having a chance to marry and have children. To avoid that, families needed to have more than a single male child, but that created a serious tension inside families. You may remember Alexandre Dumas' *The Man in the Iron Mask* (1847), a novel centered on a mysterious prisoner held in the Bastille during the reign of Louis XIV. He turned out to be the twin brother of King Louis XIV, hidden away to secure Louis' throne. An extreme case, but a dramatic illustration of the inner conflicts that could arise among brothers inside wealthy families.

About disinherited daughters, you surely remember the story of Cinderella which exists in various versions all over the world. All of them deal with the fate of a girl whose parents couldn't or wouldn't provide her with a dowry, preferring to concentrate their resources on another daughter. These stories often end with the dispossessed girl finding a trick to marry her Prince Charming. However, in the real world, it wasn't so easy to find a good fairy ready to turn a pumpkin into a coach. The problem existed in all pre-modern cultures, and we find it mentioned already in Sumerian texts that go back five thousand years ago.

Disinherited sons could still build up a career in an expanding economy by becoming warriors, explorers, or merchants. The dispossessed daughters, too, had ways to react to their bad luck. They could still find a comfortable position in society if they could marry a

promising hotshot, even though not necessarily a rich one. Things were different in a static or contracting economy, such as in early Medieval Europe. In these conditions, the penniless scion of a wealthy family could become a knight errant and engage in the search for enemies, possibly in the form of dragons. That gave rise mainly to legends and poems, but in the real world, dragons were rare, and unemployed warriors were a nuisance for everybody. They were often gotten rid of by sending them on some military adventure where they could unleash their homicidal instincts against foreigners. It is still a common strategy nowadays.

About disinherited girls, they wouldn't usually become unruly warrioress themselves, despite the many modern movies depicting sexy female fighters. But they were nevertheless a disruptive element of society, scheming to seduce powerful leaders. The resulting children were termed "bastards," not necessarily an insult in ancient times, but an element of unrest as potential claimants to the leader's wealth.

One way to avoid the tensions deriving from primogeniture rules was to limit them by law. In Islamic countries, the Holy Qur'an laid down precise rules on how to distribute inheritance, ensuring that everyone would get a fair share. In China, male heirs were privileged according to Confucianism, but the inheritance was distributed among all the heirs, although not in equal shares. India was a patchwork of different cultures, some of which practiced a relatively strict primogeniture method, but not everywhere.

Ancient Europe, instead, found a clever way to tweak the system in such a way as to make strict primogeniture possible without creating bands of penniless warriors in search of dragons to kill or scheming viragos in search of nobles to seduce. It was done by using monastic and religious orders, traditionally requiring chastity from members. Monasteries and nunneries could provide a comfortable refuge for disinherited male and female nobles who would find food, shelter, and a certain degree of comfort there. The emphasis on

chastity ensured that the cloistered nobles would leave no descendants so that the firstborn heir wouldn't risk being ousted by a nephew. The system had the additional advantage that cloistered heirs could be "de-cloistered" and brought back to the inheritance line if the first-born heir were to die. An example is that of Ferdinando de' Medici (1549 -- 1609), who inherited the title of Grand Duke of Tuscany when his older brother Francesco died in 1587, leaving no legitimate male descendants. Earlier on, Ferdinando had been ordained a cardinal, and he was supposed to pursue a religious life of chastity. But when he became Grand Duke, he had no problem in "de-cardinalizing" himself, getting married, and having children. Incidentally, Francesco's death was widely attributed to poisoning. Hence, we may suspect that his younger brother had something to do with it, but we will never know for sure.

You may think that chastity was a condition that made cloistering a heavy punishment, but that was necessarily the case. In ancient times, people saw chastity as a virtue leading to Paradise in the afterlife. Besides, monasteries were not necessarily places of penance and suffering. In comparison with the ordinary life of peasants and low-class citizens, they could be seen as even luxurious. In addition, whether monks and nuns were actually chaste is a debatable question. For obvious reasons, we will never have verifiable data on this point; however, you can gain insight by reading Boccaccio's Decameron, a collection of stories published in 1349. Boccaccio pokes fun at monks and priests, giving the impression that their chastity was considered a joke by everyone, including the monks and the nuns themselves. In other sources, nunneries were accused of being run as brothels. It is perfectly possible since, just like every institution in the real world, they needed money. An example is the story of Sister Virginia Maria (born Marianna de Leyva y Marino; 1575 – 1650), who lived in Monza in northern Italy. Sister Virginia became rather infamous in her time as "The Nun of Monza" due to an affair she had with a local aristocrat, which involved the homicide of

another nun who had threatened to reveal the story. Her life inspired one of the characters in Alessandro Manzoni's novel *The Betrothed* (1840).

Maybe chastity was taken more seriously in other places and times, but we may suspect that it was always more theoretical than real. In any case, the important point of cloistering was not chastity; it was making sure that monks and nuns would have no children, at least officially. If they did, the children were to be quietly disposed of. Sometimes they were killed, but, less drastically, they could be transferred to orphanages, which would ask no questions, raise them, and then reinsert them into society as "innocents." They could become regular citizens, and if they were female, the hospice would provide them with a small dowry, allowing them to marry and raise a family. The critical feature of these institutions was that all bonds with their original parents were forever severed; the innocents received a new name and would never know who their parents were. That made these hospices function as machines to turn nobles into commoners. It solved a problem that, much later, Peter Turchin defined as "Elite Overproduction" as a source of social instability.[82]

An interesting element of the orphanage scheme is that the abandoned children were often endowed with half a coin or other objects that, in principle, could allow them to be recognized by their parents, who kept the other half. You can still see a collection of these half-coins in the museum of the *Spedale degli Innocenti*, the Innocents' Hospital, in Florence, which catered for abandoned children for at least four centuries. These old objects are still moving to see today, when you think of how hard it must have been for the parents to give away their child forever. Indeed, the discovery of one's real parents is a common trope in modern and ancient fiction. Think of the myth of Oedipus, based on the dramatic discovery that Oedipus' wife was actually his mother. The film *Mamma Mia!* (2008) is a recent example.

The European primogeniture laws and customs were a clever arrangement that favored wealth concentration, which could then be

turned into military power. It may have been an important factor in the competition for world domination that started with the Renaissance. This idea has been proposed, among others, by David Landes (*The Wealth and Poverty of Nations,* 1998), Timur Kuran (*The Long Divergence*, 2011), and Peter Frankopan, in *The Silk Road* (2015).

Today, monasteries and nunneries are out of fashion, and the orphanages of old are mostly closed. They are no longer necessary with the rapid decline in birth rates. Nevertheless, the problem of inheritance and distribution of wealth from one generation to another remains important. But it is an ongoing story that we will see in detail in another chapter.

Polynesia: Where Malthus Ruled

Figure 18 - The Moai, the stone statues of Rapa Nui. Image by Juan Carlos Araya Mardones. Wikimedia, Creative commons

The Rapa Nui Island, also known as Easter Island, is a poster child of catastrophists. It is often described as having suffered a major population crash caused by overexploitation of the land, a few centuries before European explorers arrived. But the real story turned out to be more complicated and nuanced than this simplified version makes it appear.

Rapa Nui was discovered by the Dutch explorer Jacob Roggeveen on Easter Day, April 5, 1722, and he and his crew were the first people from outside the island to see the famous Moai, the giant stone statues. It was a fascinating discovery, suggesting that Rapa Nui had been inhabited by an advanced civilization despite being a small island of approximately 164 square kilometers.

But when Europeans first landed there, Rapa Nui didn't host anything that could be defined as an advanced civilization. Some 3000 inhabitants lived there, clearly unable to create stone statues of the size of those that their ancestors had built. The Europeans who landed there raided the island for its only natural resource, people to be sold as slaves on the continent. Later, the island was also exploited as a pasture for sheep imported from the continent, while the surviving natives were confined to a small portion of it. After a century of disasters, a census carried out by the Chilean navy in 1892 recorded only 101 inhabitants, of whom only 12 were adult men. The Rapa Nui culture and population were on the verge of extinction.

Eventually, the islanders managed to recover, and today, some 3000 people inhabit the island, most of whom are of Rapa Nui descent. But a lot has been lost. Nowadays, the Rapa Nui language is spoken by no more than a few hundred people, and the ancient culture has been so forgotten that we don't even know the original name of the Island. ("Rapa Nui" is a modern term.) The ancient Rapa Nui people had a written language known as Rongorongo, one of the most enigmatic and undeciphered writing systems in the world. Only 27 Rongorongo tablets survive today, and their meaning is forever lost.

The mystery shrouding Rapa Nui and its statues stimulated the fantasy of Western explorers. Thor Heyerdahl (1914 – 2002), a Norwegian ethnographer, was one of the first scientists to explore the island in the 20th century. He mentioned the possibility that the Islanders had destroyed themselves by overexploitation, and he proposed that the final stages of the collapse involved wars and perhaps even cannibalism. The concept of ecological overexploitation on Rapa Nui was later discussed by John Flenley and Paul Bahn in their 1992 book *Easter Island* and then popularized in the 1994 film *Rapa-Nui*. The idea was also described by Jared Diamond in his 2005 book *Collapse: How Societies Choose to Fail or Succeed*.

The common thesis of these interpretations was that the inhabitants of Rapa Nui deforested the land to leave space for agricultural production and also for moving moai statues on tree trunks used as rollers. This led to soil erosion and loss of resources, ultimately resulting in an excess population. Without sufficient food, the population collapsed among conflicts and cultural upheaval; a Malthusian collapse if ever there was one. Therefore, the island could be seen as a model of the larger island, Planet Earth, offering us a vision of our bleak future.

It is always dangerous to theorize on the basis of a few data, and the theories on Rapa Nui's population were based on almost no data. It is not surprising that they turned out to be only partially correct, if not completely wrong. The idea that the islanders had cut down the trees was contested, proposing that the rats introduced by European visitors had caused the deforestation by eating the seeds of the island's palm trees. That was another case of a hypothesis based on nearly no data. Recent studies show that the ancient Rapa Nui trees were cut using axes. Rats surely couldn't do that.[83]

So, humans did destroy Rapa Nui's forests, but did that cause a population collapse? That was mainly a hypothesis based on the idea that the modern population of the island was too small to be able to create statues of the size of the Moai. But studies based on genomic

data revealed no evidence of a "genetic bottleneck" that would indicate a drastic reduction in population before the arrival of Europeans.[84] Evidently, the Rapa Nui people were able to maintain food production at a level sufficient to avoid a major population collapse, despite having deforested their island. If you think about that, indeed, there is no obvious reason why deforestation should have caused famine and depopulation. Rapa Nui is a minuscule green spot in the vast Pacific Ocean. Its climate is tropical, characterized by high humidity. The volcanic mountain Maunga Terevaka reaches 505 meters in height, and it affects the climate by creating rain out of wet winds that blow over the island. Whether Rapa Nui is forested or not, the weather pattern remains approximately the same. Of course, without trees, there is always a risk of soil erosion, but we have archaeological traces showing that the islanders took care of their cultivations by making rock barriers against soil loss. The lack of trees must have made it difficult for the islanders to cook their main agricultural product: sweet potatoes. But, again, it seems that the island had sufficient shrubs and dry grass to make this possible.

The results of the genome examination of Rapa Nui inhabitants led to an active phase of "Diamond-bashing," in which critics accused him of twisting data to suit his preconceived ideas. However, as usual, excessive leaning in one direction or another doesn't lead you closer to the truth. The Rapa Nui islanders may not have suffered a population collapse, but at the very minimum, they saw an abrupt cultural change. They abruptly stopped making the Moai, leaving some of them unfinished in the caves where they manufactured them.

One fashionable theory popular up to not long ago was that deforestation forced the islanders to stop manufacturing the Moais due to the lack of wooden logs as rollers to transport them. But this idea is nowadays largely abandoned. It is believed that the islanders "walked" the statues to their places by a controlled rocking method while pulling them with ropes. It may be more likely that the cultural change was caused by the loss of the capability to build boats.

Despite its isolation, Rapa Nui probably maintained contacts with other Pacific Islands and maybe with the South American coasts. There is robust genetic evidence for intermixing between the Rapa Nui people and Native South American populations, occurring well before European contact in 1722. This admixture is estimated at about 8–10%. It is remarkable how the Islanders covered a distance of nearly 4,000 km from Rapa Nui, and then back; a distance equivalent to that from London to New York. But the Polynesian double canoes were sophisticated ocean vessels that could make the trip in a month or so, carrying enough water and food to sustain the crew during the voyage.[85] Losing the supply of wood necessary to make canoes locked the islanders forever on their island, and that may have led to a loss of cultural and genetic exchanges, weakening the Rapa Nui culture and leading them to abandon some of their traditions.

But if Rapa Nui cannot be a model for global population collapse, there are cases of Polynesian islands where resource overexploitation did lead to collapse, as Diamond himself reports in his book. One fascinating case is that of the Pitcairn Islands, a group of four volcanic islands located in the southern Pacific Ocean. Two of them, Pitcairn and Henderson, were inhabited for a few centuries by Polynesians who arrived there probably during the 11th Century CE from Mangareva Island, 540 kilometers to the northwest. All these islands are much smaller than Rapa Nui. Mangareva has an area of approximately 15 square kilometers, Pitcairn Island has an area of 4.6 square kilometers, and Henderson Island has an area of 37.3 square kilometers. Living on such small islands must have posed enormous survival problems to the inhabitants. Even though they could rely on fishing for their food, they still needed wood for their canoes and stone for their tools. Their survival appears to have been based on trade. Mangareva supplied oyster shells for fishhooks and ornaments, and also wood for canoes. Pitcairn supplied basalt for adzes and obsidian for cutting tools, while Henderson supplied turtle and bird eggs, bird feathers, and fish.

Something went wrong during the 15th century, when trade between these three islands ceased. Most likely, it was the result of the deforestation of Mangareva, the only one of the three islands that could supply the timber needed to make canoes. Indeed, when Europeans arrived in Mangareva in the 18th century, they found that the inhabitants had rafts but no canoes.[86] It seems that the three islands, Pitcairn, Henderson, and Mangareva, could exist only by supplying each other with commodities that couldn't be produced locally. But only Mangareva could host a human population in isolation. Pitcairn couldn't produce sufficient food. Henderson, could produce seafood, fish, and bird eggs, but it couldn't produce stone for tools and wood for canoes. In both cases, the populations died out or left. Pitcairn was resettled in 1790 by nine of the mutineers from the British ship HMS Bounty, who landed there along with six Tahitian men, 11 Tahitian women, and a baby girl. They survived in precarious conditions up to the present day, reaching a maximum of more than 200 inhabitants during the 19th century. Today, it is reported that there are only 47 permanent inhabitants, and the island may see a second human extinction in the near future.

So, although deforestation didn't cause a population collapse on Rapa Nui, it did on smaller Pacific islands. Apparently, there is a critical size that makes it impossible for the inhabitants of an island to survive on local resources only. This limit depends on the geology of the island and its fertility. Evidently, the 5 square km of Pitcairn and the 37 square km of Henderson are too small for a permanent settlement. For these islands, the Malthusian limit was effectively zero, and the population had to adapt to that limit, reaching zero inhabitants. Instead, the 164 square km of Rapa Nui were enough to sustain a human population in isolation, at least for several centuries.

The size of Earth's land surface is much larger than that of any island in the Pacific Ocean, and that would seem to make human extinction in the near future unlikely. Indeed, the Earth's ecosystem has survived for more than three billion years, and modern humans

have been living on Earth for a few hundred thousand years. But that doesn't mean we cannot destroy Earth's ecosystem to a level that would make its Malthusian limit for us equal to zero. Maybe we could move to Space colonies or to Mars, as Elon Musk is proposing nowadays. But these colonies might be too small, too, to survive on local resources only, and the colonists might face the same fate as the inhabitants of Pitcairn.

Greenland: Colonizing a Remote Planet

The saga of the Norse colonization of Greenland is another small-scale example of what could be humankind's destiny at the global level. A remote and forbidding land that was nevertheless colonized and inhabited for a few centuries, until the colonists had to give up and leave.

Europeans sighted Greenland for the first time when a Norseman named Gunnbjörn Ulfsson sailed in the vicinity in the late 10th century CE. The first recorded landing was by Erik the Red, an Icelandic Viking who was exiled for murder around 982 CE and was seeking a haven for himself and his followers. Erik the Red explored the southwestern coast of the place he had found and named it "Greenland." The name was a little misplaced for a land that, then as now, was mostly covered with a thick ice layer. But it is also true that the region where the Norse landed and settled was covered with green grass at that time, just as it is today. Greenland's glaciers are not visible from there, being tens of kilometers inland, and the Norse may not even have known that they existed.

Figure 19 - A modern reproduction of Thjodhild's church in Greenland. It gives some idea of the environment in which the Norse lived in Greenland. Image by Brattachur, Wikimedia, Public Domain

Erik the Red returned to Iceland, and then he led a larger expedition to Greenland in 985 CE. The Norse established two main colonies: the Eastern Settlement, located near present-day Qaqortoq, and the Western Settlement, situated near present-day Nuuk. These names are confusing: both settlements were in Western Greenland, and the "Eastern" Settlement was actually North of the "Western" one. In any case, the Norse settled in the only large ice-free region of Greenland.

The settlers created colonies that had all the characteristics of Norwegian society in Europe. They engaged in a combination of farming, hunting, and fishing, and they brought with them the whole menagerie of domestic animals they had in Europe: cattle, sheep, pigs, goats, and even horses. They also undertook expeditions to the North, where they could hunt walruses for ivory, furs, and meat. That was a vital part of Greenland's economy. Exporting ivory and furs to Europe made it possible for Greenlanders to import supplies of the resources that Greenland couldn't produce, such as wood for ships and iron for tools and weapons. The Greenlanders even traveled to Labrador, on the North American continent, probably to get timber. For some reason, though, they never settled there. If they had, they might have

colonized North America much before the Pilgrim Fathers arrived there in 1620. In that case, this book would have been written in Old Norse, or maybe in Iroquoian.

The Norse colony in Greenland thrived for a few centuries, a fascinating chapter in history. From an initial settlement of probably just a few hundred people in the late 10th century, the population is estimated to have grown to about 1500 by the 12th century. At its peak, during the 13th century, the population reached between 2,000 and 2,500 people, with some estimates suggesting even 5,000.

The decline of the colony began in the mid-13th century and accelerated during the 14th century. By the early 15th century, the Western Settlement had collapsed, with the survivors probably taking refuge in the Eastern Settlement. By the mid-15th century, the Eastern Settlement was also abandoned. Some of the inhabitants may have managed to return to Europe, but most of them died, leaving no descendants. In Europe, nobody knew about the fate of this remote outpost. When Norwegian missionary Hans Egede reached Greenland again, in 1721, he found Inuit people living there, but no descendants of the old Norse settlements.

What happened to the Greenlanders that wiped them out of history? The "Little Ice Age," the cooling trend of early modern times in the Northern Hemisphere is often seen as the culprit. But it is not a satisfactory explanation since it overlaps only marginally with the timeline of the Norse settlements. When the Little Ice Age hit really hard, during the 17th century, the Greenlanders had disappeared more than one century before. We will probably never know exactly what happened, but it may be that it was the result of Shakespeare's Principle that "troubles come in battalions," a sentence pronounced by Polonius in Hamlet. The Norse colony was hit by a series of problems that reinforced each other and, eventually, destroyed it. The main one may have been the same that doomed the inhabitants of the Pitcairn Islands in the Pacific Ocean: the collapse of long-range trade.

The European Great Famine of the early 14th century and the Black Death of a few decades later coincide with the start of the decline of the Greenland colonies. With the European economy in shambles, the trade of luxury items with Greenland dwindled. Europeans couldn't afford anymore the walrus ivory and fur that they used to appreciate. That didn't necessarily mean that the people of Greenland were to starve. There is no evidence that they imported food from Europe, and it is clear that they relied mostly on local food sources for their subsistence. The problem was that Greenland's economy was too small to afford iron smelting from iron ore, and there is evidence that it fully relied on Europe for iron nails and tools. In addition, there are no suitable trees for building boats in Greenland. That could perhaps have been overcome by getting timber from Labrador, and the Greenlanders may have attempted to do just that. But transporting wood from Labrador to Greenland required large boats, and no nails meant no boats.

You see how problems came in battalions. Without boats, the Norse couldn't get timber from Labrador. And they couldn't even organize hunting expeditions to the North for walrus furs and ivory. Without walrus furs and ivory, they couldn't pay for importing nails from Europe. And without nails, they couldn't make boats. A vicious circle, if there ever was one. The result must have been that their trade-based economy collapsed. There is some archaeological evidence of severe nutritional stress for them, although there is no evidence of a major wave of famine-generated deaths. In any case, they may well have concluded that it made no sense for them to stay in a gloomy and cold place that offered them nothing but a poor diet and poverty. So, most of them decided to leave when they still had a chance to. Maybe they saw themselves not as "Greenlanders" but as an outpost of their homeland, where they were always planning to return one day or another.

The disappearance of the Norse settlements in Greenland gives us a chance to note how historical events can be completely

misunderstood in our times. In the book *Collapse* (2005), Jared Diamond pokes fun at the settlers for not attempting to eat fish to survive, noting that fish are abundant in the seas around Greenland. He attributes its absence in the Greenlanders' diet to superstition, "a taboo against eating fish," maybe because some of the early settlers had suffered from food poisoning by eating spoiled fish. If the Greenlanders had been smarter, Diamond implies, they would have survived.

I am not a fan of "Diamond-bashing," but in this case, it is true that he completely missed the point. As usual, the absence of data doesn't mean that something doesn't exist. Some archaeological remains of fish bones in Greenland's settlements have been found recently, and, in any case, it would have been weird for the Greenlanders to have developed a taboo against eating fish. They came from Norway, where everyone eats fish, and a lot of it; no taboo whatsoever exists about that. And Greenland's colony was never completely isolated from the mainland.

The problem is not about taboos. It is that, as we already discussed in this book, no society in history has ever survived on fish only. It is because of the unreliability of the yield of fishing and the difficulties of conserving fish for a long time. In Europe, Norwegians had developed effective fish-drying techniques, but they could never survive on fish alone. In any case, drying fish Norway-style was possible only in the dry climate of Norway. In the wetter and colder polar climate of Greenland, drying fish is nearly impossible. Note also that Greenland had no salt resources, so fish couldn't be preserved by salting. In short, the Greenlanders simply couldn't survive on fishing only.

We may speculate on whether the Norse could have adopted the lifestyle of the Inuit, who, at that time, were living in Northern Greenland. The Inuit were stone-age hunters who had taken to the sea, and they had developed a remarkable set of technologies that allowed them to survive in extreme polar conditions. They used light

boats called *kayaks* and *umiaks*, made with a frame of bone or wood, covered with animal skins, without the need for timber to make planks, or of nails to keep them together. They hunted and fished with stone-tipped spears, and they could conserve meat and fat for long periods in their cold climate. Contrary to the common belief, Greenland's Inuit did not normally live in the classic snow-block igloos typical of the Canadian Arctic Region. They tended to live in semi-subterranean houses with thick walls and roofs made of stone and turf (grass/soil blocks).

The Greenland Norse never adopted these techniques. Probably, they didn't have enough time to learn, and it appears that their contacts with the Inuit were sporadic and often unfriendly. In addition, the lifestyles of the Norse and of the Inuit were completely different. For instance, the Norse needed large enclosed spaces for their livestock, and that was nearly impossible to obtain with the small Inuit houses. We may wonder whether some of the last Norse of Greenland could have been adopted by the Inuit and survived the collapse of their colony. It is not impossible, but modern studies have found no genetic evidence of mixing between the two populations during Medieval times. When the last Norse left Greenland, or died, the colony disappeared completely

The story of the Norse colony in Greenland may tell us something about the current idea of colonizing Mars, proposed by Elon Musk, and also a staple idea of Science Fiction. In many ways, it would be a task similar to the colonization of Greenland: a group of adventurous people settles in a remote and cold place with the idea of living away from the mainland. But, just like the Norse Greenland colony, a Martian colony could survive and become self-sufficient only if it could engage in a reciprocally advantageous trade with the mother planet, Earth. Earthlings wouldn't be happy to supply their colony for a long time without getting something back in exchange. But what products could a Martian colony ship back to Earth? For sure, there are no walruses on Mars that could be hunted to ship

walrus ivory to Earth. Maybe Mars could develop a product that can be manufactured only on Mars, but what? "Unobtanium," produced on Planet Pandora in the *Avatar* movie series, is a purely fictional concept. Nevertheless, Mars might have some abundant mineral resources generated during its long geological history and then frozen because no more geological evolution has taken place there during the past 3 billion years or so. The cost of shipping minerals from other planets to Earth is not necessarily insurmountable. Space travel is prohibitively expensive when it involves human beings who cannot withstand high accelerations and need complex and expensive life support systems. But interplanetary shipping could be done using electromagnetic catapults, propelling a payload pod to high speeds by means of electromagnetic fields.

Gerard O'Neill, the proposer of large-scale space settlements, is credited with having pioneered the idea of magnetic catapults, or "mass drivers," with his book *The High Frontier* (1976). But the first mention of magnetic catapults launching payloads into space may have been by Robert A. Heinlein with his *The Moon is a Harsh Mistress* (1966). It was a science fiction novel in which he imagined that the human colonies on the Moon could produce grain in underground cultivations and ship it to Earth to feed a population that had become so large that it couldn't rely solely on Earth's agriculture.

One of these catapults works very much like a maglev train, except that it operates under a vacuum. Hence, it can reach much higher speeds than any vehicle running on Earth's surface. Several experimental tests have been performed, and the concept appears feasible, although so far, no payload has been sent to orbit from Earth by one of these machines. Besides, a human being shot to space by an electromagnetic catapult would be squashed flat to something thinner than when Wile E. Coyote is run over by a road roller in cartoons. But such high accelerations would do no damage to bulk commodities such as metals.

So, would it be possible to move large numbers of people to other planets to overcome the limits of Planet Earth? In the 1978 book *Doomsday Has Been Cancelled* by J. Peter Vajk and Carolyn Henson, the authors developed an optimistic rebuttal to *The Limits to Growth,* proposing that space colonization—through space habitats, mass drivers, and solar power—can overcome Earth's resource and population constraints. By expanding humanity's resource base and living space, the authors argued that the collapse scenarios could be delayed or avoided.Not impossible, but at present very unlikely, to say the least. As things stand, at best, a Martian colony could operate like the modern settlements in Antarctica. They are scientific outposts where people live only for limited periods, and where nobody would like to live for their whole life. To date, only 11 people are reported to have been born in Antarctica. And note that Antarctica is not as cold, barren, and distant as Mars.

The human adventure on Earth shows that traveling and colonizing remote lands is a difficult and risk-filled enterprise. But, in many historical cases, brave and resilient explorers could overcome all difficulties and settle in remote and barren lands. We don't know if, in the future, it will be possible for humans to colonize space or other planets. But our silicon children, robots, don't need oxygen or special conditions of temperature. In the future, they may expand where no human beings could survive.

Ireland: The Great Famine

Ireland's great famine, known as *An Gorta Mór* in Gaelic, is perhaps the best-known example of how famine can cause the collapse of a human population. It began in 1845 and, in a few years,

about half of the Irish population had disappeared, directly killed by starvation, or by sickness, or forced to emigrate. It was a shocking event when it occurred, and it is still shocking for us after nearly two centuries. How could that happen? Ireland in the 19th century was part of a world in which there were, in principle, resources and technologies that could have avoided the disaster or at least mitigated it. But, as it often happens, disasters occur because people do too little, too late to cope with them.

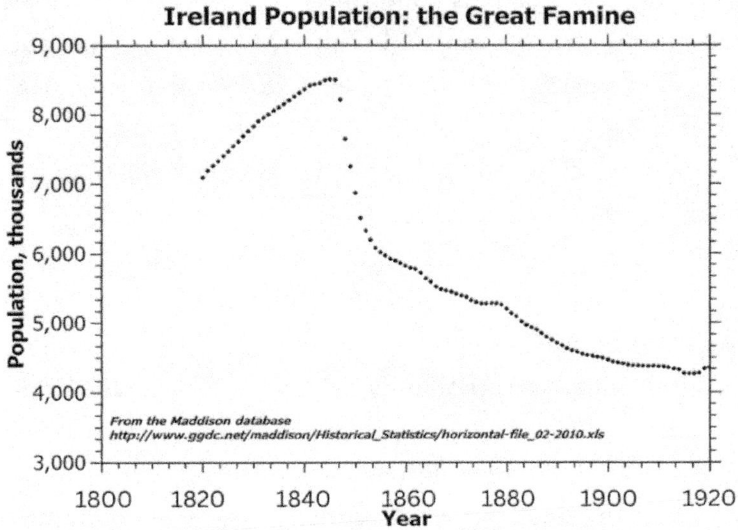

Figure 20 – Ireland's population before and after the Great Famine. Data from the Maddison Foundation

In ancient times, Ireland was a sparsely populated land covered with thick forests. It was too poor and too far away to be worth conquering, and so the Roman legionnaires never set foot there in force. With the fall of the Roman Empire, Ireland was shielded by its isolation from the wars and invasions that occurred in Europe. As a relatively unscathed region, it played an important cultural role in early medieval Europe by saving many ancient manuscripts,

conserved and copied by Irish monks. But, as continental Europe recovered from the collapse, it became clear that Ireland was too small and too weak to compete with the new European powers. Of these, England was the closest and the most dangerous one.

There were several waves of invasion of Ireland by English armies. The final one was led by Oliver Cromwell and ended in 1653 with the complete conquest of Ireland and the collapse of the Irish social structure. The ancient Irish nobility was exterminated or sent into exile. The surviving Irish lost all their lands, had little or no civil rights, could not carry weapons, and couldn't vote or have representatives. All economic activities fell into the hands of the English rulers, while the Irish were relegated to the roles of peasants or workers. Ireland was the first colony of what would later be called the British Empire, even though it was never formally declared one.

According to the data by Cullen in *An Economic History of Ireland Since 1660* (1972), after the conquest, Ireland quickly became an economic asset and a food provider for England. So much that it was called "England's larder," or "England's breadbasket." It could produce meat, cheese, butter, honey, and other high-quality food for the English, while the Irish had to content themselves with potatoes. Yet, despite intermittent hard times, an Irish family could get enough food to survive from a relatively small patch of land by cultivating potatoes and cooking them using local peat as fuel. When they were not working on their potatoes, they worked for their landlord in order to pay the rent. For the landlords, it was the perfect arrangement: they had manpower for free. For the Irish, it was far less than perfect, but at least they could survive. They lived in mud cabins or cottages with walls made of mud, clay, or sods (stacked turf). Floors were often just packed earth, windows were small or absent, and of course, there was nothing like running water and toilets. These cabins had one room shared by families, and often also by livestock. Furnishing consisted of a few stools and straw beds. Several commenters of the time mentioned that overseas "savages" lived better than the Irish.

But the problem for the Irish was not the appalling conditions of their daily life. It was that relying on a single crop is risky, and intermittent famines were a normal feature in Ireland. It was one of these periodic famines that led Jonathan Swift to write his pamphlet *A Modest Proposal*, (1729), where he satirically proposed to solve the problem of hunger in Ireland by having the Irish eat their children. He preceded by two and a half centuries the idea of *Soylent Green*, fictional food made from human flesh, that would appear in a 1973 movie with that title.

We don't know whether the rapid growth of the Irish population before the Great Famine was actively encouraged by the English landlords in order to have more manpower available. It may also be that the Irish reasoned as all peasants in the world do: more arms in the family, more wealth. Perhaps they also dreamed that their growing numbers would one day enable them to rid themselves of their hated English masters. Whatever the case, Ireland experienced a real explosion in population during the British rule. There had been fewer than two million people in Ireland at the time of the English conquest. By 1840, the historical population maximum had been reached: more than 8 million.

At the same time, making room for food production spelled the end of the Irish forests. We don't have to think that before the English conquest Ireland was still covered with the lush forests of the time of the mythical hero Cuchulainn. But the data reported by Michael Williams in his *Deforesting the Earth* (2003) show that Ireland in the 17th century still maintained about 12% of the land covered with trees, significantly more than most European countries of that time. The deforestation of Ireland is described in Eileen McCracken's book *The Irish Woods since Tudor times* (1971), in which we read that Ireland ceased to be an exporter of wood and became an importer by the late 18th century. Not just forests were destroyed, but also the species that inhabited them. Squirrels and deer went extinct, to be reintroduced only in the 20th century. The last wolf of Ireland is reported to have

been shot in 1770. Travelers in Ireland at that time reported a treeless, bleak landscape. The loss of biodiversity and the erosion of the soil were elements of a disaster waiting to take place. And it did.

In 1845, the leaves of the Irish potato plants started turning black and curled, then rotted. Nobody knew that it was because of a fungal infestation, but that mattered little; the potato harvest was ruined, and at the end of the year, the Great Famine began. About one million people died of starvation in a few years. Another half a million died of diseases related to starvation. Many tried to escape and, in many cases, they left Ireland for the United States on ships that were totally inadequate in terms of hygienic conditions and lacked sufficient food and water. These vessels were termed "coffin ships" and caused the death of an untold number of Irish emigrants. Eventually, the famine caused Ireland to lose about half of its population, four million people.

Remarkably, even during the worst years of the famine, Ireland continued to produce food to export to England. That generated the legend of the "Irish Holocaust," which blames the English for having willingly created the famine to get rid of a large number of their Irish subjects. But if the British wanted to get rid of the Irish, they could have used the method that Cromwell had successfully used a couple of centuries before: bullets. Since the Irish had no army, no weapons, and no training in military matters, they couldn't possibly have resisted the extermination treatment that the US government was inflicting on the Native Americans at the same time. More likely, the British government had no interest in exterminating the Irish, a population that was already working for them at essentially zero cost. The British poor, then, had much better prospects of emigrating overseas than of becoming even poorer by settling in Ireland, where their only perspective was a diet of potatoes and a life in mud cabins.

Unfortunately, if the British had no interest in exterminating the Irish, they had no interest in their survival, either. They didn't care about people whom they considered unruly, unskilled, and speaking

a barbarous language that nobody could understand. Nevertheless, when the famine came, the British government initially provided some relief. The government headed by Robert Peel (1841–1846) repealed the Corn Laws that imposed a tax on imported grains. Indian maize was purchased specifically to be sent to Ireland, and help was provided in the form of "soup kitchens." Most likely, what these kitchens served wasn't exactly gourmet food, but they saved hundreds of thousands of people during the initial phases of the famine. But these attempts were discontinued by the government of Lord John Russell, who succeeded Peel in June 1846. Russell's government reinstated the corn laws and dismantled the soup kitchens, leaving the Irish to paddle their own coracles, so to speak. And that created the disaster.

So, the British didn't plan the Irish genocide, but they made it possible by omission. They chose to let the Irish starve and die. Why did they do that? After all, other European countries, such as the Netherlands and France, behaved differently, and the potato blight didn't cause mass starvation because emergency food relief was provided to the poor. If we go back to the debate in the English documents and newspapers of the time, we see how the Irish are often described as an inferior race and culture; lazy and good-for-nothing people who created by themselves the disaster that befell them. Jonah Barrington, English landlord, describes the Irish peasant of his times (late 18th century) as a mixture of the troll and the hobbit; sometimes dangerous, sometimes funny, never fully human. Benjamin Disraeli (who became prime minister after the Irish crisis was over) is reported to have said, "The Irish hate our order, our civilization, our enterprising industry, our pure religion" (we read this sentence on page 6 of Cahill's book *How the Irish Saved Civilization* (1995). Apart from the insults, the general idea was that helping the Irish would have done more harm than good by creating a persistent dependency. Charles Trevelyan (1807-1886), assistant secretary to the treasury, expressed the concept as "If the Irish once find out that there are any

circumstances in which they can get free government grants, we shall have a system of mendicancy such as the world never knew."

In the end, the Irish population collapse was a good illustration of how complex systems collapse: they never do that as the result of a single factor, but as many factors converging, all pushing in the same direction. And when that happens, the result is not just decline, but collapse – it is the Seneca Effect. The Irish society didn't collapse just because a fungal infection hit the potato crops. It collapsed because the infection triggered a series of consequences that were built into the structure of the Irish society. As soon as the infection unbalanced the system a little, all these factors started to play their role: overpopulation, lack of road transportation, lack of good ports in the Southern region, absence of large scale social networks, religious hatred between different sections of society, and, worst of all, a central government which didn't care about the welfare of its Irish subjects.

So, what had to happen, happened. Can it happen again on a larger scale in our modern world? Earth is a large island in comparison to Ireland, but it is still an island. And we cannot discount the possibility that events similar to the *An Gorta Mor* will unfold on a much larger scale in the future.

North America. Depopulation by Culling

During the 19th century, the largest genocide in the history of humankind took place in North America. It was the culminating phase of a cycle that started when Columbus reached the New World in 1492. Already, the first contact between Europeans and Natives resulted in local conflicts, but the early centuries of interactions also involved considerable cultural interchanges and reciprocal influences.

What doomed the Natives had a specific name: the Industrial Revolution.

It started in the United States in the 18th century, with the first coal mine established in 1748 in Virginia. By the late 18th century, the Eastern coast of the US was already in a full industrialization phase with textile mills, forges, and the production of weapons and ammunition. The American Revolutionary War (1775-1783) showed that the US industry could support a war effort to match an established world power such as Britain.

The booming economy of the East Coast led to a gradual process of expansion of the Whites. The Natives tried to resist by military means, initially with some success. At the Battle of the Wabash in 1791, the Natives were able to inflict on the Whites possibly the worst defeat ever experienced by the US army in its history. But, from then on, it was all downhill for the Natives, who were able to defeat the US forces only occasionally in local skirmishes. That was what you would expect when a society that was at a stone age technology level faced a modern industrial power.

The 19th century saw the expulsion of the Natives from their lands, and their gradual extermination. The Indian Removal Act (1830) under President Andrew Jackson led to the "Trail of Tears" when eastern tribes (e.g., Cherokee, Creek, Choctaw, Chickasaw, Seminole) were forced to relocate to lands west of the Mississippi River. Over 60,000 people marched along the Trail of Tears. Many died along the road of disease or starvation. Many others died or were killed later as they couldn't adapt to the new lands. The Seminole population in Florida was nearly completely exterminated between 1816 and 1858. In 1832, the Sauk and Fox tribes were pushed out of Illinois and Wisconsin, and most of them died in an equivalent of a new Trail of Tears. Later, around 1876-1877, it was the time of the Lakota, Cheyenne, and Arapaho, led by figures like Sitting Bull and Crazy Horse. It was the time of the last Native victory at the Little Bighorn (1876), but that had no effect on the outcome of the war. The

surviving Natives were forced onto reservations chosen among unproductive lands where they could only live in conditions of extreme poverty. The massacre of Wounded Knee was the last event of some relevance in this war of extermination.

It is estimated that the Native American population in the U.S. dropped from an estimated 5–15 million (pre-Columbian) to under 250,000 by 1900. Estimates vary about the fraction of the Native American population exterminated; some are as high as 98%, others suggest a less drastic "culling" of about 70%-80%. At that point, Native Americans controlled less than 2% of their original territories in the U.S. Their cultures were thoroughly suppressed, and very little remains of them, with only a fraction of US citizens of Native descent still speaking the old languages.

It was one of the largest, most thorough, and most ruthless exterminations ever reported in human history, although maybe not so ruthless as the extermination of the Amalekites, a population living in Palestine, carried out by the Jews in biblical times. According to the Bible, God ordered the Jews to kill not only the Amalekite men, but also the women and the children, and even their livestock. Maybe this extermination was not so thorough as God had commanded it to be, but we have plenty of data about more recent ones. We may consider the Belgian Atrocities in the Congo Free State (1885–1908), the Herero and Nama Genocide by the Germans in Africa (1904–1908), the Armenian extermination by the Ottoman Empire (1915–1923), the holocaust of the Jews and other groups in Germany (1941-1945), the Rwandan Genocide (1994) and others ongoing right now. But the extermination of the Native Americans preceded all these cases, and was much larger in terms of absolute numbers and thoroughness.

As I discuss in my book *Exterminations* (2024), when certain conditions are satisfied, extermination is nearly unavoidable. It happens when a subgroup is 1) easily identifiable, 2) unable to provide strong military resistance, and 3) provides monetary gains for the exterminators. In addition, an extermination needs to be

accompanied by a certain degree of hate. Killing a person in cold blood is possible only when the killer is somehow convinced that it is proper and necessary to do so. That's the job of modern propaganda, which usually succeeds in the task.

When these conditions hold, eliminating people who don't belong to one's country or ethnic group has never been especially difficult in history. President Andrew Jackson (1767 – 1845) is reported to have used the phrase "Nits make lice" to justify the extermination of Native women and children. Then, of course, talking about exterminators, Adolf Hitler is supposed to be the one who rules them all. However, we have to note that he took inspiration from the way White Americans treated the American Natives.

In addition to the extermination of the Jews and other minorities, Hitler's Nazi government is credited with having planned a culling that would have been the largest in history if it had been carried out to completion. It was the *Generalplan Ost* (General Plan for the East), also known as the Ostplan, which was developed in 1942 during World War II. The proposers of the plan had in mind the concept of overpopulation and thought that the Slavs living in Eastern Europe were a "surplus" that could be conveniently removed to leave space for the superior German race. They imagined that, after having defeated the Soviet Union, the lands West of the Urals were to be occupied by 6 to 12 million German farmer-warriors, the *Herrenvolk* (master race), while several tens of millions of ethnic Slavs were to be killed in place, or pushed on the other side of the Urals to die of starvation. It would have been an operation very much like the "Trail of Tears" of the Native Americans of 1830, but on a much larger scale.

The example of the *Ostplan* is one of the several large-scale culling operations that were imagined but, fortunately, never put into practice. Unfortunately, though, in our crowded world, the idea of the wholesale elimination of disliked people remains popular. There are plenty of possibilities for governments to engage in major culling operations. They are already demonstrating that they can do that

perfectly well by engaging in a series of major wars when we desperately need to conserve energy and resources to face the challenges ahead. But this is the way the human mind works.

Japan: Stability During the Edo Period

During the Edo period (1603-1868), Japan was nearly completely isolated from the rest of the world, and the Japanese had to survive on no more than what they could produce in their islands. This period can be seen as a test bed for Malthus' ideas. There was a limited territory available and, as a consequence, a limit to the food supply that could be produced. How would the Japanese population adapt?

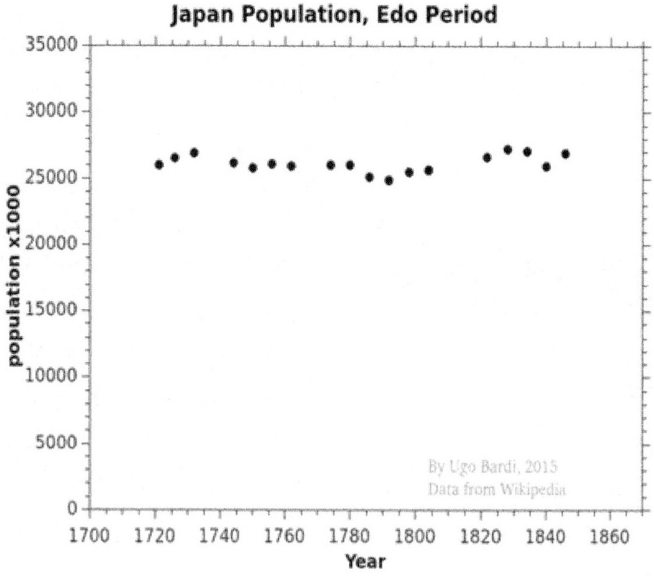

Figure 21. The Japanese population during the Edo Period

Apparently, they succeeded at the task. The population of Japan remained nearly constant, around 27-28 million inhabitants, without suffering large famines. It was a remarkable success considering how another island on the opposite side of Eurasia, Ireland, saw a succession of tragic famines.

The Japanese of the 19th century knew the work of Malthus, but we have no evidence that their government relied on Malthus' theory. Their approach was mostly pragmatic, influenced by the neo-Confucian views from China, which emphasized harmony between humans and nature. Since Japan was an island, the Japanese didn't face immediate threats from their neighbors, nor were they in a condition to attack them. So, the Government had no interest in having expendable cannon fodder, but rather in having a stable population. Stabilization was obtained mainly by "bottom-up" strategies enacted by single women or families. The Japanese used various contraception methods and, only when that was not enough, infanticide, called *Mabiki* ("thinning," a term borrowed from rice farming). Occasional famines were caused by bad weather or volcanic eruptions, but they never had more than a limited impact on the population. It was a remarkably successful story that generated the blossoming of a sophisticated civilization, of which we still admire art and poetry.

Things changed when Japan ceased to be an isolated land because of new technological developments and the economic expansion of the West. In 1854, a small fleet of American warships arrived in the Bay of Tokyo. They were called the "Black Ships" by the Japanese. The admiral of the fleet, Commodore Perry, forced the Shogunate government to open the country to foreign commerce. It was the start of a profound transformation of Japanese society, and one of the results was a population boom that continued up to the early 2000s. You see in the figure a plot of the population increase that

went from less than 30 million in 1850 to a peak of 128 million people; an increase of more than a factor of four.

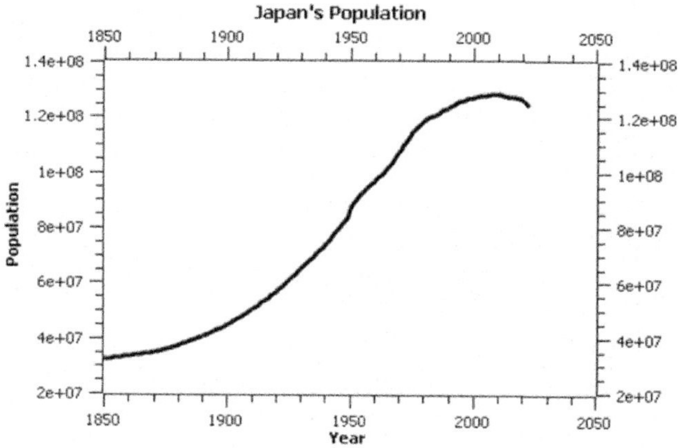

Figure 22 – Historical Japan's population. Data from Our World in Data

Today, the Japanese population is approximately 123 million, slightly lower than what it was at the peak in 2010. It is still a large number, and the problem is clear. During the Edo Period, the Japanese agriculture could feed no more than 30 million people. How can it feed more than a hundred million people today? Mainly, it is because of artificial fertilizers and other innovations; nevertheless, more than 60% of the calories consumed in Japan today come from imported food. Hence, in terms of food supply, Japan is one of the most import-dependent nations among developed countries. At present, the Japanese economy is healthy enough to be able to pay for these imports. Still, it is unsettling to think of what could happen to Japan if the economy were to decline while the world is facing a food shortage.

Fortunately, the Japanese population has started declining, prefiguring a possible return to conditions of self-sufficiency. Nevertheless, with the current annual degrowth rate of -0.54%, it would take more than two centuries for the Japanese population to

return to the level of the Edo period of approximately 25 million people. But the decline is accelerating, so that Japan may return to sustainable conditions in a much shorter time. But would that be possible fast enough and, at the same time, without a traumatic collapse?

Recently, public awareness of the risk of food shortages has been growing in Japan, and the government is launching campaigns promoting more domestic production, while some citizens are stockpiling food. Surveys show rising anxiety, especially post-COVID and amid recent global instability. So far, it is nothing that could be defined as panic; it is more like a simmering unease. Would Japan face the same destiny as Ireland or some Polynesian islands? We cannot say, but we can only hope that the Japanese can manage a non-violent population decline that will lead them to a safer situation.

China: Birth Control and the One-Child Policy

China is the only country in the world that engaged in a birth control policy that involved direct government intervention to limit the number of children that a couple could have. A series of regulations were enacted starting in 1979-1980 under the name of the "One Child" policy. Having more than one child was not a crime, but it was treated as an administrative violation that carried financial penalties. The regulations remained in force until 2015, although they were progressively relaxed from the early 2000s.The Chinese birth control policy is normally described as a success for the purposes for which it was enacted, that is, reducing population growth. Indeed, the Chinese fertility rate rapidly declined from the 1970s onward. However, in the West, this policy is generally criticized and

condemned as a mark of dictatorship and oppression. The debate is clouded with thick layers of propaganda, but the real story may be more complex and nuanced than the way it is normally presented. Why exactly did the Chinese government embark on this policy? And was it really effective? Understanding this matter requires revisiting the history of China and its population.

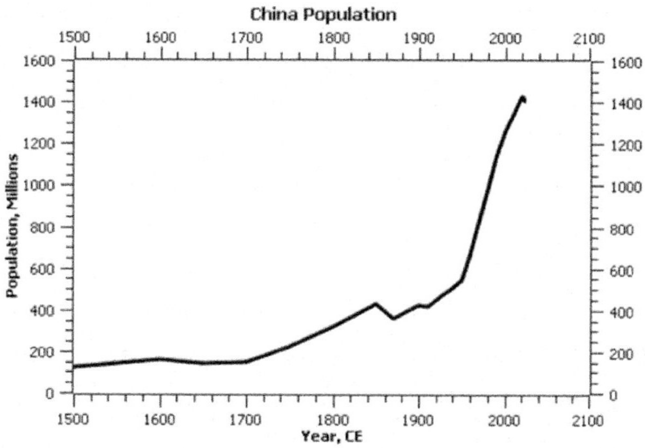

Figure 23 - The Chinese Population during the past 500 years. Data from Wikipedia

In ancient times, during the first unified Chinese empire under the Qin Dynasty (221-206 BCE), China's population was around 20-40 million people. Through the various dynasties that followed, the population grew and declined during alternating periods of peace and turmoil, but it remained always below 200 million. Things changed with the Qing Dynasty (1644-1912) when the population started growing, reaching more than 400 million by the mid-19th century.

This burst of population growth can be explained by the role that China played during the age of expansion of the European powers. The Industrial Revolution started in the mid-18th century, and it gave Europeans a technological and economic advantage that allowed them to embark on the conquest of nearly the whole world.

China was too big for Europe to conquer, but too weak to join the Europeans in their expansion. Nevertheless, with the proliferation of global markets and the opening of commercial sea routes, China could recover after the collapse of the paper currency used during the Ming dynasty, which generated inflation and counterfeiting in the 1540s.

China accomplished this task by importing the Spanish "Carolus" dollar, minted using silver mined mainly in Mexico. These coins were a tremendous boost to the economy, which geared up to pay for the silver by exporting earthenware, porcelain, textiles, silk, tea, and more overseas. During this period, China accounted for 30–33% of global GDP, it imported about 30% of the world's silver production, and it was the world's largest economy. It is not surprising that the booming economy led to a corresponding increase in birth rates and population growth.

However, this pattern came to a stop in the early 19th century, when the gradual depletion of the silver mines in Mexico and Bolivia made extraction expensive. That caused political unrest that led the former Spanish colonies in Latin America to gain their independence. That led to a further decline in silver production, since smelting silver required mercury that was mined in Almaden, in Spain. The consequence was a dearth of silver in China that led to an economic crisis, internal rebellion, and the reversal of the silver trade direction. Now, silver started moving out of China in the form of strange boat-shaped ingots called "sycees." On top of that, the British government thought it could make good money by selling the Chinese opium cultivated in India and so squeezing out the remaining Chinese silver (incidentally, opium imports are normally considered the cause of the Chinese decline, but the problems had started much earlier)

The result was generalized chaos. In a famous incident that took place in 1839, Chinese official Lin Zexu seized large amounts of opium from foreign ships, then had it thrown into the sea. The British reacted by invading China. It was the start of the Opium Wars and of the "century of humiliation" in which China was repeatedly invaded

and defeated by coalitions of foreign powers. The Qing government couldn't effectively counter the Western aggression, since it was engaged in quelling internal rebellions. In addition, China hadn't adopted the Western industrialization method, unlike what Japan did during the same period. So, the Chinese military forces were technologically inferior to the Western ones.

Perhaps it was the availability of low-cost human power that discouraged the use of production machinery, although bureaucracy and cultural factors also played a role. Whatever the case, China remained militarily and economically weak for a long time, and the Western attitude remained aggressive, not just in terms of periodic military attacks. Chinese immigrants in the US were subjected to all sorts of violence and intimidation. As an example of what was floating inside Westerners' minds, in 1909, Jack London, well known as the author of *White Fang*, wrote a short story titled *The Unparalleled Invasion* (1910). In it, he described the total extermination of the Chinese population by biological warfare. China is then colonized by the Western powers, opening the way to a "joyous epoch of splendid mechanical, intellectual, and art output."

The establishment of the People's Republic of China in 1949 marked the start of an economic and social renaissance and a new population boom. It was Chen Yun (1905-1995), head of Central Finance and Economic Commission, who redressed the monetary disaster by pegging the value of the Chinese Renminbi to real commodities that the government controlled: grain and cotton. Chen Yun's insight was revolutionary: he understood that currency is merely accounting for physical resource flows. By pegging the renminbi to state-controlled commodities rather than to scarce metals or foreign currencies, he broke China's centuries-old dependency on external monetary standards. This created the stable foundation for China's subsequent industrialization and population boom. The Korean War (1950 – 1953) saw China again fighting a coalition of

Western forces. The war ended in a draw, but it officially marked the end of the century of humiliation.

In the new phase of economic expansion, the Chinese population started a rapid growth, fueled by the introduction of new agricultural technologies. The government initially saw population growth as a good thing, and it enacted laws to limit birth control and subsidize large families. But already in the 1950s, worries about overpopulation were surfacing. The debate was affected by the "Great Famine" that struck China in 1960, during the "Great Leap Forward" designed to generate a rapid industrialization of the country. The reported number of victims from the famine has often been exaggerated, but today, estimations tend to converge to 15-20 million. A tragic event, in part due to droughts and bad weather, but in large part due to the misallocation of resources to industrialization, penalizing agriculture.

The Great Famine showed that the Chinese agricultural system was fragile. Nevertheless, the idea that China had an overpopulation problem was strongly resisted. During the Cultural Revolution (1966-1976), the natalist position was predominant. At the UN Conference on Population in Bucharest in 1970, a coalition of industrialized countries proposed that Third World Nations needed to implement birth control measures to avoid overpopulation. China sided with the Third World, forcefully condemning the proposal. The Chinese delegation maintained that world poverty was not caused by overpopulation, but by the imperialist policies of the rich world.

The Natalist position was often expressed in simplified terms as "more is better," and it was associated with the "Gang of Four," which dominated Chinese politics during the Cultural Revolution. These ideas fell out of favor after the death of Chairman Mao Zedong in 1976. With Deng Xiaoping at the helm, from 1978, the Chinese government completely reversed its position, rapidly pivoting to a set of policies and regulations designed to curb population growth.

How did the Chinese government arrive at this position? From what we can read in the 1981 book *China&Population, Problems&Prospects*, a collection of papers from Chinese scientists, it seems clear that it was the result of an extensive debate among scientists, administrators, and party members. The discussion was anchored on Marxist principles; for instance, noting how Engels himself had stated in 1891 that "a communist society should one day be compelled to regulate the production of human beings as it regulates the production of goods." Chairman Mao Zedong had also maintained in a 1957 speech that it was a task for the state to control the population in such a way as to optimize productivity. Apart from this ideological veneer, however, the debate in China was pragmatic. It was centered around a basic question: how should the population be managed to support the highest industrial output? Was it better to increase the number of workers or the productivity of each worker? The answer came from the studies carried out by the Chinese scientists working on demography.

From the beginning of its existence, the PRC government had encouraged scientific research with a view to competing with the West. In the 1970s, the Chinese school of demography went in parallel with the Western one in developing new statistical and quantitative methods of study. At that time, the main actors were Liu Zheng, director of the Research Institute of Demography of the Chinese People's University, and Song Jan, a scientific maverick who had started his career as a rocket scientist, later moving to demographic studies. Both Liu and Song were also prominent members of the Chinese Communist Party (CCP). Together with several other scientists, they framed the Chinese demographic future.

Liu and Song were part of different schools of thought: while Liu was a sociologist by formation, Song was a mathematician expert in control systems, a field sometimes termed "cybernetics." These two schools were partially in contrast with each other, and, in the West, cybernetics applied to social sciences was soon expelled and

marginalized. In China, instead, conventional social sciences and social cybernetics seemed to be able to live together, probably because both claimed that their approaches adhered to the basic Marxist principles.

The 1981 book *China&Population* contains a long article by Liu Zheng that describes the goals of the Chinese demographic policy as part of the general planning of the economy. Liu strongly promoted the view that population growth should not become a burden for the progress of industrialization. In the same book, Song Jian presented similar ideas, but went into the details. First, Song evaluated the "optimal" Chinese population, estimated as 600-700 million. Then, Song sketched how this number could be reached in about one century after having overshot it to about 1.2 billion, and then carefully controlling the fertility rate of Chinese women in such a way as to avoid an excessive imbalance of the age distribution. Song published several more papers in English on his work in the international literature describing his mathematical model of population growth.[87] Song's book, titled *Population System Control*,[88] coauthored by Jingyuan Yu, provides more details.

It is difficult to say how strongly the Chinese government was influenced by the scientific arguments of Chinese demographers. Additional strategic considerations may have played an important role. From the documents of the time, it is clear that the Chinese leadership was seriously worried about the possibility of a new famine that could have destroyed the effort toward industrialization and military security of the country. In addition, the memory of the military failure of the Chinese against the Western invasions during the century of humiliation was still present in the minds of administrators. They may have reasoned that the reliance on cheap manpower during the Qing dynasty was one of the factors that prevented China from industrializing, and they didn't want to make the same mistake again. Whatever the case, after the downfall of the Gang of Four in 1976, a general agreement was obtained within the

Chinese Government that it was necessary to control population growth.

The Chinese birth-control action started in the mid-1970s. In an initial phase, no compulsory restrictions on family size were implemented; then, in 1980, the one-child policy was introduced. It was a set of regulations and administrative measures enforced by the National Population and Family Planning Commission. These regulations were never completely rigid, and they admitted several exceptions. In 1984, the policy was adjusted to allow a second child for families in rural areas if the first child was a daughter. Starting in 2006, in some provinces, couples who were both only children were allowed to have two children. In 2013, an exemption was introduced, allowing two children in families where one parent was an only child. In 2015, the Chinese government announced that all couples would be allowed to have two children, effectively ending the one-child policy. Today, the government is encouraging larger families.

But what was the effect of the one-child policy in China? Was it really effective, as it is commonly said to have been. Let's take a look at the data

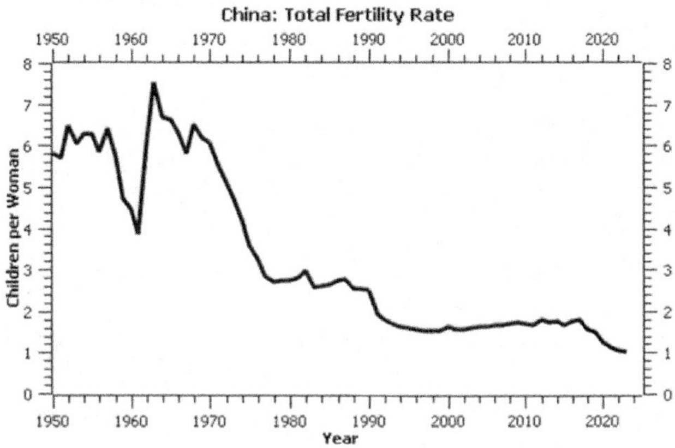

Figure 24. China's total fertility rate after 1950.

The strong oscillations of the fertility rate around 1960 are likely related to the famine of 1960 and the turmoil of the Great Leap Forward. People reacted to stressful conditions by reducing the number of births, and then by overcompensating for the previous decline. In any case, the early 1970s marked the beginning of a rapid decline in the fertility rate, which started well before the enactment of birth control policies. On the contrary, the TFR rose slightly after the one-child policy started, probably as a result of the large cohort of people born in the late 1960s entering their reproductive age. The elimination of the policy during the 21st century didn't generate a significant return to high fertility. Recently, China's total fertility rate (TFR) declined even further. Paradoxically, China reached the goal of one child per family only after the one-child policy was abolished.[88]

Further insight comes by comparing the Chinese fertility data to that of the four South-Asian "Tigers:" Singapore, Hong Kong, Taiwan, and South Korea. This comparison is significant because these countries are culturally and economically similar to China. Here is the relative graph.

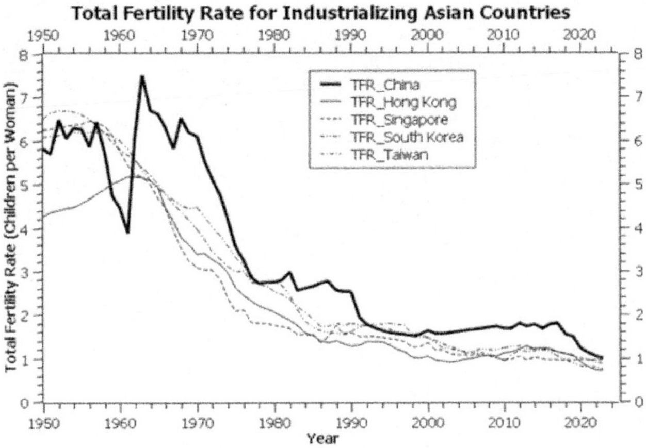

Figure 25 - Comparison of the Total Fertility Rate for China (solid curve) and some Southern Asian Countries

Remarkably, the fertility curves for all five countries are very similar, despite the fact that only China implemented a one-child policy. Today, all these countries have basically the same low fertility rate, well below the population replacement level. Does this mean that the one-child policy in China had no effect? Not necessarily, but, evidently, it was no more effective than the less drastic policy interventions to reduce natality enacted in the other four countries.

The initial Western attitude toward the Chinese birth control policy was one of interest and mild criticism. For instance, in a 1985 article,[89] Bongaart and Greenhalgh argue that the one-child policy was not necessary, but not against the necessity of reducing the Chinese fertility rate. Nevertheless, today, China is universally criticized in the West for the birth control policies enacted up to 2015. The criticism is based on four fundamental points.

- Government-enacted birth control is a mark of dictatorship and hence unacceptable on political and moral grounds.
- The one-child policy led to a large increase in the number of abortions.
- The one-child policy led to a strong imbalance in the sex ratio of newborn children.
- The one-child policy was counterproductive, leading to the current collapse of birthrates.

The first point of the list, unacceptable dictatorial policy, is a legitimate political opinion, but it is also used as an excuse for various exercises in China-bashing. As I discuss in a blog post,[90] articles on the one-child policy in the Western mainstream media liberally mix reality and fantasy, presenting a distorted view of the story in terms of a conspiracy somehow created by a coalition of Chinese Communists and Western evil forces. These articles appear to derive

their criticism from an academic paper published in 2005 by Susan Greenhalgh.[91]

It would be out of place here to go into the details, but let me just say that Greenhalgh's thesis but let me just say that Greenhalgh's thesis effectively denies agency to Chinese demographers, suggesting they were either manipulated by Western ideas or incapable of independent scientific analysis—a patronizing view that ignores the sophisticated quantitative work being done by Chinese researchers throughout the 1970s.

In addition, Greenhalgh proposes a nefarious role of the Club of Rome, which she describes as a misguided organization of alarmists in her later book *Just one Child* (2008). However, nowhere does Song cite as an inspiration the *Limits to Growth* report that the Club of Rome sponsored in 1972, nor is there evidence of contacts between Song and the members of the Club. In any case, if Song read that report, he must have found it not very interesting. He was working on practical methods of population control, a subject that *The Limits to Growth* did not discuss. The best that Greenhalgh can do to support her interpretation is to state that "one exceptionally knowledgeable researcher maintained that Song had read and was directly influenced by the work of the Club of Rome" (note 17 at page 352 of her 2008 book). This source is said to be "confidential" and hence must remain anonymous. Why having read *The Limits to Growth* should be something confidential is surprising, to say the least. It is even more surprising if you consider that a Chinese translation was published in 1980 with a foreword by Premier Zhao Ziyang (then one of China's top leaders). But we are not here to discuss conspiracy theories, so let's move on.

The second item in the list of criticisms of China's policies is that the one-child policy caused an increase in the abortion rate in China. This is possible, although the data do not show a large effect.[92] The number of abortions did not significantly increase after the one-child law was enacted in 1980; they actually declined in the 1990s. The

abortion rate picked up again after 2015, when the one-child law was abandoned, a trend hardly compatible with a direct effect of the one-child policy. In any case, modern contraceptive methods were widely available to Chinese couples from the mid-1960s onward. So, abortion was not the only possible way to comply with birth control policies. It may have been used nevertheless, because abortion is not normally seen as a moral issue in China, but as a practical birth control method.

The third item in the list is that the one-child policy caused, or increased, the gender imbalance in China, that is, the birth of more women than men. This is not a new problem for China, where a traditional preference for male heirs led to gender imbalance already during the Han dynasty (2nd century CE). From the Song dynasty onward, Confucian moralists repeatedly condemned female infanticide as a widespread practice. It seems that the highest imbalance was seen during the Qing dynasty (18th-19th century CE), when the male to female ratio was reported as about 110-150 to 100. Some provinces even reported values of the order of 200. These data can be found in the 1999 book by James Lee and Wang Feng, *One Quarter of Humanity*.

In ancient times, the gender imbalance was mainly the result of infanticide. In ancient China, "raising babies in the bucket" was a euphemism for drowning baby girls that seemed to be widely understood. In modern times, however, selective abortion can obtain the same result, since it is possible to determine the sex of a fetus before it is born by means of ultrasound examination. The Chinese census data indicate a slight increase in the male/female gender ratio after the introduction of the one-child policy in 1980, from the natural ratio of 105/100 to about 107/100. In the 1990s, when ultrasound techniques became widely available in China, the ratio rose to 114, and then to about 120 in the early 2000s. Since then, it has declined, being now around 110/100. For comparison, Taiwan now has a gender ratio of 107/100, despite never having implemented compulsory birth control policies. Today, induced abortion remains broadly legal in

China, but selective abortion is strictly forbidden. The gender imbalance is disappearing in urban areas, although it continues to exist in rural ones. We can conclude that the one-child policy may have contributed to an existing tendency to a higher male/female imbalance. Still, it was not the only factor involved, and perhaps not even the most important.

Finally, how about the accusation that the one-child policy was so effective that it is leading to the destruction of China by depopulation? (See, for instance, the 2021 article by Dominic Pino on National Review[93]). Honestly, it is impossible to take it seriously. It would mean that a policy that was abolished in 2015 is still affecting the behavior of Chinese families today, causing them to keep their fertility ratio at the levels that were required in 1980. A little unlikely, to say the least. After all, do the Chinese still use pots and pans as drums to chase away the invisible dragon that's eating the sun during eclipses?

In the end, what can we say about the Chinese experience in birth control? One conclusion is that the one-child policy was not an evil conspiracy to depopulate China. It was the result of well-founded concerns about the future of China, and it aimed at avoiding new famines and supporting an efficient industrial economy. It was devised and enacted on the basis of the best data and theoretical models available at the time. Unfortunately, it is well known that, in theory, practice and theory are the same thing, but, in practice, they are not. The Chinese planners of the 1970s were still reasoning according to the old idea that human birthrates are determined by an "urge to reproduce," and hence that a top-down intervention was critically necessary to keep the rates low. It was only in the early 1990s that it became clear that a widespread, sustained global fertility decline had begun, making birth control unnecessary as a way to reduce population growth. So, the one-child policy in China may be archived as a well-intentioned attempt, but ineffective and unnecessary.

Today, China is no longer facing the overpopulation problem it was facing half a century ago. Just like other industrialized countries, China's fertility rate is now well below the level needed to maintain the current population. In 2024, the Chinese population declined for the first time after the boom of the 1950s, and China is now losing about one million inhabitants per year. With a total population of about one and a half billion, such a loss cannot have significant effects on anything, but the decline may accelerate in the future.

A debate is presently ongoing in China on how to cope with the declining birthrates, just as it is happening in other Asian countries and in the West. Everywhere, governments are attempting to encourage births by financial and social incentives, but these measures don't seem to be having significant effects. That's not surprising because the social factors that lead to low fertility are deeply embedded in the structure of modern societies, including the Chinese one. In addition, China is affected by the same pollution factors that tend to reduce fertility everywhere by damaging the human reproductive system. Pollution is deeply embedded in the industrial production system, and the effort needed to abate it is enormous. No matter whether social or chemical factors are responsible for the decline (probably both), reversing the trend would require truly drastic actions. At present, it looks likely that the Chinese, just like other industrial economies, won't be able to do much more than mitigate the problems caused by an elderly population. Perhaps automation and robotics will provide the necessary workforce that was once provided by young human beings. But only the future will tell us how much governments will be able to use their influence to maintain a fertility rate able to stabilize the population.

Soviet Union: Economic Collapse

The collapse of the Soviet Union in 1991 was a classic example of a system that had overshot its resources. The Soviet Government had tried to do too many things at once: being a military superpower, managing a large empire, exploring space, and keeping pace with the richer and larger Western Bloc. It wasn't possible. The last straw was the invasion of Afghanistan in 1979, which led to ten years of indecisive war until the Soviet troops left the country in 1989. The campaign badly strained the financial resources of the state. Two years later, in 1991, the Soviet Union imploded. In a few months, it went from one of the two most powerful blocs on the planet to an ensemble of failed states, with an economy in shambles and no significant military power. Afghanistan is known to be an empire destroyer, and in this case, it confirmed its traditional role.

Miraculously, the collapse of the Soviet Union didn't involve significant bloodshed. The countries that formed the Union went their own way, new governments were established, and the disappearance of Communism as an official state ideology seemed to open the way to a new era of prosperity that could come by adopting the practices and economic structures of the Western world. But it wasn't to be so. The former Soviet Union states plunged into a dark world of poverty and economic decline. The largest country of the Union, Russia, didn't fare much better than the others. The government went nearly bankrupt, and its national currency, the ruble, was so badly devalued that for a few years it was replaced by the US dollar even in everyday transactions.

The economic collapse weighed heavily on everyone in the main former Soviet country, Russia. Although nobody starved, the quality of the diet of the average citizen worsened considerably. The loss of jobs led to depression, alcoholism, and drug dependence. Suicides spiked up. Both the fertility rate and the total population plummeted.

Fortunately, the bad times didn't last forever. Gradually, the economy recovered, the ruble became stable, and it returned to being used as a normal currency. The government restarted paying salaries to employees, the police cracked down on the criminal gangs, and the population began to grow again, although it didn't reach the peak level of 1990.

Figure 26 - Russian Fertility Rate. Data from Our World in Data.

Figure 27 - Russian population, data from Our World in Data.

Recently, the war against Ukraine has been affecting not only the Russian economy but also the fertility rate of Russian women, which has been going down. It is probably for this reason that in 2025,

Russia's Federal State Statistics Service *(Rosstat)* stopped publishing data that it collects on the country's demographic situation. Nevertheless, we know that the Russian TFR (total fertility rate) is now at a historical low of 1.4, well below the replacement rate of 2.1. And that's remarkable because 2024 was proclaimed to be the "Year of the Family" by the Russian authorities. Providing large families with preferential mortgages, tax refunds, free school meals, and discounts for public transport, among other benefits, was supposed to raise the TFR, but it didn't help. We may doubt that the planned "demographic task force" that the Russian government announced as being created in 2025 will do much better.

Overall, Russia is in the same quandary as most Western countries; no matter what the government does, the natality and the population continue to plummet. The collapse of the Soviet Union had much worse effects on Ukraine.

In Ukraine, the population decline was truly dramatic and took place in two phases. The first started immediately after the collapse of the Soviet Union. The second started with the conflict with Russia in the Donbass region. Note how, before the collapse, Ukraine was a relatively prosperous country, and the population was growing, reaching more than 52 million inhabitants. Today, it is around 38 million, the same as it was in 1950. Not all the missing Ukrainians are dead or never were born. Many emigrated to escape the war, and, in principle, they could return. But it is unlikely that the declining trend could be reversed.

Figure 28 Ukraine's total fertility rate. Data from Our World in Data.

Figure 29 – Ukraine's Population. Data from Our World in Data.

If we examine other countries of the former Soviet Union, we observe a trend. All the Asian republics, Uzbekistan, Turkmenistan, Kazakhstan, Azerbaijan, and Kyrgyzstan, show population growth. All the European republics, Belarus, Moldova, Latvia, Lithuania, and Estonia, show a decline, although not so sharp as Ukraine. In all these cases, the common factor that characterizes growth or decline trends is the availability of mineral resources. The Asian republics are rich in a wide variety of minerals. Kazakhstan has about 12% of the world's uranium reserves and is a strategic producer of enriched uranium as

fuel for nuclear reactors. It has also copper, chromium, and more, plus oil and gas in the Caspian Sea region. Uzbekistan has gold and copper, plus oil and gas. Turkmenistan has some of the largest gas reserves in the world. Kyrgyzstan and Tajikistan have gold, silver, lead, zinc, and more. And, of course, the Asiatic part of Russia, Siberia, has vast mineral resources, including some of the world's largest oil and gas reserves.

Conversely, the former Soviet Republics in Europe have little in terms of mineral resources: Ukraine, in particular, has some coal and some iron, but neither is very valuable in the world's market. The fabled Ukrainian rare earth deposits, the object of much hubbub when Donald Trump started his second presidential term, simply do not exist as exploitable deposits, as you can read in the database of the United States Geological Survey (USGS). The story of these mythical "rare earths" that Trump was said to want as compensation for helping Ukraine fight Russia is a typical example of how fads appear in the Western mediasphere. For a while, they seem to be all-important, and then they just disappear in a puff of smoke.

Having mineral resources guarantees an income from exports that can keep an economic system alive even during dramatic times of political upheaval. A little prosperity helps people maintain their willingness to have children, and that's what's happening in the Asian republics and also in Russia. Except for Russia and Azerbaijan, they all have total fertility rates well above the replacement rate, and in one case, Uzbekistan, the rate is increasing – an exception in the world trends. Instead, the Former Soviet republics in Europe suffered badly from the collapse, and the declining economic situation discouraged families from having children.

The message that arrives from the former Soviet Union is that the economy is a fundamental factor in keeping society stable and avoiding a demographic collapse. Avoiding wars is also an excellent idea, and not just for this reason. That spells serious problems for Western Europe, whose economy is declining together with its fertility

rate, with a serious risk of a Soviet-like general collapse. To say nothing about the rapidly growing warlike attitude of Western European Leaders. We will see where all that will lead us, but of one thing we can be sure: wars are not a good idea to improve a demographic crisis.

Ethiopia and Africa: The Other Side of Depopulation

Ethiopia is a fascinating country. It is in Africa, but it is unlike any other African country. On its high plateau, it has a long history largely independent from that of the rest of the world, almost like another planet. And it is one of the countries with the highest population growth rate in the world.

Throughout history, Ethiopia was a mix of cultures and races. In ancient times, it was a trading powerhouse, linking Rome, India, and Persia via the Red Sea Port of Adulis. In the 4th century CE, as the Roman Empire was collapsing, King Ezana of Ethiopia converted to Christianity, making Ethiopia one of the world's first Christian states, alongside Armenia and Rome. The Ethiopian Orthodox Tewahedo Church, rooted in this region, remains a cornerstone of national identity. Attempts by Muslim rulers to invade Ethiopia failed, just as the attempts by Europeans to convert Ethiopians to Catholicism.

In 1935, Ethiopia was the only country in Africa that was not under the control of a European power. At that point, Benito Mussolini, Italy's government leader, decided that the concept of *Lebensraum* (vital space) popular in Germany could be applied to Italy, too. Furthermore, the vital space that Italy needed (renamed "a place in the sun") could be found in Ethiopia. At that time, Italy had 42 million inhabitants occupying 300,000 square km. Ethiopia had 20

million inhabitants over an area of 1.1 million square km. So, there was a certain perverse logic in the idea of moving part of the Italian population to a much less densely populated region. But it was one of those cases in which a political ruler thinks he has a simple solution for a complex problem. It never works. The idea of invading Ethiopia generated an unmitigated disaster for all the actors involved.

From a military viewpoint, Italy managed to occupy Ethiopia in a relatively short time, even though the Ethiopian resistance was strong and had to be crushed by aerial bombing and poison gas. But the invasion nearly bankrupted Italy, and it was soon discovered that the poor Italian peasants had no intention of moving to an arid place where they would become even poorer. They correctly judged that they had more than enough sun in Italy. The Ethiopians, in their turn, suffered massive destruction and large human losses.

When WW2 arrived, the Italian troops in Ethiopia could not be resupplied from the mainland, and they were rapidly defeated by a coalition of British and Ethiopian *Arbegnoch* (patriot) fighters. One may wonder what would have been the final result of World War II if the more than 100,000 fully equipped Italian troops in Ethiopia had been available in the Mediterranean war theater. But this is not a book about historical fiction, so let's skip this subject.

The post-war period was difficult for Ethiopia: political upheavals and civil wars erupted. The 1984–1985 famine, claimed over a million lives. Nevertheless, Ethiopia's economy kept growing. At the same time, the population literally exploded, reaching 120 million in 2024. Note, however, that Ethiopia is nearly three times larger in terms of land area than its historical nemesis, Italy. So, in terms of population density, Italy (195 people per square km) is still more populated than Ethiopia. (114 people per square km.) The difference is that Italy's fertility rate is now below the replacement rate, while that of Ethiopia remains well above it.

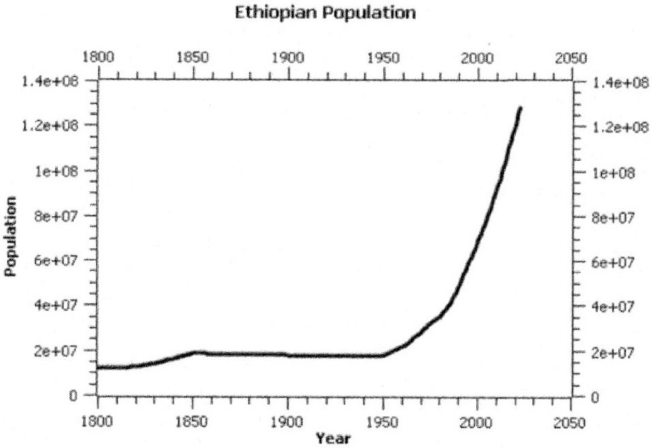

Figure 30 - Ethiopian Population. Data from the United Nations.

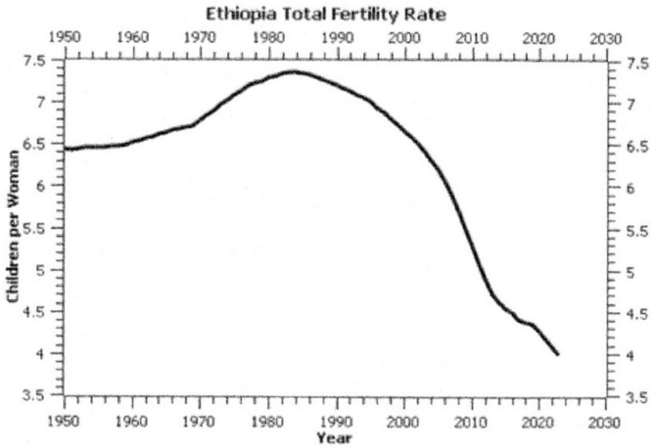

Figure 31- Ethiopia's Fertility rate. Data from Our World in Data.

In the 1980s, Ethiopian women had more than seven children each, a large country. Then, fertility declined rapidly, but it is still well above the replacement rate of 2.1 children per woman.

What about the future? With over four children per woman and a large cohort of young women able to reproduce, Ethiopia's population is destined to keep growing for some time, possibly

throughout the 21st century, with the statistical projections showing that it could reach more than 300 million inhabitants in the early 22nd century, when it should start declining. These data look impressive, but, again, numbers have to be placed in context. With 300 million inhabitants, Ethiopia would still have a lower population density than Japan today.

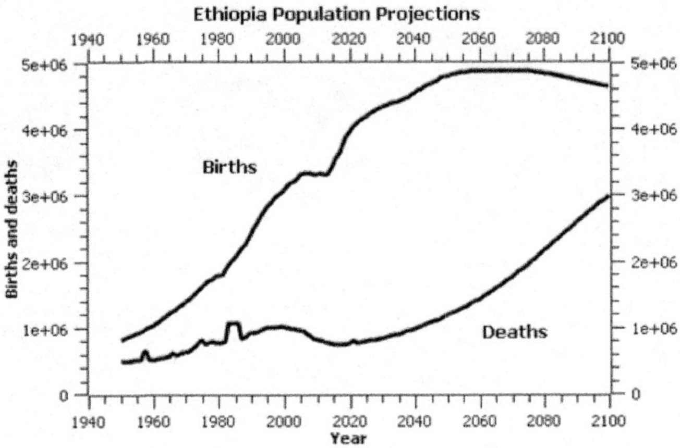

Figure 32- Ethiopia births and deaths, projected to 2100. UN data.

The population trends for Ethiopia parallel those for central Africa, but they are very different in the regions North of the Sahara Desert, where fertility is declining in the same way as in industrialized Western Countries. Overall, Africa's population trends are dominated by those of the central region, including Ethiopia

If nothing changes, Africa's population could reach about 40% of the world's population by the next century, up from the current value of 18%. Perhaps, Africa could reach a population of 4 billion people, and even more, according to some projections.

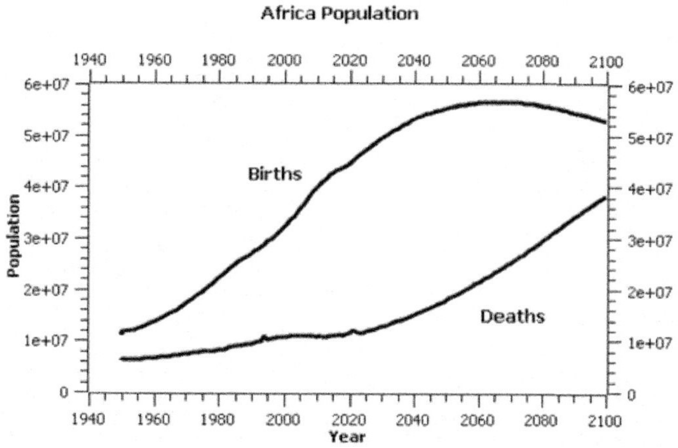

Figure 33 - Africa Birth and Death trends. UN data

Nevertheless, these long-term projections have to be taken with extreme caution. Whereas the North expanded in a period of abundant resources, largely provided by the South, now the South doesn't have an equivalent resource basin, and might well encounter a Malthusian barrier to reach population density levels comparable to those of the North. Eventually, the demographic trends in different countries will have to be compatible with each other, and we can only hope that it won't involve violence

The Future.

Technology can relieve the symptoms of a problem without affecting the underlying causes. Faith in technology as the ultimate solution to all problems can thus divert our attention from the most fundamental problem — the problem of growth in a finite system — and prevent us from taking effective action to solve it – Dennis Meadows

Figure 34 - A detail of the painting by the Italian painter Telemaco Signorini L'Alzaia (The Riverbank) 1894. It shows the plight of human beings used as energy sources. Wikimedia, Public Domain.

Taking a peek into the future of the human population, it is clear that we are approaching a "perfect storm" where several effects may coalesce to create a rapid population decline that we may call collapse. It is a thorny subject, loaded with political overtones of all sorts.

Predicting when and if the world population could crash down from the current levels turned out to be a honey trap for catastrophists, in which many people who should have known better fell, such as when Paul Ehrlich published his book *The Population Bomb* in 1968, predicting famines and assorted disasters in the short term. That book provided endless ammunition for the cornucopians to poke fun at the funny antics of catastrophists. Yes, but it is also true that famines and disasters did occur in the past, even though never at the

planetary scale and not during the past few decades. So, without falling into the trap of predicting dates, what can we say about the population trends in a not-too-remote future? Let's play the scenario game.

Food Production: Malthus' Return?

Food is the most obvious element that determines the population level, and its availability will be a crucial factor in the future of humankind in the coming decades. The limit to food production on a given extent of surface varies depending on several factors, but there is an upper limit given by the flow of solar light that powers photosynthesis. The actual limit is usually much smaller, given by other factors such as the availability of nutrients, water, and the range of temperatures in which plants can live and prosper. It also depends on the efficiency with which the products of the land or the sea can be harvested, processed, and stored. We can call this production level the "Malthusian Limit." It is not an absolute limit, but there is no doubt that it exists.

Ancient civilizations operated close to their Malthusian limit, as shown by recurrent famines. It was on the basis of this observation that Malthus proposed his model. But how close are we to the limit in our modern times? The data about global famines show a declining trend that started in the mid-20th century. Evidently, during the past few decades, the world's agriculture could match the demand for food worldwide. Some people took such data as evidence that famines have disappeared forever. One was Julian Simon with his *The Ultimate Resource* (1996). A more recent work by Steven Pinker, *The Better Angels of Our Nature* (2011), deals mainly with the disappearance of violence and conflicts, but also proposes that famines have

disappeared for good.

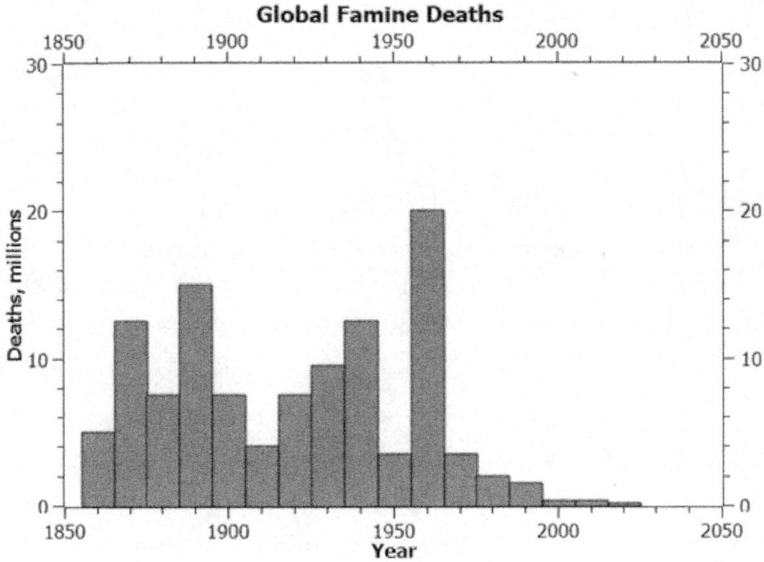

Figure 35 – Famine victims worldwide

At this point, you could argue that Malthus was dead wrong. But that would be an excess of optimism. Necessarily, for a famine to occur, it must be preceded by a period of abundance that leads the population to increase beyond its limits. It is reported that, in the 1840s, potato harvests were so abundant in Ireland that some had to be thrown away into ditches. You might have taken that as proof that Ireland would never suffer from famines again, but, alas, that wasn't the case. The great famine of 1846 was just around the corner.

The fact that we haven't seen global famines ongoing during the past 75 years doesn't mean we won't see them again. A lull of less than a century in a history that spans several thousands of years is not enough to state that the worst devils of our nature aren't waiting in the shadows to hit us again. Even if the risk of large-scale famines does not seem to be immediate, we do have a problem of food security, with

many people, even in the rich world, who aren't sure that they will have enough to eat every day. According to FAO, today, about 10% of the world's population suffers from severe food insecurity, and almost as many are undernourished. Many of the remaining fraction are not appropriately nourished because obesity and type II diabetes are rampant diseases. If the trend continues, half of the world's population is going to suffer from one or another form of diabetes, including the dreary "type III" form, which is the way some people call dementia. These trends are increasing, according to FAO.

Several possible conditions could lead to a contraction in the availability of food for a large fraction of the world's population. The main factor is, of course, the economic system's capability to keep producing food at the current levels. In this section, I will concentrate on agriculture and the associated livestock raising, leaving the other main food supplies, fishing and aquaculture, aside since they are minor sources in comparison, or largely depend on agriculture for their existence.

Today, agriculture has grown to a major planetary force. It is highly mechanized with the use of tractors, harvesters, and other machinery, significantly reducing manual labor and increasing the scale of farming operations. Industrial methods have led to specialization, where farms focus on a single crop or animal species to optimize efficiency. High-input agriculture is where large amounts of resources like water, fertilizers, and pesticides are used to maximize yield per unit area. The use of Genetically Modified Organisms (GMOs) is expanding, with genetically engineered crops leading to pest resistance, herbicide tolerance, and improved nutritional content. The newest trend is "Precision Agriculture," where farmers use technologies like GPS, sensors, drones, satellite imagery, and the like to optimize parameters such as the application of water, fertilizers, and pesticides. Theoretically, this approach reduces resource use and the environmental impact.

These improvements are all part of a series of changes promoted to make it possible to feed a growing number of people. But agriculture is a complex system that involves a variety of technologies that interact with each other, not always with good results. Consider GMOs: sometimes, they are lionized as proof of human ingenuity that reaches stellar levels. GMOs can indeed increase the amount of calories produced per unit surface in industrialized agricultural systems, but the result is not necessarily positive. The use of GMOs generates a cascade of effects that reverberate in the whole system, typically transforming a resilient rural production system into a fragile, heavily industrialized system. To say nothing about the fact that these technologies often worsen the food's nutritional quality.

To exploit the increased yield of GMOs, you need fertilizers, pesticides, irrigation, agricultural machinery, storage facilities, and more. Even if you can manage to upgrade all that, very often, the result is to make the system more vulnerable to external shocks, for example, increases in the cost of supplies, such as fuels and fertilizers. An economic crash or an increase in the cost of fossil fuels from which pesticides and fertilizers are created might make GMOs as obsolete as steam locomotives.

There are other examples of deeply flawed strategies in food production. One is the idea that we can increase supply by eliminating food waste and arriving at or near a "zero waste" condition. This idea is often presented together with images showing how a large amount of food, nowadays, is thrown away into waste bins, especially in Western countries. Sometimes, though, a little waste may not be a bad thing, and it is well known that perfectly optimized systems are also perfectly fragile.

As an example, years ago, the student cafeteria of the University of Florence had a conveyor belt that went through the hall and carried the trays with the lunch leftovers back to the kitchen. The trays often contained plenty of edible food, and some of the local poor had taken the habit of sitting near the end of the conveyor belt to catch

the food before it disappeared into the kitchen. They were a quiet presence that bothered nobody, and some good-natured students would purposefully leave some intact food for them in their trays. Unfortunately, the idea that the poor would eat the students' leftovers was considered unseemly and somewhat subversive by the university managers. The cafeteria was rearranged in such a way that the students themselves would bring back their trays to the entrance of the kitchen in the same way as is commonly done in fast-food restaurants. Then, the edible leftovers were thrown away. A big improvement, don't you think?

This story highlights how our society is poorly organized to cycle its resources, and still operates according to obsolete dreams of abundance. Much food is wasted in restaurants, but collecting it for the poor is not often done. Sometimes it is forbidden by law, although sometimes it is mandated, such as in France. It is a complex story that varies from country to country, involving different rules, laws, and cultural factors. An interesting story is that of the Canadian "binners," the people who collect food from waste bins. The practice is forbidden by law, and it is reported that sometimes the police would stand on guard in front of waste bins or run after binners. Surely not a way to optimize the use of societal resources.

We see the same story for traditional gleaning; once a common feature of peasant societies, today it is sometimes tolerated, but more often forbidden. In the 1930s, in the Soviet Union, gleaning was declared a criminal activity that could be punished with death. Fortunately, it is reported that the law was rarely applied in full. Nevertheless, reusing food waste is sometimes seen as degrading for the poor and offensive for everybody, as it goes against the idea that there exist technological solutions for everything. In practice, eliminating food waste would not just be impossible, but it would involve high costs and would make the system more fragile and vulnerable to shocks.

That doesn't mean that waste is unavoidable. Natural ecosystems are zero-waste systems; they recycle everything. But they are organized in a different way from the human food production system. An ecosystem is an ensemble of subsystems that work on the principle that "waste is food." That is, what is waste for one subsystem is food for another. But we humans are far from being able to do the same. The industrial system would have to be rebuilt from scratch, imitating the way natural systems work. But, at present, it is not done at a significant scale anywhere in the world.

Another apparent solution to food scarcity is expressed as, "If we all went vegetarian, there would be plenty of food for everyone." The production of animal proteins is indeed a wasteful process that uses agricultural products as feedstock for animals. If the areas presently used for livestock were turned to agriculture, more food would be available, at least in terms of calories. But switching to vegetarian food has plenty of problems, the main one being the difficulty of providing sufficient protein. Furthermore, "green" food is bulky and hence expensive to transport. It also spoils easily, and so you need refrigeration, and so on.

Similar concepts are shown by the "let's go local" strategy, that is, eat only food that's produced near where you live. That eliminates the cost of transportation, but involves huge problems, too. How do you deal with the unavoidable fluctuations in local production? Once upon a time, these fluctuations were the cause of periodic famines, often accepted as a fact of life. Going back to that is not exactly a way to solve the food supply problem.

How about the newest poster child of agricultural technologies, precision fermentation? It is a biotech process that uses microorganisms, like bacteria, yeast, or fungi, to produce high-value chemical compounds. It is a little miracle of genetic engineering that allows people to hack the DNA of bacteria to insert the sequence that generates the protein they want. Each bacterium then becomes a tiny factory that churns out whatever the DNA sequence is assembling.

The modified microbes go into a bioreactor: a water-filled tank with nutrients (usually sugars or starches), and the right temperature and acidity. It's like a brewery vat, but instead of beer, the vats grow custom molecules that can be harvested as food. You may get, for instance, an artificial burger or artificial cheese. You can also indulge in spectacular claims, such as creating mammoth meat, a food that no human has tasted for probably a few thousand years. Actually, the "mammoth meatball" story was just an advertising stunt. We don't have the DNA sequence of extinct mammoths, so it was impossible to recreate real mammoth meat.

Impressive as these technologies are, what can they do in addition to giving us the illusion of being paleolithic hunters? There are reasons why precision fermentation could be a game-changer in several fields of food production. Suppose you want to create meat proteins. You need to raise cattle, pigs, or chickens, and then kill them. Hopefully, it is done "humanely," but it is still killing living beings. Moving the production of proteins to fermentation plants, you could re-naturalize huge swaths of land with great advantages for the health of the planet. It is also fast: you can produce a lot in a short time, without worrying about changing seasons and the natural cycles of animals.

On the other hand, fermentation plants function with anaerobic organisms that don't perform photosynthesis. So, what they can do is to transform sugar into more sophisticated food. But they can't do what plants do: produce sugar out of atmospheric CO_2. You still need plantations to do that. Can we remove the dependence of the bioreactors on cultivated sugar? Yes, in principle, you could utilize a less valuable vegetable product, such as corn stalks. With appropriate genetic programming, the bacteria could break down hard plant biomass into glucose and then use it to manufacture food. Some bacteria (e.g., gluconobacter) already make gluconic acid (a glucose derivative) commercially via fermentation. Marketing these products,

we would become able to eat wood as termites do. A major metabolic change for humans.

With some creativity, we could also direct bacteria to transform electrical energy into food. Renewable energy plants produce plenty of electric energy, and in periods of low demand, this energy comes at zero cost. There doesn't seem to be a way to power the natural photosynthesis machinery of plants using electrons. Still, electrons can be turned into photons with good efficiency using, for instance, LED lights. Using electric energy directly produced by renewable plants, or stored in batteries, it would be possible to create farms completely independent from solar light. Then, it may be possible to hack the DNA of blue-green algae and make them produce food for humans in bioreactors, just as is done today using biofermentation. It is not clear whether that would be more efficient than using natural plants, but it could have significant advantages in comparison to traditional agricultural processes.

All is well and beautiful with these ideas, but one must also take into account that humans need not just sugar and proteins. They need all the micronutrients that plants obtain from the living soil. They need nitrogen, phosphorus, potassium, magnesium, sodium, and many other minerals in small amounts. They also need vitamins. And here things get complicated: we can instruct bacteria to create the basic proteins of meat or milk, but natural food contains compounds in microscopic amounts whose role in nutrition is probably important, but not completely understood. One thing is to eat natural meat that once was part of a living animal; another is to eat meat in the form of proteins created by bacteria. They may look the same, and even taste the same. But in terms of trace nutrients, they won't be the same. So, can people thrive on a diet of bacteria-made food? We don't know, and it will be an interesting experiment to do.Another problem with food production is that the modern food industry can be seen as a way to transform fossil fuels into food with some help from sunlight. Fuels are needed in the fields as fertilizers, pesticides, and fuel for

agricultural machinery. Once the food is produced, it needs fossil fuels for transportation, processing, refrigeration, packaging, and storage. Agriculture directly uses about 3-5% of global fossil fuels. The broader food industry, including transport, processing, and packaging, accounts for roughly 15-20%. Numbers vary by region and efficiency, but these are the numbers. And you see what the problem is: fossil fuels are not and cannot be eternal, and they are also the main source of carbon dioxide, generating global warming. Right now, if you take away the fuel, billions of people starve.

Figure 36 - The author, Ugo Bardi (right), with Paolo Pasquini (center) and Toufic El Asmar (left), together with the RAMSES electric tractor. Photo by the author

Eventually, we'll have to learn how to produce food and supply it to consumers without using fossil fuels – it is not easy, but it is possible. My coworkers and I discussed that in a paper aptly titled *Turning Electricity into Food*[94] We even built an electric agricultural truck/tractor to demonstrate how it could be done.

Despite the efforts to push agriculture to a lower reliance on fossil fuels, the problem is rarely taken into account in agricultural planning. When fuel prices rise, the immediate reaction of farmers and government officials alike is to provide subsidies to reduce the impact. But that means simply shifting resources from one sector of

the economy to another. It doesn't change the fact that fossil fuels will not last forever and that they are already doing enormous damage to the ecosystem with their emissions of pollutants.

In a longer time frame (but maybe not so long), we have to consider how climate change is going to affect agriculture, and how it is already affecting it. Climate change is disrupting weather patterns and creating havoc in traditional cultivations almost everywhere in the world. Droughts, in particular, are becoming harsher and more frequent in many regions of the world. The problem can be eased by switching to different crops, and it is at least in part compensated by the warming effect that makes it possible to produce cereals in northern regions, where it was too cold to do so in the past. On the whole, extreme effects of climate change are said to be unlikely to happen for at least a few decades, although we cannot exclude an acceleration of the change, which would make large parts of the world's regions too hot and dry to be cultivated.

In general, plants can't function at temperatures below 0 °C, and their vegetative rate drops rapidly above 35-40 °C. Some plants can survive up to ca. 50°C, but most will dry out and die over 40°C. This means that global warming may push temperatures in tropical regions to a level at which cultivating staple crops like maize, rice, and wheat will be difficult, if not impossible. Temperate regions may initially benefit from longer growing seasons and thawing permafrost, but beyond 1.5-2°C warming, heat waves and drought will reverse these gains. Adaptation strategies like heat-tolerant crops (e.g., drought-resistant maize), precision irrigation, and sustainable aquaculture can mitigate losses, but only within some limits. In general, the future of agricultural food production does not look good unless some radically new technologies can come to the rescue, or climate change can be contained.

Food Supply: Who's Going to Starve First?

Most of the discussion on providing food for humankind focus on the idea that we need to increase agricultural yields to increase food production. But that's just one of the elements of a problem embedded in a complex and delicate production system. Basically, the question is not just food production, but *food supply*. Two very different concepts.

What moves food from fields to plates is not the benevolence of the farmer (as Adam Smith would have said), but the capability of consumers to pay for it. This implies a working global economic system that allows people to perform some activity to earn money to buy food. The case of the Irish famine of the 19th century teaches us what the problem can be. There was food available in the world market, but the Irish didn't have the money to buy it. Hence, they starved to death. Both governments and charities can provide the money needed to help the poor, but they may not have enough or be unwilling to provide it.

The modern food processing activity is a long chain of linked activities: harvesting, processing, storing, refrigerating, transporting, packaging, marketing, and more. If just one of the steps fails, food does not arrive on plates, and people starve. A possible cause of the breakdown is the fragmentation of the global economic system into separate regions that engage in making war (commercial or kinetic) with each other, which is already happening. So, despite all the technological progress in agriculture, the situation is fragile and potentially heading for a disastrous outcome. We'll have to see how it will be possible to manage it, if it will be possible at all. Suppose, for instance, that the global economic system falters and collapses in the midst of wars and financial conflicts. Every country will have to rely on its national resources for food production. And, of course, many

countries have a production deficit, and their people can have enough food only by importing it. So, who's going to starve first?

The question is not easy to answer because most of the data reported in the various sites dealing with food import/export use monetary units, and do not distinguish between the different nutritional content of agricultural products. So, you could think that Italy has an excess of food production because it exports wine and other expensive agricultural products, and hence, the financial balance is positive in terms of food imports and exports. But, of course, not even Marie Antoinette would ever say that if the people don't have bread, they can drink Chianti wine.

For a more realistic assessment of the food movements across borders, we can use the FAO trade statistics data to convert exports in weight and monetary units into calories. Even that is a partial index because people don't just eat calories – they need good food rich in nutrients. But that will do as a first approximation. I calculated the result for 13 countries that seemed to me representative of extreme cases, or of large and important regions. The results are in the table below, based on commodity volumes and average caloric densities (e.g., cereals at ~3,300 kcal/kg, soybeans at ~350 kcal/kg). The data excludes non-foods such as wine and other alcoholic beverages. These are rough estimates, not official figures.

Country	Pop (M, 2021)	Food Exp (Tcal/y)	Food Imp (Tcal/y)	Exp-Imp (Tcal/y)	Cal def/surp per cap (kcal/d)
Japan	126.0	1.5	28.0	-26.5	-576
United Kingdom	67.0	3.0	14.0	-11.0	-450
Saudi Arabia	35.0	0.5	5.5	-5.0	-391
Italy	59.0	4.2	10.5	-6.3	-293
EU (Total)	447.0	85.0	120.0	-35.0	-215
Kenya	54.0	0.8	4.2	-3.4	-172
Mexico	129.0	4.5	11.0	-6.5	-138
China	1,425.0	20.0	65.0	-45.0	-87
Ethiopia	117.0	1.2	3.8	-2.6	-61
India	1,391.0	15.0	18.0	-3.0	-6
Russia	146.0	18.0	12.0	+6.0	+113
United States	332.0	45.0	25.0	+20.0	+165
Brazil	213.0	22.0	8.0	+14.0	+180

Table 5. Estimated annual food calorie trade (trillions of kcal) for 13 selected countries, showing imports, exports, and import-to-export ratios for a number of countries. Based on FAO trade statistics. Data spans 2020-2023, sorted by increasing ratio, starting from net exporters (e.g., Brazil, ratio 0.05-0.13) to net importers.

The second and third columns list the food imports and exports in trillions of calories (or tera-calories). The subsequent column is the difference between imports and exports. A negative value means that a country has a deficit in calorie production. The last column lists the

deficit/surplus in terms of calories missing or in excess per person. So, the countries at the top of the table are those which are most dependent on imports and whose citizens would be the first to starve if worse came to worst. China, Saudi Arabia, and Japan are in a bad situation. Instead, Brazil, the USA, and Russia are doing very well. Surprisingly, even India does reasonably well, despite its large population and its fame as a place where people often experience famines. That's the miracle of the green revolution and its fertilizers, pesticides, GMOs, and the like.

The table above gives only a partial view of the situation. As we saw in a previous chapter, agriculture needs energy to produce, and this energy nowadays comes mainly from fossil fuels. The countries that can produce large amounts of food today wouldn't be able to do that in a situation of a lack of energy supply, currently mainly in the form of fossil energy. So, I took into account this factor to evaluate national food security risks amid potential global supply disruptions. Let me summarize how I did it.

First, I started from the same data from the Food and Agriculture Organization (FAO) used to create table 5. Fossil fuel dependency (FFD) was estimated directly from 2022 energy import dependency ratios sourced from the World Bank and International Energy Agency (IEA), expressed as percentages of total primary energy consumption; for net energy-exporting nations (e.g., Brazil, Russia, United States), FFD was capped at 0% to reflect negligible import risk. The adjusted net balance, accounting for vulnerability in domestic production to energy shortages, was calculated as Adj Net = Net × (1 - FFD/100). This is an ad hoc hypothesis that serves to establish a reasonable weight of the use of fossil fuels in agriculture. Finally, per capita risk was derived by dividing Adj Net by 2022 population estimates (from United Nations data) and scaling to daily kcal/person: Adj Net Per Cap = (Adj Net × 10^{12} kcal/Tcal / 365 days) / population.

In table 6, countries were ranked by Adjusted Net calories imports (most negative first) to prioritize those facing the greatest aggregate caloric shortfalls. The table also shows the relative risk per person, taking into account the population of each country. (data from 2022 from FAO and World Bank)

Country	Imp Tcal/y	Exp Tcal/y	Net Tcal/y	FFD %	Adj-Net Tcal/y	Adj-Net/cap kcal/d
Saudi Arabia	-25	2	-23	0	-23	-1749
EU (Total)	-800	400	-400	62.5	-150	-919
China	-600	100	-500	20	-400	-776
Mexico	-60	20	-40	16	-33.6	-730
UK	-30	10	-20	34	-13.2	-539
Kenya	-15	5	-10	22	-7.8	-395
Japan	-120	10	-110	87	-14.3	-313
Italy	-40	15	-25	77	-5.75	-267
India	-250	150	-100	35	-65	-126
Ethiopi a	-10	5	-5	11	-4.45	-102
United States	-80	180	100	0	100	822
Russia	-50	250	200	0	200	3803
Brazil	-120	530	410	0	410	5221

Table 6 – Food imports and exports taking into account the production of fossil fuels

The new table shows several interesting elements. Now, the countries at risk in terms of food resilience are those that need to

import fossil fuels. It is because agriculture needs these fuels. Do not pay too much attention to the absolute numbers; the influence of fossil fuels was estimated only qualitatively.

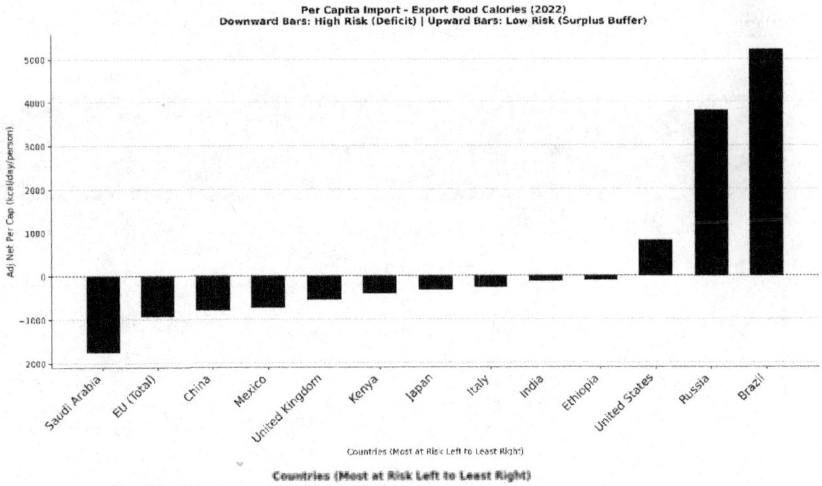

Figure 37 – Net food production for selected countries, taking into account the production of fossil fuels. Upward bars: low risk of starvation. Downward bars: high risk.

But the table tells us that Brazil and Russia have a positive adjusted net import-export ratio when you take into account fossil fuel production, and the same is true for the US. All of them have abundant fossil fuel resources and plenty of available land. The Netherlands is the only European country with a positive balance because of the availability of offshore natural gas. All the other countries have negative net import-export calorie values. Saudi Arabia has a highly negative net value despite being a fossil fuel exporter because it produces very little food. Note that a person needs 2,000 to 2,500 calories per day, even though, in practice, people in industrialized countries are accustomed to more than that. In any case, the results shown in the table are better visualized in a bar chart. The chart indicates that in the case of a major disruption of the global commercial system, most EU countries could lose a significant

fraction of their calorie supply per person. In other words, people would starve. China faces the same problem, and this is probably the reason why it is pushing so hard on renewable energy to guarantee the energy supply needed for agriculture.

Of course, these calculations have to be taken with a lot of caution. One problem is that the table does not take into account climate change. Increasing temperatures and droughts are expected to affect countries closer to the equator, so, again, they should favor Russia. At the same time, they could badly damage India, which depends on its yearly monsoon for the water needed for cultivation. Even Mediterranean countries are expected to suffer from droughts according to the models used to calculate the effects of global warming.

These are the negative factors that could affect food supply in the future. But, of course, things never stand still, and, in the future, depletion might considerably change the values and bring some producers to the negative side of the food supply balance. Consider also that agriculture adapts, changes, and improves over time, together with climate, social, and political changes. So, the negative effect of climate change could be countered by adaptation, while new agricultural technologies could benefit from the low-cost renewable energy that can be produced nowadays using photovoltaic and wind plants. Nevertheless, the risk of a Malthusian catastrophe in a non-remote future cannot be completely discounted. As usual, the future always surprises us.

The End of Economic Growth

How is the economy going to react to a population decline? A case in point is Japan, whose population peaked at 128.1 million in

2008 and has been sliding down ever since, being at around 123 million in 2024. Fertility in Japan is stuck at 1.3 births per woman, well below the 2.1 replacement rate. According to data from the Japanese Ministry of Internal Affairs and Communications, in 2024 alone, the loss was about 899,000 inhabitants, close to 1% of the total. It corresponds to a drop of about 4.3% in 15 years, with projections of a 16.3% decline by 2050.

However, Japan remains a prosperous country. It is no longer the engine of growth it was a few decades ago, but it still has some of the world's highest standards of living and highest life expectancies (85 years). So, Japan shows that it is possible to keep an industrialized society alive and functional while losing about 1% of the population every year and, at the same time, moving the average age of the residents toward geriatric levels. Evidently, a population decline does not necessarily lead to catastrophic situations that could look like a Mad Max movie. Some studies based on economic models indicate that an aging population generates a decline in GDP growth, but not necessarily an absolute decline.[95]

But what about faster rates of decline? At present, we have no examples among modern industrialized countries of population declines so rapid and abrupt as to have caused the complete collapse of a country's economic system. The worst example is that of Ukraine, which, as we saw in a previous chapter, lost about 4% of its population per year after the collapse of the Soviet Union, and even more during the current conflict. Ukraine was able to survive as an organized state, but only with the support of a massive inflow of capital from Western States.

There are worse cases, even though not among industrialized countries. There are plenty of "failed states" in the world; states that theoretically exist, but where the government does not rule or control most of its territory. However, none of these failed states appears to have been associated to population decline. For instance, in the 1960s, Syria built a relatively modern state by exploiting its crude oil

resources. It even arrived at a point where its government could dream of a "Greater Syria," challenging in military terms other local powers, including Israel. But, in the 1990s, with the decline of oil production caused by depletion, the Syrian economy declined, too, and the government had to stop dreaming about territorial expansion. It was still possible to keep the state functioning by turning Syria into a world manufacturing center of Captagon, a powerful amphetamine, illegal in most countries. Even that activity collapsed in 2024, possibly because of internal rivalries or sabotage by external powers. In 2025, the government was unable to pay its soldiers and the Syrian army collapsed in a few days when the country was invaded by a less-than-impressive force formed by a coalition of Sunni Islamist organizations. Now, Syria is fragmented into several semi-independent regions, in part controlled by foreign states. Nevertheless, Syria's population continues to increase, having reached nearly 26 million people in 2025.

From these examples, we see how difficult it is to predict the effects of the ongoing demographic decline when it enters high gear and rapidly drives down the population. Economists are obsessed with growth and see as a disaster the possibility of even a moderate reduction in the growth rate, for instance, from 2% to 1% annually in nations like Germany or Italy by 2040. But, most likely, we are not facing just a decline in the GDP growth rate. We are facing simply a decline that some people politely call "negative growth." That may already be happening, but it is masked by the adjustments made to the GDP, for instance, by including "hedonic factors," designed to make it always grow. With these arbitrary corrections, the GDP may no longer faithfully represent the state of a country's economy.

The problem is that a decreasing population reduces the labor force and also the demand for goods and services. Industries like housing and retail suffer first; fewer people need fewer homes. Deflationary pressures may emerge as businesses cut prices to attract scarce consumers, further squeezing profits. Unexpectedly, per-capita GDP could rise if productivity gains outpace population loss, as seen

in some Scandinavian countries with high automation. Yet, without policy shifts, such as higher immigration, incentives for births, or extended working ages, most developed economies face a significant structural drag on growth.

In the future, labor dynamics may shift toward automation and outsourcing. McKinsey estimates that automation could raise global productivity by 0.8-1.4% annually through the 2030s,[96] and this is a conservative estimate. It could be much more. For Western countries, adopting robotics and AI is critical to sustaining GDP with fewer workers. However, workers displaced by automation are also a problem. Most tasks that people normally perform in their jobs involve nothing more than moving things from one place to another. These things may be physical entities (say, you are a mailman or a truck driver), or numbers/strings of letters (say, you are a clerk, or a government bureaucrat). Or, maybe, your job is to try to move a chunk of lead from the inside of a gun barrel into someone else's body, but it is basically the same idea. Human brains have a certain capability to evaluate the position of things in space and to act on them. And that's what they are used for. But, recently, automated systems have become capable of performing these tasks better and faster, including the skill involved with putting chunks of lead inside people's bodies.

So, what kind of jobs can be found for people whose skills have become useless? Apart from removing them from the job market by means of the robotic skill of moving chunks of lead around, the very idea that everyone must have a job of some kind may be challenged. Yet, the current political views emphasize concepts that may be totally obsolete in a world where robots and AI will take over tasks that once only humans could perform. Politicians seem to promise us a world in which men will be the breadwinners, going to work every day, while women will be sweet wives waiting for them at home, taking care of the kids, and preparing good meals for the whole family. That world, alas, looks now as remote as the science fiction magazine covers of the 1950s, including the robot-butler vacuuming the carpet

and carrying the Margaritas around.

In the future, pensions will also face a crisis as population decline accelerates. With fewer young workers supporting more retirees, dependency ratios worsen. In the EU, the old-age dependency ratio (retirees per working-age person) is projected to rise from 32% in 2020 to 50% by 2050. Pay-as-you-go pension systems, common in Western nations, are heavily strained under this imbalance. For instance, Italy's pension spending already exceeds 15% of the GDP, and a shrinking workforce could push that to 20% by 2040, risking insolvency without reforms like higher taxes or reduced benefits. Shifts with longer work hours are also considered as a response. [96] A smaller labor pool forces employers to compete for talent, potentially raising wages but also increasing per-worker hours. In Germany, where the working-age population could drop by 20% by 2050, firms already report labor shortages. Some companies push for 42-hour workweeks over the standard 38. As you may imagine, not every worker is happy about that. Alternatively, part-time work may rise for older workers, as governments incentivize delayed retirement. However, cultural resistance to these ideas is strong.

We must accept that in a stable or slowly declining society, we will have a large fraction of elderly people. We need to help them to remain in good health, and active and productive citizens. That will maintain the society's economy alive, and will also be good for the elderly if we stop considering them a burden. During the long history of humankind, grandparents have been a critical asset for families to help parents raise and educate their children. Nowadays, we tend to lock grandparents into nursing homes, where their only perspective is to watch TV while sliding into a vegetative state until they die. It is a lost opportunity for the young generations to learn from their elders, just as it is a terrible financial burden for families. Remedying this disaster is a huge challenge for society, but we must start thinking about it.

MORE GENERATIONS LIVING TOGETHER ARE NOT ALWAYS HAPPIER. MANY ELDERLY PEOPLE LIVE IN THEIR OWN HOMES.

Figure 38 - An Italian Family in 2021. From right to left, Liliana (100), Grazia (68), Donata (33) and Aurora (1). Grazia is the wife of the author of this book. Photo by the author.

Plenty of horror stories can be found on the Web about how the elderly are mistreated in these homes. This phenomenon is well known in the scientific literature, and it even has an acronym, EA, for "elder abuse," which can go from simple neglect or verbal abuse to much more serious forms involving emotional, financial, and even sexual abuse. Some recent reports are truly chilling, for instance, a recent survey carried out in Germany[97] shows that more than half of people over 80 in nursing homes report having experienced EA. Not only are we horribly mistreating our parents and grandparents, but it is a loss Ultimately, the fate of the economic system hinges on adaptability. Countries that embrace high tech, reform pensions, and balance labor policies could turn decline into a manageable transition. Those countries that don't, or can't, risk stagnation, decline, and a diminished global role. How states will manage these challenges is all to be seen, but, in principle, it is not an impossible challenge in a world where the population decline eases the dramatic lack of resources and

DON'T IDEALISE THE EXTENDED FAMILY.

the damage caused by climate change. Old age is not a sickness; we have to learn how to live with it.

LIVING IN NURSING HOMES ISN'T ALWAYS WORSE THAN A LIVING WITH RELATIVES.

Money is a Gas: Inequality and Population

In 1988, two American economists, Bennett Harrison and Barry Bluestone, were among the first to note the inversion of the tendency toward higher equality in the US that started in the 1960s. Something had placed the country on a path of higher inequality that it is still following nowadays. Most Western countries show the same behavior and some recently industrialized countries, such as China and India, are also seeing an increase in inequality.

But what generated this trend? Harrison and Bluestone proposed several explanations; all related to specific US conditions. Eventually, they concluded that it was the result of a reorganization of the US businesses and corporations designed to maximize profits by attacking labor costs and relocating manufacturing overseas. This is a reasonable interpretation for the US situation, but the fact that the inequality is increasing everywhere, worldwide, indicates that there is something much deeper in this story. I can propose that it is related, at least in part, to the worldwide demographic transition that brought down fertility. But that needs an in-depth explanation.

First of all, what are the causes of inequality? Is it something intrinsic in the way humans are? Or has it to do with the way society is structured? Surely, it is related to money, but how is it that some people have more money than others? In 1976, Pink Floyd created a song titled *Money is a Gas*, which turned out to be a term remarkably apt at describing the distribution of wealth in society according to the "econophysical" approach. It is a vast field, but some studies by Victor

Yakovenko and his coworkers used the "money is a gas" analogy to describe their work on the income distribution in modern times.[98]

To understand their approach in detail, you would need to know something about statistical physics. But the basic idea is simple: they modeled the economy in terms of random exchanges among economic agents. These models are called "money exchange models." The idea is that inequality is a natural result of the statistics of the exchanges, not of special skills or abilities. Money behaves like gas molecules: just like some molecules have more energy than others, some people have more money than others. The models reproduce reasonably well the distribution of money in the real world, where the probability of being rich goes down exponentially with the size of one's stash. In mathematical terms, both money and the energy of gas molecules follow the law called the "Gibbs-Boltzmann" distribution. It is, incidentally, a distribution that maximizes the entropy of the system, making it stable. These results show that a certain degree of inequality is unavoidable in a free market. It may not be a bad thing, provided that it is not excessive.

The rich, however, follow a different pattern, a curve called the "Pareto" or "Fat Tail" distribution, accumulating much more money than the gas model would predict. It is this distribution that gave rise to the commonly heard statement attributed to Vilfredo Pareto, that "20% of the people earn 80% of the income." Why that? Are the rich able to defeat the laws of thermodynamics? No, but they can exploit the fact that there is no such thing as a "free market" in the real world. In the real economic system, people engage in money-exchanging activities not with everyone at random, but mostly with people who are close to them physically and socially. In common parlance, we call this phenomenon "the old boy network." It means that if you have rich friends, you are more likely to be exposed to more opportunities to become rich yourself. In this way, Madame Entropy can be tricked and made to maximize herself only at the local level. That explains the

existence and the persistence of the multibillionaires (soon trillionaires) of today.

These models do not take into consideration population growth or decline, but these are very important factors. You know that when you die, you can't take your money with you to Paradise (or Hell, if you have a lot of it). So, death could be a powerful wealth equalizing factor if the inheritance were to be distributed among many heirs. But declining birth rates are changing the rules of the game, shifting the system even more toward the Pareto rules. That is, the rich inherit from the rich, and wealth accumulates rather than being redistributed.

We are seeing a phenomenon similar to the wealth accumulation of the heirs of noble families that was typical of ancient times, and that is described in a previous chapter of this book. The difference is that, in ancient times, rich people had plenty of troubles to make sure that only one of their several heirs would inherit the family's wealth. Today, the problem doesn't exist because many families have only a few children, or just one. No need to cloister anyone; the mechanism functions by itself as a wealth accumulation machine.

The early economists noted the problem. David Ricardo, in particular, noted how landlords, who often inherited large estates, earned "rent" simply by owning scarce land, not through productive effort. Large inheritances created inequality without merit, fostering a class of idle rich who consumed resources without contributing to production, harming economic progress. Later, Socialists often proposed to abolish inheritance altogether, with the wealth of the deceased going all to the state. That, of course, is considered abhorrent nowadays, mainly because the rich see it in that way for obvious reasons.

The Economist magazine rediscovered the problem in an article titled *The New Inheritocracy* on February 27, 2025. It examined the growing importance of inherited wealth in advanced economies and its implications for society. According to the article, the total wealth

transfer to inheritance in rich countries was about $6 trillion in 2025. It is equivalent to about 10% of the average GDP of these countries, a value that has doubled in comparison to the mid-20th century. This surge is largely driven by the baby boomer generation passing on wealth, especially in the form of real estate. With the cost of apartments skyrocketing, the gap between heirs and non-heirs is widening in terms of the kind of housing families can afford. If you were lucky enough to inherit a home from your parents, you are in Paradise, and you can dream of your next vacation to Hawai'i. If you didn't, you are in Hell, with a heavy mortgage or rent to pay, and the risk that if you miss a few installments, you'll end up sleeping in Skid Row.

Interestingly, the article in The Economist does not mention low birth rates as a factor in its discussion of inherited wealth. But with fewer and fewer heirs appearing to collect their parents' accumulated wealth, if we wanted to avoid phenomena of extreme accumulation, we would need laws to tax inheritance. Unfortunately, there is no evidence that governments are moving in that direction. We see, actually, the opposite trend. In the US, the federal estate tax remains stable with a 40% rate and an exemption of $13.61 million in 2024. In practice, it affects less than 1% of estates. Some states are imposing additional estate taxes, but most are phasing them out (e.g., Delaware, New Jersey) or are increasing exemption levels. The trend seems to be the same all over the world: many countries are reducing or eliminating estate and inheritance taxes. Even when these taxes still exist, there are usually ways to circumvent them by various legal tricks. It is not surprising: with inequality increasing, the rich are pushing for reducing taxes affecting their wealth, and they surely have more clout than the poor. The process feeds on itself as the rich become richer, and there are fewer of them. Eventually, the poor may not have anything anymore to pass to their heirs.

Given these factors, it seems unavoidable that a shrinking population will lead to increasing wealth inequality. Indeed, it is

happening in the countries that experienced the demographic transition. This increase in inequality is often accompanied by the dismantling of the social services that the state used to provide, such as health care, education, social security, and the like. Not only that, but we are also seeing an ideological trend toward assuming that this is the way things should be. The political forces that traditionally defended the poor are in decline or have completely disappeared. Leaders such as Javier Milei in Argentina and Donald Trump in the US represent the trend very well: they want to dismantle the welfare state and replace its services with those provided by private enterprises. Those who can't afford to pay, well, they must learn how to paddle their own yacht, or drown. We can only hope that some trends will slow down if we can find a way to stop the decline and stabilize the population level.

Technology: The Changes Ahead

Typically, we tend to think about technological progress as if scientists were the equivalent of Santa Claus, assumed to bring only good things. But technology may bring coal lumps to everybody, and not just to bad kids. So, in the rush of optimism of the 1950s, people thought we would have flying cars, space colonies, robot butlers, immortality pills, and similar gadgetry. Nobody could imagine things like the Internet, social media, genetic engineering, photovoltaic energy, and the like. Nor could we have imagined the disasters that these wonderful technologies would bring in terms of pollution, climate change, erosion, ecosystem disruption, loss of biodiversity, and more.

The only rule that we can extract from about a century of technological forecasting is that the technologies that are most touted

are those that tend to fail. A good case in point is that of the "hydrogen-based economy," which governments doggedly continue to push and finance, but which never worked and probably never will. But new technologies are having big effects on many fields of the world's economy. What will be their effect on the human population trends? Let's see a list of what we may expect, with the elements in no particular order.

Artificial Intelligence. AIs have burst onto the scene during the past few years, making human work obsolete in many fields. In terms of human population trends, AIs cannot directly affect the production of food or human fertility, but they may affect the economic system in various ways, mainly because they will change the value of human beings as workers and soldiers. If humans become less valuable, there may be a lower interest in increasing the population, and that may lead AIs to become powerful population-limiting factors. A further possibility is that people will become so addicted to AIs that they'll lose interest in everything else, including sex and reproduction. "Sexbots" may become powerful birth control factors, enhancing the already existing ones. It is also possible that AIs could turn out to be not so friendly as they seem to be nowadays. And that would mean bad news for us, puny humans.

Renewable Energy. The Industrial Revolution started during the late 18th century as the offspring of fossil fuels. Coal first, then oil, and later natural gas provided the energy to move the giant machine we call the "economic system." By now, fossil fuels are obsolete; solar photovoltaic and wind energies are revolutionizing energy supply at costs vastly inferior to what fossil fuels can produce. That promises the capability of staving off the collapse caused by a lack of energy, which is still believed to be coming. Renewable energy can power the many processes of agriculture and, in principle, help generate abundant food for human beings. The problem is that building a new

energy system based on renewable energy will take time and money, and we seriously risk an energy crisis before the transition is completed. In addition, we are currently seeing a propaganda attack against renewables, likely supported by the fossil industry. This attack is turning renewable energy into anathema for many people, especially on the right side of the political spectrum. Not for nothing, President Trump said that renewable energy is a scam and a "con job" in his 2025 speech at the United Nations. It may be that before we understand how much we really need renewable energy, we need a Seneca Cliff in energy production that will sweep away fossil fuels from the energy system. That, unfortunately, won't be painless, and it may generate a parallel Seneca Cliff of the world population.

Lean Technologies. The Industrial Revolution was ushered in by an abundance of mineral resources. Not just fossil fuels but all the elements of the periodic table have been mined and lavishly used as if there were no tomorrow. Now, the industry is facing a dearth of essential minerals, e.g., copper for conductors, rare earths for magnets, noble metals as catalysts, and more. This trend is forcing a complete rearrangement of the industrial system according to the "three golden rules of mining," which I sketched in my 2014 book *Extracted* (2014). Inspired by the working of the biological ecosystem, these rules are 1) Use only what's abundant, 2) Use sparingly, and 3) Recycle ferociously. By using these rules, Earth's ecosystem has been thriving for a few billion years without ever running out of anything. Unfortunately, that's not the way the human economy works: it is wasteful, inefficient, and scarcely interested in recycling. So, the risk of running short of critical minerals is not negligible. Nevertheless, current critical technologies can be re-engineered to work according to these rules. For instance, PV panels use elements abundant in Earth's crust: silicon and aluminum. At the same time, the transmission of electrical energy can be done by replacing the rare element copper with the abundant aluminum. Mineral depletion is a

problem that population stabilization and decline can substantially ease.

Genetic Engineering. Theoretically, hacking the DNA of living beings opens immense possibilities. In terms of the effects on the human population, one of their potential uses in medicine is to lengthen the human lifespan. So far, however, the global trend is tapering off worldwide at about 73 years of life expectancy at birth. Even the nations that have the longest lifespan, Italy and Japan, have seen their life expectancy no longer increase. The "pill of immortality" that was envisaged in the 1950s doesn't seem to be coming, just as we don't have miracle cures for sicknesses such as cancer, dementia, diabetes, and more. The miracle cure for obesity, Ozempic, is now being adopted everywhere in developed countries. However, it has the problem that once people start taking it, they can't stop; otherwise, they will become obese again. And we are not sure of the long-term side effects of this drug. Yet, this field is in motion, and it is still possible that new technological developments could substantially increase the human lifespan. In this case, there would be consequences on the global population curve, with the population peak being delayed and the social structure being even more dominated by elderly people.

A society dominated by the elderly ("senocracy" or "gerontocracy"), is a condition never experienced in the past. It was only described in fictional form by Jonathan Swift in his 1726 book, Gulliver's Travels. In the story, the *Struldbrugs* are people born with a red spot on their forehead who are immortal but do not have eternal youth. By the time they reach old age, they are decrepit, miserable, senile, in constant pain, unable to enjoy anything, and legally dead (they lose all civil rights at 80). They become an unbearable burden to themselves and society, envying the ordinary people who are lucky enough to die. Is this our dark destiny? Maybe it is, considering Fran

Lebowitz's quip that "my objective is to become decrepit, because the alternative is worse."

Robot Soldiers. Robots, under the name of "drones," are revolutionizing many fields, including warfare. In a chapter I wrote for the book *2052 –A Global Forecast for the Next Forty Years* (2012), I discussed the consequences of drones replacing human beings on the battlefield, arguing that it wouldn't be a bad thing. We are seeing it happening right now in Ukraine. Drones haven't yet made infantry completely obsolete, but we are moving in that direction. So, are we going to see a human-free battlefield in which drones will fight each other in a sort of huge ball-wrecking game? Something similar to the British TV series, Robot Wars, aired from 1998 to 2004 and from 2016 to 2018. It featured clumsy robots fighting each other with hammers, circular saws, and other mechanical devices. Why people found that fun is difficult to explain, but at least it was a harmless pastime.

In any case, the idea that robots will fight for us is at least a bad waste of resources and energy, but all wars are like that. The real problem is that robots may also be programmed to fight human beings, and that would provide a cheap and effective weapon of mass destruction. We can only hope that they will remain under the control of sane human beings.

The New Green Revolution: Precision Fermentation. The conventional Green Revolution was a set of technologies mainly based on mechanization, fertilizers, and pesticides, in turn, all based on the availability of cheap fossil fuels. This approach has now exhausted its capability for further improvements. But if we move to precision fermentation powered by renewable energy, then, in principle, it would be possible to increase food production and sustain a much larger population than the current one. The result would be humankind further expanding into the ecosystem and leaving even less space for non-human creatures. It is not impossible to conceive

such a dystopic scenario, reminiscent of Asimov's short story, *2430 A.D.* (1970). Philip Dick also explored this theme in his *Do Androids Dream of Electric Sheep?* (1968), which was the basis of the *Blade Runner* movie (1982). The common theme of these stories is that humans would increase their numbers so much that they would cause the extinction of most animal species. Some people seem to think that this is a good thing, such as some religious fundamentalist groups and a loose group of Silicon Valley thinkers, transhumanists, and futurists (e.g., Ray Kurzweil, Peter Diamandis, and others). It is, after all, what's happening right now with a new mass extinction in full swing in Earth's ecosystem. On the other hand, even assuming that technological developments could feed several tens of billions of people, there are stumbling blocks that could make it impossible. One is that humans still need a functioning ecosystem to which they are adapted as a result of millions of years of evolution. A one-species, human-only ecosystem may be simply impossible to maintain in stable conditions. It could crash because of pollution, lack of nutrients, or perturbations we can't yet imagine.

These considerations describe some of the main trends of technological progress, those which are likely to have a significant effect on population trends. But the situation is complex, and one characteristic of technological progress is that it always takes us by surprise. It could lead the human population to tens, or perhaps hundreds, of billions. Or, conversely, it could rapidly lead to the extinction of the human species. Unfortunately, the future will not be what we think it should be.

Global Warming: The Ultimate Threat

The current debate on population growth often deals with the question of whether a population decline will reduce emissions and save humankind (and the ecosystem as well) from the grim reality of global warming. It is grim because Earth's atmosphere has a "memory" of the past; it remembers the accumulated emissions in the past. So, we don't just need to stop emitting greenhouse gases, but we should take steps to reabsorb the already emitted amounts.

Unfortunately, the current political ideas are not favorable to an effort to reduce emissions, to say nothing about doing something to restore the atmospheric composition to the pre-industrial characteristics. On the contrary, many governments are pushing for an increasing use of fossil fuels, while major ones openly define the global warming problem as a "scam," as the US President, Donald Trump, did.

Given the situation, could the expected decline in humankind's population reduce the warming threat? Fewer people mean lower emissions, and that's a trend that goes in the right direction. In practice, though, the question is extremely complex and involves a large number of parameters having to do with accumulated climate factors and the complex way in which the Earth's ecosystem is reacting to the perturbation. There have been only a few studies on how population decline could affect Earth's climate, probably because the idea that the global population is close to its peak has not yet penetrated the general perception of the scientific community engaged in climate science studies. Typically, climate models only tell us how much temperatures will increase in dependence on greenhouse emissions and, in most cases, emissions are simply expected to increase with population, unless they are curbed by internationally agreed legal actions.

Only a few studies have explicitly attempted to quantify the consequences of population trends on climate. These models are called "Integrated Assessment Models" (IAMs) and try to describe not just the climate system, but the coupled economic and climate system. A recent review of these models can be found in the paper by Krawczyk and Braun.[99] The problems with these models are many. Krawczyk and Braun describe the "Superhero Syndrome" that affects IAMs, that is they can

> "... be compared to Hollywood superheroes, fixating on defeating one villain, like emissions, while overlooking the bigger picture. Despite their heroic efforts, IAMs and superheroes overlook the broader systemic issues, and thus they mark the prevailing crisis-ridden societal conditions as rational and legitimate. In other words, IAMs examine futures to find solutions to mitigate the climate crisis, but the way they do it stabilizes the status quo and thus the path into the climate crisis. "

My personal experience with these models is based on the MEDEAS one, which I helped develop,[100]It was a complex and powerful model but, in my opinion, the large number of parameters involved in the computation made it subject to biases and uncertainties. This problem exists for all large and complex models. Conversely, some IAMs are oversimplified and unable to provide reliable results. This is the case of the first of these models, the one called DICE (Dynamic Integrated Climate Economy) model, which is today the most common and most influential among IAMs. Unfortunately, this model suffers from serious biases and problems.

The DICE model has its origins in the work of William Nordhaus. In the 1970s and 1980s, he focused on modeling the effects of mineral depletion, criticizing the results of the world models generated by system dynamics, such as The Limits to Growth. I describe this approach in detail in my book *The Limits to Growth*

Revisited (2011). For this purpose, Nordhaus used a simple model based on the concept of "production function" and, taking into account the effect of technological progress, argued that the global economy would keep growing exponentially for the foreseeable future. Later, Nordhaus introduced global warming as a parameter of the model. The result was the DICE model, proposed for the first time in 1992,[101] and later upgraded in various versions. On the basis of his model, Nordhaus and others typically arrived at the conclusion that climate change would only marginally affect the economy, and that mitigation efforts should not be undertaken at levels high enough to reduce economic growth. Nordhaus was awarded the Nobel Prize in economics in 2018 in large part because of this work.

Here, it would be out of place to enter into a detailed discussion of the DICE model. Briefly, anyway, it is based on the assumptions typical of the neoclassical economic approach. The output of an economy is proportional to the product of two main parameters, capital and labor, affected by an entity called "total factor productivity," which is supposed to represent the exponential increase of technological progress. Population is an exogenous parameter; that is, it is not determined by the inner parameters of the model, but by external projections generated, for instance, using the UN demographic models. Emissions are proportional to the economic output, and are supposed to decline via carbon-saving technologies. Temperature is also an exogenous parameter, supposed to vary according to the IPCC estimates.

The limits of this approach are many. For instance, increasing temperatures are not supposed to cause extreme events such as hurricanes or generate disastrous "tipping points" such as the melting of the polar ice caps or the collapse of the Atlantic Meridional Overturning Current (AMOC). Additionally, rising temperatures do not directly affect population growth at all. The only effect of Global Warming in the model is on the GDP, assumed to face a decline

proportional to the square of the temperature increase (or "temperature anomaly" in the climatologists' jargon).

Apart from being an arbitrary assumption, the effect of temperature appears to be badly underestimated in the DICE model. Just consider that a temperature increase of 2-3 °C only generates a loss of a few percentage points of the world's GDP, which appears overoptimistic, to say the least. Larger increases, of the order of 6 degrees or more, have no disastrous effects, apart from a modest decline in the global GDP. In addition, the fact that the damage function increases with the square of the temperature anomaly naturally leads to postponing efforts to mitigate the effect to the far future, when the damage will be really serious. The same is true for the steep "discount rate" embedded in the model, which evaluates long-term damage at a lower cost than short-term ones. That encourages postponing investments until the problem can no longer be ignored.

How the consequences of the DICE model are understood by economists is spelled out clearly in the book by Dean Spears and Michael Geruso, *After the Spike* (2025). On the basis of a recent version of the model, they extrapolate that the human population will grow to about 10-12 billion people at the end of the century, then it will stabilize itself, or start a slow decline. The GDP will continue increasing, leading to a richer world. Temperatures will not increase above ca. 4 °C, and that will cause no disastrous damage.

The gist of the idea of Spears and Geruso is that a large human population will have a higher economic output and will be able to develop new technologies and field a larger climate change mitigation effect in the future. As a consequence, no action should be attempted now to face a problem that is expected to be easier to solve in the future. The system will optimize itself to a high level of prosperity for everyone. In short, it is a view based on something similar to the "invisible hand" concept introduced long ago by Adam Smith, now

supposed to allocate resources in the optimal way to solve the climate problems while maintaining economic growth.

Unfortunately, the DICE model is not only overoptimistic, but it also lacks the features that would be necessary for a realistic representation of the effects of rising temperatures on the various elements of the ecosystem and of the human economy. That is, it lacks the effect of *feedbacks.* Earth's climate is not a static entity that we humans just happened to find when we evolved. It is part of a complex system dynamically controlled by the biosphere. It can react to perturbations by abrupt changes.

Think, for instance, of the possibility that in some regions, temperatures will become too hot for human beings to live in. North Australia, central India, and the Persian Gulf areas are all places where temperatures are expected to exceed the "Wet Bulb Temperature" at which people die of thermal shock if they stay in the open for more than a short time. But you don't need to arrive at that point to experience famines caused by food production decline, or lack of water access, or simply living a miserable life in summer if you can't afford air conditioning. And don't forget extreme events: you and your home may be swept away by hurricanes, and the rising water level will make it easier for tsunami waves to reach you. Wildfires are another problem enhanced by increasing temperatures. Finally, you need to take into account that carbon dioxide is not just a climate forcing agent. It is a chemically active substance active in the metabolism of the biosphere, including the metabolism of human beings. In some cases, it may be seen as "food for plants," but for those of us who are not plants, it can have all sorts of harmful effects, including a decline in cognitive capabilities.[102]

Unfortunately, while a lack of models is a bad thing, wrong models are even worse. The DICE model and its subsequent version may be leading decision makers into a false sense of security by generating scenarios that promote economic growth in place of mitigation. If Earth's ecosystem goes through one of these points, say,

the collapse of the Gulf Stream, it will no longer be a question of maintaining economic growth; it will be a question of survival for humankind as a whole.

So, abandoning the optimistic DICE model, what can we say about the effect of a slow population decline on climate? World models based on system dynamics do not normally have global temperatures as a parameter. Nevertheless, from the start of the field, in the early 1970s, these models included a parameter called "pollution," or "persistent pollution."[9,10]. At the time, the threat of global warming was not completely understood, yet, but later it became commonplace to consider the pollution stock as a "proxy" for the concentration of CO_2 in the atmosphere.[111,112]

System dynamics models can therefore tell us what to expect will happen to the CO_2 atmospheric concentration and, hence, the future global temperature trends. We cannot expect these models to have the same degree of refinement as the current climate models, but they can give us at least some hint about what to expect as a result of the interplay of the various parameters Let's skip the results of the early studies and focus on a relatively recent version of *The Limits to Growth: the 30-Year Update*, published in 2004.[33]

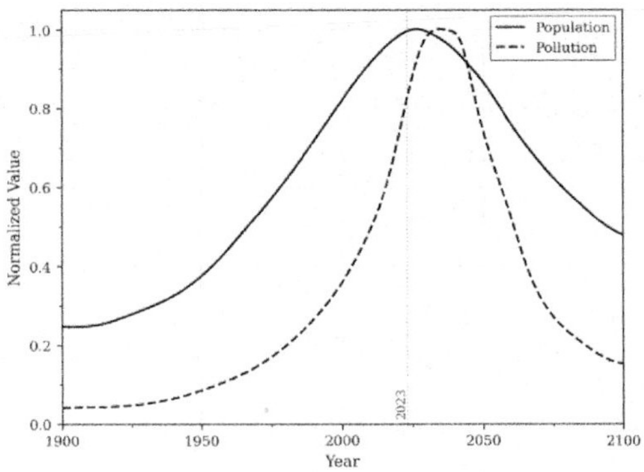

Figure 39 -- The data for population and pollution parameters from the "base case" scenario of The Limits to Growth, the 30 years update (2004)

do that. In this way, the population could be stabilized without the need to force anyone to have or not to have children.

Let's start by supposing that the fertility decline is mainly the result of socio-economic factors. That is, fertility declines because people tend to manage their family size in order to maximize their well-being and that of their children. In this case, fertility could be regulated by interventions in the socio-economic sphere. Financial support, facilities to take care of children, bonuses for working mothers, and other forms of help for families with children are all good things that could lead to a return to higher birth rates. This idea is already being tried in several countries in various measures. The problem is that it appears to be ineffective: birth rates are not increasing.

A compendium of the current data on this approach can be seen in a recent article by John Burn-Murdoch in The Financial Times of March 29, 2024, appropriately titled "*Why family-friendly policies don't boost birth rates.*" Between 1980 and 2019, the world's most developed countries roughly tripled their spending on child benefits, but they all saw birth rates decline, sometimes at increasing speeds. In addition to the cases reported in this article, we may cite that of Russia, which is implementing several measures to encourage women to have more children, so far with meager results. There are no examples, so far, of a country where government intervention to favor natality led to a consistent reversal of the declining trend.

Maybe governments didn't pay enough? Indeed, the government subsidies tried so far are paltry sums in comparison to the cost of raising a child to adulthood. Let's consider the case of the US, where a middle-income, married-couple family with two children is reported to spend about 200-300 thousand dollars (USDA data) to raise one child from birth to age 17. This is necessary in terms of housing, food, childcare, education (pre-college), healthcare, transportation, and more. It equates to about $15-20 thousand per year per child, up to age 17. In practice, in most cases, the family will

continue to support their children for several more years. We also know that in the US, there are about 80 million underage people. Assuming a yearly cost of $20,000 per year, the total is roughly $1.5 trillion per year. It is a huge sum. The U.S. federal budget for fiscal year 2024 was approximately $6.8 trillion. A $1.5 trillion extra subsidy for underage people would represent about a quarter of that total. Subsidizing families for 100% of the cost of raising a child would only be possible by raising taxes or cutting other government expenses by the same amount.

In the current political climate, raising taxes at the necessary levels is simply unthinkable. About cutting other government expenses, not even the budget of the mighty DOD, the Department of Defense (now DOW, Department of War), would be enough; it is today under one trillion dollars per year. And, in any case, the idea of using a large fraction of the military budget to finance child raising is even more unthinkable and unspeakable at a time when the development of drones has made human cannon fodder useless. These results are for the US, but wouldn't be very different in other industrialized countries.

Even if the government were able to increase support for childbirth and child raising, would it solve the depopulation problem? Never forget the Easter Island fallacy: "Our problems will be solved if we just build bigger statues." In our time, it is expressed as "if we throw enough money at the problem, eventually it will go away." The thorny issues with child-raising subsidies are many, not just that the amounts that can be reasonably paid are too small. How to distribute subsidies? For what specific purposes? Subsidies might overcompensate some families (e.g., the lower-class ones, which are spending less per child) and undercompensate upper middle-class ones. To say nothing about racial, religious, and ethnic issues that would put different sections of the population in conflict with each other, and to grab subsidies that would allow their groups to expand in numbers at the expense of other groups.

typically work on symptoms rather than on the sources of the problems. Regarding fertility, there are no approved medical treatments to eliminate endocrine-disrupting substances from people's bodies and restore fertility and sex drive in people who have been heavily exposed to them. At present, the only technology that can reverse the fertility decline is in vitro fertilization.

"In vitro" is a term that comes from the Latin word *vitrum,* which means glass or crystal. It is a method that begins with hormonal stimulation of the ovaries of the woman to produce multiple mature eggs, which are then surgically retrieved. The eggs are fertilized in a laboratory dish by sperm cells obtained from a male donor. When embryos form, one is selected and transferred into the woman's uterus, then a normal pregnancy ensues. The method bypasses all the problems that the poor little sperm cells have with having to swim all the way along the fallopian tubes. It also overcomes the decline in sperm cell numbers: only one of the tiny creatures is needed to fertilize an egg. In vitro fertilization is already relatively common in industrialized countries. According to the American Society for Reproductive Medicine (ASRM), about 98,000 children were born in this way in 2023, and the number has been increasing from the values of the previous years. It represents 2.7% of all U.S. births, out of about three million and a half in total. Not a large fraction, but not negligible, either.

Could the method be expanded to have a more significant impact on fertility rates? In principle, yes, although at a high cost. At present, a single fertilization cycle goes for about $20,000 in the US. For women under 35, in vitro live birth rates per cycle are around 40-50%. Over 40, it drops to 10-20%. So, multiple cycles are often needed, and the cost rises in proportion. However, prices may go down in the future if in vitro fertilization becomes common. Already now, they are much lower in some countries, and, among other possibilities, a woman may try Ukraine, where one cycle of in-vitro fertilization is reported to cost less than $3000. So, it is perfectly possible that in vitro

fertilization will become a common way to give birth to children, perhaps even the most common one if the current trends continue. After all, one hundred years ago, the idea that most children would be born in hospitals would have been nearly unthinkable. So, in the future, it may become perfectly normal that nearly all children will be created in a glass vial.

Even if we arrive at an extensive use of in vitro fertilization, it doesn't mean that all problems will be solved. Some factors that damage natural fertilization remain; for instance, the quality of the DNA carried by the sperm and egg cells. The main questions, though, are social and economic. In the technique known as "gestational surrogacy," the woman carrying the pregnancy need not provide the egg, allowing her to serve purely as a "womb for hire." This role is indeed a paid service. Sperm, meanwhile, may come from the mother's partner or an external donor, who might also receive payment as a sperm provider. These possibilities carry substantial additional costs for assisted reproduction, making it accessible mainly to the rich. In this case, in vitro fertilization would reinforce the current socioeconomic trend of having fewer children by the average population.

A deeper danger associated with these technologies would be that they can pave the way for eugenic practices once deemed impossible. For instance, with in vitro fertilization, it is possible to determine the sex of the embryo before it is implanted. Hence, parents can select the sex of their child without the need to resort to abortion. That could imbalance the sex ratio in those cultures where male children are preferred. This method is illegal in many countries (although not in the US), but we all know that laws are not always respected.

Another new possibility offered by in vitro fertilization is screening the fertilized embryos for potential genetic defects and discarding those that would produce defective babies. The technology has arrived to the point that the embryos can be screened by

7. Conclusion: What can you do?

The angel Gabriel was sent from God to a town of Galilee called Nazareth, to a virgin betrothed to a man named Joseph, of the house of David, and the virgin's name was Mary. And coming to her, he said, "Hail, favored one! The Lord is with you. Do not be afraid, Mary, for you have found favor with God. Behold, you will conceive in your womb and bear a son – Luke 1:26-28

Figure 42 -Raphael's 'Madonna della Seggiola' (1513-1514), Galleria degli Uffizi, Firenze. Public Domain.

It is a tradition for books dealing with potentially catastrophic futures to end with suggestions for practical action. Yet, this attitude is locked in a common way of thinking that automatically assumes that for every problem there is a solution. This idea is deeply embedded in the political discourse, with politicians forever chasing

solutions to the problem of the moment. Somehow, though, despite solutions being continuously thrown at problems, the problems never seem to go away; they return, larger, nastier, and more dangerous than before. It is a rigid way of thinking that aims at maintaining things unchanged, while everything changes. In war, it leads you to more war. In commerce, it leads to bankruptcy. In love, to hate.

So, when discussing population trends, we start by trying to identify what the problem is. And we immediately bog down in a morass where what some people see as problems, others see as solutions. Are we too many? Are we becoming too few? Is more always better? What's the ideal world population? What space should we leave to the other species inhabiting planet Earth? And even before having decided what the problem is, we start throwing solutions at it.

But from what we saw in this book, the attempts by governments to intervene in population matters were often ineffective, unnecessary, or inhumane. The framing of population as a problem that must be solved is itself a trap. It's an engineer's or politician's reflex: every dial must be adjustable; every lever needs to have a predictable effect. But fertility is not a dial, it is not a lever. It's an emergent outcome of millions of individual decisions shaped by culture, economics, technology, religion, and by the very fact of being human. Central planners have been trying to turn the dial or push the levers in one or another direction. We saw pronatalism in Italy, Germany, Romania, and Hungary; anti-natalist campaigns in China, India, and other Asian countries. The scorecard is almost always disastrous: temporary blips at best, horrific human cost at worst, and in nearly every case, the trend eventually reasserted itself in the opposite direction once the effort ended.

If you are honest when you look at certain problems, you'll see that they have no solution in the common sense given to the term. That is, there is no way that governments can force natality to go the way they want it to go, and even if they could, people would disagree on which direction it should go. At the same time, there is little we can do

Visualizing Population Growth and Decline

The first step to solving a problem is to understand that it exists, and the way to do that implies the capability of collecting data about it and visualizing its trends. "Population" is an abstract concept, not directly visible to any single person. It needs to be quantified by a laborious counting process called "census" (from a Latin word meaning "to assess"). Obviously, tribal societies didn't have this capability, but the need for censuses emerged with agrarian societies, where counting the population was necessary for tax and military purposes. The Ancient Romans of imperial times performed a census every five years, an interval that gives us some idea of how expensive and time-consuming it was. One of these surveys was enacted by Emperor Tiberius around 0 CE, and it is mentioned in Luke's gospel. Censuses have been a feature of human society up to our times, part of the general tendency of governments to measure and classify everything.

The ancients used censuses to evaluate their current population, but their comments on trends of growth and decline were episodic. The Greek historian Polybius (ca. 200–118 BCE) offers a rare, direct reflection on population decline in his Histories. In Book 36, he observes that cities were emptying, fields were untended, and families had fewer children. He was probably observing the result of the agricultural collapse that occurred as a result of the overexploitation of the Greek land. In China, the scholar Ban Gu, author of the Book of Han (ca. 111 CE), records population figures from Han censuses—59 million in 2 CE, then a crash to 21 million by 57 CE after rebellions and floods. He didn't explicitly analyze "growth" or "decline" as concepts, but his matter-of-fact reporting implies rulers tracked these shifts to assess the empire's health. In Rome, the historian Livy (*Ab Urbe Condita*, 27 BCE–9 CE) described how the number of Roman citizens

dropped because of the military defeats that Rome suffered against Carthage.

During the Middle Ages in Europe, there was no central authority that could carry out a census of the population. People could only understand that an epidemic was taking its toll by seeing people dying around them. That was sufficient evidence to perform appropriate rituals, or maybe to vent people's anger against whatever ethnic minority was used as a scapegoat at that time. There was no way to plot the progress of the epidemic on a graph, nor to extrapolate the trend to the future. But dramatic images, such as the "Triumph of Death" subject, served to carry the message that something was badly wrong.

In modern times, data about population growth became available, but there remained the need for a way to visualize how the population was growing or shrinking with time. That became possible with the development of graphs. For us, graphs are a normal feature of what we read and what we see on screens, but they are a modern invention. René Descartes (1596 – 1650), also known by his Latin name Cartesius, is credited with the development of the Cartesian coordinate system, the basis of "Cartesian diagrams" or "Cartesian graphs." It is said that he was inspired by watching a fly walking on a ceiling, imagining that its coordinates could be described using numbers. It is probably an apocryphal story, but in his 1637 work, La Géométrie (part of Discours de la Méthode), Descartes introduced the coordinate system that today takes his name. But it doesn't seem that he ever used what we now call a "Cartesian Graph;" these graphs popped up only in the 19th century.

on a grass-covered island, and you'll soon see young rabbits appearing. These young rabbits will spawn new young rabbits, and the more rabbits there are, the faster the population will grow, at least initially. It is not just a theory; it is what happened in Australia when someone brought a few rabbits from England for the pleasure of hunting them. Disaster ensued, with rabbits growing to invade the whole of Australia, no matter how diligently human hunters tried (and still try) to exterminate them. The concept that growth generates itself is known as "positive" or "enhancing" feedback in the field of system dynamics. In chemistry, you call this behavior "autocatalytic," and in the financial world, you call it "compound interest." In mathematical terms, people speak of "geometric growth" and "exponential growth."

These are two similar, but not identical, concepts. Geometric growth nicely describes the growth of a population of, say, bacteria, that doubles at each cycle of reproduction by cellular divisions. You start with one, then you have two, then four, then eight, then 16, and so on. This is an ideal model that doesn't often occur in nature, and, in any case, it doesn't last for long. A real-world example is that of elephants in the Kruger National Park in South Africa. .

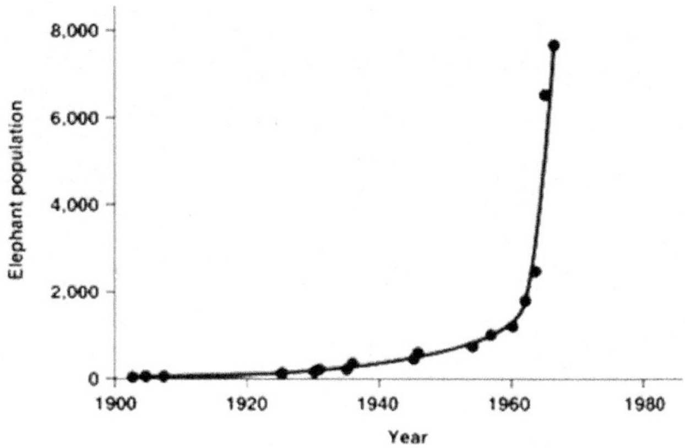

Figure 47 – Elephant population in the Kruger National Park in South Africa. Data from https://www.bio1152.nicerweb.com/

Until 1905, the park didn't host elephants, but that year, a small troop of 10 was observed, having likely moved in from a nearby region. The number of elephants rose rapidly, following a nearly exponential curve, and incidentally, demonstrating that even large animals, and not just bacteria, can show this growth pattern

Logistic growth. This idea was introduced in 1838 by the Belgian mathematician Pierre Verhulst (1804 – 1849). Verhulst wanted to give a mathematical form to Malthus' idea that the growth of a population cannot continue forever. So, he added a constraint to the equation describing exponential growth: a negative term proportional to the square of the size of the population. Since the square of the population grows faster than the population itself, this term causes growth to slow down and eventually stop. Today, it is called the "carrying capacity" of the system.

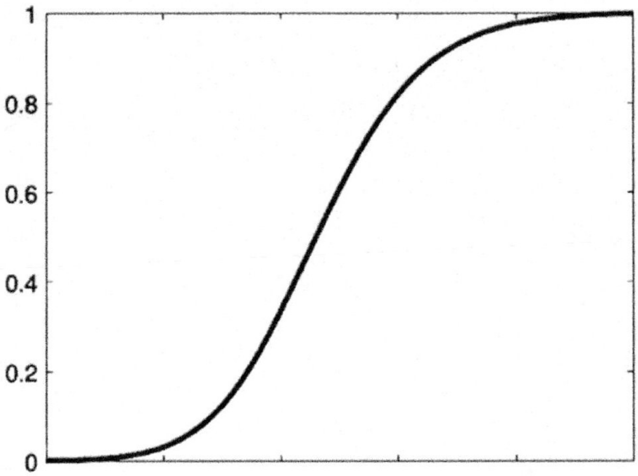

Figure 48 – the Logistic or Verhulst curve

On a Cartesian graph, the result is an "S-shaped" curve, now known as "logistic," for reasons that have to do with "skill in calculations." The idea is that the S-shaped curve provides a mathematical frame that fits with Malthus's idea that populations cannot keep growing forever. The problem with the logistic equation

sometimes the "prey/predator" or "Rabbits/Foxes" model. In its simplest version, the Lotka-Volterra model is nearly identical to the SIR model, with the "susceptible" stock called "prey," and the "infected" stock called the "predator." The only difference is that in the LV model, the prey population reproduces and can grow, while in the SIR model, it does not. There are several variants to the LV model that can become much more complicated on the basis of different assumptions. [52]

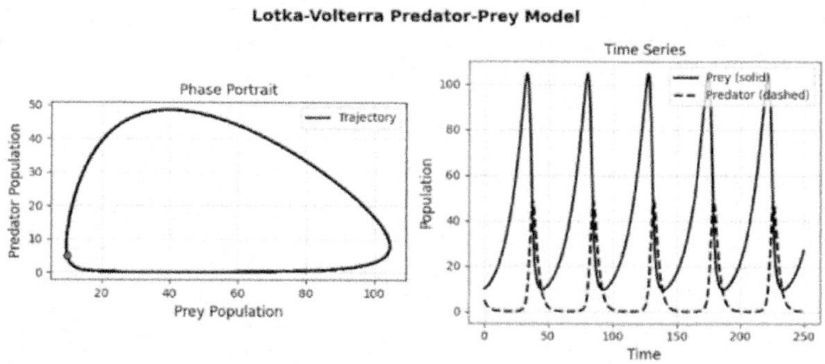

Figure 52 - Typical results of the Lotka-Volterra model. Calculated using the standard LV equations

In the LV model, the predators never succeed at completely exterminating their prey. But they can reduce the number of preys to a level so low that it can't support so many predators. At this point, predators start dying, and the prey population starts re-growing. The result of the simplest version of the LV model is a series of oscillations that extends to infinity. The "phase portrait" graph plots the number of predators as a function of the number of the prey stock. Note how the two populations chase each other without ever reaching a stable point. If the model is modified by adding a "friction" term, then the predator and prey stock will eventually reach a condition of stability. In the natural world, populations seem to be able to reach that condition, unless they are influenced by external perturbations.

The Lotka-Volterra model becomes the same as the SIR model if you remove the term that generates the growth of the prey. In this case, it is sometimes called the "Single-cycle Lotka-Volterra" (SCLV) model[107]. This model is related to the one called the "Hubbert" model, which was developed outside population studies but turned out to be part of the family. Marion King Hubbert (1903-1989) was a US petroleum geologist who developed a model on the oil extraction cycle in the 1950s.

The Seneca Curve.

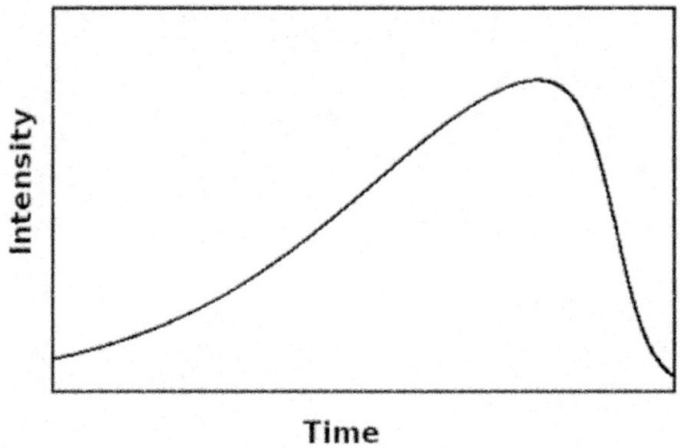

Figure 53 - The Seneca curve. Growth is slow, but collapse is rapid. Calculated according to the model described in Ugo Bardi's Book The Seneca Effect (2017)

The "Seneca Curve" or "Seneca Effect" are terms derived from a statement by the Roman Philosopher Lucius Annaeus Seneca, who, in one of his letters, noted how "Growth is slow, but ruin is rapid." It is a concept that describes well how some populations tend to crash rather than just decline.

The Seneca Model can be described mathematically by a set of three differential equations. In simpler terms, it is the result of a "perfect storm" that affects a growing population. If the decline is caused by a single factor, such as running out of food, then the curve tends to be the symmetric, bell-shaped one described in the previous section. However, if additional factors appear together to weigh on

Dynamic Models: The Limits to Growth

From Malthus onward, modeling population trends was a question of using equations that could be written on paper and solved by hand. That was often laborious and time-consuming. The revolution came with the development of the first digital computers in the 1950s and 1960s. At that point, the drudgery of finding approximate solutions to a set of equations could be left to the machine, while humans could concentrate on the structure of the model. This kind of modeling was initially developed for military applications, but it was very versatile and could be dedicated to modeling population growth and decline.

One of the pioneers in this field was a professor at the Massachusetts Institute of Technology in the 1960s, Jay Forrester (1918-2016), who built his own advanced computers to run his sophisticated models. Forrester developed a new field of modeling called "System Dynamics," which used a specific programming language called DYNAMO. Already in the 1960s, Forrester thought that he could use his computers and his models to study the evolution of the world's economic system, including the trajectory of the human population.

In 1969, Forrester was a faculty member of MIT when he was contacted by Aurelio Peccei, the president of the recently formed Club of Rome. At that time, Peccei was interested in understanding how Earth's resources could be distributed among the people of the world. But no data or models were available to understand how exactly the economic system would evolve in a situation that, at that time, seemed to promise a future of abundance. Would there be enough for a fair share for everyone? But how would the production of goods adapt to a growing population? The existing models were either partial or oversimplified.

Forrester's calculation methods promised to generate answers to these questions. After discussing with Forrester, Peccei found a sponsor for the project with the Volkswagen Foundation, which provided a grant. That led to the creation of the first "world models," which examined the whole Earth's economic system, taking into account the physical constraints of the environment.

The first study was created by Forrester himself and published in 1971 with the title *World Dynamics* [9]. A second study, published in 1972 by a group of Forrester's coworkers, carried the title The Limits to Growth (LTG)[10]. These studies were milestones in the understanding of the evolution of the human population as a function of the economy. The results were similar and showed that Malthus was an optimist.

Far from reaching the limits to growth and staying there, human civilization was to overshoot the limits and then crash down. The figure shows the results of the "business as usual" (or "base case") scenario

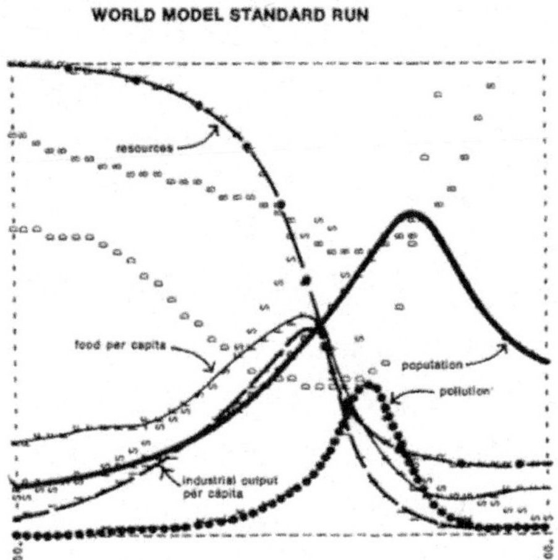

Figure 56 - The "base case" scenario of the 1972 edition of The Limits to Growth. Image courtesy of Dennis Meadows

10. References

(1) Láng-Ritter, J.; Keskinen, M.; Tenkanen, H. Global Gridded Population Datasets Systematically Underrepresent Rural Population. *Nat. Commun.* **2025,** *16* (1), 2170. https://doi.org/10.1038/s41467-025-56906-7.

(2) Greenspoon, L.; Krieger, E.; Sender, R.; Rosenberg, Y.; Bar-On, Y. M.; Moran, U.; Antman, T.; Meiri, S.; Roll, U.; Noor, E.; Milo, R. The Global Biomass of Wild Mammals. *Proc. Natl. Acad. Sci.* **2023**, *120* (10), e2204892120. https://doi.org/10.1073/pnas.2204892120.

(3) Rockström, J.; Steffen, W.; Noone, K.; Persson, Å.; Chapin, F. S.; Lambin, E. F.; Lenton, T. M.; Scheffer, M.; Folke, C.; Schellnhuber, H. J.; Nykvist, B.; de Wit, C. A.; Hughes, T.; van der Leeuw, S.; Rodhe, H.; Sörlin, S.; Snyder, P. K.; Costanza, R.; Svedin, U.; Falkenmark, M.; Karlberg, L.; Corell, R. W.; Fabry, V. J.; Hansen, J.; Walker, B.; Liverman, D.; Richardson, K.; Crutzen, P.; Foley, J. A. A Safe Operating Space for Humanity. *Nature* **2009**, *461* (7263), 472–475. https://doi.org/10.1038/461472a.

(4) *Earth beyond six of nine planetary boundaries.* https://doi.org/10.1126/sciadv.adh2458.

(5) United Nations. *World Population Prospects*. United Nations. https://population.un.org/wpp/ (accessed 2025-04-07).

(6) Dhakad S. et al. *Updating the Shared Socioeconomic Pathways (SSPs) Global Population and Human Capital Projections.*; IIASA. http://iiasa.ac.at/models-tools-data/ssp-2023 (accessed 2025-04-07).

(7) Lee, H.; Romero, J. *Sixth Assessment Report — IPCC*; IPCC, 2024. https://www.ipcc.ch/assessment-report/ar6/ (accessed 2024-07-23).

(8) Vollset, S. E.; Goren, E.; Yuan, C.-W.; Cao, J.; Smith, A. E.; Hsiao, T.; Bisignano, C.; Azhar, G. S.; Castro, E.; Chalek, J.; Dolgert, A. J.; Frank, T.; Fukutaki, K.; Hay, S. I.; Lozano, R.; Mokdad, A. H.; Nandakumar, V.; Pierce, M.; Pletcher, M.; Robalik, T.; Steuben, K. M.; Wunrow, H. Y.; Zlavog, B. S.; Murray, C. J. L. Fertility, Mortality, Migration, and Population Scenarios for 195 Countries and Territories from 2017 to 2100: A Forecasting Analysis for the Global Burden of Disease Study. *The Lancet*

2020, *396* (10258), 1285–1306. https://doi.org/10.1016/S0140-6736(20)30677-2.
(9) Forrester, J. *World Dynamics*; Wright-Allen Press: Cambridge, Massachusetts, 1971.
(10) Meadows, D.; Meadows, D. H.; Randers, J.; Behrens, W., Jr. *The Limits to Growth*; Potomac Associates, 1972.
(11) Ugo Bardi. *The Seneca Effect. Why Growth Is Slow but Collapse Is Rapid.*; Springer Verlag, 2017.
(12) Levine, H.; Jørgensen, N.; Martino-Andrade, A.; Mendiola, J.; Weksler-Derri, D.; Mindlis, I.; Pinotti, R.; Swan, S. H. Temporal Trends in Sperm Count: A Systematic Review and Meta-Regression Analysis. *Hum. Reprod. Update* **2017**, *23* (6), 646–659. https://doi.org/10.1093/humupd/dmx022.
(13) Calhoun, J. B. Death Squared: The Explosive Growth and Demise of a Mouse Population. *Proc. R. Soc. Med.* **1973**, *66* (1 Pt 2), 80–88. https://doi.org/10.1177/00359157730661P202.
(14) Herculano-Houzel, S. *The Human Advantage: A New Understanding of How Our Brain Became Remarkable*; The MIT Press, 2016. https://doi.org/10.7551/mitpress/9780262034258.001.0001.
(15) Pinson, A.; Xing, L.; Namba, T.; Kalebic, N.; Peters, J.; Oegema, C. E.; Traikov, S.; Reppe, K.; Riesenberg, S.; Maricic, T.; Derihaci, R.; Wimberger, P.; Pääbo, S.; Huttner, W. B. Human TKTL1 Implies Greater Neurogenesis in Frontal Neocortex of Modern Humans than Neanderthals. *Science* **2022**, *377* (6611), eabl6422. https://doi.org/10.1126/science.abl6422.
(16) Bardi, U. The Role of Carbon Dioxide in the Evolution of Intelligence: Solving the Dinosauroid Question. *Qeios* **2025**. https://doi.org/10.32388/IKNUZU.
(17) Morris, D. *The Naked Ape*; Jonathan Cape, 1967.
(18) Gould, S. J.; Vrba, E. S. Exaptation-A Missing Term in the Science of Form. *Paleobiology* **1982**, *8* (1), 4–15.
(19) Bartsiokas, A.; Arsuaga, J.-L. Hibernation in Hominins from Atapuerca, Spain Half a Million Years Ago. *L'Anthropologie* **2020**, *124* (5), 102797. https://doi.org/10.1016/j.anthro.2020.102797.
(20) Roebroeks, W.; MacDonald, K.; Scherjon, F.; Bakels, C.; Kindler, L.; Nikulina, A.; Pop, E.; Gaudzinski-Windheuser, S. Landscape Modification by Last Interglacial Neanderthals. *Sci. Adv.* **2021**, *7* (51), eabj5567. https://doi.org/10.1126/sciadv.abj5567.

(66) UNEP, U. N. *Chemicals in Plastics - A Technical Report*; UNEP, 2023. http://www.unep.org/resources/report/chemicals-plastics-technical-report (accessed 2024-06-11).
(67) Mastrantonio, M.; Bai, E.; Uccelli, R.; Cordiano, V.; Screpanti, A.; Crosignani, P. Drinking Water Contamination from Perfluoroalkyl Substances (PFAS): An Ecological Mortality Study in the Veneto Region, Italy. *Eur. J. Public Health* **2018**, *28* (1), 180–185. https://doi.org/10.1093/eurpub/ckx066.
(68) Di Nisio, A.; Sabovic, I.; Valente, U.; Tescari, S.; Rocca, M. S.; Guidolin, D.; Dall'Acqua, S.; Acquasaliente, L.; Pozzi, N.; Plebani, M.; Garolla, A.; Foresta, C. Endocrine Disruption of Androgenic Activity by Perfluoroalkyl Substances: Clinical and Experimental Evidence. *J. Clin. Endocrinol. Metab.* **2019**, *104* (4), 1259–1271. https://doi.org/10.1210/jc.2018-01855.
(69) Edaes, F. S.; de Souza, C. B. BPS and BPF Are as Carcinogenic as BPA and Are Not Viable Alternatives for Its Replacement. *Endocr. Metab. Immune Disord. Drug Targets* **2022**, *22* (9), 927–934. https://doi.org/10.2174/1871530322666220316141032.
(70) Chao, F.; Gerland, P.; Cook, A. R.; Alkema, L. Systematic Assessment of the Sex Ratio at Birth for All Countries and Estimation of National Imbalances and Regional Reference Levels. *Proc. Natl. Acad. Sci.* **2019**, *116* (19), 9303–9311. https://doi.org/10.1073/pnas.1812593116.
(71) Press, A. More than 63 Million Women "missing" in India, Statistics Show. *The Guardian*. January 30, 2018. https://www.theguardian.com/world/2018/jan/30/more-than-63-million-women-missing-in-india-statistics-show (accessed 2025-11-27).
(72) Miguel, E. Poverty and Witch Killing. *Rev. Econ. Stud.* **2005**, *72* (4), 1153–1172.
(73) United, N. *World Population Prospects as Assessed in 1963*; 41; 1966. https://www.un.org/development/desa/pd/content/world-population-prospects-assessed-1963 (accessed 2025-02-16).
(74) UCSUSA. *1992 World Scientists' Warning to Humanity"*. https://www.ucsusa.org/resources/1992-world-scientists-warning-humanity (accessed 2025-02-22).
(75) Simmons, M. *Revisiting The Limits to Growth: Could the Club of Rome have been correct, after all? An energy white paper.*

http://www.greatchange.org/ov-simmons,club_of_rome_revisted.html (accessed 2014-01-01).
(76) Gilfilan, S. C. Lead Poisoning and the Fall of Rome. *J. Occup. Environ. Med.* **1965**, *7* (1), 53–60.
(77) Cilliers, L.; Retief, F. Lead Poisoning and the Downfall of Rome: Reality or Myth? In *History of Toxicology and Environmental Health: Toxicology in Antiquity*; Wexler, P., Ed.; Elsevier: Amsterdam, Boston, Heidelberg, London, Nw York, Oxford, Paris, San Diego, San Francisco, Singapore, Sydney, Tokyo, 2014.
(78) Colás, R. Ancient Lead, Mercury, and Tin. In *Reverse Engineering of Ancient Metals*; Carrizo, P. S., Ed.; Springer International Publishing: Cham, 2021; pp 29–40. https://doi.org/10.1007/978-3-030-72842-7_3.
(79) Büntgen, U. European Climate Variability and Human Susceptibility over the Past 2500 Years. **2010**.
(80) Makarieva, A. M.; Nefiodov, A. V.; Nobre, A. D.; Baudena, M.; Bardi, U.; Sheil, D.; Saleska, S. R.; Molina, R. D.; Rammig, A. The Role of Ecosystem Transpiration in Creating Alternate Moisture Regimes by Influencing Atmospheric Moisture Convergence. *Glob. Change Biol.* **2023**, *29* (9), 2536–2556. https://doi.org/10.1111/gcb.16644.
(81) DeWitte, S. The Anthropology of Plague: Insights from Bioarcheological Analyses of Epidemic Cemeteries. *Mediev. Globe* **2014**, *1* (1), 97–124.
(82) Turchin, P. Modeling Social Pressures Toward Political Instability. *Cliodynamics* **2013**, *4* (2). https://doi.org/10.21237/C7clio4221333.
(83) Mieth, A.; Bork, H.-R. Humans, Climate or Introduced Rats – Which Is to Blame for the Woodland Destruction on Prehistoric Rapa Nui (Easter Island)? *J. Archaeol. Sci.* **2010**, *37* (2), 417–426. https://doi.org/10.1016/j.jas.2009.10.006.
(84) Moreno-Mayar, J. V.; Rasmussen, S.; Seguin-Orlando, A.; Rasmussen, M.; Liang, M.; Flåm, S. T.; Lie, B. A.; Gilfillan, G. D.; Nielsen, R.; Thorsby, E.; Willerslev, E.; Malaspinas, A.-S. Genome-Wide Ancestry Patterns in Rapanui Suggest Pre-European Admixture with Native Americans. *Curr. Biol.* **2014**, *24* (21), 2518–2525. https://doi.org/10.1016/j.cub.2014.09.057.
(85) Finney, B. Polynesian-South America Round Trip Canoe Voyages. **1994**.

Printed in Dunstable, United Kingdom

84347386R00171

The figure shows the data for two of the parameters, population and pollution, for the "base case" scenario of the 2004 study, that is, the one based on the data available at that time and which assumes no action to steer the economy in the direction of a lower use of resources or reducing pollution. In this calculation, the global population peaks in ca. 2027-2028, pollution peaks about 10 years later, and then rapidly goes down. This is a scenario that describes a future we may see as not so bad. In these assumptions, the gradual decline of the world's population may save us from the worst damage generated by climate change. Note, though, that it won't save us from a bad crash of the economic system generated by the depletion of natural resources.

Unfortunately, this nice scenario is the result of a specific choice of parameters, and we can't expect the universe to make the choices we would like it to make. Let me show you another scenario from the same study. This is called "BAU2," and it assumes that the available natural resources are twice as large as in the BAU1 scenario. It is equivalent to assuming that better technologies will allow the industrial system to use resources more efficiently, or to find new ones

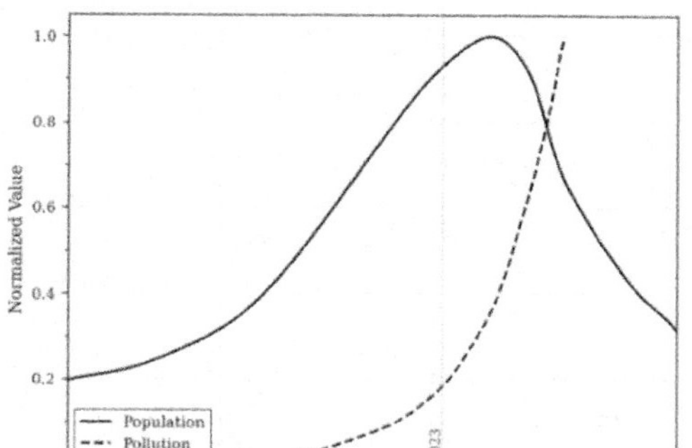

Figure 40 - The data for population and pollution parameters from the BAU2 scenario of The Limits to Growth, the 30 years update (2004). This scenario assumes a higher availability of natural resources.

In the BAU2 scenario, the population peaks around 2048 and then crashes down in the typical shape of the "Seneca Cliff," while

pollution shoots through the roof. If we see the pollution parameter as proportional to the concentration of CO_2 in the atmosphere, as it is commonly done in these studies, it would bring Earth back to a situation comparable to that of the End-Permian catastrophe that led to the near extinction of the biosphere.

These calculations were made more than 20 years ago; we have a more recent version with the study by Nebel et al. [28] who recalibrated the Limits to Growth base case scenario, adapting it to the data available in 2023.In the 2024 recalibration, the global population peaks in the 2030s. Pollution keeps growing for at least 30 years afterward and starts declining only after ca. 2070. Considering that the pollution level at the peak is about three times larger than it is now, we might estimate that in this scenario, the CO_2 concentration would rise to well above 1000 ppm, generating a temperature rise of 5-6 °C. A condition that humankind would probably not survive.

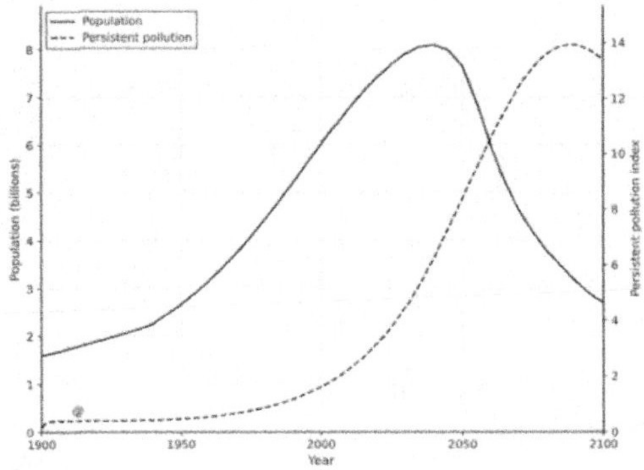

Figure 41 – The data for population and pollution parameters according to a recalibration of the WORLD3 model performed in 2024 28

This romp on modeling should be useful to understand the basic features of the global warming threat. For one thing, the uncertainty is large when projecting a vast and complex system such as Earth's climate into a long-term future. You saw how different models and a different choice of parameters could lead to scenarios

that go from a world similar to the scorched Earth of the early Mesozoic to a world where only minor adjustments need to be made in order to keep the economy growing. There are many more models, and you can play with your own. But only the Universe knows which is the right model and what the right parameters are.

Unfortunately, uncertainty is often used as a tool to favor financial or political interests. It is a propaganda technique that has been known for a long time, described in detail in the book *Merchants of Doubt* (2010) by Naomi Oreskes and Erik Conway. It was extensively used by the tobacco industry in the 1950s, during the debate on the health effects of smoking. If you have been involved in debates on climate and similar subjects, you surely encountered the attitude that goes as "since the damage that global warming creates is uncertain, then we should do nothing until we know better." In many fields of life, this attitude would be labeled as criminal. Imagine someone telling you, "Since it is uncertain whether you'll have a car accident or not, you shouldn't have your child wear seat belts." We react correctly to this attitude when it deals with things we know well, but climate change is sufficiently remote from our everyday experience that the "uncertainty" technique is effective.

But uncertainty is not a bug; it is a feature of models. Nobody can predict the future, and prediction is not the job of models. Their purpose is not to tell us what the future *will* be; it is to tell us what the future *could* be. Just as you can't forget that car accidents happen, you can't forget that abrupt bursts of increasing temperatures happened in the geological history of our planet. And if they happened in the past, they could happen in the future. What we have done so far has been sufficient to unbalance the system enough that it might go through one of those transformations and bring us to another world. It is the scenario that Bill McKibben named *Eaarth* in his 2010 book with that title. The models tell us a few fundamental points; the main one is that we can't expect population decline to solve the climate problem automatically. But it can also be of considerable help to

reduce the damage. The destiny of humankind lies between these boundaries.

Reversing the Fertility Decline?

Population decline is not a bad thing in itself. We may discuss its disadvantages, but a positive feature of it is that it can reduce the impact of humankind on a heavily strained global ecosystem. It means having more resources available per person and less pollution overall. But there also exists the concept of "too much of a good thing." Without input from new generations, states and societies could decline, or even collapse, unable to maintain the social and economic structures they had been able to build with the contribution of a larger population. So, could the future population trend maintain the good things of our society, including social security, health care, public education, and the like? Ideally, the fertility could stabilize at a level that ensures generational exchange, while slowly having the population decline to levels that the ecosystem can support. The process should be slow enough that it could maintain a working economy.

Could that happen? The answer depends on the factors that affect fertility. We saw in this book that there are at least four factors involved in controlling population size: famines and wars, socio-economic factors, pollution, and stress. Fortunately, right now, famines and wars are not playing an important role, while stress doesn't appear to be significant, either. But we still have to take into account socioeconomic factors and pollution. It is unlikely that the fertility will adjust itself to the ideal levels we would like it to be, so we need governments to intervene on these factors: creating socioeconomic conditions that encourage families to have children, and abating pollution in such a way as to make it possible for them to

Seen from a different viewpoint, large subsidies would amount to paying women to have children, which would give a new meaning to the concept of "proletariat" of Marxist times. We might think of some extreme scenarios in which government subsidies would bring about a profound restructuring of the social order, with some women taking childbearing as a profession. At the limit, society could organize itself in forms resembling the story told by Margaret Atwood in her novel *The Handmaid's Tale* (1985). It describes a dystopian society based on a distorted reading of the Bible, where fertile women are enslaved in order to produce children for the state. Society would then turn into a "eusocial" arrangement in which reproduction is a task taken by a small number of females, as is the case for some insects such as ants and bees. Some mammals adopt this arrangement, for instance, the naked mole rat (*Heterocephalus Glaber*), a creature native to the Horn of Africa and parts of Kenya. Those small creatures are said to have developed this social structure in order to survive the extremely harsh conditions of their environment. Maybe we will have to learn something from those rats? Right now, it looks unthinkable, but the recent years have seen so many previously unthinkable things becoming obvious truths that we can't completely discount anything.

A less complicated strategy to increase fertility could be the stick instead of the carrot. That is, penalizing people and families without children. This is a known approach, traditionally applied to men. In the past, several countries enforced "bachelor taxes" designed to encourage marriages. In Italy, the Fascist government introduced a tax on celibacy in 1927. During Nazi times, Germany introduced taxes to promote the "Three Ks," *Kirche, Küche, Kinder* (Church, Kitchen, and Children), which were supposed to be the main occupations of women. Probably not exactly what we want in the West today.

In any case, there is little evidence that these methods had any effect, but we cannot exclude the possibility that they will be tried again. They have the advantage that they cost nothing; on the contrary, they bring money to governments. But forcing people to

marry is one thing; forcing them to have children is another. Taxation on childless people would be unfair for those who can't have children for health reasons, in addition to bringing many more social and political problems.

Another method to raise fertility could be to use the best weapon that governments have to convince people to do things they don't want to do: propaganda. Having children could be praised and presented as something that provides prestige for the women who engage in the task. In the 1950s, it was common to present happy families with four to five children in advertising. In Eastern countries, natalist propaganda had a more socialist slant, but it had similar themes. The perfect Soviet mother was termed a "heroine" and was sometimes shown with 8-10 children. As it is typical of propaganda, these ideas faded out with the stark reality of the high cost of having children becoming clear to families. This method may well be tried again, but it is unlikely that it will have a large effect.

A different approach to propaganda is based on demonization. You probably know that, as Machiavelli never said, the art of politics consists in finding a culprit. So, this culprit could be found in childless families, working women, women who have a culture, and similar targets. Working women would lose their jobs, girls would be discouraged from attending school, illiterate women would be praised, while cultured women would be shunned and considered evil people. That would lead to a situation not unlike the way witches were demonized and despised in ancient times. Could society arrive at a new round of active witch-hunting to get rid of those pesky women who insist on thinking with their own heads? Again, it is an extreme scenario, but in recent times, we have seen the unthinkable becoming perfectly thinkable, and the current debate on social media seems to be moving exactly in that direction.

What if, instead, the fertility decline is mainly the result of pollution? In this case, the problem is much more difficult in political terms. Whereas laws and financial subsidies are the normal terrain of

action of governments, doing something against pollution is more difficult and more expensive. One problem is that it goes against the sacred principle of economic growth. Another is that polluters have powerful weapons to influence government choices that damage their profits: propaganda, lobbying, and good old corruption of government officials. The strong resistance of the polluters' lobby may be one of the main reasons why the idea that pollution is the main cause of fertility decline is mostly ignored nowadays. Nevertheless, there are several examples of successful policy actions designed to curb pollution. It has been possible to eliminate at least some major deadly pollutants: lead, cadmium, beryllium, CFCs, DDT, and others. A much-touted example is that of the elimination of the chlorofluorocarbon (CFC) compounds that were destroying the ozone layer in the upper atmosphere.

The problem is that in the current situation, the government engagement should be stepped up to cover much more dangerous and common pollutants known to cause infertility. That is, plastics, which are the main source of endocrine-disrupting molecules such as BPA, PFAS, pesticides, and more. Then, we should also curb the production of heavy metals and all those industrial activities that indirectly affect human health, primarily the emission of greenhouse gases.

Unfortunately, fighting pollution is expensive and unpopular, especially in the current political climate. The public perception of the pollution problem appears to have gone full circle: from the indifference of the first half of the 20th century to the worries that started being common in the 1960s. Nowadays, we see a return to neglecting the problem, while those who are raising the alarm are demonized and ignored. A good example of the trend is how the recent turn to right-wing policies is working at undoing regulations that were protecting people. Think of the recent *Plan 2025*, prepared by the Heritage Foundation, a prominent conservative think tank, in partnership with over 100 conservative organizations. It is said to be a manifesto of the current right-wing views and, among many other

things, it contains the specific proposal to "revisit the designation of PFAS chemicals as 'hazardous substances.' In practice, that means to deregulate the PFAS concentration in drinking water and food, throwing away all the evidence that it causes not only infertility but also serious health damage to people. Plan 2025 says nothing about other endocrine-disrupting substances, probably because the authors didn't know they existed. But there are other examples of failures in the attempts to control pollution. One is the recent attempt to remove carbon dioxide, CO_2, from the list of polluting substances.

Do these people drink the same water and breathe the same air as we do? Do they think they are invulnerable? Are they human beings? Or maybe Reptilian Aliens? More simply, these people may genuinely believe that they have been bothered enough with all those sacrifices that governments have been asking us to make to combat climate change and pollution. That is, we are burdened with expensive requests, unable to solve the problems they claim to solve – assuming that these problems exist. According to this view, the idea that PFAS is bad for people's health is just another scam perpetrated on us by those dishonest scientists who want to get money for their research grants.

With the current political turns that emphasize profit at the expense of protecting people from pollution, the possibility of significantly abating the concentration of endocrine-disrupting substances and other pollutants appears slim. Eventually, though, a declining population will also cause the decline of pollution, since industrial production will decline. Unfortunately, scenarios such as those calculated by *The Limits to Growth* series of studies tell us that worldwide pollution will start to fall decades after the collapse of the industrial system. Hence, we are destined to live with the pollution we created in the past, and we are still creating.

Can the fertility decline problem be solved by technological solutions? Much can be done in this sense, but new technologies

sophisticated DNA analysis techniques in order to choose which embryo is the most likely to produce a healthy baby, unaffected in late life by common forms of illness, such as high blood pressure or diabetes.

The possibilities offered by in vitro fertilization are multiple, and not all positive. For instance, governments could impose which eggs and sperm can unite in a Petri dish under laws favoring genetic optimization. What was once a private choice of partners could become a state-orchestrated selection; a dystopia we rightly view as abhorrent today. Yet history tells us that when something becomes possible, then it may well become reality. We all know how, in the recent past, there have been governments engaged in eugenic procedures to improve human beings of selected races. Could these ideas return? Hopefully not, but we can't be sure about that.

So, what is the likelihood that population decline may be slowed down without resorting to extreme technological or social measures? The best we can say is that governments should be careful to avoid worsening a situation that may be worrisome, but not yet catastrophic. There is no reason to panic: population decline is a natural phenomenon that will not lead to the extinction of the human species. First, even though we don't know whether pollution is the most important factor causing fertility decline, cleaning up the environment as much as possible is a good idea for many reasons. Cleaning up the air we breathe, the water we drink, and the spaces in which we live will surely improve people's health and will also reduce the societal costs for health measures.

We also need to help families to have and raise children, without expecting them to return to the fertility levels of the times before the Industrial Revolution. No one could, or should, be forced to have children, or enticed to have them by propaganda or other tricks. If we can achieve a clean, harmonious, less stressful, and more balanced society, it is perfectly possible that fertility will return to the replacement level that we need to keep our society alive and well.

Beyond Earth's Limits or Extinction?

Discussing the global human population trends often starts with the question, "How many people can Earth support?" The implication often is that we are already too many, and sometimes that it could support many more. But the question doesn't make sense unless a condition is specified: for how long? There is no doubt that the current global food production system can support eight billion people because it is doing exactly that. But how about the situation in a few decades from now, with fertilizers and pesticides becoming more expensive because of fossil fuel depletion? How about the effects of global warming, with the associated droughts and extreme events? How about pollution reducing fertility to levels that cannot sustain the human population? It is clear that "population" is a dynamic element of our future: it can, and most likely will, change, increasing or decreasing depending on human actions and on how the ecosystem will react to the increasing human pressure. The only thing we can be sure of is that the future is never what we expect it to be. Nevertheless, the point of reasoning about the future is to be prepared for it. So, what can we reasonably expect?

There are plenty of extreme population scenarios floating on the Web. On the pessimistic side (at least from the human viewpoint), we have extinction. It could hardly be caused by a single factor, but rather by a combination of events, including famines, plagues, wars, and assorted disasters. Climate change alone could make Earth uninhabitable by human beings, and that would conclude the human adventure on this planet. Extreme, indeed, but not impossible. After all, it is the normal destiny of species to go extinct. Why should humans be an exception?

Less extreme views do not imply extinction, but a return to conditions typical of ancient human societies. The "Olduvai Scenario," proposed by Richard Duncan,[103] posits the return to hunting and gathering. Other scenarios foresee the return to a purely

agricultural economy, similar to the conditions of Europe during the Middle Ages. In both cases, a regression to ancient times would be caused by the increasing cost of mineral extraction, which would make it impossible to sustain an industrial civilization. Both scenarios imply a huge reduction in the human population, considering that it had always been well under one billion individuals before the Industrial Revolution started in the late 18th century.

On the opposite side, we have optimistic views that see technology propping up human expansion, overcoming all the doomsday views that have been fashionable during the past few decades. Maybe we will find an energy source truly "too cheap to meter," as was dreamed of in the 1950s. Then, we could couple it with planetary engineering in such a way as to control the atmosphere's composition and temperature. Using artificial food, we could decouple humankind from Earth's limited resources. At this point, we could colonize the Moon and Mars; terraform Venus, and colonize it too. If you really trust technology, we could colonize space and build huge orbiting habitats around Earth or other planets.

We could even build a "Dyson Sphere," a huge shell around the sun that would collect all the light that the sun emits and use it to create a biosphere on the inner surface. That's beyond what current or even imaginable human technologies could do. Still, if it were possible, it would provide the definitive answer to the question of the ultimate limit of how many human beings could be alive at the same time. The habitable area inside the Dyson sphere could be, conservatively, at least 100 million times larger than that of Earth, maybe half a billion times larger. So, if we were to populate it with humans at a density comparable to that of the early industrial age, about 100 quadrillion (thousand trillion) humans could live there. Maybe this is what God meant when he told Adam and Eve, "Be fruitful and increase in number." But this is more than a little extreme, so we'd better explore more reasonable scenarios.

In practice, a moderate population decline may be the most likely scenario. On the positive side, it would help reduce the pressure on the environment due to industrial and agricultural activity. It would also help us to maintain a certain flow of resources into the economy, presently being depleted at an impressively fast rate. It will also reduce the need for wars, often created by expanding populations in search of vital space. It is not a bad future, but it will not be a paradise. With a declining population, we need to accept that the economy is also likely to decline. That's not a catastrophe, and cases such as Japan show that a prosperous economy can survive a population decline of about 1% per year. The use of robotics and AI may reduce the need for human power in many areas, so that it will be possible to keep the system humming along even with a smaller participation of human beings in productive tasks. But the damage already done to Earth's ecosystem is large enough that it will take a long time for it to be reabsorbed by natural processes. Its most evident manifestation is global warming. Unfortunately, even rather extreme hypotheses implying a rapid numeric decline of the human population would not necessarily reverse the warming trend.

So, what does the future have in store for humankind? From the extremes of extinction to expansion into space, there are plenty of intermediate scenarios, from the not-so-bad to the pretty good. The beauty of the future is that it is always full of possibilities.

by making individual decisions. If humans go extinct, it won't be because you decided not to have children. Nor, if they will survive, will it be because you decided to have them.

We can't engineer population trends, but we can stop pretending we could or we should. Humankind has been around for at least 300 thousand years. Our ancestors knew how to survive and how to play the reproduction game in terms of how many children to have and when. They made the right choices, and that's why we are here. Our ancestral heritage is a powerful force, and maybe, at some internal level of our minds, we understand that we have overshot the limits of this planet, and we are making a collective choice to reverse our trajectory before it is too late. Of course, we have no proof of that, and probably we never will. But we cannot, and we should not force people to make choices they don't want to make. We can focus on making whatever population trend emerges in the future more humane, ensuring people have genuine choice, reducing suffering, creating prosperity, and building resilient systems.

Nevertheless, no species lasts forever, and why should humans be an exception? Maybe we'll go extinct after having ruined the ecosystem. In that case, Earth will have to wait for a few million years to recover by itself and, perhaps, generate new sentient species who may do better than we did. Or maybe we'll find a way to stop wrecking everything around us and turn Earth into a garden. That may be what the Bible meant when it told Adam and Eve to "be fertile and multiply." Maybe we even have a chance to expand to space, and, if not us, our silicon children, the robots, will be able to do that.

We know that the future will always surprise us, and so, our job isn't to control it but to be less destructive and more adaptive as it unfolds. We need a different attitude, a way of thinking that doesn't lead us to escalation, that makes us accept the unavoidable and move along with it. In war, this attitude leads to peace; in commerce, to prosperity; in love, to love. This book is an invitation to see more

clearly, resist false solutions, and participate more effectively in the open-ended story we're all still writing.

8. Acknowledgements

No part of this book was written by artificial intelligence systems, but, with the disappearance of human assistant writers, Grok 4 and Claude turned out to be good as replacements, although always with limits and a horrible tendency to hallucinate. Other AI tools I used for this book were Manus for some of the graphs, Grammarly for grammar and syntax checking, and, occasionally, DeepL for translations. Miguel Martinez (a human being) provided the final editing and smoothing of the book.

Among other human beings, I would thank the members of the Club of Rome who encouraged me to embark on this enterprise, in particular the Secretary General Carlos Álvarez Pereira, the Communication Manager Philippa Baumgartner, and the Co-presidents Paul Shrivastava and Silvia Zimmerman. I would also like to thank Chandran Nair, another Club member, for his critical review of the chapter on China. Special thanks to Dennis Meadows for having made a critical evaluation of the book and suggested the present title. I would also cite David Samways as a source of inspiration for his work with the *Journal of Population and Sustainability*. I'd like to thank my coworkers for many scientific projects in which we have been engaged together, among them Stefano Caporali, Toufic El Asmar, Sara Falsini, Alessandro Lavacchi, Gianluca Martelloni, and Ilaria Perissi. I would also like to thank the Consorzio Nazionale for the Science and Technology of Materials (INSTM) for supporting my work. The ideas of this book were inspired by many people who acted as guides for me, among them Colin Campbell, Jean Laherrere, Jorgen Randers, Matthew Simmons, and many others.

9. Appendix: Mathematical Models of Population Trends

And it came to pass in those days that a decree went out from Caesar Augustus that all the world should be registered. This census first took place while Quirinius was governing Syria. Luke 2:1-2.

Figure 42 - The Triumph of Death (Prado, Madrid), by the Flemish painter Peter Bruegel the Elder (1525-1569). Public domain. This image is communicating the severity of the plague, but it does not provide quantitative data about it. Public Domain

The appendix is dedicated to how population trends can be understood and modeled. It starts with the first attempts to measure population by means of censuses, already in use in ancient times, and then it moves on to the modern population models based on sophisticated computer-based calculations.

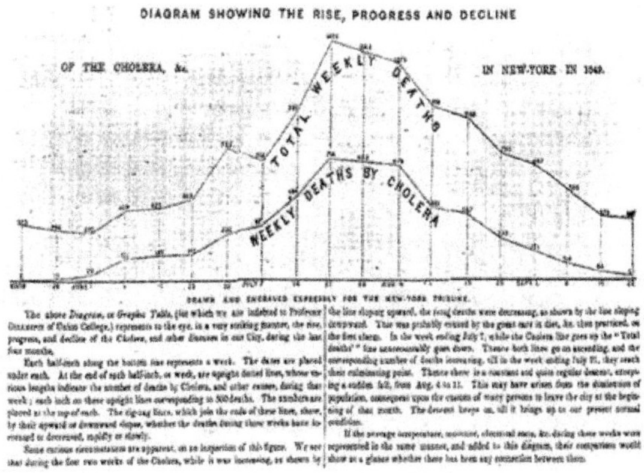

Figure 43 - Graph of the progress of the Cholera epidemic in New York up to 1849. Published in the New York Daily Tribune, it was probably the first ever published Cartesian graph.

Perhaps the first modern Cartesian Graph to be publicly available was printed in the New York Daily Tribune in 1849, which was a population graph, although dedicated to a bacterial population rather than a human one.[104]

The graph reported the progress of a cholera epidemic at the time. It was an innovation that most readers must have found challenging to understand, and, indeed, note how the editors made an effort to explain to readers the meaning of what they were seeing. From the discussions about the pandemics of 2020, it appears that even in modern times, most people were still not familiar with this kind of graph. But for anyone who has more than a passing interest in these matters, graphs are a fundamental tool. It took time before modern population graphs appeared in print. Here is the oldest example I could find: it is in the "U.S. population growth from 1790 to 1890 in the Statistical Atlas of the Eleventh Census" by Henry Gannett.[105]

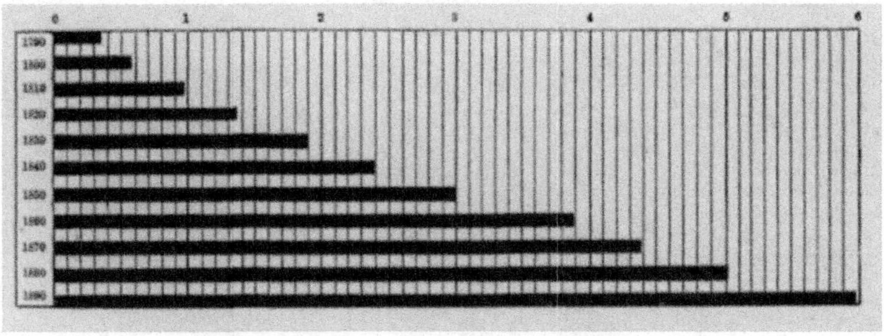

Figure 44 -- Possibly the first Cartesian graph ever published to illustrate the growth of a human population. From the "Statistical Atlas of the Eleventh Census" by Henry Gannett.

It is a Cartesian graph, but a little quirky if seen from our modern viewpoint. We tend to place the time on the x-axis, growing toward the right. Here, instead, the time goes *down* on the Y axis. But if you imagine turning the image 90 degrees anti-clockwise, the graph appears in a way that we can readily understand: a typical bar graph showing the growth trends of some quantity. Note how New York's population appears to grow exponentially, a typical behavior of a population during its early stages of expansion.

Cartesian plots of time series allow us to visualize the trends of population growth (or de-growth) in a way that tables or lists of numbers never could. Graphs make the population "alive" on paper; its history and trends bounce up to our eyes, clear and unmistakable. Over time, Cartesian graphs have evolved to describe a variety of phenomena, but their use to show the evolution of some entity as a time series remains probably the most common one.

Simple Models of Population Trends

To begin, when we refer to "population," we typically mean human or animal populations; however, nothing prevents us from

using the term for non-human and non-biological entities, cats, dogs, cars, planes, etc. That said, all populations tend to follow similar laws and often predictable patterns. They may grow, remain stable, or decline.

Figure 45 – Ugo Bardi explaining the various population growth modes to his class. Note "Amelia the Amoeba," a character used to enliven the presentation. Photo by the author.

Growth. The simplest case is that of a population that expands in the environment that supports it. Typically, it doesn't just grow; it grows faster and faster: more people (or rabbits, or flies, or whatever) mean more hatchlings, and more hatchlings mean more people. Of course, no real-world population is known to have followed this growth mode forever, but this mechanism does occur for limited times.

Stability. The physical limitations of the environment dictate the limits of a population: resources or predation by another species. A population reaching this limit may attain stability, although it will often oscillate around it. Sometimes, people call that level an "attractor," and some attractors are said to be "strange" (as per the first Jurassic Park movie). It means that the oscillations are chaotic and

never exactly repeat the same pattern. But that changes little to the behavior of the population.

Decline. The population may also decline or even collapse after having overcome its limits, having reached a state of "overshoot." That is, it has exploited its resources beyond their capability to reform. Often, the decline is much faster than growth as a result of additional constraints, typically pollution; in this case, one speaks of the "Seneca Effect."

Now, let's examine the details of how these mechanisms work.

Exponential (or "geometric") growth. The idea that populations tend to expand geometrically was probably known for a long time. Today, the concept of exponential economic growth is embedded in the current ways of economic thinking, but it is also common in biology. .

Figure 46 -- Exponential Growth

You may describe this kind of growth as in the common saying that some creatures reproduce "like rabbits." Put a couple of rabbits

is that it is rare to see real-world populations that follow this growth mechanism, at least in a natural environment. To cite a case, we can go back to the example of the elephants in the Kruger National Park in South Africa. After reaching a number that appeared excessive to humans, elephants began to be culled in order to keep their numbers within a limit that seemed appropriate. The result was a growth curve that could be interpreted as a logistic. However, it was not a natural behavior; it was the result of an external intervention by human beings. In recent times, culling has been abandoned, and elephants have restarted growing again in a curve that, so far, looks exponential. It does not appear that elephants can reduce their growth rate to match the sustainability limits imposed by their environment, and that may prefigure an uncertain destiny for them.

The idea of the carrying capacity is that the growing creatures find that life becomes more and more difficult as they approach the limits of their environment to sustain their life. Herbivores have a limited area of grass to graze on, while carnivores have a limited number of herbivores to prey on. So, short of food, they reproduce more and more slowly until they reach a level where the newborn creatures replace those that die. At this point, the population becomes stable. The stability can also be generated by a predator that "culls" the population at a rate proportional to its size.

Bell-shaped curves. Malthus was an optimist when he thought that a population would reach an upper limit and then stay there. Things are not so simple in the real world, and consuming the resources that make people (or animals) live cannot be without negative consequences. In practice, populations don't just stabilize when they reach the limits of the resources that sustain them. They tend to destroy them, sometimes forever, and the result is not stabilization but collapse. In several cases, the population curve follows a "bell-shaped" curve.

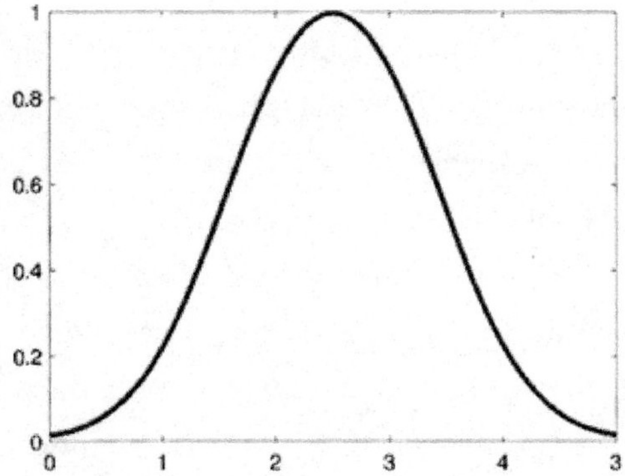

Figure 49 - A typical, bell-shaped curve The size of the population is on the Y-axis; time is on the X-axis

There is a whole fauna of mathematical functions that produce this kind of curve: the Gaussian, the derivative of a logistic, the Gompertz curve, the Dirac curve, and several others. All these curves can be used to describe the growth and decline of a biological population that runs out of the resources that make it live. It is typical of some laboratory systems, such as microorganisms grown in Petri dishes. We saw earlier the graph of the Cholera epidemic in New York in 1849. In the figure, you see another example: a curve drawn in the 1850s to illustrate the progress of the cholera pandemic in London. Pathogens can be seen as predators that live on the human population. But there is just a limited number of humans to exploit, and they gradually either die or become immune to the pathogen. When the virus, or the bacterium, has no more "food" to grow on, its population declines and eventually disappears.

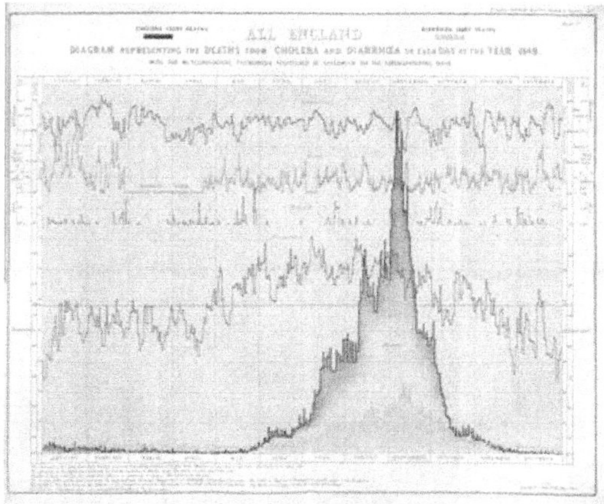

Figure 50 - Time chart of the Cholera epidemic in London in 1849. The blue line indicates the number of deaths attributed to cholera. Wikimedia Creative Commons. https://wellcomecollection.org/

The empirical observation that microorganism populations tend to follow these curves led to the development of a mathematical model to describe their behavior. In the 1920s, three British researchers, Kermack, McKendrick, and Walker, proposed the "SIR" model for the evolution of epidemics. SIR stands for "Susceptible," "Infected," and "Recovered."[106]

These models are also called "compartmental," because they divide the population into compartments. In the jargon of these studies, the number of individuals belonging to each of these categories is referred to as a "stock." Note also that the model is based on data on the effects of the pathogen, not directly on the pathogen population, which is usually impossible to measure. Instead, the number of infected people is a proxy for the number of microorganisms. The idea of the SIR model is that a population starts with a small fraction of its members infected. As more people get infected, the number of susceptible individuals declines while that of infected ones increases. As time goes by, infected people recover and become "immune" (or die). Eventually, the pathogens don't find enough targets to continue spreading, and their population (counted

in terms of the number of infected people) starts declining, too. At that point, the human population is said to have reached "herd immunity," and the epidemic doesn't grow anymore. In time, the epidemic abates, and the microorganism population goes down to zero. Epidemiological models exist in several variants, and there are plenty of bells and whistles that can be added to simple models to make them complicated (and often not more reliable). In some cases, these additional elements can be used to torture the data until it confesses to whatever an investigator wants it to confess. But that's true for all models.

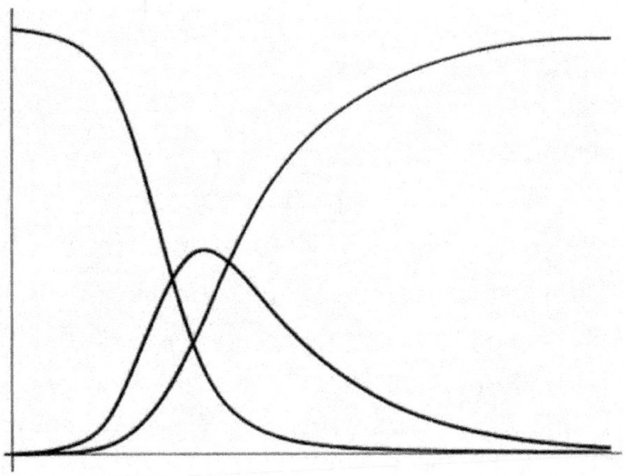

Figure 51 - Typical results of the SIR model. The time is on the x-axis, while the three curves describe, respectively, the number of susceptible, infected, and recovered people107

Nothing prevents the SIR model from being applied to populations other than microorganisms. In practice, however, it remains traditionally confined to medical studies. In the more general field of population biology, similar models are used, but with different names. The ancestor of these models was independently developed a few years before the SIR model by Alfred Lotka (a physical chemist) and Vito Volterra (a mathematician). Today, the model takes the name of the "Lotka-Volterra" or "LV" model,

the population, then decline is typically faster than growth. An example can be the role of predators, added to the lack of food. In the case of a human population, famine may be coupled to a plague or, in recent times, to pollution

.

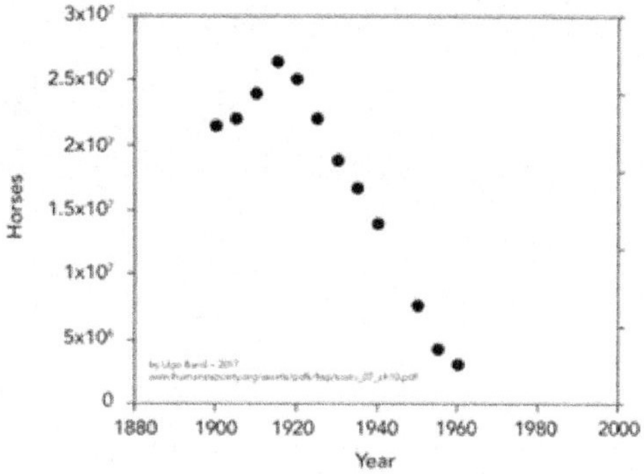

Figure 54 - The Horse population in the United States. Data from www.thehumanesociety.org (no longer available).

A typical example of a real-world population collapse that followed a Seneca trajectory is that of the horse population in the United States, which rapidly declined after horses were no longer used as a means of transportation. Later, the horse population restarted growing, but it remains today much smaller than it was at its peak.

The "Hokusai Model" – Using this term, I am referring to the famous print of "The Wave" by the Japanese painter Katsushika Hokusai

Figure 55 - Katsushika Hokusai, 'The Great Wave off Kanagawa' (c. 1830-1833), from the series 'Thirty-Six Views of Mount Fuji.

It is a visual help to understand that when things go bad, they gang together to do much worse things. As Shakespeare said in "Hamlet," troubles come "not as single spies, but in battalions." A population collapse may come in the shape of a Seneca Curve, but even though the curve shows a sharp downward trajectory, it is still a smooth curve. The "Hokusai model" refers to a situation in which the system goes chaotic or unpredictable. It refers to the various forms of rapid collapse, which are sometimes referred to as "Black Swans" [108] or "Dragon Kings,"[109] part of the general field of "critical" phenomena. [110] These are real phenomena that happen in the real world. Examples are earthquakes, avalanches, landslides, tsunamis, and more.

The models described here are at the basis of population studies in biology and medicine. They are also often used to describe the behavior of human populations, but they form a separate and different compartment of science from the main field of human population study: demography. It is a field strongly influenced by economics, and uses an approach mainly based on curve fitting. Demographers tend to try to learn about population trends starting

from historical data, rather than supposing that the curve will follow a specific curve or theoretical model.

Demographic studies use sophisticated statistical methods to analyze data, identify trends, and project them into the future. "Curve Fitting" is a process in which the experimental or historical data are compared to a curve obtained by a model or an equation. The correspondence will never be perfect, and there exist sophisticated statistical treatments that can quantify the discrepancy between theory and the real world. These methods can be used to decide whether a specific model is good or not to describe a process, for instance, the spreading of an epidemic. Once a model has been tested and shown to produce a good fit, it can be extrapolated to obtain a peek at the future. It is an ensemble of methods that goes under the name of "MLE," "Maximum Likelihood Estimation." Sometimes, these routines are based on the basic population models described here, or it is possible to ask the calculating routines to estimate the equation or set of equations that's behind the historical trends. Then, the system can extrapolate the trend into the future. As you may easily understand, this approach is fraught with uncertainties.

The model used by the United Nations for the World Population Prospects (WPP) is one of the most advanced. It relies on a variety of data sources to build its models, such as National Censuses to provide baseline population counts, typically conducted every 5–10 years by countries. Birth and death registrations from national systems are also used, and special surveys are often carried out. For countries with limited or unreliable data, the UN uses statistical methods to estimate missing figures based on historical trends or data from similar regions.

The model is based on a cohort-component method, a standard demographic technique, to project population changes over time. It tracks population by age and sex, factoring in three key drivers: 1) the Total Fertility Rate (TFR), or average number of births per woman, 2) Mortality, and 3) Migrations. Assumptions about future fertility,

mortality, and migration are based on trends in education, healthcare, economic development, and policy. Each "cohort" (e.g., women aged 20–24) moves through time, aging and experiencing these demographic processes, which are calculated in five-year intervals.

Since the future is uncertain, the UN uses a Bayesian hierarchical model to generate probabilistic projections (introduced in the 2015 WPP and refined since), incorporating uncertainty by producing thousands of possible trajectories for TFR and life expectancy. The output is a median projection (most likely scenario) alongside ranges (e.g., 80% or 95% confidence intervals), reflecting high and low variants.

The UN model, sophisticated as it is, does not include factors such as climate change, effects of pollution, and resource depletion. They are supposed to be incorporated in the past trends, and hence to be "virtually" accounted for in the future. There is growing pressure to better integrate climate change into demographic modeling through interdisciplinary models that merge climate, economic, and population dynamics. However, the problem is that including more details adds uncertainty to the calculations and makes the models less robust.

One problem is that since historical data do not usually involve population crashes, the method will never predict a possible future crash. Predicting the future is always difficult, and no matter how good your model is, it will never be the same as the real world. There will always be something in the real world that its virtual counterpart in the memory of a computer didn't take into account, but which turned out to be important. Nevertheless, we all know that life is fraught with uncertainties, and often, scientific forecasters can't do much better than the average guy in the street. Otherwise, they would be richer and more successful. So, we keep going, trying to do our best.

. You can see in the figure the original graph that was printed in the first edition of LTG, plotted in black and white with the limited plotting capabilities of the time. It is the so-called "base case" scenario, a projection of how the world's social and economic system would evolve if the trends of the time were to be maintained. It was based on the best available data on the quantities of mineral resources, land, and industrial capital. The results for the global population are shown as the black curve, the one that reaches the highest level in the mid-21st century and then rapidly declines.

It was a revolutionary result. It was the first time that a population was quantitatively studied not as an independent variable based on statistical trends, but as part of a complex system that dynamically changes over time. Not that people hadn't realized that the population would depend on such factors as the availability of food and energy, but before the development of system dynamics, it wasn't impossible to calculate all these factors together.

Let's describe more in detail how the "world modeling" approach worked. In the case of The Limits to Growth, its first appearance in 1972 was based on a mathematical model called "World3." It had the "3" index because it was the third of a series that had been started earlier on by Forrester, who had used the "World2" model for the study he published in 1971. The World3 model was remarkably complex for its time. It had hundreds of parameters arranged in a complicated network of interactions. Nevertheless, the model was based on five main parameters:

- Human Population
- Non-renewable Resources (minerals)
- Renewable Resources (agriculture)
- Capital Resources
- Pollution

These five elements, also called "stocks," interact with each other by exchanging materials, energy, and money. The main results of the model could be explained in qualitative terms by describing how the stocks evolved together. The combined effects of resource depletion and pollution accumulation gradually reduced the ability of the industrial system to accumulate capital, which was created by the resources and had to be spent to fight pollution. With less capital available, both the industrial system and the agricultural one slowed down their growth and, eventually, reached a peak and then declined. Later, the population stock would follow the same trajectory, as impoverished families would be unable to form families and have children. With the collapse, pollution, too, would decline since it was created mainly by the industrial system.

These results were not to be taken as predictions but just as answers to the question "what if?" They formed a series of scenarios that demonstrated the robustness of the tendency toward collapse. Unless some specific interventions were to be carried out, or some miraculous new technology developed, a global collapse was unavoidable at some moment during the 21st century, probably during the first half of it. Only specific policies to curb growth could avoid it. In general, the "base-case" scenario, the one that assumed no changes in the current policies at that time, produced results that turned out to describe the world's situation as it is today. Re-examinations of the study, such as the one by Graham Turner in 2008[111] and by Gaia Herrington in 2021[112] showed that the correspondence with the historical trends was not perfect, but remarkably good considering that it spanned more than half a century.

The population parameter in *The Limits to Growth* was one of the most uncertain and most difficult to deal with. Most of the parameters of the model could be treated in terms of the standard assumptions of economics. That is, it could be assumed that people would operate in such a way to maximize their economic benefit in

the short run. In more mundane terms, you would say that they were trying to make as much money as they could. But population growth (or decline) depends on choices that cannot be based on monetary gains, but on the more vaporous concept of "utility." That implies proposing what factors make people decide to have children or not. It is a decision that most likely results from a series of factors combining: food availability, cost of living, future prospects for one's children, local customs and morals, and more. The authors of the first Limits to Growth study used the known historical data on the relationship between wealth and birthrate. This relation is far from being linear: poor people tend to have more children when they get a little richer. But, over a certain limit, the "population transition" kicks in, and birthrates decline. It is a well-known phenomenon, normally ascribed to social factors.

If we assume that the correlation remains valid when economic growth becomes a decline, then one would expect that people would have more children. That explains why the Limits to Growth model shows population growing while everything else collapses. But that's hardly a realistic assumption: hungry and sick people are unlikely to think very much of sex. Besides, the assumption doesn't correspond to the data we have about societies that actually collapsed in recent times, such as the states that once formed the Soviet Union. In all recent cases, the population went down rapidly, together with the economy.

This problem was noted by the authors of the 1972 study, and it was corrected with more realistic assumptions that placed more importance on wealth and resources on people's willingness to have children. In the new versions of the study, the decline of the world's population starts about one decade after the start of the decline of food availability. Other studies based on system dynamics provided similar results.

Most dynamic models generate the turning point at some moment during the first half of the 21st century. It is a prediction that

still needs to be verified, but it looks reasonable considering that already today, one-third of the world's population lives in countries where the population is declining. As always, the future is not exactly predictable, but these models provide us with tools to be prepared for what will befall us.

(21) Hawks, J. Significance of Neandertal and Denisovan Genomes in Human Evolution*. *Annu. Rev. Anthropol.* **2013**, *42* (Volume 42, 2013), 433–449. https://doi.org/10.1146/annurev-anthro-092412-155548.

(22) Bardi, U. *Chimeras: Inanna and Ebih: a report of an ancient ecological catastrophe?*. Chimeras. https://chimeramyth.blogspot.com/2015/08/inanna-and-ebih-report-of-ancient.html (accessed 2021-11-09).

(23) Bairoch, P. *Cities and Economic Development: From the Dawn of History to the Present*; University of Chicago Press: Chicago, Il, 1988.

(24) Varia. *World Population Prospects*. World Population Prospects. https://population.un.org/wpp/ (accessed 2025-09-14).

(25) Greiling, W. *Wie werden wir leben?*; Econ-Verlag, 1954.

(26) Lutz, W.; Sanderson, W.; Scherbov, S. Doubling of World Population Unlikely. *Nature* **1997**, *387* (6635), 803–805. https://doi.org/10.1038/42935.

(27) Lutz, W.; Sanderson, W.; Scherbov, S. The End of World Population Growth. In *The End of World Population Growth in the 21st Century*; Lutz, W., Sanderson, W., Scherbov, S., Eds.; Earthscan: London, 2004; pp 17–84.

(28) Nebel, A.; Kling, A.; Willamowski, R.; Schell, T. Recalibration of Limits to Growth: An Update of the World3 Model. *J. Ind. Ecol.* **2024**, *28* (1), 87–99. https://doi.org/10.1111/jiec.13442.

(29) Bystroff, C. Footprints to Singularity: A Global Population Model Explains Late 20th Century Slow-down and Predicts Peak within Ten Years. *PLoS ONE* **2021**, *16* (5), e0247214. https://doi.org/10.1371/journal.pone.0247214.

(30) Randers, J. *2052: A Global Forecast for the Next Forty Years*, Illustrated edition.; Chelsea Green: White River Junction, Vermont, 2012.

(31) Dixson-Decleve, S.; Gaffney, O.; Ghosh, J.; Randers, J.; Rockstrom, J.; Stoknes, P. E. *Earth for All: A Survival Guide for Humanity*; New Society Publishers: Gabriola Island, British Columbia, Canada, 2022.

(32) Meadows, D. H.; Meadows, D. L.; Randers, J. *Beyond the Limits*; Chelsea Green: Post Mills, Vermont, USA, 1992.

(33) Meadows, D. H.; Randers, J.; Meadows, D. L. *Limits to Growth: The 30 Year Update*; Chelsea Green: White River Junction, 2004.

(34) Hotelling, H. The Economics of Eshaustible Resources. *J. Polit. Econ.* **1931**, *39* (2), 137–175.
(35) Zimmermann, E. W. *World Resources and Industries;: A Functional Appraisal of the Availability of Agricultural and Industrial Resources,*; Harper & Brothers: New York, 1933.
(36) Daly, H. E. Georgescu-Roegen versus Solow/Stiglitz. *Ecol. Econ.* **1997**, *22* (3), 261–266. https://doi.org/10.1016/S0921-8009(97)00080-3.
(37) Hall, C.; Lindenberger, D.; Kümmel, R. The Need to Reintegrate the Natural Sciences with Economics: Neoclassical Economics, the Dominant Form of Economics Today, Has at Least Three Fundamental Flaws. *BioScience* **2001**.
(38) Hubbert, M. K. Nuclear Energy and the Fossil Fuels. In *Spring Meeting of the Southern District, American Petroleum Institute, Plaza Hotel, San Antonio, Texas, March 7–8-9,*; San Antonio, Texas, 1956.
(39) Bardi, U.; Lavacchi, A. A Simple Interpretation of Hubbert's Model of Resource Exploitation. *Energies* **2009**, *2* (3), 646–661. https://doi.org/10.3390/en20300646.
(40) Hardin, G. The Tragedy of the Commons. *Science* **1968**, *162* (13 December), 1243–1248.
(41) Ostrom, E. *Governing the Commons: The Evolution of Institutions for Collective Action*; Cambridge University Press: Cambridge, UK, 1990.
(42) Moxnes, E. Not Only the Tragedy of the Commons: Misperceptions of Feedback and Policies for Sustainable Development. *Syst. Dyn. Rev.* **2000**, *16* (4), 325–348.
(43) Gorshkov, V.G; Makarieva, A.M. Biotic Pump of Atmospheric Moisture as Driver of the Hydrological Cycle on Land. *Hydrol. Earth Syst. Sci. Discuss.* **2006**, *3*, 2621–2673.
(44) Kralj-Fišer, S.; Čelik, T.; Lokovšek, T.; Šuen, K.; Šiling, R.; Kuntner, M. Development and Growth in Synanthropic Species: Plasticity and Constraints. *Naturwissenschaften* **2014**, *101* (7), 565–575. https://doi.org/10.1007/s00114-014-1194-y.
(45) Calhoun, J. B. A Behavioral Sink. In *Roots of Behavior*; National Institutes of Health, 1962.
(46) Ramsden, E.; Adams, J. Escaping the Laboratory: The Rodent Experiments of John B. Calhoun & Their Cultural Influence. *J. Soc. Hist.* **2009**, *42* (3), 761–792.

(47) *Guide for the Care and Use of Laboratory Animals: Eighth ...* m.moam.info. https://m.moam.info/guide-for-the-care-and-use-of-laboratory-animals-eighth-_59c5d0d01723dd42ad22462f.html (accessed 2025-05-15).

(48) Terman, C. R. A Study of Population Growth and Control Exhibited in the Laboratory by Prairie Deermice. *Ecology* **1965**, *46* (6), 890–895. https://doi.org/10.2307/1934030.

(49) Suvorov, A. Population Numbers and Reproductive Health. *Endocrinology* **2021**, *162* (11), bqab154. https://doi.org/10.1210/endocr/bqab154.

(50) Dolnik, V. R. How Many People Is the Earth Designed For? *Priroda* **1992**, *6* (922), 3–16.

(51) Bonenfant, C.; Gaillard, J.; Coulson, T.; Festa-Bianchet, M.; Loison, A.; Garel, M.; Loe, L. E.; Blanchard, P.; Pettorelli, N.; Owen-Smith, N.; Du Toit, J.; Duncan, P. Chapter 5 Empirical Evidence of Density-Dependence in Populations of Large Herbivores. In *Advances in Ecological Research*; Academic Press, 2009; Vol. 41, pp 313–357. https://doi.org/10.1016/S0065-2504(09)00405-X.

(52) Tyutyunov, Y.; Titova, L. From Lotka-Volterra to Arditi-Ginzburg: 90 Years of Evolving Trophic Functions // Biology Bulletin Reviews. **2020**, *10*, 167–185. https://doi.org/10.1134/S207908642003007X.

(53) Sibly, R. M.; Barker, D.; Denham, M. C.; Hone, J.; Pagel, M. On the Regulation of Populations of Mammals, Birds, Fish, and Insects. *Science* **2005**, *309* (5734), 607–610. https://doi.org/10.1126/science.1110760.

(54) Peen, J.; Schoevers, R. A.; Beekman, A. T.; Dekker, J. The Current Status of Urban-Rural Differences in Psychiatric Disorders. *Acta Psychiatr. Scand.* **2010**, *121* (2), 84–93. https://doi.org/10.1111/j.1600-0447.2009.01438.x.

(55) Makarieva, A. *Does the concept of 'pollution' match the complexity of human–biosphere interactions?* Biotic Regulation and Biotic Pump. https://bioticregulation.substack.com/p/does-the-concept-of-pollution-match (accessed 2025-05-09).

(56) NIH. *Mental Illness - National Institute of Mental Health (NIMH).* https://www.nimh.nih.gov/health/statistics/mental-illness (accessed 2025-04-11).

(57) Ridenour, N. *Mental Health in the United States, a Fifty-Year History*; Cambridge, Mass., Commonwealth Fund, 1961.
(58) Inc, G. *Global Emotions Report*; 2024. https://www.gallup.com/analytics/349280/gallup-global-emotions-report.aspx (accessed 2025-04-03).
(59) MacLeod, J. The Metabolism of Human Spermatozoa. *Proc. Soc. Exp. Biol. Med.* **1939**, *42* (1), 153–155. https://doi.org/10.3181/00379727-42-10830.
(60) Carlsen, E.; Giwercman, A.; Keiding, N.; Skakkebaek, N. E. Evidence for Decreasing Quality of Semen during Past 50 Years. *BMJ* **1992**, *305* (6854), 609–613. https://doi.org/10.1136/bmj.305.6854.609.
(61) Wang, C.; Mbizvo, M.; Festin, M. P.; Björndahl, L.; Toskin, I. Evolution of the WHO "Semen" Processing Manual from the First (1980) to the Sixth Edition (2021). *Fertil. Steril.* **2022**, *117* (2), 237–245. https://doi.org/10.1016/j.fertnstert.2021.11.037.
(62) Rahban, R.; Priskorn, L.; Senn, A.; Stettler, E.; Galli, F.; Vargas, J.; Van den Bergh, M.; Fusconi, A.; Garlantezec, R.; Jensen, T. K.; Multigner, L.; Skakkebæk, N. E.; Germond, M.; Jørgensen, N.; Nef, S.; Group, the N. W. Semen Quality of Young Men in Switzerland: A Nationwide Cross-Sectional Population-Based Study. *Andrology* **2019**, *7* (6), 818–826. https://doi.org/10.1111/andr.12645.
(63) Fierz, L. *Kastriert im Mutterleib: Jeder ist Versuchskaninchen*; BoD – Books on Demand: Hamburg, 2025.
(64) Nihart, A. J.; Garcia, M. A.; El Hayek, E.; Liu, R.; Olewine, M.; Kingston, J. D.; Castillo, E. F.; Gullapalli, R. R.; Howard, T.; Bleske, B.; Scott, J.; Gonzalez-Estrella, J.; Gross, J. M.; Spilde, M.; Adolphi, N. L.; Gallego, D. F.; Jarrell, H. S.; Dvorscak, G.; Zuluaga-Ruiz, M. E.; West, A. B.; Campen, M. J. Bioaccumulation of Microplastics in Decedent Human Brains. *Nat. Med.* **2025**, 1–6. https://doi.org/10.1038/s41591-024-03453-1.
(65) Ponnana, S. R.; Rajagopalan, T.; Zhang, T.; Chen, Z.; Sirasapalli, S. K.; Deo, S. Microplastic Concentration, Social, and Environmental Features and Their Association with Chronic Disease Prevalence: An Analysis across u.s. Census Tracts. *JACC* **2025**, *85* (12_Supplement), 374–374. https://doi.org/10.1016/S0735-1097(25)00858-7.

(86) Archive, H. *Reefs and Atolls Around Mangareva and Rapa Nui*. https://archive.hokulea.com/rapanui/reefs.html (accessed 2025-02-15).
(87) SYSTEMS SCIENCE AND CHINA'S ECONOMIC REFORMS. In *Control Science and Technology for Development*; Pergamon, 1986; pp 1–7. https://doi.org/10.1016/B978-0-08-033473-8.50006-1.
(88) Chen, T.; Hou, P.; Wang, B.; Yang, J. Analysis of Fertility Policy Differences Based on Policy Continuity and Policy Effectiveness in China. *Biodemography Soc. Biol.* **2025**, *70* (3), 138–164. https://doi.org/10.1080/19485565.2025.2527033.
(89) Bongaarts, J.; Greenhalgh, S. An Alternative to the One-Child Policy in China. *Popul. Dev. Rev.* **1985**, *11* (4), 585–617.
(90) Bardi, U. *Pixie Dust and Overpopulation: What are the Origins of the "One Child" China's Population Policy?* The Seneca Effect. https://senecaeffect.substack.com/p/pixie-dust-and-overpopulation-what (accessed 2025-11-25).
(91) Greenhalgh, S. Missile Science, Population Science: The Origins of China's One-Child Policy. *China Q.* **2005**, No. 182, 253–276.
(92) Wang, T.; Jiang, Q. Recent Trend and Correlates of Induced Abortion in China: Evidence from the 2017 China Fertility Survey. *BMC Womens Health* **2022**, *22* (1), 469. https://doi.org/10.1186/s12905-022-02074-5.
(93) Pino, D. *China's Population Policy: A Failure and a Test*. National Review. https://www.nationalreview.com/corner/chinas-population-policy-a-failure-and-a-test/ (accessed 2025-11-28).
(94) Bardi, U.; El Asmar, T.; Lavacchi, A. Turning Electricity into Food: The Role of Renewable Energy in the Future of Agriculture. *J. Clean. Prod.* **2013**, *53*, 224–231. https://doi.org/10.1016/j.jclepro.2013.04.014.
(95) Maestas, N.; Mullen, K. J.; Powell, D. The Effect of Population Aging on Economic Growth, the Labor Force, and Productivity. *Am. Econ. J. Macroecon.* **2023**, *15* (2), 306–332. https://doi.org/10.1257/mac.20190196.
(96) Anu Madgavacar. *Confronting the Consequences of a New Demographic Reality | McKinsey*; McKinsey Institute, 2025. https://www.mckinsey.com/mgi/our-research/dependency-and-depopulation-confronting-the-consequences-of-a-new-demographic-reality (accessed 2025-03-24).

(97) Brijoux, T.; Neise, M.; Zank, S. Elder Abuse in the Oldest Old: Prevalence, Risk Factors and Consequences. *Z. Für Gerontol. Geriatr.* **2021**, *54* (2), 132–137. https://doi.org/10.1007/s00391-021-01945-0.

(98) Banerjee, A.; Yakovenko, V. Universal Patterns of Inequality. *New J. Phys.* **2010**, *12* (7), 075032. https://doi.org/10.1088/1367-2630/12/7/075032.

(99) Krawczyk, F.; Braun, A. Ch. Models like Heroes? Making Integrated Assessment Models (IAMs) Ready for Deep Decarbonization and a Socio-Economic Transformation. *Energy Res. Soc. Sci.* **2025**, *121*, 103959. https://doi.org/10.1016/j.erss.2025.103959.

(100) Solé, J.; Samsó, R.; García-Ladona, E.; García-Olivares, A.; Ballabrera-Poy, J.; Madurell, T.; Turiel, A.; Osychenko, O.; Álvarez, D.; Bardi, U.; Baumann, M.; Buchmann, K.; Capellán-Pérez, Í.; Černý, M.; Carpintero, Ó.; De Blas, I.; De Castro, C.; De Lathouwer, J.-D.; Duce, C.; Eggler, L.; Enríquez, J. M.; Falsini, S.; Feng, K.; Ferreras, N.; Frechoso, F.; Hubacek, K.; Jones, A.; Kaclíková, R.; Kerschner, C.; Kimmich, C.; Lobejón, L. F.; Lomas, P. L.; Martelloni, G.; Mediavilla, M.; Miguel, L. J.; Natalini, D.; Nieto, J.; Nikolaev, A.; Parrado, G.; Papagianni, S.; Perissi, I.; Ploiner, C.; Radulov, L.; Rodrigo, P.; Sun, L.; Theofilidi, M. Modelling the Renewable Transition: Scenarios and Pathways for a Decarbonized Future Using *Pymedeas*, a New Open-Source Energy Systems Model. *Renew. Sustain. Energy Rev.* **2020**, *132*, 110105. https://doi.org/10.1016/j.rser.2020.110105.

(101) Nordhaus, W. *The "DICE" Model: Background and Structure of a Dynamic Integrated Climate-Economy Model of the Economics of Global Warming*; Cowles Foundation Discussion Papers; Working paper 1009; Cowles Foundation for Research in Economics, Yale University, 1992. https://EconPapers.repec.org/RePEc:cwl:cwldpp:1009 (accessed 2025-08-06).

(102) Bardi, U.; Bierwirth, P.; Huang, K.-W.; MacIntyre, J. Carbon Dioxide as a Pollutant. The Risks on Human Health and the Stability of the Biosphere. *Environ. Sci. Adv.* **2025**. https://doi.org/10.1039/D5VA00017C.

(103) Duncan, R.C. The Olduvai Theory, Sliding Towards a Post-Industrial Stone Age. *Soc. Contract* **2005**, *16* (2), 1–12.

(104) Klein, S. *Infographics in the Time of Cholera*. ProPublica. https://www.propublica.org/nerds/infographics-in-the-time-of-cholera (accessed 2025-03-13).

(105) Gannett, H. *Statistical Atlas of the United States, Based upon the Results of the Eleventh Census*; United States. Census office. 11th census, 1890., 1893.

(106) Kermack, W. O.; McKendrick, A. G.; Walker, G. T. A Contribution to the Mathematical Theory of Epidemics. *Proc. R. Soc. Lond. Ser. Contain. Pap. Math. Phys. Character* **1927**, *115* (772), 700–721. https://doi.org/10.1098/rspa.1927.0118.

(107) Perissi, I.; Lavacchi, A.; Bardi, U. Peaking Dynamics of the Production Cycle of a Nonrenewable Resource. *Sustainability* **2023**, *15* (8), 1–11.

(108) Taleb, N. *The Black Swan*; Random House, 2007.

(109) Sornette, D. Dragon-Kings, Black Swans and the Prediction of Crises. *ArXiv09074290v1 Physicsdata-An* **2009**, 18.

(110) Bak, P. *How Nature Works. The Science of Self-Organized Criticality.*; Copernicus: New York, 1996.

(111) Turner, G. A Comparison of The Limits to Growth with 30 Years of Reality. *Glob. Environ. Change* **2008**, *18* (3), 397–411. https://doi.org/10.1016/j.gloenvcha.2008.05.001.

(112) Herrington, G. Update to Limits to Growth: Comparing the World3 Model with Empirical Data. *J. Ind. Ecol.* **2021**, *25* (3), 614–626. https://doi.org/10.1111/jiec.13084.

4560061R00161

Printed in Great Britain
by Amazon.co.uk, Ltd.,
Marston Gate.